THE
KINGDOM
OF
DADRIA
A LAMB AMONGST WOLVES

THE
KINGDOM
OF

DADRIA

A LAMB AMONGST WOLVES

N. J. HANSON

Ink Drop Press,
Chico, California

Also by N. J. Hanson:

Stand Alone Works:

The Last Stand of the Dragon

Frost Bite: Cannibal in the Forest

The Ravenwood Hauntings:

An Empty Swing

The Broken Chain

The Kingdom of Dadria:

A Lamb Amongst Wolves

The Blood of Wolves and War

Co-authored with Hope Hill:

Secrets Under the Skin

PART I
THE PRINCESS
OF DADRIA

I.
DARREN

Sir Darren rode at the head of a small caravan. He snapped the reins of his horse. The animal snorted and shook its mane. It moved forward, the constant clop of its hooves echoing through the still forest air. All around him stood enormous trees, taller than most watchtowers and with trunks thicker than castle walls. Massive trees for a massive forest, it seemed to stretch forever. In the distance he could see the snow capped peaks of the Dragon's Teeth mountains. In that rugged terrain, nestled in the only mountain pass for two hundred leagues north or south, was their destination; the Kingdom of Dadria.

"Sir Darren!" A familiar, grating voice called from behind him. With a groan, he pulled on the reins to stop his horse, and then raised a clenched fist. The eight knights behind him came to a halt.

All but Sir Darren were dressed from head to toe in reddish gold armor with face concealing helmets and deep blue cloaks. They were assembled in sets of four, one set rode in front and the other rode behind with the front and rear pair each carrying deep blue banners adorned with a red elk against a gold shield, the royal crest of Kendrick, King of Kahren. Unlike them, Sir Darren wore pure black leather armor with light plating. His cloak, boots, gloves, and even his hair and beard were black. The only color on his uniform was the five-pointed gold crown on his chest with a sword stabbed through it from above. It signaled Sir Darren's status as one of the Black Swords of the King, the most elite order of knights in Kahren. They answered only to Kendrick himself, no one else had authority over them.

A carriage was nestled in the center of the caravan. Like the other knights, it too was highly ornate, painted a lavish red with gold trim around the door and windows. Its four wheels were all plated in gold. Sir Darren turned around and marched his horse back to the carriage and tapped his knuckles against the door. "You summoned me, your grace?" This carriage, or rather its lone occupant, was the sole reason they were here.

The door came unlatched and swung open. A boy stepped out; Prince Sedrick, brother of King Kendrick and heir to the throne. He was a large boy for his age of five and ten years, with light-chestnut colored blonde hair and fair skin. His cheeks were puffy and belly rounder than other children his age, with short stubby legs. His garb was a glimmering gold that hurt the eyes to look upon, even in this dim light. His gold cloak shown the brightest of all, with only the deep lavender underside to offset it. Most important of all was the crown that rested atop his head, signifying his royal standing.

"Sir Darren, how much further to Dadria?" Prince Sedrick asked.

"We are still almost a day's ride from the Walls." Sir Darren tightly gripped the reins in his hands.

"Is King Cassius's escort on its way?" Sedrick asked.

"They are probably waiting for us further along the road. We would be making better time, however, if we didn't have to stop every time you needed to take a piss." Sir Darren's tone was soft, but forceful. He did not mince words.

"Oh," Sedrick said as he stepped down from the carriage. "Speaking of, that might be a good idea." He hurried off into the woods, his awkward gait a sign both of his discomfort and of being unused to walking outdoors.

10

Sir Darren watched the boy with a mixture of irritation and resigned disappointment. The boy was pampered, simple as that. Kendrick kept him isolated inside the castle most of the time, trying to teach him how to be a king. The sight of this clumsy child waddling off to use a tree as a latrine filled Darren with dread for the future of the kingdom.

The black knight let out a sigh before dismounting his horse and following after the child. He moved off the well worn trade route and into the dense forest. In the woods, the shadows crept in close, cutting off most of the light from the sun. A thick layer of twisting ferns blanketed the forest floor and grew as high as the knight's knees. Moving through these woods on foot was difficult.

Those in Dadria called these the Red Woods, for the color of the soft fibrous bark that covered the tree trunks. Sir Darren, however, preferred the Kahren name: the Forest of Wayward Souls. It's said that if anyone wandered off the path and lost sight of it, they'd never find it again and instead be doomed to wander in the wood forever, their voice added to the wailing screams that can sometimes be heard in the dead of night.

Sir Darren took these rumors with little seriousness. Thick and difficult to maneuver through perhaps, but it was unlikely these woods were haunted in anyway. However, there were wolves, panthers, and even bears in these woods. In the dim light, he would have little chance of spotting one before it would be upon him.

It did not take long for Darren to find the prince. Sedrick stood facing a tree with the tinkling sound of his relief obvious. Sir Darren turned his head away to give the young man some privacy. "Your grace, you can not run off into the woods like that without an escort. If you were to get lost or injured, your brother would have my head on a spike."

"I'm sorry. I'm just nervous is all." The trickle came to a stop and Sedrick readjusted himself. He moved away from the tree and faced the knight. "I'm supposed to meet with King Cassius tomorrow and ask for his daughter's hand. My brother says it's a good match, but I do not know. Is she pretty? Will she like me? Kendrick says it's very important that I make a good impression, but I do not know what I should do." The boy spoke quicker and his voice grew higher. His fingers began to twitch and fidget, his gaze fell to the forest floor.

"I would not worry about it." Sir Darren placed his hand over the pommel of his sword. "If the girl is only half as beautiful as her father claims, then Princess Endelynn will still be the most stunning young woman in the world. Now are you finished pissing?"

"Um, yes." Princes Sedrick answered awkwardly.

"Then we should return. We're already late for the rendezvous and losing daylight."

A twig snapped nearby. Sir Darren froze in place. His eyes shifted back and forth in the dark shadows, looking for any movement. He listened, tilting his head quizzically from one direction to the other, but now the woods had fallen eerily silent. Before there had been the rustling of ground squirrels in the ferns and the knocking of a woodpecker in the far distance, but now there was nothing.

"Sir Darren?" The prince asked as the watched the knight's strange behavior. "What's going on?"

"Shh!" Darren raised a finger to the boy, silencing him. He did not turn to address Sedrick, instead kept his attention on the trees and foliage all around them. He beckoned the boy closer, and when he was in arm's reach he grasped Prince Sedrick's tunic and pulled him in.

"Stay quiet." He whispered in a low, scratchy voice. He drew his sword, a long shimmering steel blade, and held it up before him. "Now, step where I step, and do not make a sound."

His heart rate was elevated, drops of sweat accumulated on

his forehead, but Darren did not let his fear show. The young prince, however, was on the verge of a breakdown. From the moment he drew his sword, Sir Darren saw the look on Sedrick's face turn to terror. He raised a foot off the ground and settled it back into the soft earth.

Prince Sedrick followed closely behind, but the boy did not move with the same caution as the older, more experienced soldier. His breathing was erratic and shallow, and the steps he took were less precise. His feet squished into the earth and popped back out with each step.

Darren silently cursed under his breath. The prince's constant noise was drowning out the ambiance of the woods. A light breeze stirred the pine bows far overhead and the speckles of sunlight danced around the forest floor.

A sudden flash of movement caught the knight's attention. He jerked his eyes to the left and glimpsed a large dark shadow run between the trees. Sir Darren stopped, and placed a hand across Sedrick's chest to stop him. "Shh." He whispered. "do not make a sound."

Then he heard it. A low, raspy, growl. Darren slowly turned and looked over his shoulder. Behind them, hidden in the shade of the redwoods, stood a large black wolf, back hunched and fur bristled. Its eyes emanated a piercing amber glow, and fangs bared and dripped with saliva.

Darren's blood ran cold. This wolf was larger than any he had ever seen, nearly the size of a small horse, and where there was one wolf there are usually more. "Your grace, run!" He grabbed the prince by the collar and shoved him forward. They took off running and the wolf gave chase.

It charged after them, powerful hind legs propelling it forward in great leaps. With great raspy breaths as it closed in on them. As the wolf pounced, Sir Darren threw Sedrick to the ground. The knight spun on his heels, gripped his sword in both hands and swung down towards the wolf. The beast halted and veered off the left, dodging the blade. The sword embedded in the ground. The wolf ran back into the shadows and vanished into the darkness.

Darren pulled his sword from the earth, black specks of dirt clinging to the blade. The wolf had disappeared and the woods were silent again. Then, a set of eyes opened, and another, and another. A half dozen pairs of glowing amber eyes appeared between the trees. The low growling reverberated through the air.

The knight grabbed Prince Sedrick by the collar and yanked him back to his feet. "Move!" He screamed at the boy. They turned from the wolves and raced for the edge of the forest. The pack gave chase, a dark mass of fur, claws, and fangs. Darren doubled his speed, dragging the prince behind him. Together, they burst from the trees and emerged on the path. "Wolves!" He shouted to his men.

The large, black wolf charged out of the forest behind them, gnashing its teeth. One of the mounted knights kicked his horse, and the animal broke away at a gallop, bearing down on the wolf. The mounted knight drew his sword and swung low. The wolf evaded, darting back into the forest.

The pack hovered on the edge of the trees, their teeth bared. Then all the mounted knights drew their swords and formed a protective circle around Sir Darren and Prince Sedrick. "Your grace," the black knight said, "get back in the carriage and latch the door. Do not open it again until I say."

"But," the prince said between breaths, "what about– "

"Do as I say!" Sir Darren shoved the boy towards the open carriage door.

A wolf snarled. It lunged towards the prince in a sudden burst of speed, its mouth agape and claws extended. A mounted knight placed himself between the wolf and prince, his horse reared up and kicked at the wolf, stopping it in its tracks. The wolf growled and snapped its jaws, but the knight and horse

14

did not budge.

While he was distracted, another wolf bolted out from the trees and leapt at the knight. He had no time to react before it pounced on him and knocked the man from his horse. The startled mount kicked and bucked before racing away from the scene, only to find itself getting brought down by another pair of large black wolves. They jumped on its back and forced it to the ground, then closed their jaws tightly around its throat, crushing the airway. The horse was dead in seconds.

The knight was not much better off. The attacking wolf pinned him to the ground. He held his arm up to protect his face, the wolf's jaws clamped over his plated forearm, teeth pierced through the metal and into his flesh. The knight cried out in pain.

Just as Sir Darren moved to aid his fellow, the rest of the pack attacked. They rushed the soldiers, barking and snapping their jaws. They leapt at the horses, biting their flanks and nipping at their heels. The mounts, many of them trained since the time they were foals for combat, were now surrounded by predators. Their combat training was forgotten and most of the animals panicked, their eyes white with terror, and threw their riders to the ground.

The horses attached to Prince Sedrick's carriage roared in fear. Their hooves dug into the earth as they raced ahead at full gallop, dragging the prince away with them. A pair of wolves broke away from the attack and gave chase. Sir Darren could only watch as the prince's carriage was taken by the frightened animals. Once the predators began their pursuit, he ran for his own horse to follow. Distracted, he didn't notice the other wolf leaping for him until it was already in the air.

With only a second to react, he brace his sword across his chest just as the beast landed. The weight of the animal forced him on his back, the wolf's powerful jaws gnawed at the blade in its mouth. It pawed at his face, the claws tore the skin over

Sir Darren's eye. He winced and groaned, his eye clamped shut.

His elbows braced against the ground, one hand gripped the pommel of his sword, and the other held the blade. The wolf was kept at bay, but it would not last. Every second, the prince grew further away from him and closer to death.

The sword was useless while in the wolf's mouth, but he had a dagger on his belt. If he could get it, Darren could stab the wild dog and force it away. But he knew once he released his hold on the sword, those sharp, white fangs would be in his throat.

That was the gamble he chose to take. Holding firm on the pommel, the black knight released his grip on the blade and the sword fell at an angle over his neck, the wolf lurched forward, startled by the sudden loss of resistance.

Seizing his chance, Sir Darren pulled the short dagger from its sheath and plunged it into the wolf's gut. The beast howled in pain, pulling away from the sword. The black knight braced his foot against the wolf and kicked it away, yanking his dagger from its stomach. Blood spurted from the wound.

The wolf staggered away, yowling and whimpering, a trail of blood dripped down its leg and stained the ground red. A she-wolf ran to its side, inspected the wound with its snout and licked it before nudging the injured animal away. Together, they retreated into the forest.

Sir Darren placed a hand against his injured eye. It stung, throbbed with pain, and when he pulled his hand away a smear of blood had formed on his glove. He couldn't worry about that now. He'd gotten the beast off him, but all that did was slow him down. The prince was now further away.

He cleaned the dagger, sheathed it, then whistled to his horse. His mount, a large black stallion, roared as it kicked a wolf away and raced for him. As the horse approached, he grasped the bridal, hooked his foot into the stirrup, and swung his leg over the animal's back to landed with a thump in the saddle, all without the horse slowing its pace. His sworn duty was to the king, and King Kendrick had ordered him to ensure the safety of Prince Sedrick. Even if it meant dying, he would do everything in his power to fulfill that cause.

The carriage had come to a halt. The two horses squirmed and pulled against their restraints, they kicked and bucked. A pair of black wolves circled around them. One wolf stood in front of the horses, it crouched low to the ground with its back hunched and fur bristled. It snapped at the animal's hooves, the horse kicked and stomped at the earth, but the predator would not leave. Just as it prepared to pounce, the wolf stopped. Its ears twitched. Something was coming.

Sir Darren saw them first, a quartet of fully armored soldiers storming down the beaten forest path, a trail of dust kicked up under the hooves of their mounts. They rode on the backs of rams, big horned mountain sheep the size of oxen. The leader charged ahead, his ram lowered its head and aimed for the nearest wolf.

They collided, the wolf flew through the air and crashed back to the earth with a bone-crunching thud. It whined and twisted, scrambling to its feet. The ram snorted, scraped its hooves against the ground as it prepared for another attack. A second wolf crept around the mounted soldier, its legs coiled under its body as the vicious carnivore readied its attack. Before it could pounce, an arrow fell from the sky and stuck in the ground at its feet.

The marksman drew another arrow from the quiver at his side. He notched it and took aim, the bowstring strained. The wolf wasted no time, it turned tail and ran.

The first wolf, the one still limping from the ram attack, lifted its head skyward and howled. The rest of the pack perked up their ears at attention, then retreated back into the woods. Only after the rest were gone did the last wolf, the pack leader, depart. It raced away into the woods, disappearing into the shadows between the trees.

Exhausted, drained, Sir Darren sheathed his sword. His body ached from the attack, but that was nothing a day's rest and an ale would not fix. He tugged on the reins, directing his horse over to the other knights. "Greetings," he waved to the closest ram-mounted soldier. "You are Dadrian knights, are you not?"

"That we are." The armored man dismounted and removed his helmet. His vibrant red hair flowed down across his shoulders like a fiery waterfall. "I am Sir Aridain, personal guard of King Cassius and Queen Beatrice. They sent me to be your escort, and it appears we arrived just in time. The wolves of the Red Woods are not always so easily frightened away." Aridain looked quizzically at Sir Darren's facial injury. "That eye doesn't look good."

"It's fine. Now, if you'll excuse me." Darren climbed down from his horse and walked past Aridain to the prince's carriage. He struck his knuckles against the door. "Your grace?" He called. "It is safe. You can come out now."

The door unlatched and a severely shaken Prince Sedrick emerged. His cloak was ruffled and crown askew, but otherwise well preserved. "Are they gone? The wolves, I mean?"

"They are, your grace," Darren said.

"Sir Darren, your eye!" The prince shouted. "What happened?"

"It's nothing. A small scratch from a wolf's claws," The knight said. "We had some aide in that regard. Our escorts from Dadria intervened just in time." The black knight motioned to the four armored soldiers and their battle rams.

The Dadrian knight bringing up the rear carried a large red banner which flapped in the wind. It bore the coat of arms of Clan Rambourne, the Dadrian royal house; a white mountain ram majestic against a purple shield, with a pair of gold ferns flanking it from the sides, and a crown hovering above. The Dadrian knight fell to one knee, placed his helmet on the ground, and bowed his head. "It is an honor to meet you, Prince Sedrick, son of Osrick, brother of Kendrick. I am Sir Aridain, knight of Dadria."

"So it's true." Sedrick looked past the knight to his steed, it seemed so strange to have a saddle and reins attached to a ram, much less the armor plating over its face and flank. "Dadrians ride sheep into battle. I thought that was a jest."

"Rams are important to our society." Sir Aridain grabbed his helmet and stood up. "They are the best means of travel through these mountains. But do not worry, we have a few paths and trails that will accommodate horses as well."

"Once we've rounded as many of those blasted animals up as possible, then we can accept your escort." Darren said.

Aridain gave a quick hand signal to the other Dadrian's. They set off to scout the area and retrieve the missing horses. Aridain returned to his steed and climbed back in the saddle to join them. "Do not worry, we'll find your horses soon enough, and once we reach Dadria we will have our royal physicians tend to your injury. In truth, we were expecting you earlier and only came searching when you didn't arrive at the rendezvous at the designated time."

Sir Darren chuckled. "You can blame our tardiness on a nervous bladder."

II.
ENDELYNN

A pillar of sunlight fell across the floor as the curtains were drawn back. It came to land on the pillow and face of the Dadrian princess; Endelynn. She squirmed and blinked, twisting on the bed to avoid the light. With an annoyed groan, she rolled over and pulled the pillow over her face.

"My lady," an elderly woman spoke, "It's time to get up."

"No." Endelynn's muffled voice came from under the pillow. "Can't you give me a few more minutes, Winifred?"

"I'm afraid you cannot sleep in today. You have an important guest waiting for you." Winifred, the elderly lady-in-waiting, finished pulling the window curtains open, allowing the full sunlight in.

Slowly, meticulously, the princess lifted herself up from the bed. She stretched and yawned, her long, vibrant, fiery red hair burst around in all directions. Endelynn pushed it away from her face as she rubbed the sleep from her eyes. "A guest? Who could that-" She stopped and her eyes snapped wide open. "The prince!" Endelynn leapt from her bed, the sheets and blankets flew away in a mess. "Prince Sedrick is here, isn't he?"

"He is, my lady." Winifred gave a nod. "We should prepare to meet him."

Endelynn moved over to her her vanity mirror, her thin

20

pink nightgown flowed behind her. She placed herself on the small cushioned stool and faced the reflective glass. "Yes we should. Just be delicate."

"Of course, my lady." Winifred took the brush from the vanity and got to work straightening the princess's rebellious hair. It was a daily ritual the handmaiden and princess shared, and Winifred had years of practice.

"Tell me," The elder woman said as she stroked the brush through Endelynn's red locks. "Who is Prince Sedrick? What do you know about him?"

The princess tilted her head to the side to look at her handmaiden in the vanity mirror. "Why are you asking me? What can I tell you that you don't already know?"

"Nothing," Winifred stated as she yanked out a particularly troublesome knot. Endelynn winced, her shoulders hunched. Winifred placed her hand gently on the princess's shoulder, calming the girl before returning to the task at hand. "But I need to test you to make sure you haven't forgotten anything. Now tell me, who is Prince Sedrick?"

Taking a deep breath, Endelynn closed her eyes and straightened her back. "Sedrick is the third born son of Osrick, the previous king of Kahren."

"Who is the current king?" Winifred asked.

"Sedrick's older brother, Kendrick."

Winifred nodded her approval. "Good. You are doing well." Her questions continued. "How many brothers does Sedrick have?"

"He had two." Endelynn answered. "His eldest brother was the crowned-prince, Roddrick, who tragically died in a hunting accident eight years ago. Kendrick was second born, with Sedrick as the youngest. His mother, the last queen, passed away giving birth to him."

"Very good." Winifred planted a small kiss on the top of Endelynn's head. "I hadn't asked about that, but nonetheless, you remembered. Although I'd advise you not to bring this up to the prince himself."

"Of course not," Endelynn said. "Am I done with the test?"

"Not yet." The handmaiden set the brush down on the vanity and separated Endelynn's hair into three segments. As she began to braid the hair, she asked, "What is Sedrick's clan name? What is on his banner, and what are the colors used to depict it?"

Endelynn sighed. She understood the reason, but still felt irritated with her caretaker's questioning. She knew all of this, they'd been reading about it and studying this subject for hours a day for the past month. Ever since her father had arranged for the young prince to visit. "Sedrick is of House Stagghart," Endelynn said at last. "His family's banner is deep blue, emblazoned with a gold crown and shield, upon which is depicted a red elk."

Once the braid was pulled tight, Endelynn's hair was done. "You did well." Winifred complemented the princess's correct answers. "I understand it might seem a little tedious to continually address these same points, but it is important that you remember them."

"I know." Endelynn replied.

Winifred moved on to applying make-up, jewelry, and a suitable dress for the princess.

Endelynn watched the process unfold, first in her vanity and then in a full length mirror. Her dress was long and elegantly sewn, lavender with white lace trim along the edges, sleeves, and collar. It clasped around her neck, adorned with a large, deep blue sapphire resting on her collarbone.

She gazed at herself in the mirror, tilted her head from one side and then to the other, smiling all the while. Every girl in the kingdom, nay the world, wishes they could have this kind of treatment. Endelynn twirled around on the balls of her feet, her dress lifted just above her ankles before falling back to the floor.

"My lady, please. You should not indulge in such child-like behavior." Winifred said.

"Am I not a child? I still feel as though I were one." Endelynn responded, her eyes never left the mirror. She posed, her back arched and foot lifted off the ground, she giggled all the while.

"You may still feel so, but now that your sixteenth year has come, you are a woman. Please," Winifred motioned to the stool. Endelynn rested herself on it while the older woman applied her shoes. "Not just any woman, but a lady of the court. And someday, you may even become queen."

"I've always been destined to become queen." Endelynn said.

"That you are, my lady." The handmaiden ran her hands long the seams of the dress and sleeves. She checked the princess's hair, making sure not a single strand was out of place. "There," Winifred said with a satisfied smile. "You are now presentable. Now, we had better hurry along. Your father and mother are awaiting you in the banquet hall."

A radiant smile grew over Endelynn's face. She gave a curtsy to her lady-in-waiting, who then returned the favor, and together they hurried out the door. The princess held the edges of her dress between her fingers as they walked briskly down the long and spacious halls of the castle. Servants moved about the corridors, cleaning the windows, sweeping the floors, lighting the candles if needed. They stopped and bowed as the princess approached before returning to their task once she'd passed. Endelynn barely noticed them, she was more concerned about what awaited her.

A young servant girl greeted the princess at the doors to the banquet hall. "Good morning, milady," she said and pushed the great doors open.

Two rows of red marble columns ran the length of the hall,

supporting the ceiling which reached over twelve feet high. A chandelier lit with fifty candles was suspended over the three tables. One ran along the wall at the far end of the hall and was raised higher than the other two. The tables themselves were carved from the trunk of an old Redwood tree, sanded and finished with a glossy shine. They shimmered with the light cast upon them from the standing fire baskets.

At the high table; the one reserved only for the royal family and their visiting guests, sat the High King Cassius and his wife, Queen Beatrice. "Good morning, Father. Good morning, Mother." Endelynn pinched the edges of her dress between her forefinger and thumb to curtsy.

The king pushed himself up from the table and dabbed his mouth and short beard with a napkin. "My daughter," his voice reverberated throughout the hall, "I'm glad you decided to join us this morning. Although, you are later than I had expected." He stepped down from the table and stood over the princess, his long shadow cast over her. His face was stern, eyes fierce. He crossed his arms over his burly chest. "Care to explain?"

Endelynn paused. She slowly straightened herself up and placed her hands together, her eyes still turned on the floor and away from her father's gaze. She opened her mouth to speak then stopped, unable to form her thoughts and excuses into words. She didn't want to give her father an excuse.

Her fear dissipated when she saw the smirk appear on the corners of the old man's lips. He stifled a giggle, then threw his head back and bellowed a powerful laugh. "Aha ha ha! Oh, Endelynn, your face was priceless." Before she could react, the king embraced her in his arms and lifted Endelynn off the ground, spinning her through the air. "Happy birthday" he said as he set her down, "Look at you, you look so grown up and proper today. No doubt I know the reason. Some pretty boy here to see you."

She laughed along with her father, kissing him on the cheek

and returning his hug. While she would never admit it, even to herself, she much preferred her father's company over that of her mother. "Yes, Father." She said. "Is he here? I don't see him." She looked around the banquet hall but only saw her parents and the few servants that served them.

"He arrived last night, they'll come to meet us later this morning after breakfast." The king explained as he led her to the table. A servant quickly pulled Endelynn's chair out for her and pushed her in once seated.

"That's unfortunate," Princess Endelynn said as she looked back at Winifred over her shoulder. "I was led to believe he was meeting me here."

"Not exactly, my dear." Queen Beatrice spoke for the first time since her daughter entered the room. She delicately held a knife and fork and cut at the venison before her. "But you need not worry. We will go to the throne room where the prince will present himself after breakfast." She placed the meat in he mouth and chewed quietly. Once swallowed, she spoke again. "However, it might take an extra moment to get your father prepared."

The king downed a pint of ale, his third for the morning, and set the mug down on the table. "I have no idea what you mean, my sweet." He belched and placed his hand over his mouth again. Then smiled sheepishly. "Let's not make this about me. This is our daughter's special day, we should be celebrating her."

Endelynn's face became warm. She smiled and turned away, trying to hide her embarrassment.

"In fact," Cassius rose from his chair again and addressed Winifred. "Bring the princess's birthday present."

"Yes, your grace." Winifred nodded and hurried out of the room.

"Dear, we agreed not to give that to her until her wedding day." Beatrice said scornfully.

25

"Now, please, my queen. It's her special day, it's deserving of a special gift." The king stated. Winifred returned to the banquet hall carrying a large, hinge latched box. She handed it over to King Cassius. "Ah, thank you." Cassius stood and cleared his throat. "Endelynn," he said with his powerful voice. "You are my beloved daughter and only child. And more than that, you are the princess and heir to the throne." He opened the box and revealed its contents. Inside was a circlet crown made of gold. It glistened and shined in the dancing candle light.

Endelynn gasped, the tips of her fingers brushed her lips. It was beautiful, more dazzling than the sun. "Oh, my... is that for me?"

Cassius nodded. "I had it specifically made for you while you were still a baby by the finest craftsman in the kingdom specifically for today. It's my birthday present to you." The king set the box down on the table and lifted the crown out. "I would be honored if you wore it for me."

With tears of joy peeking from the corners of her eyes, Endelynn smiled and gave a quick nod. She placed her hands together and bowed her head low. Cassius raised the crown up, then placed it atop the princess's vibrant red hair. It rested heavily on her, pushing down on her scalp, but Endelynn didn't care. This belonged to her, a magnificent crown that she could call her own. "Thank you, Father."

III.
SHUNKA

Shunka grit his teeth together and hissed. The wet, slimy mush that the shaman smeared on his wound was supposed to alleviate the pain, but it only caused more discomfort. The tribal medicine man held a small, stone bowl mortar in one hand and a wooden grinding pestle in the other. He crushed berries, leaves, and herbs into a thick, purple mixture that he then applied to the stab wound on Shunka's stomach.

The mixture hissed when it came in contact with the blood. Shunka groaned and turned his head away, but otherwise did not flinch. To do so would invite even more mockery from the tribe than he'd received since his return.

The hunting party had been lead by his older brother; Mingan, the strongest young warrior in the village. It consisted of himself, Shunka, their mutual friend, Tala, and several other warriors from the tribe, most of them the same age or younger. While on the hunt, they had found a small number of horse mounted soldiers and a carriage moving northeast from the coast towards the mountains and chose to follow them. When a pair of these invaders left the path and entered the forest, that's when Mingan gave the order to attack. But it was during this encounter, when Shunka had one of the soldier's pinned to the ground, that the man caught him off guard and stabbed him in the stomach with a hidden knife. Shunka was forced to retreat,

27

and Tala had to carry him on her back the final leg of the journey.

Shunka had almost bled out by the time they returned to the village. To say his father; Ahote Chaa, was displeased with the young warrior-in-training's hunting and battle performance would be a gross understatement. It was only the critical state of his injuries that prevented the Chaa from berating his son in front of the whole village. Tala had taken Shunka to the Longhouse of her father, the shaman, and he'd been there ever since.

"You need to relax, child." The shaman said as he dabbed more of the fuchsia berry and herb mix into the young man's injury. "The more tense you are, the longer your recovery will take."

"I know. You tell me all the time." Shunka lay on his back across a wooden table. A blanket was placed under him, another draped on top which was pulled down to his hips.

"If I tell you so often, why do you not listen?" The shaman, Alo, placed a bone needle into a small woven basket full of water. The strands were woven so tight no water could seep out. He then retrieved a stone from the nearby fire pit, picking it up with a forked branch, and dropped it in the water. The stone hissed and steamed, bubbles swirled around it. Once the water had settled, he removed the bone needle. "A child should always listen to his elders, even the child of the Chaa." The shaman looped a thread through the needle-eye. "You may end up leading us someday, and will need all the wisdom you can get."

"Not likely," Shunka said. "Mingan is the eldest, and strongest, of Ahote's children. If the Chaa Rantuuk gives leadership to anyone, it'll be him." The young warrior tensed up. A spasm wracked through his body as the shaman poured the remaining hot water across his wound. It washed away the berry juice and excess blood, leaving the injury clean. The blood and water dribbled down into a round wooden bowl on the floor.

"This may hurt a little." The medicine man warned as he prepared the needle. It pierced the tender flesh around Shunka's wound, and the young warrior winced. A sharp intake of breath and the clenching of both fists signaled his discomfort, but he did not budge. "You should not worry about your future. Whether you are given titles by your father or not, it will not matter." The shaman spoke as he stitched the young man's wound closed. "You are of a great heritage, a child of-"

"Yes, I know!" Shunka cut him off. "A child of Wahyuk, the great savior of all wolves. The blood of heroes flows through my veins, I've heard this all before!" A trickle of sweat ran down his forehead. His outburst was as much from discomfort as it was annoyance, with a little self loathing. "So far, I've done nothing worthy of being a hero, or even the child of one."

The shaman finished stitching the wound. He cut the thread and tied it off. Then placed his hands together and stared judgmentally at Shunka. The young warrior looked over at the much older man, the shaman's face stretched long with age and set with deep creases. His hair, once as black as raven feathers in his youth now gray as ash, stretched down to his waist.

After a long while, the medicine man spoke. "Would you like to see what your future holds? Maybe discover what the Great Spirit has in store for you?"

"You aren't serious, are you?" Shunka asked.

The shaman did not reply. He simply stood, taking the bowl of blood mixed with water, and walked over to the fire. From a pouch on his waist, he pulled a fine blue powder and sprinkled it into the bowl and began chanting. The phrases were indiscernible to Shunka, magical spells taught only from one shaman to his apprentice. Once the powder was fully mixed in the bowl, the medicine man threw it onto the fire.

An enormous explosion of steam rose into the air. Instead of being extinguished, the flames grew larger and brighter, they roared louder than an angry bear. Lilac smoke filled the Longhouse.

Alo swirled his hands through the smoke, catching and changing it. He inhaled deeply though his nose, and then breathed out his mouth. The shaman's eyes had turned the color of early morning fog. "This is strange." He murmured. "I see something for you."

"Like what?" Shunka asked, more interested than before.

"You will go on a patrol. Just you, Tala, and Mingan. You will find someone out in the woods. A girl, one of the pale-faced people of the walled kingdoms." The shaman said. "Her hair is like fire, and eyes green as the sequoia pine."

"Why do I care what she looks like?" Shunka said. "If she's from inside the walls and off the path, then she has no business being in our forest. She will be killed like all the others."

"This one you will not harm, rather you will protect her."

Shunka balked at this. "Protect her? An outsider, one of the invaders that nearly destroyed our forest and used to hunt our people? Why should I protect anyone such as that?"

"Because she is the Aleutsi." The shaman said.

Shunka's eyes snapped open. He tried to sit up, but the pain of his stomach wound forced him back down. "You are serious? Some outsider girl is the Aleutsi? The Great Spirit would never be so cruel to twist our fate like that. It'll never happen."

The shaman was lost in his vision. His eyes drawn skyward with smoke dancing around him. "The Aleutsi, the Great Mother. To think I would live to see the day of her return. And the rebirth of the hero."

"It's not going to happen." Shunka lay back on the table and turned away. "No outsider girl is going to be the Aleutsi."

"You will meet her on the next patrol, as I've said." The

30

shaman blinked and his eyes returned to normal. The smoke drifted up through the circular hole in the roof, clearing the air within the Longhouse. "Before the next full moon. It is fated."

The cloth flap across the door lifted, letting a pillar of light fall in, and a young woman stood in the doorway. Like the rest of her tribe, her skin was a dark hazel, and long hair a shiny black. A pair of feathers were woven in her hair, white with black tips pointed towards the floor. And the same as her other tribesmen, her eyes were amber-gold. "Father," she said, "I need to take Shunka."

"For what purpose?" The shaman sat next to the fire pit, his legs crossed and hands rested on his knees. The flames had simmered down to a low burn, barely whisking off the blackened coals.

"Ahote Chaa wants to speak with him." The young woman, Tala, spoke. She dropped the flap behind her as she stepped into the Longhouse. Moving away from the entrance, she sat across the fire from her father. Tala turned to address Shunka on the table. "He's still upset over what happened on patrol yesterday. Says you've shamed him somehow."

Shunka let out a long, tired breath. "My father has always been shamed by me. I promise, if it was Mingan who got a knife in his gut, Father would be praising how bravely he fought and the sacrifice he made for our tribe. Songs would be sung and legends told of the warrior who shrugged off a stab wound. But since it's me, he's only interested in my failures and disappointments."

Tala folded her arms and glared at Shunka. "You act as though you were the only one injured in the attack. It's not as if you were struck by an armored ram. Or had an arrow lodged in your back. All of us fought, and many were injured, not just you."

"Yes, but no one else had a knife plunged in their stomach." Shunka continued, hardly acknowledging what she said. "If

31

father wants to discipline me, then he should come here."

Tala closed her eyes and shook her head in irritation. "I guess you leave me no choice." She stood, walked over to the wooden slab Shunka lay upon, and placed both hands under one side. With a quick heave, Tala lifted the slab and flipped it over.

At first, Shunka was too startled to do much. One moment he was fine, the next he was falling to the dirt floor with a wooden slab pressed against his back. It knocked his breath away, and aggravated the wound in his stomach. He coughed and groaned in pain. As he tried to push himself up, he was shoved back down by Tala.

She pressed her foot down on the slab, forcing Shunka's face into the dirt. "You're being a childish brat. You always have been. Your father might hold Mingan in higher regard than you, but he has a good reason to. You are not fit to be Chaa. You get yourself injured too often, need everyone else to rescue you when you get in trouble, and are too selfish for your own good. Ahote will probably tell you the same thing."

He didn't respond. Her words rained down upon him, and rather than retort he just laid there and took it. He hated it, but wouldn't give anyone, least of all her, the satisfaction of seeing him so hurt.

The pressure lifted from his back. Tala pulled the slab away and brought Shunka to his feet. "Now," she said, brushing the dirt off his body. "Your father wishes an audience with you."

Shunka nodded. He did not speak, instead walked past her and out of the Longhouse. He walked through the village, rows of wooden lodges and Longhouses all leading up to the Council of Elders, where his father and the tribal elders were waiting.

He didn't want to see them. The last thing he needed now was another scolding from Ahote Chaa, father or not. He caught the gazes of other tribal members, seeing them silently judging him from a distance, but none of them said a thing. He wanted neither their thoughts nor criticism. He didn't need it. Nevertheless, it still hurt.

Lost in his thoughts, he was upon his father's Longhouse before he knew it. He stood at the entrance, trying to muster the courage to step inside. With a deep breath, he opened the flap, and entered.

"My son," Ahote Chaa spoke as the young warrior stood before him. "You have come."

Inside the Longhouse, Shunka found himself facing down not just his father, but four of the five Council of Elders; the oldest, wisest, and most respected members of the tribe. They were all seated in a row along the far wall, Ahote Chaa in the center.

There was Kitchi, the oldest warrior in the tribe and one of its greatest fighters. Kiyiya, a builder and gatherer. And lastly, Onatah the den mother. The only council member not present was Alo, the shaman and medicine man.

There was one more man in the Longhouse, he sat cross-legged beside Ahote Chaa with his arms folded and his face stern. Shunka recognized this man, he'd seen him before but only from a distance. This was Orumaku, Chaa of the Hawk Tribe.

"Shunka," Ahote spoke, his voice resonated through the Longhouse, echoing off the walls. What little whispering there was before had fallen silent with the sound of his words. "Come forward, my boy."

The young warrior did as he was bid. Walking towards the council, each step caused throbbing pain in his side. Even with the stitching holding it closed, blood still seeped ever so slowly from the gash in his side. It was agonizing, but he tried not to express it. No weakness, not for this wolf warrior.

Shunka seated himself before his father. He crossed his legs and placed his hands upon his knees. His back was straight, and chin raised high. He waited in quiet stillness, watching the

Elders as they watched him in return. No one moved, and no one spoke.

"My son," Ahote broke the spell of silence, "a proposition has been offered by Orumaku." He turned to the man at his side and gave a swift nod.

Orumaku Chaa stood. "Shunka, son of Ahote and Kakahoya, I have spoken with your father and asked to arrange a union between you and my daughter, Shikoba." The Hawk Chaa sat down again, leaving Shunka in shock.

"You wish... a union with your daughter?" Shunka asked in confusion. "I don't know what to say."

"You don't have to say anything." Ahote raised his hand to silence his son. "I have spoken of your achievements in battle, and how faithfully you've defended our lands from the Pale Invaders." The Chaa pointed to Shunka's injury. "Even the way you entered, still in pain from your last encounter with them, and not showing the slightest weakness. It has impressed me. It has impressed Orumaku as well. He would be honored for you to join his clan."

They weren't asking for his opinion, rather they were informing him of the decision they had already reached. "So it has already been decided." Shunka said, understanding. He wondered, had Orumaku's daughter been informed in this same way? Did she have any say in the matter, or would it be as much a shock as it was to him?

Or, as it was sometimes done, had she asked for him by name? And if so, why would she choose a man such as he? Shunka was neither the strongest nor the wisest of the young warriors in the Wolf Tribe, why would anyone choose him?

"The choice has been made." Ahote said. "In two moon's time an envoy from the Hawk Tribe will come to our village and accompany you back to their lands, where you will meet Shikoba and be united with her. That is all, you may go."

Shunka felt his heart sink. A pit formed in his stomach

34

much heavier that the throbbing pain. He bowed his head, "As you say, Father." He pushed himself back to his feet, his arms and legs still felt weak and he strained to stand, but stand he did under his own strength. It was important to show he was still capable of caring for himself.

Turning on his heels, he walked out of the Longhouse. Once outside, he allowed his emotions to flow. He ran. Allowed his feet to take him away from the village, picking up speed and disappeared into the forest.

The trees blurred past him as he ran, ferns trampled under his feet. The pain flared up in his side, but he hardly noticed and cared less. He just wanted to go, leave and be someplace else. He hurtled over fallen logs, took running leaps from jutting rocks, even the cold water of streams didn't bring him any discomfort as he splashed through them.

His human form fell away the same way one might throw off dirty clothes or a snake would shed its old skin. He fell on all fours, thick black fur sprouted all along his body, hands and feet became paws, his face stretched into a muzzle full of sharp teeth. He was no longer a man, he had allowed the wolf to take over.

He raced through the woods. The forest was now open to all his senses. Sharper smell allowed him to pick up the three day old trail of a chipmunk that had scampered here. He could hear the pecking of a woodpecker over ten miles away. While the colors in his eyes grew weaker than in human form, the forest was more diverse and saturated than before.

Shunka could have run for hours, even days in his wolf form if he was at full strength. But as the rush of anger and anxiety wore off, the gash in his side flared again. He slowed to a stop, whimpering in pain. Only once he was still did he notice the streaks of blood that ran down his leg, leaving a trail of red on the leaves and plants behind him.

A howl alerted him to the arrival of another pair of wolves.

They came rushing through the woods behind him, following his trail of blood. They emerged from the shadows between the trees and encircled him. He knew these wolves, had known them his whole life. The older, stronger male was his brother Mingan, while the she-wolf was Tala.

They reverted back to human form, prompting him to do the same. "Where were you trying to go?" Mingan asked. "In your state, I'm amazed you got this far."

"I wasn't going anyplace." Shunka said, he averted his eyes from his brother. "I just wanted to run. Try and clear my head."

"But what for?" Tala asked as she finished her changing.

Shunka huffed. "You know who was with my father? Orumaku Chaa of the Hawk Clan."

"So?" Tala said dismissively.

"They were talking about a union with Orumaku's daughter, Shikoba." Shunka continued. "They wanted to unite me with her."

"Oh," Tala's eyebrows raised, her mouth falling slightly agape. "I see. But, isn't that good news?"

"You'd think." Shunka continued. He hobbled over to a tree, his right leg suddenly too stiff to move, He braced his back against the bark covered trunk and slid to the ground. "But they made this arrangement without my consent, or even my knowledge. They just sprung it on me."

Tala sat next to him, she placed her hand on his shoulder. "It's not going to be that bad. You don't know, maybe a union with Shikoba won't be so bad."

"I'm not concerned about that." Shunka said. "If I join a union with her, I would have to leave the tribe to live with the Hawks and join their clan."

A heavy silence fell between them. No one spoke, though all could feel the weight of the situation bear down on them. "I won't let them." Mingan spoke at last. "I can talk to father, get him to change his mind."

"It's too late now." Shunka said. "Nor does it matter. This is what father wants, for me to leave so I won't disappoint him anymore."

"This isn't right." Mingan shook his head. "Mother wouldn't want this. She always stood against arranged unions, told us ever since we were children to choose our own love, why would father ignore her wishes?"

"Mother is dead. And father has always been more interested in tradition and the old ways than she." Shunka tried to stand, he braced himself against the tree and pushed himself back to his feet. The gash in his side flared with hot bolts and his face twisted in pain as his legs buckled. He would have fallen is Tala hadn't caught him.

"Come." Tala said as she settled his weight over her back. "We should return. My father needs to tend to your wound again."

Before they could leave, a new sound caught Shunka's ear. A yipping sound, like a small animal in distress. "Wait," he said. Regaining his strength, Shunka stepped away from Tala and followed the animals cries.

He soon found it, a small fox's head poking out from a hole in a hollowed out log. The poor creature must have chased some prey animal through the log and tried to follow it out the hole only to get stuck. It barked and yipped, struggled to pull itself free, but unable to escape.

Shunka knelt beside the log. Upon seeing him, the fox began to panic. It tugged and struggled more fiercely, but to equally fruitless results. "Sssshhhh," Shunka hushed as he reached for the fox, extending his arm slowly so as to not frighten the animal further. "It's going to be alright." His words changed as he spoke, turning from the words of his tribe to the language of animals. The fox's thrashing slowed and it came to relax as Shunka's hand stroked the fur along its ears.

"I'll get you out of there. Don't worry." With his free hand,

37

Shunka delicately chipped away at the rotting wood around the fox's head. Little by little, the pieces fell away and the hole in the log grew until it was just wide enough for the fox to slip its head back through. Once freed, the small animal bolted away, disappearing into the underbrush.

Shunka watched it go, caught sight once or twice of its red fur flash beneath the dark green fronds. *Yes, go,* he thought. *Be free. How I long for your freedom.*

IV.
ARIDAIN

A row of horn blowers stood at attention, awaiting orders from the king. The royal couple, King Cassius and Queen Beatrice, sat beside one another on their thrones, each dressed in their most extravagant and regal attire with a crown upon both their heads. King Cassius's back was pressed straight against the throne, his chin held high. Princess Endelynn stood between them, her fingers laced together delicately and her new crown resting upon her head. A tapestry depicting the white ram on a purple shield hung on the wall behind them.

Sir Aridain and a row of knights stood guard around the royal family. They were rigid and unmoving. But still Aridain kept his eye on the king and queen. It was his sworn duty to serve them from the day he was knighted until his death. Most of all, he wished to serve the princess. He had watched her from a distance most of his life, ever since being welcomed into the castle as a royal guard. Her beauty, her grace, her warmth had won him over from the first day, but he knew they could never be together. She was a princess and he was just a knight. Even the greatest of knights would be unworthy of her.

Aridain noticed Endelynn's face turn a deeper shade of pink. Her gaze fell to the floor, and she began tapping her thumbs together. She fidgeted, and leaned from one side to the other.

39

The knight looked over toward Beatrice, caught the woman's attention, then shifted his eyes over to the princess. The queen noticed Endelynn's twitching, she reached over and took the younger girl's hand. "Stop your fussing." Beatrice's voice was low and warm. "You have nothing to worry about. You look beautiful." The queen gave Endelynn a reassuring smile. This small gesture seemed to soothe the princess's nerves. She took a deep breath, let it out, then straightened herself out, confident and ready.

Aridain could not agree more with the queen's statement. When she was self assured, Endelynn was at her most radiant. No doubt the girl was both excited and terrified of meeting this prince, not that Aridain remembered anything particularly special about the boy. Prince Sedrick was young and attractive, as prince's go, but nothing out of the norm. In fact, from his performance with the wolf pack, Sir Aridain would consider Sedrick a poor match for Endelynn.

A knock came from the large wooden doors. The whole room froze in an instant and turned to the sound. Sir Aridain looked up at the king. Cassius gave him a quick nod, and with his king's order the knight stepped away from the thrones, grabbed the large iron rung of the door, and pulled it open.

A messenger came in and bowed. He faced the king, unrolled a scroll, and began to read. "In the name of his esteemed majesty, Kendrick the First, King of Kahren, it is my honor to present unto you Sedrick, the crown prince of Kahren!"

The prince approached from the darkly lit hallway. His row of fully armored knights followed closely behind him. All the trumpeters in the hall lifted their instruments to their lips and played a royal march. Aridain's eyes never left the prince as the younger man and his knights moved towards the king's thrones.

He caught the attention of the one knight in black, Sir Darren. Aridain remembered him as the knight with the damaged eye. The healers had tended to him the night before, and he now wore a bandage around that side of his face. The black knight gave Aridain a quick look of acknowledgment before continuing on.

Endelynn's reaction to the prince was hard to miss. Her eyes widened in awe and lips parted in a smile. While Aridain didn't care to see what she saw, it appeared that the princess was enamored with the young Prince Sedrick. Her face flushed red and Sir Aridain could see how she forced herself not to squirm.

As he came to the foot of the steps leading to the king's throne, Prince Sedrick bent his knee to the ground, rested his arm over his leg, and lowered his head. "Great King Cassius of Dadria, it is an honor to meet you in person."

"Prince Sedrick, of course," the king flexed his fingers upward. "Stand, my boy. No need to address me on your knees like a commoner. It is an equal honor to accept the brother of Kendrick into our halls."

The prince stood, his hand came to rest on the pommel of his sword in an action of relaxation rather than threat. "Your grace, I have journeyed from afar to seek your daughter's hand."

Aridain was certain the princess would faint, but somehow the girl kept her feet. Endelynn shyly waved to the prince, turning her ever reddening face away, but still keeping her eyes on him.

"Don't just stand there like a mute, girl," King Cassius belted to his daughter. "This young man has come a long way just to meet you. You should address him."

With her face almost as red as her hair, Endelynn stepped forward. "It is a pleasure to meet you, Prince Sedrick." She curtsied and held out her hand.

Sedrick took her hand in his and kissed it. "The pleasure is all mine. I had been told of your beauty, but the tales fall

41

utterly short of the truth of your magnificence."

Sir Aridain rolled his eyes. This sickeningly sweet exchange made him want to vomit. He knew the endgame here, and knew this charm was only skin-deep. The king continued to exchange pleasantries with the prince, they talked about the requirements and stipulations in place for a marriage between Endelynn and Sedrick, all the while the princess made love-eyes at the prince long after Aridain stopped paying attention. These political marriage speeches were all the same.

Soon the discussions came to a stop. King Cassius stood and stretched his arms. "I believe we've talked on this long enough for one day. I have other matters to attend to, and I am certain my little girl would love to get out of those dreadful shoes." He shoot Endelynn a smile, then held his hand out for Beatrice. "My queen?"

The lady took his hand and delicately rose from her throne. "Dinner will be served in the main banquet hall at sundown. We expect to see you there, young prince, and hope you will enjoy your stay with us. Sir Aridain?"

The sound of his name brought the knight's immediate attention. "Yes, my king?"

"Would you please escort Prince Sedrick and his party back to their rooms." Cassius said as he, the queen, and princess left together with Endelynn waving to the prince.

"Of course, your grace." The knight turned to face Prince Sedrick and his knight bodyguards. He resettled the helmet tucked under his arm and cleared his throat. "Your highness, if you will follow me, I will show you to your quarters."

"I remember very well where they are." The prince pushed past Sir Aridain and strutted out into the hallway, acting as though he owned this castle.

"That may be, your grace," Sir Aridain moved quickly and stepped in front of the prince, stopping the boy, "but King Cassius has commanded me to escort you." The knight's voice elevated, respectful but stern. "So since my king has ordered it, I will do as he says."

Sedrick stared up at the older knight, his face was twisted in pent up rage, as if trying desperately not to lash out. Aridain studied the boy closely, and while he was still dressed in the fine lavender tunic and gold cloak of royalty with a crown on his head, Sedrick emoted less a prince and more like a spoiled child.

Aridain looked away from the boy and caught the gaze of the Kahrenian knights, all of whom stared daggers at him. He was not afraid of them, save the black knight at the end, whose hand already gripped the pommel of his sword. Sir Aridain stepped away from the prince. "You are a guest in this kingdom, so do allow me the honor of escorting you to your chambers." His voice more restrained. He turned and began walking down the stone hallway, soon followed by the footsteps of the boy and his guards.

Sir Aridain directed each of the knights to their own separate rooms before coming lastly to the prince's chambers. He unlatched the door and pushed it open, revealing the silken sheet-covered bed, hearth of polished stone, a large wardrobe, and small round table with two chairs. "I do hope you enjoy your stay in Dadria, your grace."

"I'm sure I will." Prince Sedrick entered the room, then paused. He turned back to Sir Aridain and smirked. "The princess is lovely, isn't she?"

The knight raised an eyebrow at Sedrick's question. He stood silently in the hallway, thinking of the right words to use to not insult her grace, his heart beating faster the longer he thought.

"You don't need to answer, I can see it all over your face." Sedrick continued, his voice irritating and juvenile. "It's true, she is a most beautiful girl, and I can only hope she is just as lovely out of those dresses. I suppose I'll discover soon enough,

43

a pity you won't, however."

Rage surged within Sir Aridain's chest. His face felt hot and his fist clenched tighter around his helmet. At that moment, he wanted nothing more than to strike that smug look from Sedrick's face.

Before he could respond, however, the black knight slipped between him and the prince. "Your grace," the Kahrenian knight said, "you need to prepare for tonight. Go inside, I wish to have a word with this man in private."

"Is that so? And if I wanted to listen in?" Prince Sedrick continued his taunting, at least until the black knight set his hand against the boy's chest.

"You will not." He shoved the prince forcefully into the room. Sedrick cried out as he fell and landed with a thud, a look of shock came over his face. The black knight then closed the door on him and latched it shut.

The black knight turned his attention away from the muffled, angry shouts of the prince and towards Sir Aridain. "I apologize for his rudeness. It appears his brother has not quite disciplined him enough. I will take this up with the king when we return to Kahren."

"Apology accepted, although I'd rather receive one from the prince than his bodyguard." Sir Aridain strained. "But it was not me who was insulted, rather the princess."

"I disagree," the Kahrenian knight said, "the prince is young and willful, but would never insult the one he's set to wed. I assure you, the insult was directed at you. And I can understand why."

"I have no idea what you mean."

"I'm sure you do. I saw how you looked at the girl in the throne room, your eyes never left her even when her father bartered her off." The black knight smirked. "You have eyes for the princess, don't you?" He continued when Aridain did not respond. "There's no need to hide it. She is a beautiful young woman, a fine prize for any man."

"Princess Endelynn is not a prize." Aridain hissed.

"Of course not. Insinuating she's a prize would i there was some sort of contest, of which there is not." The black knight bantered. "Rather, she is to be given away to the first prince to ask."

Sir Aridain did not rise to the taunts. His lips pressed tightly together and eyes narrowed. He noticed the bandage across the man's face. "I haven't had the chance to ask yet, how's the eye?"

The black knight's face turned to a grimace. "It's fine." He sneered.

"Oh, good. I hope the damage isn't permanent, that might end your service to your king." Aridain gave a shrug, "But then, I don't know. I've never allowed a wolf to get the better of me like it did to you." He looked the foreign knight up and down, pausing at the emblem on his chest and the sword at his waist. "You are a member of the Black Swords of the King, are you not?"

"I am." The black knight said. "My name is Sir Darren."

"That means you have some skill with a blade." Aridain leaned in close so they were eye-to-eye. "I would love to test my steel against a knight of your caliber some day."

Darren smirked. "I'd be happy to answer the call. When the time comes, I'm more than willing."

"Very well. But only once you've recovered. There would be no honor in besting a man who was half blind." Aridain turned to leave."I hope you enjoy your stay, and give my regards to the prince."

Sir Darren pushed open the door to Prince Sedrick's chambers and stepped inside. "I'll do that." The sound of the door latching behind him echoed through the halls.

V.

DARREN

"**H**ow dare you!" Prince Sedrick was on his feet, shouting at Sir Darren. "You have no right to lay a hand on me! When my brother hears of this, he'll have you drawn and quartered!"

"Of that I sincerely doubt." Sir Darren stepped away from the closed door. "I will be sending my report back to King Kendrick shortly, and I will do the same every night for as long as we're guests in this kingdom. And I'm sure he's not going to be happy to hear you tried to pick a fight with one of the royal guards."

"I did not." Sedrick stomped against the ground. He stormed back and forth around the room, his arms folded and lower lip stuck out.

"Wars have been started for less than what you said to that knight." Sir Darren sat in one of the small chairs and propped his feet on the table. "This set up with the princess is quite convenient for us. She's an only child of an only child, King Cassius has no sons to inherit the throne, and no brothers to challenge him for it. Endelynn will be the queen of Dadria. The only question is, will you keep yourself in line long enough to ensure you become its king?"

"Why wouldn't I be? Kahren is their closest ally, uniting the kingdoms would be the best thing for them." Sedrick said.

"Plus I was the first prince to answer her father's call for suitors."

The knight scoffed. Sedrick was speaking, but these were not the prince's words. Rather he was parroting what his brother Kendrick told him to say. "If you think being the first one here gives you any advantage, you are surely mistaken." He took his boots off the table and stood. "The king has been rejecting suitors for Endelynn's hand for the past three years, mostly the sons of noblemen from within Dadria. Cassius only accepted Kendrick's invitation after he exhausted all other options. You were not the first, and if you keep this attitude, you will not be the last. You have the princess's eye, which is good, but you have to win over the king and queen. Making enemies with the people sworn to serve them is not a good idea." Sir Darren approached the prince, grabbed the boy by the collar, and lifted him off the ground. He brought Sedrick's face close to his own and stared him in the eye. Through gritted teeth, he hissed, "Think about that the next time you try mouthing off."

Sedrick's eyes were wide with fear. He tried to pull away, but Sir Darren was too strong. Sweat rolled down his face. He squirmed, his eyes closed and lips started quivering. After relishing in the sight of the lofty prince brought low, the knight released his hold and Sedrick dropped back to the floor.

Darren cleared his throat. His expression melted back to one of stern calmness. He adjusted his cloak and tugged at his gloves. "Now," he said, "make sure you get yourself prepared for tonight. I have some things I have to see to."

"Wh– where are you going?" Sedrick managed to choke out.

"I just said, I have things to do. Special orders your brother gave me to carry out while we're here." The knight stepped back to the door and pulled it open before stopping in the archway. "I'll return shortly." He then closed and latched it behind him.

Sir Darren walked hurriedly down the hall, his cape fluttering behind him. The corridors were empty, lit by the few open windows. They held no glass, only wood shutters.

He paused by one of the windows. Looking out past the jagged mountain peaks and the mighty walls encircling the kingdom, he saw the Wayward Forest. An enormous sea of trees that stretched all the way to the horizon, and beyond that was the sea. From here in the mountains it did not look as intimidating as it had been to travel through. He ran his fingers over his bandaged right eye. It still throbbed.

That blasted wolf. If Sir Darren had his way, he would burn that accursed forest to the ground. He would slaughter every one of those vile beasts and decorate his walls with their pelts. And the head of the one that scared him would be mounted over his fireplace. If this injury cost him his knighthood, he'd make sure to kill them all.

He sneered at the forest, then turned away and continued down the corridor. King Kendrick was counting on him to complete his mission, and Sir Darren was nothing if not loyal to his king. He spotted a young servant girl emerging from another room and called to her. "Young lady," he said as he approached.

She jumped, startled, almost dropping the basket of sheets and linens in her hands. She quickly bowed in greetings to the knight. "How may I be of service, sir?"

"I have some questions for you." Sir Darren said. "The banquet tonight, do you know what is being prepared?"

"Of course." The girl's voice was low and stuttered. She set her laundry basket on the floor and clasped her hands together in front, her eyes never raised from the floor. "His majesty is preparing wild venison and boar. I believe red wine will be served."

"What about nuts?" The black knight asked. "Any pine

nuts?"

"I..." Her shoulders hunched up, she began to tremble. "I don't know. I'm sorry for my incompetence." The girl started to break down.

Sir Darren placed his hand under her chin and raised her head up. She was crying, her eyes wide with fear, tears streaming down her face, and lips quivered. "Hey, it's not an issue if you don't know." He said in a comforting voice. His eyes were full of false compassion. "I don't expect you to have information about everything in this castle. How about you go down to the kitchen and learn if they're preparing the food with nuts. And if they are," he pulled a small glass vial full of lavender liquid from the pouch at his side, "ask them to put this in the wine."

She grabbed the vial delicately, staring into it. "What is it?"

"Medicine." Sir Darren said. "The prince, Sedrick, is deathly allergic to nuts. If he ingests even a little bit, it could kill him. But this is a medicine that will allow him to eat all he wants without worry." He produced three silver coins from his pouch and held them out for her. "Will you put it in the wine for me?"

The girl looked awestruck at the coins. She glanced up at the knight, then scooped the money out of his hand. "Yes, sir. As you ask."

"Good girl." He straightened himself up and turned to walk away, then stopped. "Oh," he said, "might I ask, which way to the aviary?"

"You keep going down this hall, take a left at the second passageway, then up two flights of stairs to the highest tower. That's where we keep the messenger falcons." The servant girl quickly stuffed the vial and coins down her shirt, then grabbed the laundry basket. "If there's anything else I can do to help you, sir, I will gladly do it."

"It's greatly appreciated." He took another coin and tossed

it behind him where it clinked against the stone floor. The girl quickly gathered it then headed in the opposite direction.

Sir Darren watched her go, then turned to depart. The maid girl had not been altogether unattractive. As he headed towards the aviary, he thought more and more of this young, naive servant girl. Perhaps she might be willing to aid him more in his ventures. And maybe, for enough silver coins, she could warm his bed.

He found the stairways. A pair of spiral steps circled around the central column of the southernmost tower. He followed them up until he came to a closed door. A sign above the door labeled the room as the falcon's roost.

Sir Darren rapped his knuckles against the door. A slot in the door opened at face level and a pair of eyes peered out at him. "Who goes there? What is your business?" The man behind the door asked.

"I am Sir Darren, knight of Kahren, bodyguard of Prince Sedrick, and captain of the Black Swords of the King." The black knight said. "I need to send a message to Kendrick of Kahren."

The eye slot closed. The door unlatched from within and pulled inward away from Sir Darren. An old man stood beside the door. He wore robes which fell to his feet and covered his hands. The man's head was shaved bald, a long beard grew down from his chin. "Welcome, Sir." The old man said. He stepped aside to allow Sir Darren's entrance.

Slots dotted the walls of the aviary, all with a hinged barred door like a cage. Housed within each was a single falcon, a black and white speckled bird with long pointed talons and a hooked beak. Every falcon had a hood over its eyes.

A small desk and chair were set against a wall next to an open window. A nearly melted candle stood next to the stack of paper, with a bottle of ink and feather quill beside it. A small stub of red wax rested next to the candle.

"You will find matches in the left drawer." The elderly bird-keeper said.

"Thank you." Sir Darren seated himself at the desk, dipped the quill in the ink, and wrote his message.

> *"My King,*
> *Your brother arrived safely in Dadria. The princess appears to have interest in him, but the boy's made enemies with some of the royal guards. I have scolded him, but I fear this development may hinder your plans for a union of him and Endelynn.*
> *Otherwise, things are proceeding as planned. I've given the prince's medicine to the serving staff to have it prepared with his meals.*
> *-Sir Darren, Black Sword of the King."*

Sir Darren finished the letter and set the quill feather aside. After a moment to let the ink dry, he folded the parchment thrice. Striking a match to light the candle, he melted a seal of red wax atop the folded paper. Then, while the seal was still wet, he removed the glove from his left hand.

He bore a ring on his third finger, bronze with the sigil of the Black Swords carved into the flat top. He removed the ring and pressed it into the setting wax, marking it. Once finished, he set the ring back on his finger and replaced his glove. "My message is complete." Sir Darren said.

A cage door creaked open. The old bird-keeper brought over a falcon, the bird nestled on his gloved hand with a hood covering its eyes. He took the letter from Sir Darren and slipped it into the cylindrical compartment attached to the bird's back. He moved to the open window and raised the falcon. "Kahren." He spoke to the bird before removing its hood.

The falcon leapt from his hand. It's wings spread and caught the air, lifting the bird up and away from the tower. It veered to the south, heading away from Dadria, over the Wayward Forest, and towards Kahren. Sir Darren raised himself from the desk, thanked the bird-keeper for his help, and gave him a silver coin.

The knight then made his way back down the tower to the room of the prince, still locked from the outside. Sir Darren lifted the latch, pushed the door inward, and stepped inside. "I have returned, my prince." He said. "I trust you've not been too bored while I was away– " he froze as he gazed upon an empty room.

The prince was gone.

VI.
ENDELYNN

Princess Endelynn hurried down the stone corridor, she gripped the edges of her dress and raised it above her ankles to allow better strides. She moved quickly and with a purpose. While she had spent some time with Sedrick in the throne room with her parents and royal guards, what she really wanted was some time alone with the prince.

As she approached the prince's chambers, voices reached her ears. One was deep, gruff, and unfamiliar. The other was much softer and more timid, Endelynn recognized it as one of the wash maids.

She came to the corner and paused. Peeking around the edge, she saw them. The owner of the gruff voice was a tall man dressed entirely in black, with dark hair and a beard, and a patch over his left eye. An emblem was embroidered on his chest, a gold sword stabbing down through a five-point crown. She did not know his name, but Endelynn recognized him from the throne room, one of the Kahren knights who served Sedrick.

The two finished talking and the knight handed something to the maid, who snatched it from his hand. She gathered her basket of dirty sheets and turned down the hall away from the knight and towards Endelynn.

The princess moved back behind the stone corner. She waited until the maid past before looking out again, only catching the flutter of the knight's cape as he headed towards the towers. Once the hall was empty, she moved over to Sedrick's chambers.

Just as she came to the door, Endelynn stopped. Her hand hovered an inch from the door, but she did not knock. She wanted to, more than anything all she wanted to do was call out to Sedrick, but something was holding her back. She knew her father would disapprove of this meeting, and her mother would likely scold her.

She was nervous. That's what this was, just flutters in the stomach. She took a deep breath, stretched out her arm, and tapped her knuckles against the door.

"Who's there?" The prince called out from within.

"It is I." The princess said. "Endelynn."

There was a moment of silence, and then the prince spoke again. "To what do I owe your presence, my lady?"

She found herself at a loss for words. She hadn't actually expected to get this far, and knew not what to talk about. "I just wanted to see you again, more personally this time." She noticed the beam placed across the door. "Do you know your chambers are locked from the outside?"

"Yes, I know." Sedrick said through the door. "My bodyguard decided to seal it when he left. I don't know where he went or how soon he will return."

"I just saw him." Endelynn said. "He was talking to one of the servants, and then headed off towards the aviary."

"Oh," Sedrick said. "I get it now."

"I wanted to know," Endelynn stuttered as she found her words, "if it was alright with you, I'd like to take you on a tour of the castle." The door was quiet. She stood in the hallway, waiting for a response, but none came. "I mean, if you don't want to, that's okay."

"I would, actually." The prince spoke. "I'd greatly enjoy your company. But as you've seen, I'm locked within. If you could undo the latch, that would be wonderful."

"Oh, alright." Endelynn said. She placed her hands under the wooden beam across the door and lifted. It was heavier than she expected. Her arms strained and teeth gritted, but it steadily rose. Once beam was removed, the door sung inward and Prince Sedrick emerged.

"Many thanks, my lady." He said. Sedrick took the wooden beam from the princess and placed it over the door again, making it appear as though he were still inside. "You have freed me, and offered me a tour of your home." He held his arm out, crooked at the elbow. "Lead the way."

"Yes, as you wish." Endelynn slid her arm around his, placing her hand against his bicep. They walked together down the hall away from the prince's quarters. "What would you like to see first?"

Sedrick thought for a moment. "Actually, I'm interested in seeing those animals you ride. Those giant ram things."

"The raox?" Endelynn corrected him.

"What's a raox?"

"That's what they're called; raox." The princess said. "If you'd like, sure. I can take you to the stables."

She led the prince along, walking casually down the corridors of the castle, passing windows, tapestries, and portraits along the way. They came to one such painting and Sedrick stopped. He looked up at it, tilting his head quizzically. "What's this?"

Endelynn looked up at the painted canvas. It depicted a great king on the back of a raox, his army of white knights behind him. He had a beard of red hair, a gold crown, and swung a sword overhead, leading his advancing forces against a field of dark-skinned savage men who ran away hunched over like animals. "This," the princess said, "is called Thaddeus's victory at the Mountain Pass."

"Who's Thaddeus?" Sedrick asked.

"You never heard of him?" Endelynn asked. When Sedrick shook his head, she began to explain. "Thaddeus was the first king of Dadria. He helped establish the first fortress in these mountains, which would later become this very castle. He fought and defended the people during the Savage Wars after the first settlers from the Old World came here across the Endless Sea." Endelynn ran her hand under the picture frame. "He established Dadria and named it after his wife, the first queen."

"Hm," Sedrick glanced back up at the portrait and they continued walking. "You mentioned something called the Savage Wars. What where those?"

"You don't know?" Endelynn said in shock. "Didn't anyone teach you history? It's the history of both our kingdoms. How they were settled and how they came to be. I know even of your first king, Haddrick the First who established Kahren at the mouth of the Blue Serpent river. He'd later expand Kahren to encompass all of Serpent's Mouth bay and set the capital at the Fang."

Sedrick rolled his eyes. "Of course I know that, but you didn't answer me. What were the Savage Wars?"

"Alright." Endelynn said. "When the first settlers arrived from the Old World they thought this land was free from people. But as they soon learned, there were tribes of wild, uncultured, savage men. Our ancestors tried to live in peace with them, but the wild men would sneak into the camps and villages and started attacking. They're even said to have practiced cannibalism and skinned their victims alive."

Sedrick shuddered.

"Haddrick and Thaddeus wouldn't stand for this." Endelynn continued. "They amassed what forces they could and marched into the forests, finding the villages and dispensing righteous justice. Soon a war broke out, which we have called the Savage Wars."

56

"So, we obviously won, right?" Sedrick asked.

"Yes, after a long and bloody war." Endelynn said. "But it came with a cost. Once the wild men were gone, something happened to the animals of the forest. The predators; wolves, panthers, bears, and even hawks started attacking the settlers. And not just regular animals either, enormous bloodthirsty beasts. They would sneak into the cities and attack people in their homes, even dragging them back to the woods. Because of this, the great walls were built. The walls of Kahren were named Haddrick's Mercy, and Dadria's walls named God's Grace."

"Oh, I know about them." Sedrick said. "The beasts and monsters. My caravan was beset by a pack of those wolves on our way here."

"Oh, my!" Endelynn placed a hand over her mouth. "Really?"

"Yes." He pointed to his right eye. "That's how my body-guard, Sir Darren, got injured."

"That sounds terrible." The princess said.

"It was." Sedrick spoke. "A horrible encounter. You see, we were riding along the path through the forest when suddenly we came to a stop." The prince recounted. "I got out of my carriage and saw a pair of eyes in the trees. Big, glowing, red eyes. And then another, and another. All these red eyes. Just then, a whole bunch of wolves came rushing out of the woods. They jumped at us, tried to bite and claw us, but I was brave."

Sedrick held his arm out as if he had a sword. He took a fighting stance and swished his hand through the air, slashing imaginary foes. "One came at me, but I dodged it. It tried to bite me, wanted to tear me to shreds, but I held it back with my sword. I pushed my sword in its mouth, I did. Forced the beast away."

Endelynn listened, enthralled by the prince's story. He moved and danced around the hall, fighting invisible wolves.

"Then, I noticed Sir Darren." Sedrick pointed to the ground, indicating where the knight would have lain. "There was a wolf on top of him. It was biting and slashing at him. It's claws scratched over his eye. I knew I had to help him, I was the only one who could." Sedrick rushed over and stabbed at the air. "I thrust my sword into the foul beast's rotten belly. It howled and ran away, like a frightened dog."

Endelynn clapped her hands together, cheering for the prince's victory. "What happened next? I must know."

"Next, well," Sedrick paused. "That's about when your knights appeared riding those... " He snapped his fingers as he thought. "What were they called?"

"The raox." Endelynn smirked.

"Yes, those. The raox." Sedrick said. "We're still on our way to the stables, right?"

"Of course." Endelynn laced her arm through his again and they continued down the corridor.

As they walked, she pulled him closer, just a little at a time. He didn't seem to notice the small gap between them diminishing bit by bit until she placed her head against his shoulder. Sedrick felt her soft hair press against him, and tuned in surprise.

"I'm sorry," Endelynn pulled away. "I just thought it'd be more romantic this way. If you'd prefer, I won't."

"No, it's quite alright." Sedrick said. "Do as you'd like."

Endelynn felt as though she would faint. Her heart raced and her face felt warm, she was sure her cheeks had turned bright red again. Even so, she placed her hand through the crook of his arm and lay her head upon his shoulder. Silently, she embraced the moment.

VII.
BEATRICE

"I don't like this boy." King Cassius stood at the balcony overlooking his kingdom. In the distance the great wall, God's Grace, circled around Dadria's borders, and a massive gate stood locked. Outside those walls was the Red Woods, or the Wayward Forest as the Kahrenian's called it. "Sedrick is too childish, too immature for our daughter."

"Now, dear, I think you're overreacting." Beatrice stood in the center of the room, a trio of servant women encircled her. They worked to apply the queen's dress, her precious jewels, everything she might need to look proper for the banquet tonight. "You've hardly met the boy, you can't be so quick to judge."

"It's not just me," Cassius placed his hands together behind his back. "We spoke with him in the throne room, yes, but Sir Aridain has just reported to me that-"

"Ah, so that's why." The queen interrupted.

Cassius turned to his wife. "Why what?"

"Why you gave the visiting prince an escort back to his room." Beatrice said, a knowing smile on her lips. "It made no sense before, but it does now. Young Sedrick and his guards already knew where their sleeping quarters where, you just wanted someone to listen in on them while you weren't around

59

to hear."

"Of course I did." King Cassius stroked his beard in a proud manner. "What one says to a king usually differs greatly from what one says in private. And I wanted to know what the boy really thought."

"I take it you were not pleased."

Cassius shook his head. "No, I wasn't. His remarks about our daughter were crude. According to Sir Aridain, the boy is childish and spoiled. He was goading our knights and disrespecting Endelynn. I think we should wait until we find a better suitor."

"In what way was he disrespectful?" Beatrice asked.

The king took out the note given him by his knight. "Sir Aridain reported that Sedrick wanted to know if our daughter was as lovely out of her dresses as in them."

Beatrice scoffed. "Is that all? He's young, it's all he thinks about." She groaned as her dress was tied together in the back, tightening around her rib cage. "As I recall, you were very eager to get me out of my bridal gown on our wedding night."

Cassius's cheeks turned a light pink. He smirked and looked skyward. "Yes, that was a good night."

Beatrice laughed. "I'm glad someone had fun." The king froze, then turned to his wife, but she placed her fingers across his lips to silence him. "My point is, Sedrick is still a child. He has yet to gain the age and wisdom of a man. He's young and restless, the weight of a king's crown will settle him. We cannot judge the prince yet if he doesn't reach the impossible standards you've set."

"My standards are not impossible to reach." Cassius said. "I just want what's best for our daughter. She is our only child, and to this day I still regret not being able to give you more."

"That is not your fault." Beatrice said. "It was that raox during the tournament celebrating Endelynn's birth. If it hadn't gotten spooked and knocked you down, you wouldn't have been hurt."

"And we'd have children running throughout the castle." Cassius said with sadness in his eyes.

"Is that what this is really about?" Beatrice said. A servant girl ran a brush through the queen's chestnut-brown hair. "You're worried about losing our daughter. Our only daughter." Cassius didn't respond, he merely turned his back to the queen and looked out the window again. "You're concerned for her, I can see that. You want her to wed someone kind and gentle, but that won't happen if you keep her shut in forever. Do you remember the first night she bled?"

"You mean her first cycle?" Cassius shuddered. "I remember that night well. All the screaming, all the shouting, it's burned in my mind."

"Yes," the queen smirked, "screaming and shouting mostly came from you." The king looked back at Beatrice, annoyance on his face. Beatrice just smirked. "Once word had reached the lords and nobles of Endelynn's ability to bare children, everyone in Dadria with even an ounce of titles or authority tried to proposition their sons for marriage. And you turned them all away. You kept making up any excuse you could as to why they were unfit for your little girl."

"They were unfit." Cassius spouted. "Do you remember that one boy? Giribald, son of Lord Cathwalth of the Northern Province? That boy had a clubfoot and a lazy eye. And then Wauldon, son of Lord Marigold of Southhaim. He was dimmer than a candle made of mud."

"That's two, my dear." Beatrice retorted. "Out of how many? Over the last three years, dozens of men and their sons opted for Endelynn's hand, and you turned them all away. It's not that all of them were unfit, you were simply afraid of losing our little girl. Our only girl."

King Cassius looked solemnly off the balcony, his hands placed upon the railings. He didn't speak a word, but Beatrice know what he was thinking, as those thoughts were in her mind as well. "But she's not a girl anymore. She's becoming a woman, and nothing you or I can do will ever change that. It's already been three years, it's time to let her go."

"I know," Cassius said, choking on his tears. "I should let her live her own life, but I'm not ready to let go."

Beatrice stepped away from her dressing maids. The trio of women began to object, but a single raised finger from the queen silenced them. She came up behind her husband, rested her hands upon his shoulders and placed her face against his back. She could hear his heartbeat, powerful and rhythmic.

"Everything's going to be alright." The queen whispered in his ear. She traced her arms around his body, embracing her husband from behind. "Never forget that I love you, and Endelynn loves you, too. No matter what happens, nothing is going to bring us apart."

A knock came from the door, thrice struck before a voice called. "Your majesty's, someone seeks an audience."

Cassius groaned. "Can it wait?"

A new voice replaced the first. "It is a matter of some urgency." This person was not recognized by their voice alone. They sounded deep and gruff, and spoke with authority. "It concerns the visiting prince, and your daughter."

Upon hearing this, Beatrice pulled away from her husband. She stepped back to her previous spot, and the dressing maids resumed their work. Cassius moved to the door.

Standing on the other side was the black knight, the one who accompanied Prince Sedrick. Sir Darren. "Your grace," he fell to a knee, "I apologize for this intrusion. I would not disturb you like this if it wasn't important."

The king raised his hand, palm facing up. "Stand." As the black knight came to his feet, Cassius folded his arms over his chest. "What is the matter?"

"Your grace, it is the prince." The Kahrenian knight said.

"He is missing. Gone somewhere I know not, and I believe it was by your daughter's hand."

The Dadrian king's eyes widened. His lips tightened in anger. "What do you insinuate about my daughter?"

"Nothing, your grace." The black knight backtracked his words. "All I know is this. I left the prince alone in his chambers with the door firmly locked while I procured a falcon to send to my king. When I returned, young Sedrick was gone."

"And should you have not kept better track of him?" Cassius said.

"As I had said, your grace," The Black Swordsman replied, "I had the prince's chambers locked from the outside when I left. Upon my return, he was gone. Someone must have let him out."

The king placed his hand against his chin, he lightly plucked at his beard. "And you believe my daughter was the one to do this?"

"I can think of no one else."

"Very well," Cassius said, "I will summon her handmaiden to assess the princess's whereabouts. If she is not where she should be, I'll form a search party and find them."

"Thank you, your grace." The Kahrenian knight bowed again, then turned and left.

Cassius closed the door. He let out a heavy sigh and brought his hand to his forehead, pressing his fingers firmly against his brow. "That girl is going to be the death of me."

"My love," Beatrice said, "we still don't know that Endelynn has done anything wrong. The knight has a suspicion, not an absolute."

"You saw how enamored she was in the throne room." The king said. "Her eyes couldn't leave the boy. I want them found. I want to be sure the boy hasn't stolen my daughter away and taken advantage of her."

But, of course, the knight had said Sedrick was locked in

his room. If anyone has been stolen away, it would be the prince, and Endelynn would have done the stealing. Beatrice knew this, but her husband would not accept that. Endelynn would always be a child, always his little girl for as long as Cassius lived.

"We will find them," she pressed herself against him, placing her hands on his chest. "They can't leave the castle grounds."

VIII.
ENDELYNN

She couldn't help but giggle, placing her hand over her mouth to stop herself from laughing. Her cheeks ached from the constant grin brought on by the sight before her. Sedrick, the brave boy prince who saved his own bodyguard from a vicious bloodthirsty wolf all on his own, was now afraid of a simple raox.

The prince stood with his arm stretched out and fingers clenched around a handful of hay. His eyes were shut and face turned away from the opened mouth and reaching tongue of the raox still in its stable. The large ram, at least a tall as a horse and weighing nearly as much, strained its neck out over the wooden stable door and flexed its fleshy lips for the food in Sedrick's hand. But still, the prince would not move any closer.

"You can't stand so far back." Endelynn said, managing to contain her laughter. "What are you so afraid of? I thought you were a brave fighter and swordsman. Didn't you fight a wolf just yesterday?"

"I am!" Sedrick insisted. He stomped his foot. "I did!"

"Then give the food to the raox. He may be big, but he's still just a sheep. Here," she tore a patch of hay from the nearby bale and brought it over to the stable. "Like this."

The princess lifted her hand with the food in it, her palm flat and open, up to the raox. The animal's attention shifted from the prince over to her, and it scooped the dry grass out of her hand as though it were nothing. Within a second, there was no sign or trace of the hay. The raox chewed and swallowed quickly, then went back to reaching for what Sedrick held.

"It won't hurt me?" Prince Sedrick asked.

"Of course not." Endelynn placed her hand against the creature's neck, feeling the powerful muscles beneath her fingertips. "If it helps, just think of it as a horse." A mean thought came to her mind and she couldn't stop herself from speaking it. "A horse with an enormous set of curved horns as wide as its shoulders and more solid than stone that can easily batter down this stable door if it were so inclined."

She watched with amusement as his eyes grew wide and he swallowed in fear. He took several deep breaths as a way to steady himself, then rolled the sleeve of his tunic up to his elbow, and lifted his hand with the hay again. He took two small steps towards the beast.

The raox's slimy lips and tongue slurped against his hand, finally catching the food. Sedrick yanked his arm back in a frantic rush. "Yech!" He cried out in disgust. He trembled and shook his arm up and down, trying to get the film of the animal's green spit off his hand. "That's disgusting!"

Endelynn giggled again. "Awww, it's alright, Gallant," she said to the raox and she ran her hand over the fur on its neck. "He didn't mean to be so rude."

The raox craned its neck to look at her, its eyes were large and glassy with long, flat, oval shaped pupils. It bleated in response, then stepped back into the stable.

"Is it true what you said?" The prince pulled a handkerchief from his pocket and used it to clean his hand, then after looking as the saliva on the cloth, tossed it aside. "That he could break down the stable door if he wanted?"

"Probably." Endelynn folded her hands together. "They are quite powerful. Supposedly they were used as literal battering rams to knock down fortress gates in times of war. But war has not come to Dadria for a long time."

As Sedrick rolled his sleeve down, Endelynn noticed a patch of raised, red skin on his arm. It had a peculiar shape, almost like a deer's head with a set of mighty antlers. "What is that?" She gestured to his arm.

Sedrick looked down to his wrist. "Oh, this." He pressed a finger against the red skin. "It's the birthmark of my family. Everyone born from House Stagghart has this mark on their arm. It's a sign of my royal lineage." He finished fixing his sleeve, then looked back to the raox and shook his head. "Such strange things. How can you stand to be around them? Why not just use horses?"

"Horses do not work well in these mountains." Endelynn explained. "They can be easier to train and control, but the terrain is too uneven and rocky, and the winters too harsh outside our city walls for them. The mountain rams, on the other hand, have been living along these slopes for thousands of years. They've adapted to the harshness. So after we settled these lands we captured and domesticated them.

"The raox are our finest mounts, strong and dependable, able to scale even the sharpest cliff faces and steepest mountains. During the Savage Wars, the first king of Dadria took it as the name of his new clan, House Rambourne. And my family words, 'Strong as the Mountain' reflect the power of the raox, as only something this strong can survive up here." She grabbed another handful of hay and held it out to Gallant. "Also, feeding them is easy. They can survive on almost anything." The great ram ate the straw from her hand. "Come on," she said and she dusted her hands together to knock away the smallest pieces of dried grass, "I'll show you mine."

"Yours?" Sedrick asked. "This one isn't yours?"

"You mean Gallant? Oh, no. Not him. He's Sir Aridain's." She couldn't help but chuckle. "Mine is this way." She led him down the stable corridor, passing row after row of raox. At the very end of the hall, penned within a waist high wooden fence, with straw bedding covering the fenced-in ground, was a young lamb. It had a simple fleece with a tiny pair of budding horns sprouted from its head. The lamb munched contently from a trough of grains. Endelynn whistled. "Sleppa, come here, girl."

The lamb's ears perked. It looked up from its food, and upon seeing Endelynn, ran towards her. It jumped and bounded along on it's little hooves as though they were springs, kicking and wheeling in the air like it had lost control of itself. The lamb raced up to the fence, placed its hooves along the top rung, and stuck its face against Endelynn's cheek. The princess laughed, giggling like a small girl as the soft, fluffy face nuzzled against hers.

"This one is yours?" Sedrick asked, confused by the animal's display.

"Yes," Endelynn pulled her face away as the lamb tried to lick her. She wrapped her arms around its neck and hugged it. "This is Sleppa. She was born a runt and her mother abandoned her. Father was going to have her made into lamb stew, but I talked him out of it and got to keep her as my personal raox."

"She?" Sedrick glanced down at the lamb, then back to Endelynn. "Why does she have horns? I mean, they look small, but they're still there. Don't only rams have horns?"

"The female's horns are smaller, but they have them." Endelynn said. She scratched the little raox behind its ears. "In the wild, mothers and their offspring are always in danger from predators. Wolves, bears, and panthers would love to dine on raox lamb chops. So, the females have to be prepared to fight them. They're really protective parents."

"Hm," Sedrick pressed his lips together and nodded. "Is that why they're on your sigil?"

"Yes." Endelynn said. She lightly pushed Sleppa away and the baby raox set itself back on the ground. It stood next to her, letting the princess run her fingers along its back and through its soft wool. "They're the most important animal to our society. Without them, we wouldn't be able to survive in the mountains."

She bent down to face level with the lamb. "Okay, Sleppa, go back." She pointed to the trough. Sleppa walked back over to the grain and continued eating. "Someday she'll be strong enough to ride, and I'll have her take me anywhere I want."

"Where do you want to go?" Sedrick asked.

"Anywhere." Endelynn laced her fingers together over her waist as she spoke, the same way Mother always taught her to. "Everywhere. I want to see the world. Someday I want to visit Kahren and sail through Serpent's Mouth bay. To gaze upon the black, Endless Sea and watch the gray whales as they swim north, maybe even witness a hunt by the black orca whales."

Sedrick step beside her. "Why don't you? Tell your father what you want and make him give it to you."

"He won't." Endelynn said. "I've asked to go on survey and scouting missions into the Red Woods or deeper into the Dragon's Teeth, but he always refuses. He says, 'that's not suited for a princess.' So I just spend most of my time in the castle library reading about places I wish to someday visit."

At the mention of the library, Sedrick's eyes grew wide with shock. "You have a library? You can read?"

"Of course I can." She answered. "I've been learning since before my fifth year. Can't you?"

"Not very well." He said. "My father brought scholars to teach me, but after he died and my brother became king, Kendrick decided to stop my lessons. He said I would always have people to read for me, so I didn't need to learn."

It struck Endelynn as quite odd. She knew that many of the common people could not read as it was not important for their simple lives, but for the prince, more than that the heir to the throne of a powerful kingdom, to be unable to read seemed unfathomable. She faced the prince again. "Is there anything else you wanted to see? I did offer you a tour of the castle."

"How about you decide this time." Sedrick bowed and extended his arm. "I asked for the stables, and I saw them, but you should choose what to show me next."

"Oh, well if you insist." Endelynn placed a hand against her chin in thought. An idea came to mind and her face lit up. It would make perfect sense. The prince couldn't read well, but she could. And all her favorite books were in the library. "How about next we see –"

"The inside of the prince's chambers." A deep, gruff voice boomed behind the princess. She froze in place, her words caught in her throat. Sedrick looked on with terror written on his face.

Endelynn slowly turned around. She hesitated, and then saw the source of that voice. It was Sedrick's bodyguard, the knight dressed all in black. Endelynn recognized the emblem on his chest, the one of sword piercing downward through a five-point crown. That emblem identified him as one of the Black Swords of the King.

"Sir Darren," Sedrick's voice trembled, "nice of you to join us."

"You have the castle in an uproar." The black knight said. He didn't seem to care about position or ceremony, addressing the prince as he would any peasant, servant, or stable boy. "The castle guards have been searching for you and the princess for the better part of an hour. Do you understand what kind of fury you've upset with the king?"

"Please, sir," Endelynn placed herself between the prince and the black knight, her hand raised in defense. "It wasn't his fault. I asked him to accompany me, I am to blame."

"I know." Sir Darren said, only briefly shifting his attention to the princess. "He could not have gotten out of that room without help, so I discerned you were likely the culprit.

70

However," his gaze returned to Sedrick, "he should have known better than to leave without a bodyguard, or at least securing permission."

"Permission?" Sedrick vehemently spat. "I am a prince! I don't need permission!"

"I'm afraid you do." Sir Darren stepped around the princess and advanced on Sedrick. The young prince took a step back, a twinkle of fear in his eye. "As I said before, we are guests here. You cannot go running around the castle on your own, even if the young lady joins you. The king is furious with you, and any chance you might have had could now be ruined." Darren stood over the prince, his arms folded and face stern. His long shadow fell over Sedrick, casting the young man completely in the dark. "The only way you can hope to fix any of this will be to go before King Cassius, explain what happened and beg his forgiveness. And maybe then, he'll be gracious enough to allow us depart in the morning rather than tonight."

"Depart?" Endelynn interjected. "No, Father can't do that. I'll speak with him myself and make sure he doesn't send you away."

Sir Darren turned around to face the princess. "As nice as that sentiment is, my lady, I don't believe it will change much." The knight said.

"He'll listen to me." Endelynn said. "He has to."

"In any case, now that I've found you I am to bring you back to the throne room where you will speak directly to the king." Sir Darren gripped Sedrick's shoulder and pushed the boy forward. He herded the young prince back from the stables, up to the castle and through its many corridors. Endelynn followed closely behind, her hands folded together over her dress as she walked.

What would father do to him? Was Sedrick to be sent back to Kahren? Was the wedding to be called off? All because she took the prince on a small tour alone? She wouldn't let him. If

71

she could get a moment alone with father, she could convince him otherwise and give Sedrick another chance. Endelynn would not let her father send another suitor away, not this time.

Walking through the courtyard, and then through the corridors and hallways, Endelynn felt all the stares of the castle servants and workers on her. No one said a thing, leaving the only sounds in the halls their footsteps on the stone floor.

She was so preoccupied with her thoughts that they were upon the throne room doors before she realized. A pair of guards stood by the doors, one of whom she recognized as Sir Aridain. The armored men stepped aside and pushed the doors open, allowing the prince, his bodyguard, and the princess to enter.

Just as the black knight had said, her father and mother were both awaiting them. She couldn't read their faces, although they appeared less than pleased. The king leaned back in his throne, his fierce eyes staring down and his fingers laced together in front of him. The queen sat more rigid, her back held straight and chin lifted up so she looked down her nose as they entered.

At first, neither spoke. The black knight fell to his knee and lowered his head as he addressed her father. "I have retrieved the prince and princess, your grace. They were found in the stables feeding the beasts."

"You have my thanks, sir knight." Endelynn's father said. He didn't move or make any other gesture that he'd heard. As far as Endelynn could tell, he hardly blinked. "Please, take the prince back to his chambers and be sure to keep him there. I would like a word with my daughter."

"As you wish, your grace." The black knight stood and turned on his heels, never meeting the king's eyes. As he left the throne room, he grabbed Sedrick by the arm and escorted the young prince out with him. The doors closed behind the knight with a thud and a clang that echoed throughout the halls.

She stood alone in the center of the throne room, the intimidating stares of her parents bearing down on her like heat from the midday sun. They were waiting for her to say something, but she didn't know what to say. She hoped they would be the first to speak, at least accuse her of something so she could defend herself.

At last, her mother broke the silence. "Endelynn," she said, the tone in her voice both withheld and angry, a tone often used by a queen. "Your actions have angered your father and me. Do you realize what you did?"

Endelynn remained quiet. Her eyes stayed fixed on the polished stone floor and the ornate mosaic tiles that made up its design; her family's sigil, the white ram. Beneath her calm exterior emotions were boiling. What were they accusing her of? There was nothing wrong with just talking to the prince or giving him a tour around the castle, why did that make them mad?

It was just another way of controlling her. She knew, even if her parents would never admit it, they didn't like her doing things in her own time and in her own way. She looked up to meet her parents gaze. "I was merely showing Sedrick the raox stables. What was wrong with that?"

"Don't give me that smart tone, child," her father said as he placed his hands firmly on the throne's armrests. "You were wandering the castle with a visiting royal and without supervision. Something could have happened to you."

"I was in no danger." Endelynn said. "We were just talking, nothing else. If Sedrick and I are to be wed, then we should get to know each other before hand. I don't understand why you're so mad."

"I'm not upset that you wanted to spend time with him. The problem was that you did so without an escort and without his bodyguard's permission." The king said. He rose from the throne, no longer angry but still his face appeared upset.

"Endelynn, when a man or woman of royal blood travels any great distance, their lives are in danger. Any revolutionary or political rival or ambitious lord could take the opportunity to kill them, or someone they care about. In some cases it needn't be a deliberate orchestrated assassination. Prince Sedrick's party was attacked by wolves while traveling here to see you. I just want you to be safe. I don't want to see anything happen to you."

"Nothing's going to happen." Endelynn protested. She heard her father's words, but inwardly it annoyed her. He was trying to spout wisdom and be gentle, but it only came across as annoying. Judgmental. He was trying to control her as he always did. "You don't need to worry. I am not a little child anymore!" Her voice grew louder and tone harsher as she spoke. "I can handle things on my own! I don't need you to protect me!"

"You'll always need protection, young lady!" The king shouted back. "I'm not going to have my daughter, my only child, put herself in needless danger!"

"There was nothing dangerous about it!"

"I don't care!" The king's voice roared through the halls. "You're my daughter, you live in my castle and in my kingdom, and as long as that is the case, you will obey the rules I set in place for you!"

"Then maybe," Endelynn said as the rage built within her. She felt like doing something outrageous, something she knew she would regret, but right now didn't care. She lifted the gold circlet from her head. "I don't want to be your daughter!" She threw the crown away. It clattered across the floor, coming to a halt at her father's feet.

The room fell silent. No one, neither her father or mother said anything. Mother and father stared at her in shock, and Endelynn found herself surprised by her own outburst. After a moment, which felt longer than it truly was, she said, "May I be excused?"

The king nodded. "Very well. You may go. I'll see you tonight at the banquet."

Endelynn turned on her heels and marched out the door, her chin raised high. There was a rush surging through her body. She just stood up to her father, she'd talked back and told him how she felt. And she didn't regret a word.

Then why did she feel angry with herself?

IX.
ARIDAIN

The knight found himself still in shock at the princess's words and actions. Never before had Endelynn said or done anything so hurtful. It drove a spike through his heart to hear the princess speak such things to her father. Cassius fell back to the throne with a tremendous thud. His hand fell over his brow, trying to suppress the tears welling up in his eyes.

Beatrice picked up the crown and ran her fingers gently over it. She'd had it less than an a day, and already Endelynn had put a dent in it.

"Was it something I said?" Cassius spoke up. His voice was strained, trying to hold back the distress building within. "Was I too harsh on her?"

"It was nothing you did." The queen said, still gazing down at the circlet in her hands. "I was quick to anger too at her age. This is something children go through. They want freedom and independence from their parents. And besides, this is a difficult time for us all." She leaned over and placed her hand against her husband's. "The prospect of her wedding is causing a lot of stress for the young girl."

"Should I call the wedding off? Set it for a later time?" Her husband asked.

"No. We should move forward as planned." Beatrice stood. She placed a kiss on Cassius's forehead. "I'll go speak with her.

See if I can put some reason in her head." Just as the queen was about to leave, standing in the doorway, she turned back to her husband. "Endelynn still loves you. As do I."

"I know." Cassius said. He brushed the tears from his eyes and smiled. "I do, too."

Beatrice left the throne room, followed close behind by Sir Aridain, and walked along the corridor towards her daughter's chambers. There was no guarantee that Endelynn had come back this way after she stormed out, but it was always the best place to start.

She quickly came upon the bed chamber, finding the door closed and locked from within. So Endelynn had come back here. The queen lightly knocked her knuckles against the wooden door. "Endelynn," she said in a soft voice, "May I come in?"

The was no response from within. The room remained silent. "You dropped your crown back there. I've brought it for you. Would you like it back?"

The door unlatched and creaked open. Endelynn stood on the other side, her face red and eyes puffy from crying. Her hair was a disheveled mess. So the outburst had as much an impact on the young girl as it did her parents. Beatrice held out the circlet to her, which Endelynn graciously took.

"Now may I come in?"

The princess stepped aside and held the door open. As Beatrice entered, Sir Aridain turned around and took his place in the hall, outside the room. The door latched again. From within he could hear the muffled conversation between mother and daughter, but he couldn't make out the words. It was just as well, it was not his place to overhear such a private talk on such a sensitive matter.

Down the hall, he saw a young woman carrying a wicker basket full of sheets and other dirty clothes. At first, he thought nothing of it, until she turned a corner only to pause in surprise.

A black-gloved hand reached from around the corner, placed itself on her shoulder, and pulled her out of sight. His eyebrow arched. No one in the castle wore gloves such as those, but it was reminiscent of a certain Black Sword.

He glanced behind himself at the door, waiting for it to open. The voices of the queen and princess continued to discuss from within the room. They weren't coming out anytime soon. Feeling secure in his actions, he took a breath and headed towards the edge of the hall.

Aridain rounded the corner and found pretty much what he'd expected. The black knight, Sir Darren, conversing with the young servant girl. The Black Sword was holding a small vial filled with light pink fluid out to the girl, along with three silver coins. And the girl had her hand extended, eagerly awaiting both the vial and the coin.

"What is this?" Aridain elevated his voice, causing an echo through the hall. Both Darren and the servant girl froze in place, their head's whipped over to Aridain. The Dadrian knight gripped the hilt of his sword, preparing to draw if needed.

"I was merely asking a favor of this young lady." Sir Darren said. "You see, the prince as some food allergies. I wanted to make sure everything being prepared for the night's banquet is safe for him to eat. So I was having this maid take his medicine down to the kitchen for me so it could be mixed in with the food."

Aridain shifted his eyes to the vial dangling in Darren's hand. This whole exchanged seemed suspicious to him. "Why not just inform King Cassius himself of the prince's allergy and have the cooks prepare safer food? Or if that's not an option, at the very least inform someone of what you're doing rather than sneaking around like a thief?"

"I didn't want to alarm anyone." Darren said. "Some people are very particular of what goes in their food, and would rather not know."

He Dadrian knight narrowed his eyes. "Give me the vial." He ordered. The black knight complied. Aridain twisted the cork from the top and it came out with a pop. Holding the lip under his nose, he sniffed the contents. It had no discernible odor.

"See?" Darren said. "Nothing to be afraid of."

Aridain still had to be sure. He placed the tip of his finger over the opening and quickly flipped the vial upside down. He then flipped it right way up, leaving just a drop on his fingertip. He placed it on his tongue. No taste. And no effect.

"Very well." Aridain replaced the cork and handed the vial back to Darren. "It appears safe. I won't report you this time, but either go before the the king or queen or see one of us if you need anything else of this nature."

As he turned to leave, he heard the black knight speak up. "Of course. Whatever you say, Royal Guard."

"My name is Aridain." He said without turning around. "And it is Sir Aridain."

He returned to the princess's chambers just as the queen was stepping out. She gave Endelynn one last hug before leaving the young girl in her room. The queen saw him as he was walking back to his post. "Where did you go?"

"I thought I heard an altercation down the corridor." He said. "But it was nothing important. Did your talk with the princess go well?"

"Everything is fine." Beatrice spoke. "This evening when it is time for the banquet, I want you to escort Prince Sedrick and his bodyguards to the dining hall."

"As you command, your highness."

X.
DARREN

A large chandelier, covered with no less than fifty burning candles, cast its light upon the banquet hall. It was nothing Darren hadn't seen before, two tables, each with a long bench on either side, rested below along the two rows of marble columns. A third table, the one reserved for the royal family and their visiting guests, raised above on a platform just before the roaring fireplace. They were each given an individual chair rather than a bench. All the tables were carved from redwood. Supposedly, all three had come from the same slab of wood.

The hall was filled long before the royals arrived. When the time had come, it had been the red-haired knight that retrieved them. That one, Sir Aridain as he called himself. He'd come to their door a little before sundown to invite them to the feast.

Aridain escorted him and the prince, along with all the rest of Sedrick's bodyguards, down to the great doors of the banquet hall where they were greeted by the king, queen, and princess already waiting. It was only after they arrived that the servants manning the door pushed it open and allowed them entrance.

The tables full of people all stood at once as the doors opened. A pair of horn blowers trumpeted to announce the royal family's appearance. King Cassius led the march, escorting the queen at his side with her arm draped through his.

As they walked down the center between the tables, everyone bowed in respect.

They were followed closely behind by the prince and princess. Sedrick likewise held his arm out, and Endelynn placed her hand through it. There was a slight pinkish hue in her cheeks as the prince escorted her through the hall.

He and Aridain followed the royal couples up to their place at the high table. The rest of the guards, both for Sedrick and for the Dadrian family, dispersed into the crowd. They weren't officially on duty tonight, it was their time to enjoy themselves.

The king took his place at the center of the table, his queen at his right hand, and the princess Endelynn to his left. Prince Sedrick was seated one spot further down to the princess's left. Sir Darren took his place beside the prince. Once everyone was in their proper positions, Cassius brought his hands together in a mighty clap. "Bring forth the feast!"

The doors flew open again and a swarm of servants came bustling in, many carried platters of fresh meat and steaming vegetables. Plates of bread, fruits, and many bottles of wine. Everyone had a mug or a horn for drink, and all took at least one serving of the wine.

All, that is, except for King Cassius. "None for me," he said as the servant approached with an open bottle. "I'll just take an ale."

"Of course, my king." The girl said, and finished filling the glasses of Endelynn and Sedrick before hurrying off to fetch the ale.

Sedrick leaned forward and took his chalice. "Not fond of wine, your grace?" He asked.

"I never was." Cassius replied. "It never agreed with me. Always had a twisted stomach after drinking it."

The servant girl returned with a mug of ale and placed it before he king. He took it and drank heartily. Endelynn reached for her goblet, and as she cupped it turned to her mother, who nodded in approval, before placing her lips to the edge of the cup and sipping daintily.

The noise grew as food and drink traveled through the hall. Soon, it would be too loud to hear oneself think. "Endelynn," the queen said, her voice already growing elevated to raise over the ambiance of the crowd, "how would you like giving Sedrick a tour of the castle grounds tomorrow?"

The princess's knife and fork froze. She turned to her mother with her eyes wide. Before she could speak, Beatrice continued. "Supervised, or course. We never objected to you showing him around. I'm sure Sir Aridain would be willing to accompany you." She turned to the knight at her left. "Isn't that right?"

"Of course, my queen." Aridain said.

Endelynn smiled. "Yes. Thank you, mother." She said, and then after a moment, "thank you, father."

Cassius did not respond, merely drank again from his ale.

As the night wore on, as it usually did it grew louder and more rowdy. The feast lasted for hours, well into the night. Eventually, long after the candles of the chandelier had melted to stubs and the fires burned down to embers, the crowds began to disperse.

Sir Darren had allowed himself two goblets of wine before indulging in the feast, the minimum he would need and the most he could tolerate without head-splitting pain in the morning. Sedrick, however, drank enough to become inebriated and had to be carried back to his chambers once it was all over.

"It's not too bad, is it?" Endelynn had asked as Darren carried the young man off. She had only two goblets as well, it was all the queen would allow. "Will he still be able to join me on the morrow?"

"You need not worry, My lady." Darren had replied. "The prince is young, but he has the thirst of a man twice his age. He will be well come the sunrise."

The thirst of a man, but the wine tolerance of a boy. When the morning came, and the princess arrived with her bodyguard outside the prince's bed chambers, Sedrick was a mess. Any bright light or loud noise caused him pain, and it was a struggle for him to get dressed.

"The young prince is getting prepared for the day, my lady," Darren had said through the partially opened door. "He will be finished in a few moments."

Two servants were required to get the boy into his garb. Even in his finely prepared tunic and trousers with his cloak attached to the shoulders, delicately brushed and parted hair, and fine golden crown, Sedrick was obviously in a disheveled state.

"Are you alright?" The princess spoke as Sedrick came out of his chambers to greet her. "You appear to have not slept."

"I will be well after I've broken my fast." Sedrick rubbed a hand against his temple. He straightened up best as he could and extended his arm to Endelynn. "Might I have the honor of escorting a lady?"

The princess slipped her arm through his without hesitation, her head rested lightly against his shoulder, and they walked together towards the banquet hall. Sir Darren, along with the princess's bodyguard the young, red-haired knight Sir Aridain, followed the couple close behind. The two knight's eyed each other with a mutual look of disdain, but did not speak.

The king and queen were already waiting in the dining hall when Sedrick and Endelynn arrived. The king had a sickly look about him, his skin looked paler and hair less vibrant, more like tattered straw, and he appeared to be slouching further in his seat than the evening before. These changes were slight, all but invisible to anyone not searching for them, but to Sir Darren they might as well been as plain as day.

Breaking their fast was done quickly, as the princess eager

to spend her day with Sedrick. They were each served a plate with succulent roast meat, baked apples, boiled eggs, and a glass of sweet goat's milk. Endelynn downed her food almost as soon as it arrived and then waited patiently with her hands folded across her lap while the prince finished his meal. Sir Darren had been right after all, the food did help alleviate the worst of Sedrick's pain brought on by a night of drinking. Once they were finished, the prince and princess bowed to the royal couple and took their leave. The received only the barest of acknowledgment from Cassius as they headed out the door.

Endelynn led the way, dragging the prince from one location to another all throughout the castle. They stopped by the Halls of the Kings, were rows of statues carved from white marble depicted the many previous kings of Dadria. Each was adorned with a bronze plaque which listed the king's name, his house, and the dates of his rule. The most recent was of Endelynn's grandfather, King Leothuldus Rambourne.

From there they moved on to the library. A great tower with enormous shelves that housed hundreds upon thousands of books and scrolls. Sedrick expressed little interest in these, as his knowledge of reading was limited. Kendrick had taken away his language instructors not long after the death of their father, claiming it was a skill Sedrick wouldn't need. Why learn to read when he would have servants to do that for him? Endelynn, however, appeared to be quite learned in the studies of language. She took down a large, leather bound tome, and read a story from it aloud to Sedrick. An old legend of the Hero of Ages and the Four Dragons from across the sea. Darren didn't care much for the story, instead something more interesting caught his eye.

Along one wall of the library was a brightly painted mural of a mountain slope blanketed in thick, white snow with dark trees and their thick boughs covered in needles so green and thick they almost appeared black. Two mounted animals were displayed before this mural. The first was a raox, proud and strong, rearing on its hind legs with its head angled down in a charge. The second was a wolf. Its lips were pulled back to expose the white fangs beneath, and black fur shown in the light from the windows.

The claw marks across Sir Darren's eye ached anew. He'd had the bandages changed twice yesterday, and once again this morning, but it was clear these slashes would become true scars when they were fully healed. Seeing the wolf again, even a dead and mounted one, stirred anger and fear in Darren's gut. He could hear its snarls and feel the hot breath on his face. He didn't notice Sir Aridain's approach until the Dadrian knight spoke.

"His majesty killed that wolf himself." Aridain said. "Out on a hunting trip into the woods several years past. He was hunting for deer or boar, but instead found a pair of wolves and their pups. He managed to kill the she-wolf, but the father fled along with the pups." The red-haired knight turned to Darren as he spoke. "Does your king do any hunting?"

Darren took his hand away from his face. "King Kendrick's older brother was killed during a hunt. Such things bring bad memories."

"I see." Aridain replied. He turned back to face the mounted animals, locked together in their eternal duel. "The wolf has been the age old enemy of House Rambourne for hundreds of years. They hunt the wild raox who live in the mountains, but to a trained soldier and his mount, a single wolf is no match."

"As I saw when you came to our aide." Darren said.

"If you don't mind my asking, have our healers been treating you well?" Aridain asked.

A new heat rose along the nape of Darren's neck. "They have." He said. "My vision is intact. The worst I will suffer is a new set of scars along my face. But, then again, what worthwhile knight is without his share of scars?" He shifted to face Aridain and looked the young man up and down.

"I assure you, I have a collection of my own. They are just not as prominent." The Dadrian said.

"Not all of us can be as lucky." Sir Darren said. "But, who knows? Perhaps when Sedrick and Endelynn are wed, they will induct you into the Black Swords of the King. We could always use a few strong knights of your caliber."

"The day I accept that position will be the day the lamb and the wolf lay together in peace." Aridain said with a sneer. "In truth, I cannot wait until you and your pampered charge return to your kingdom."

"You will not have to wait long." Darren replied. "The prince will set out for his own lands on the next morn. And, if things go as you wish, you may never have to see him again."

The tour continued on for most of the day. They came by the armory to let the prince fawn over the many assorted weapons, and then followed out to the training fields were young men worked to break the strong-willed yearling raox.

That evening's supper was not a large, flamboyant feast as the previous night's had been. There was still a gathering in the hall, but nothing to the same degree as the first. During the evening meal, Sir Darren continued to notice the king's deteriorating state. His eyes drooped more and his skin appeared to sag in places where the night before it had been taut. The princess seemed to take no notice of her father's state, and Sedrick never bothered to look after the formal greetings.

Sedrick only had a few goblets of wine, not wanting to repeat the pain of the morning. After they finished their meal and both the prince and princess were led back to their separate bed chambers, Darren sought out the chamber maid from the previous day, the girl whom he paid to slip the potions into the evening feast's food and wine. For a few more silver coins, she indeed made a suitable bed warmer.

In the morning, their entourage gathered in the main courtyard in preparation for the journey back to Kahren. The royal family came out to see them off, and as Sir Darren mounted his great black stallion at the head of the caravan and Sedrick said his goodbyes to the princess, he took notice of King Cassius's absence.

"My husband is not feeling well this morning," the queen spoke as they readied to depart. "But he greatly appreciates your visit, and will send word to your king, Kendrick, regarding his decision about any betrothal arrangements."

"We are honored to have been his majesty's guests." Sedrick bowed to the queen and princess. "We are saddened to hear of his illness, and offer prayers to the All Father for his quick recovery."

"You have my gratitude." The queen said.

With that final exchange of words, Sir Darren snapped the reins and directed his horse forward. So began the three day journey through the Forest of Wayward Souls back to Kahren.

XI.
BEATRICE

Last night had not been so bad, but this morning was far worse. The king's fever grew with each passing moment. The windows were all thrown open and the curtains drawn away to allow better air flow. Towels soaked in cold water were placed across his face and body, but they needed to be changed every few minutes as he was so warm the damp cloths soon lost their cooling touch. Cassius' breathing was ragged and shallow, coming in small weak breaths. His face was red as a beat drenched in sweat.

All the while, Queen Beatrice watched in anxious fury. Once the business of seeing the visiting prince off and wishing him a safe journey home was complete, she returned to her husband's side and had not left for any reason. Food had been brought to her, but she could not bear to eat while her king was in such misery.

She sat beside the bed with his hand clasped in hers. At first, his grip was strong, but as the day wore on the strength from his fingers began to wane. She helped to change the wet towels multiple times herself, dabbing them across his chest and face in a vain effort to cool him down. Later in the day, servants were brought in to wave fans over the feverish king, and for a while it helped. He almost became lucid again. But soon, even that was not enough and his temperature continued to rise.

She watched him tremble on the bed, as if he were racked with terrible chills. He would twist and turn, tugging at the sheets drenched in water from the towels and his own sweat, his overworked heart beat so hard she could see his chest shake. Beatrice could do little but watch him suffer, her own heart trembling with anxiety.

During a rare moment of lucidness, he looked up at her with bloodshot eyes and mouthed three words. His voice was barely above a whisper. "I love you."

"I know, my love." She said as she ran another damp cloth across his face. "Try not to speak. You need to conserve your strength."

"No," he gasped and coughed, then spoke again, "I need to see Endelynn. I must tell her something before it's too late."

"It's not too late. Don't talk like that." Beatrice said, holding back her fears as best she could. She refused to entertain that possibility, and sought to drive it from his mind as well as her own. "You just need rest. Once your fever breaks you will be fine."

"I have to see her." Cassius insisted. He raised a hand as high as he could, barely holding it above the bed, and a handmaiden rushed to his side. "Find my daughter and bring her to me."

"At once, your grace." The servant girl bowed and hurried out of the room.

Beatrice took her husband's hand in her own again. His skin was burning to the touch, like trying to grab a hot iron from a fire, but she kept hold nonetheless.

"I won't live to see another sunrise." His lips were chapped and cracked as he spoke.

"No," Beatrice pleaded, the tears she had managed to keep back until then began to flow down her cheeks like a pair of tiny waterfalls. Droplets landed on the king's feverish skin where they began to steam. "You can't give up."

"It doesn't matter." Cassius said. "I just have to speak with her one last time. I can't let our last words spoken be a fight."

The door flew open with a loud bang as Endelynn burst into the room. Her eyes were wide with fear and her cheeks flushed red, as though she had just sprinted halfway across the castle to be here. Her gaze instantly fell upon the king. "Father!"

He turned to face her, a warm, inviting smile on his face. "My daughter," he said in a weak voice, "come here." He reached out with to her with his free hand.

Endelynn knelt beside the bed, clutching her father's hand. She winced a little as she grasped it, feeling the heat of his skin, but did not let go. "I'm here, Daddy." It had been years since the last time Endelynn referred to her father by that term, but right now no one cared.

"My time is short. I want you to know– " a spastic coughing fit overtook him. He hacked and spat, blood dribbled down his chin and onto the bed.

"My dear, stop!" Beatrice shouted as she cleaned his face with a wet cloth. "You'll kill yourself."

"It's too late for that." The king's coughing fit subsided. "Listen, Endelynn," he said as he turned back to the princess. "You are a woman now, have been for many years, and I'm sorry for not realizing earlier. I've been blind, willfully ignorant to not see.

"I'm sorry I won't be there on your wedding day," he continued, "that I won't be able to see you take the throne, or see your children."

The tears were streaming down Endelynn's face, her lips quivered. Beatrice watched her daughter and knew how it took every ounce of fortitude for her not to shriek like a child.

Cassius continued. "You should have the right to choose what you want. If you want to wed that young prince, then you may. And if you choose not to, that is also your choice. No

90

matter what you choose, you will have my blessing. I love you, Endelynn."

"I love you, Daddy." The princess kissed the back of her father's hand, struggling to hold back her sobs.

"Alright," Beatrice said, choking back her own tears. "He needs his rest. Endelynn, leave us."

The princess stood, one hand still clutched around the king's, and wiped her tears away with the other. The wet lines on her face were soon replaced with more tears. Without saying another word, she folded her laced her fingers together like a proper lady and departed the royal couple's bed chambers. It would be the last time she'd see her father alive; less than an hour later, he had passed.

XII.
ENDELYNN

Rows of trees moved past the windows of Endelynn's carriage. The princess gazed out at the magnificent forest, the massive trees as tall as a castle tower that reached to the sky. This was the first time she'd ever been outside the walls of Dadria, and the farthest she'd been from home. The road was well worn, hard packed dirt, but at the edge of the path thick ferns and undergrowth carpeted the forest floor. Shadows and pinpoints of light danced within the forest as a light breeze rustled the branches.

However, Endelynn didn't see the appeal. She saw it, and had a hollow appreciation for it, but it didn't register. Her mind was elsewhere. She wasn't in a carriage, surrounded by knights mounted on raox traveling to Kahren, she was back in Dadria at her father's funeral.

"And He sayeth unto thee, children of men, fear not the shedding of the mortal coil, for the world beyond is a land of peace and joy." A Grand Faith Lord read aloud from the Book of the All-Father. "That the land of the righteous shall be filled with the just kings of old. Weep not for those that have departed this world, for they go to a better place, the likes of which we cannot comprehend on this earth."

Despite the Faith Lord's words, Endelynn took no comfort. She wept, clinging to her mother's side in a way she hadn't done since she was a mere child. The princess, the queen

92

mother, and everyone else in the courtyard aside from the Faith Lord himself were dressed in black for mourning.

Her father's body lay upon a flat, stone altar. Stacks of wood and straw lay around the base drenched in oil. The king had been dressed in a ceremonial white gown, signifying his passage to the afterlife. A new stone statue of white marble was already being crafted, one that represented the king in his finest armor, with a crown seated upon his head, and his hands clutching the hilt of his sword.

The courtyard was filled with people from all walks of life, royal, noble, and peasant alike. All had come to pay their respects to the late King Cassius.

The Faith Lord finished the rights and closed the book. "My lady," he said, "it's time."

Endelynn sniffled and wiped her tears away. Her mother nudged her forward and the princess climbed the steps to the funeral pyre. A servant carried a torch to the Faith Lord, who took it and handed it to Endelynn. With shaking, hesitant hands, the princess gripped the flaming torch and walked over to her father's body.

As she gazed down at him, Endelynn could only think about how peaceful he appeared, like he was merely sleeping and would awake at any moment. The tears came back stronger than ever and she began to weep again.

In a mixture of anger and grief, she threw the fire down on the oil soaked wood under the king's body. The flames ignited and quickly spread over him. In a matter of seconds, the whole pyre was a roar with fire and smoke reaching up to the sky as if sending his soul to live with the All-Father. Endelynn ran back down the steps and into her mother's arms, still weeping.

More words were read from the Book of the All-Father, and songs of sadness were sung. The large gathering of mourners grew thinner as the day wore on and people returned to their lives. The flames of the pyre burned down to soot and ash, leaving only the king's charred bones on the altar. These were taken by the morticians to be placed in a tomb under the king's new marble statue. By the time they collected the bones, only Endelynn and the queen mother remained to watch.

So ended the reign of Cassius the third, son of Leothuldus the first, King of Dadria.

They left the courtyard, mother and daughter walking side by side through the halls of the castle. Endelynn made no sound aside from the scuffing of her shoes across the stone floor. Her face was warm and eyes puffy from the tears.

It was her mother that broke the silence. "I've had some sweet cakes prepared for us." She said.

"I don't feel hungry," Endelynn replied in a quiet, weak voice.

"I didn't ask if you were." The queen stated. "We have things we need to discuss, and it would be better done over food. And the sweeter the food, the easier the discussions."

She didn't want to argue, not after Father's funeral. They came to the sitting room were a small table and two chairs had been laid out. A platter of fresh sweet cakes, still steaming from the oven and drizzled in honey, and with a jug of warm cream awaited them. The delicious aroma reached her, and Endelynn's mouth began to water. Her stomach gurgled. She was hungry, as it turned out, and nothing looked nicer.

Mother seated herself at the table, and Endelynn across from her. She took the jug of cream and filled two goblets, then slid one across the table to Endelynn. "The time of succession is upon us." The Queen Mother said.

"Succession?" Endelynn asked.

"The kingdom is without a king." Her mother took one pastry and tore off a small piece before placing it in her mouth. "You have no brothers, and neither did your father. There are no male heirs, so by right, the throne and crown pass to you."

"I know." Endelynn took another pastry and held it with a

94

delicate grasp between her thumb and forefinger. It was warm and soft to the touch, her fingertips leaving impressions even from the lightest pressure. She pulled it apart, and the inside steamed. Strings of honey stretched between the pieces. "What part of succession is in question?"

"The matter of your wedding." The queen said. "As the sole heir, it is your responsibility to preserve the line. If your father hadn't been so dismissive of prospects, you would've been betrothed long ago and likely already wedded."

"As you were?" Endelynn asked out of curiosity.

"Yes. Your grandfathers, both my father and your father's father, arranged the proposal, the dowry, and the marriage." Mother continued. "But that is not the case. As it is, he left the matter in your hands." She finished her sweet cake and dabbed the corners of her mouth with a napkin before facing the princess again. "So, what would you like to do?"

The question, and all its weight, were upon her before she realized it. Now, perhaps for the first time in her life, she was fully in control of her future. So then, why was she afraid? This was what she wanted, what she'd been demanding that day when she shouted at her parents in the throne room and tossed her crown aside.

How long ago had that been? Only a few days? Now Endelynn had the freedom she desired, and the price for her newfound freedom had been her father's life. She hated herself for saying those words, hated the words themselves as if they were poison on her tongue. That day stuck in her mind like a splinter she couldn't remove. It would be a moment she would regret for the rest of her life.

Regrets could be felt later. Here, in this moment, she needed to make the choice of who she was going to marry. "Sedrick." She said, almost without realizing it. "I will go to Kahren and marry Prince Sedrick. Then I will return and take my place as Dadria's new queen."

Her mother nodded as if she expected that answer. "Very well." The queen rose from the table. "I will send a falcon to King Kendrick telling him you've accepted Sedrick's marriage proposal. And once preparations are made, you will journey to Kahren."

Endelynn turned to her mother. "Me?" She said. "What about you? Won't you be there with me?"

"Under normal circumstances, yes." Mother said. "but these events have not been normal. I have to stay and act as regent in your name. At least until you're returned."

This was her future, a wedding to Sedrick of Kahren and then she would return to Dadria as its new queen. Sitting in her carriage, glancing out the window at the passing forest. Across from the princess was her handmaiden, the elder woman Winifred, a pair of knitting needles in her hands and a ball of yarn at her side. Whatever she was knitting, be it a scarf or a pair of socks, Endelynn didn't care. "What am I to expect?"

"Excuse me?" The handmaiden stopped and looked up.

"When we get to Kahren, what should I expect?" Endelynn asked. "Will I be married immediately? Do I have a day to prepare? What will happen?"

"I cannot say for sure." Winifred answered. "It all depends on what King Kendrick chooses."

"But my marriage is to Sedrick."

"True, but Kendrick is still the king. In the end, he decides when and where any royal wedding is to be in his kingdom." The handmaiden said. "Usually, you would stay in Kahren and become a lady of the court in that kingdom, but Kendrick has chosen to not take away Dadria's sole heir."

"I suppose I should be glad for that." Endelynn said. She gazed back out the window. The sun was starting to fall behind the trees, casting its light through the boughs and bathing the earth in bright yellow and dark shadows. "I'm just not as excited about this as I thought I'd be. Before, the prospect of marriage was all I ever wanted. But now, without Father, I don't know how to feel about it."

The older woman set her knitting needles aside. Her hands folded in her lap and she looked across the carriage to meet Endelynn's eyes. "I don't pretend to have all the answers." She said. "As your servant and concierge, it is my duty to aide you in every way I can, including giving you advice when you need or ask for it." Winifred reached over and placed her old, weathered hand atop the princess's soft, youthful one. "I can't tell you how to feel or what to think, all I can do is say how proud your father would be to see you on your wedding day."

"I know. He told me so." Endelynn turned away from her handmaiden to look out the window again.

The carriage came to a halt. Endelynn jolted in her seat, the usual creaking and rocking having stopped. "What's going on?" Endelynn asked, growing more anxious.

Winifred pushed the carriage door open and stepped outside. "I will find out. Stay inside, don't come out unless I say otherwise." The handmaiden shut the door behind her, leaving Endelynn alone.

The princess fidgeted in her seat. It was growing dark outside, and even darker within. She twisted the wedding invitation between her hands, the paper tore and fell away in small flakes. She heard voices, distant and low, of Winifred and the soldiers speaking with some unknown person. They talked on and on, too far away for her to understand anything they were saying. Finally, she'd had enough. Endelynn stood up, grabbed the latch at the top of her carriage, and twisted it open. There was a hidden door on top of the cab, all the royal coaches had one. She pushed the door open and climbed out, finally able to see.

On the road ahead there was a man. His wagon lay across the path, one of its rear wheels broken and in pieces, all his cargo in the wagon spilled across the road. "I told you, my mule ran away! Startled by wolves!" He shouted. "I can't move the cart by hand, certainly not with it as damaged as it is."

"This is pointless." The captain, still mounted on his raox, groaned. "We don't have the time to sit here and argue with you." He snapped his fingers and motioned forward. Two of the other mounted soldiers rode to his side. The captain delegated orders. "Help this man lift his cart and fix his wheel as best you can. Then get it out of our way." The two soldiers climbed off their raox.

"Out of the way?" The merchant said. "You're seriously going to leave me out here alone? Monsters come out at night, I could be attacked or killed! You're Dadrian knights, can't you give me an escort back to your kingdom?"

"We have no men to spare. Already this distraction will keep us from getting to Haddrick's Keep before the sun sets." The captain said. "Besides, Dadria's walls are too far away to make it before dark anyway. If you'd like, you can accompany us to the fortress."

Out of concern, the princess cupped her hand around her mouth, and elevated her voice. "Is everything alright?" She called. And then after a moment's thought, "when can we get underway?"

Everyone turned and looked at her, frozen in shock. The knights who were lifting the cart now stood in place, the wagon held in their hands. "Milady!" Winifred shouted. "What are you doing up there? Get back inside, where it's safe!"

"There's nothing unsafe out here." Endelynn said.

Winifred sighed. She placed her hand against her face. "Milady," she said with a strained voice, "we don't know what kind of dangers could be – "

There was a wet sticking sound, like a knife plunging into ripe melon. Winifred lurched forward, her eyes bulged wide. She sputtered, coughed, and blood oozed up between her lips. It dribbled down her chin in red streaks and splattered across the front of her tunic. Her legs gave out and her fell to the ground, an arrow stuck out from her back.

Endelynn shrieked. A flock of birds cawed in response and took to the air. The captain looked on in shock, then grabbed the hilt of his sword and drew it from the sheath. "Men, to arms!" He commanded. "We're under attack!"

Just then, the merchant jumped on the back of one of the knights holding his cart. He grabbed the armored man by the helmet and yanked it back, revealing the soft neck underneath. Then, he revealed a hidden knife from his robes and slit the knight's throat. Blood spurted out in sprays of scarlet red. The knight collapsed.

The other soldier holding the cart quickly dropped it and reached for his own sword, but the merchant was too swift. He ducked under the swinging sword and stuck his knife under the exposed shoulder guard. With a groan and jets of blood, the second soldier fell.

"Sell sword scum!" The captain hissed. He brought his sword to bare and attacked the merchant, now clearly an assassin. "My lady, get back in the carriage! Latch the door and do not open it until I say otherwise!" He ordered. "Everyone, form a barrier around the princess. Protect her with your lives!"

Still in shock, her heart racing and body feeling cold, Endelynn ducked inside her carriage and slammed the hatch shut. She locked it and huddled on the floor, her arms wrapped around her legs. Outside she heard the bleating of the raox and the trampling of hooves. The sound of flying arrows was followed by the same stabbing sounds, and then the cry of pain and death from another soldier. It repeated again and again, each time Endelynn winced. The carriage rocked when a raox crashed against it. Endelynn screamed, clutching her hands over her ears.

Finally, the noises stopped. She kept her eyes closed, sitting on the floor with her knees brought up to her face and arms around her legs, waiting. For a while, nothing happened. Each moment only caused her more distress. What had happened outside? Did they win? Did the captain kill the assassin? Was she safe?

A new sound reached her ears, approaching footsteps which stopped right outside her carriage. The handle on the door turned. It stopped, still locked. Endelynn jumped in fright and moved away, she pressed herself against the far side as the door handle rattled. It stopped, and for a moment she felt relief. Then something large and heavy struck against the door. It strained and buckled, then on the third strike it gave and the door was torn from the hinges.

Outside was a trio of men, one was the merchant from before. He held a sword from fallen soldier, inspecting it, before slipping it into the stolen scabbard at his waist. The one closest to her, the one who had kicked the door open, lowered his foot. He had a an ugly face with blotchy skin, a long scar over his swollen shut left eye, and a sickening yellow beard the same color as his teeth. He wore a green hooded cloak with a quiver of arrows on his back, and gripped a crossbow in his hands.

The bowman set his crossbow aside, climbed towards Endelynn and extended a dirt stained, gnarled hand with its grime-covered fingernails for her. Endelynn shrieked and crawled away, her back pressed against the other side of the carriage, trapping her.

"Come on, lassie." He said with a thick accent. "Make this easy for all of us."

Endelynn kicked at her abductor, her foot struck him in the face. He wheeled back, rubbing his cheek. "Alright, if ya want to play that game, we can play." Pulling a knife from his belt, he reached for her again. This time when she tried to kick him away, the assaulter grasped her by the ankle, yanked her from the carriage, and threw her to the dirt. Endelynn cried out again

100

when the fiend took her braided hair and yanked her head back. She gasped as the cold blade of the knife pressed against her neck. "Give me a reason to twitch, and you'll bleed like a pig."

"Stop it," the assailant from earlier said. "Rayleigh, let her go. We need her alive and unspoiled. That was the deal."

"This little bitch kicked me in the face. Come on, just let me return the favor." The man with the knife said, his rancid breath brushed against Endelynn's face and she nearly heaved.

"No." The other assassin, it was now apparent he was the leader, ordered. "Put it away."

"After all, it's not like she could make you look any worse." The third man, a scrawny greasy-haired cretin with a hooded falcon perched on his fist, laughed.

"Shut yer trap before I carve a new one in your face!" Her captor, Rayleigh, spat. He pulled the knife away from her neck and shoved her to the ground. Endelynn lurched forward, catching herself on her hands with her face inches from the ground. Small stones dug into her palms.

Only now, once everything had slowed down, did she being to weep. All around her she saw the bodies of her fallen guards, all of whom had given their lives in vain to protect her. The ground was soaked with their blood. Even the raox were slain. She caught sight of Winifred's corpse laying face down in the dirt with an arrow protruding from the back, the clothes around it almost black with blood. The old woman who Endelynn had known since she was a child, always offering advice or comfort, now dead before her.

"Well, fearless leader," Rayleigh scoffed, "what do we do with the girl now?"

"Bind her hands. Gag her, too. Then we'll take her to the rendezvous spot and wait for or payment." The leader said. There was a tug on her dress. Endelynn jolted up in shock, she tried to run, but the leader held her down. "Don't struggle."

Rayleigh stuck his knife through the fabric of her dress,

101

which tore like paper as he ripped away strips of cloth. Once he had one long enough, he pulled her arms roughly behind her back and tied them together at the wrist. She struggled, but couldn't escape. He took another long strip and placed it over her mouth. She shook her head and held her lips tightly closed, until he grabbed her by the back of her head and forced his fingers in her mouth. She gagged, the horrid taste of his hands lingered on her tongue. With her mouth open, the assailant forced the rag between her teeth and tied the ends together behind her head. Endelynn was then forced to her feet and pushed forward. "Alright, girly. Let's get movin'."

"You," the leader pointed to the grease-haired one, "put that bird to some use and send a message to King Kendrick. Tell him we have the girl."

"Right away, boss." He scribbled a quick note and stuffed it into the canister on the bird's back. Then he whispered to it, "Kahren, Kendrick," and removed the hood. The bird took off, a flutter of wings as it headed southwest for Kahren.

Once the falcon was out of sight, they headed into the forest. The limited light of the setting sun was obscured by the thick canopy, turning the world almost black. The red fiber-like bark of the trees caught the limited sunlight and seemed to turn the color of blood.

XIII.
KENDRICK

"It was the blight, your highness." The peasant farmer groveled before the king on his knees. The throne room was a long, dark hall lined with stone columns. The only light came from the burning torches and the braziers beside the throne. "It's killed my horse, and without it I can't till my field or grow my crops." The farmer said.

"Is it not summer?" Kendrick slouched in his throne, his face propped on his fist, his lips turned up in a sneer. "Shouldn't your fields already be tilled and crops planted?"

"Your grace," the pathetic man before him pleaded, "I couldn't get to planting as I was working in your quarry, chiseling the stones for your new monument."

"So it's my fault you're late with planting your fields?"

"No, my king." The farmer fell to his hands, his palms slapping against the stone floor. "I just meant to say I was busy in the service of you, your grace."

"And I am grateful for your hard work." Kendrick said. He shifted on the throne to sit taller, his chin raised and voice elevated. "But that doesn't mean you can shirk your other responsibilities." The king stood and walked down the steps of his throne. "If I let everyone get away with every minor fault, then this great kingdom I've built will fall to ruin."

"I am sorry, my king." The peasant groveled.

"As you should be." Kendrick said. "But I am merciful."

103

He extended his hand, palm down to the poor man. "I will grant you gold enough to buy a new horse. Use it to till your field and grow your crops. Is that sufficient?"

"Yes, your grace." The peasant wept with joy. And of course it was sufficient, as he was a merciful king. But if the farmer had tried to bargain for more, Kendrick would have taken back his offer and had the man flogged. He extended his hand with the large, gold ring with a sparkling ruby, and the farmer kissed it.

"Stand," the king said, "and return to your farm." The man bowed and turned to leave. Before he was gone, the king spoke again. "Just know this, when your crops are grown and the time comes to pay your taxes, you will be responsible for repaying the treasury for the cost of the horse. If you are late with your payment," Kendrick continued, "your farm, the horse, and all your land will be forfeit to me. And you and your family will be sent to work in the mines."

The peasant trembled with fear. It exhilarated the king, watching these little people squirm like frightened animals before his presence. "A . . . as you command, your grace," he said, and bolted from the throne room.

King Kendrick fell back to his throne. "Is there anyone else?" He asked his aide.

"No, your grace." The young man to his side spoke. "He was the last."

"Good," Kendrick said. "Bring some wine."

The aide rushed away, leaving Kendrick alone in the throne room. Of course, he was not truly alone. He had his guards, the Black Swords of the King. A pair of the knights stood at his sides, one to his left and the other to his right. They had been his best idea, and his most faithful servants.

As a young man, he'd always told his father that an elite order of knights were needed to guard the royal line. Back then, there had been the Stag Knights. They served the king and his family, but Kendrick argued it wasn't enough. After his youngest brother was born and his mother's tragic death in childbirth, King Osrick finally heard reason. Soon it was discovered his mother the queen was murdered, and through the efforts of Kendrick's newly formed Black Swords the conspiracy was uncovered.

The conspirators, several members of the royal court, were captured and executed once they confessed. Bringing justice to his much beloved mother was the first shining moment of Kendrick's life, the first time people saw him as something more than just the king's second son, or the younger brother of the beloved Prince Roddrick. Among those executed was the king's previous chief adviser. Kendrick was soon moved into the court to take the adviser's place at his father's side. Since then, the Black Swords gained more influence and prominence under Kendrick's direction until, under his kingship, they completely supplanted the Stag Knights.

His aide returned with a pitcher of red wine and a goblet. The young man hurried up the steps, placed the goblet on the armrest of the throne with shaking hands, and attempted to pour the wine. The pitcher trembled and wine splashed, flowing over the lip of the goblet and landing on the king's robes.

"What are you doing?!" Kendrick roared with anger, he jumped to his feet and knocked the goblet to the floor, where it crashed and shattered. The aide fell, tumbling down the stairs and landing with a thud on his side. The pitcher spilt across the floor.

The aide scrambled to his hands and knees, face down so his nose almost touched the floor. "I am sorry, your grace." He groveled. "I don't know what came over me. I ask your forgiveness, oh good king."

There was a warble in the young man's voice. Even now, he trembled before Kendrick's might. Which he was wise to do, as while King Kendrick was a merciful ruler, he could also show his wrath, and it would be swift and just. He considered himself a just man, after all. The punishments he dealt were never unfitting of the crime.

"Guards," the called to the Black Swords to his left and right, "take this incompetent fool to the holding cells until I've thought of an appropriate punishment for him." As the guards lifted the man by his arms and dragged him from the room, Kendrick called, "Be grateful I am merciful."

With his incompetent aide gone, Kendrick relaxed in his throne. The duties of a king were so difficult some days. These little people didn't know, couldn't possibly understand the hardships he faced everyday. No one could, not even the late King Cassius of Dadria knew. After all, that kingdom was peaceful and prosperous, not having the problems of peasant rebellions happening across this country or the economic troubles and debts left by Kendrick's father after his death.

So much tragedy had befallen his family. First, his dear mother's assassination, then his elder brother's unfortunate hunting accident, followed by the old king's death of a broken heart. With all of them gone, that just left Kendrick and his younger brother, Sedrick, to pick up the pieces.

Thoughts of Sedrick brought the forthcoming wedding between his younger brother and the Dadrian princess back to the Kendrick's mind, and with it all the preparations and arrangements that needed to be taken. However, this was a welcome arrangement.

A stomping of boot steps alerted Kendrick to the approach of Sir Darren, the most senior and loyal member of the Black Swords of the King. He came up to the base of the throne and fell to one knee, his fists braced against the floor. "My king."

"Sir Darren." Kendrick said, raising one hand. "Stand, my friend. Do you have news?"

The knight carried a scroll. He held it out to the king. "A

106

falcon just arrived. It was carrying a message concerning the Dadrian Princess."

"A message from Dadria?" Kendrick asked as he took the scroll.

"Not exactly." Sir Darren said.

The king unrolled the parchment and and quickly scanned over the words. His brows furled and lips twisted in a sneer. "You've read it?"

"Yes, my king." Sir Darren confirmed. "They've taken the princess hostage and are demanding a ransom for her return."

"Then you know what must be done." Kendrick crumpled the scroll and tossed it in the brazier, where it twisted in the flames and blackened to ash. "We can't let such things go without retribution. Find my brother, assemble a squad of Black Swords, and be ready to ride by first light tomorrow."

"It will be done, my king." Darren bowed again and turned on his heels to leave.

"Sir Darren," the king called, "make sure you bring her highness back alive, and unharmed."

XIV.
TALA

It was their night again. Mingan was once again leading the patrol party, this time consisting only of him, Shunka, and Tala. A small, three man team. This patrol, however, wasn't chosen to hunt invaders, but rather to help Shunka get back on his feet.

It had been a few days since his encounter with the black knight, and since he'd gotten that knife wound to his stomach. During that time Shunka mostly stayed in the healing lodge of her father, the shaman, to recuperate. With the help of her father's knowledge of medicinal herbs and berries, along with the aid of the forest's spirits, Shunka was now recovered enough to journey out on patrol again.

And not a moment too soon. Word of the union between Shunka and Shikoba, daughter of the Hawk Tribe, had quickly spread throughout the village. Once the ceremony was performed, Shunka would have to leave and live with Shikoba's family, as was tradition. Whenever a union arrangement was made between clans, the man would always forsake his old tribe to live with his betrothed and her family. With the little time that remained until then, it was likely this would be Shunka's last patrol as a warrior of the Wolf Tribe.

Together with Mingan, she waited by the edge of the village. She stood with her back pressed against a tree, arms folded over her chest and eyes directed at the ground, looking at nothing in particular. At long last, Shunka emerged. He stepped out from the healing lodge, a slight but noticeable limp in his step. The side of his torso that took the knife was scarred over, a nasty strip of flesh on the right side of his stomach.

Just another scar. Every warrior in the tribe had their share. Tala had a particularly gruesome one on her left side just under her breast from an arrow. All of them had scars from their encounters with the pale invaders.

Her father was speaking with Shunka as they approached. "Don't put too much pressure on that side." The shaman said. "Don't overexert yourself, and try not to come back bleeding this time."

Shunka answered each of the shaman's directions with a short grunt and a nod. This was not the first time he'd been told all this. "Yes, I know." The young warrior rolled his eyes. "I'm fine, I'm not going to try anything extreme."

"I hope not." Tala's father said. The old medicine man came to a stop, then cupped his hands behind his back. "You know what you're going to find out there today."

Shunka turned to address the older man. "I doubt it. We're not going very far. A simple scouting mission, nothing more. And even if we do find something, it won't be that."

Tala's ear's perked up as they spoke. This was something new. She tried to listen in, holding her breath to hear more. "You will." Her father said to Shunka. "I have seen it. And once you do, you should remember what to do."

Alo gave a smile, then departed back to his lodge. Shunka shook his head and continued on, joining Mingan and Tala at the village's edge. "Are we ready to go?" He asked.

"You tell us. Do you think you can run?" Mingan jested. "Or are you still as weak as a newborn?"

"I can run fine." Shunka said.

Tala motioned her head towards her father. "What was that about?" She asked.

Shunka tilted his head. "What?"

"My father. He mentioned something. Said you were going to find it on patrol tonight. What is it?"

"Nothing." Shunka answered, a dismissive wave of his hand. "He saw some vision in the smoke and said it was important."

"And what was that?" Tala asked. It was beginning to sound intriguing, and strange that her father never mentioned this. He was usually forthcoming with his visions, at least to her.

"It's nothing." Shunka said. "Come on, let's set out already."

Mingan nodded to acknowledge his brother. He set off, leading the way into the woods, followed closely behind by Shunka. Trailing at the end, Tala kept a close eye on Shunka as he walked. She noted his movements, followed his footsteps, making sure he was strong enough to be out here again and not pushing himself beyond what he could do. So far, it all seemed well.

"Do you feel like running?" Mingan smirked.

"How do you mean?" Tala asked as she took her focus away from Shunka.

"You know how." Mingan steadily began to change, his fingers shortened and melded into paws, his face lengthened into a snout filled with massive white teeth, and black fur sprouted along his body.

"I could go for some real running tonight." Shunka said. His body began to shift as well, changing from human to wolf.

"Are we sure that's wise?" Tala asked. "Your brother and I will be fine, but you're still recovering. Maybe becoming the wolf is too dangerous right now."

"I told you, I'm fine." Shunka managed to say mid-shift. "I want to feel the woods again. Let me have this."

Tala sighed. "Alright." She closed her eyes and allowed the

animal power to surge. The mark on her chest grew warmer until is was burning hot to the touch. Strength rose from within, her muscles tightened.

The transformation only took a few moments. For some of the younger members of the tribe it could take much longer to change their skin. For more experienced warriors, it was almost instantaneous. Her human form was gone, replaced by a wolf with fur as black as the night.

They left the village at sunset, when the sky was darkening but with plenty of light left to see. By the time they reached the forest path it was near dark. This was normally the extent of their scouting missions, covering the distance from their village to the well worn road used by the Pale Invaders. To walk this far would take over half a day, but in their wolf skins they could make this journey and back thrice in the same amount of time.

As they approached the road, a metallic smell lingered in the air. Tala raised her snout to catch the wind, scenting the air and following the invisible trail. She knew this odor very well. The scent of blood.

Mingan lifted his head to the sky and howled. So he had smelled it too. The three of them headed deeper into the woods, charging through the underbrush and leaping fallen logs in their path. The scent of blood grew stronger the closer they came to the forest road. Her nostrils burned with the smell. It wasn't just an injured animal, something was dead up there.

They burst from the forest and came upon the site. It wasn't just death, this was a massacre. At least a dozen bodies, men and beast, lay strewn across the road. They were bristling with arrows, and most had their throats slit.

These were soldiers, mounted knights from one of the Walled Cities. They must've wandered into an ambush and found themselves outnumbered. Their beasts, the large cliff climbing rams from the eastern mountains, had been slain along with their riders.

An old woman lay among the fallen knights. A long, think arrow stuck out from her back, the cloth around it soaked black with blood, and her throat had likewise been slit. Tala inspected the corpse, sniffing and nudging it briefly with her snout before moving on.

A carriage set in the path, surrounded by the fallen bodies. It was ornate, intricately carved and brightly decorated. The kind of coach used by someone of importance in the Walled Cities. Tala placed her front paws on the footstep and looked inside. The door had been torn off. Whomever was in this carriage must've been the target of this attack.

Moving her sensitive nose back and forth within the carriage she soon discovered the scent of its occupant, a flowery, acidic smell of perfume that burned her nostrils, the scent of a young woman. She followed the smell as it left the carriage and moved towards the woods. The scent of three other men joined the first, all of them far more foul. She paused by the forest's edge, looking off into the darkening woods. She barked to the others, alerting them to her finding.

Mingan and Shunka shifted back to their human forms as they approached. Tala likewise reverted to her human self. "What did you find?" Mingan asked.

"There was someone in here. A young girl by the scent. This traveling party was attacked, but not everyone was killed. Who ever was in this carriage was taken by the attackers and led into the woods." Tala reported.

"Who was attacking?" Mingan asked, looking around at the fallen armored soldiers. "One of us? One of the other tribes?"

"No. There was no scent of our people to be found here, at least not recent enough for this. The blood has only started growing cold and they have yet to become stiff, this would have happened only a few hours ago. Besides," Tala grabbed the shaft of one of the arrows sticking from a corpse and yanked it out with a sickening pop. "These arrows were not made by our clan, or any of the forest tribes. These are weapons of the pale-faced man."

"How many do you think there were?" Mingan said.

"Four." Tala set the arrow aside. "Three attackers and one hostage."

"Then we follow them." Mingan ordered. "They can't have gotten far, not with darkness settling in. And once we find them, we will kill them. The attackers and their hostage alike."

They shifted back to their wolf forms and raced into the forest. Tala picked up the scent trail left by the invaders even before they left the road, following as it meandered through the woods.

The scent grew stronger. She found herself not needing to search anymore, it was as obvious as the moon in the sky. Soon, a chattering of voices reached her ears, speaking no tribal tongue. She couldn't understand their words, that was Shunka's task. On every scouting mission they needed to take at least one Chaowtee. A dim light appeared, it vanished every few moments as it moved behind the trees. The light of flames on a torch. The smell of smoke mixed with the ugly stench of the men.

Tala spotted them from a distance, three full grown men and a young woman with her hands bound together and a rag tied around her mouth. The men were grungy and gross with the rank scent of waste and dirt wafting off them, obvious mercenaries or low-class vagabonds. The girl with them, however, had the acidic perfume scent from the carriage and wore a purple dress with gold trim and white lace. Even in wolf form, when Tala's eyes weren't as crisp, she could see the vibrant mix of colors only intensified by the girl's brilliant red hair.

They regrouped and returned to human shape. "We found them easily enough." Tala said in a quiet voice. She kept the light from the invaders torches in view, but stayed far enough away so their voices wouldn't carry.

The words of the pale men, however, were loud and boisterous. "Shunka, what are they saying?" Mingan asked.

"They are speaking of the girl." Shunka replied. "She is their captive. They plan to sell her for money."

"We attack." Mingan said without hesitation. "Surround them and pick them off one by one until all are dead."

"Should we?" Shunka asked, both Tala and Mingan turned to him, confused by the question. "I mean, the hostage. If she was brought into our territory against her will, then do we need to kill her with the rest?"

"Why do you care?" Mingan eyed his brother with a hard gaze. "Whether she was coerced or not, she still invaded the woods. And above a certain age, all who invade our lands are subject to death." Shunka did not respond, but his discomfort with the idea was obvious. "Let's not waste anymore time." Mingan said, and the trio shifted back into wolves.

They trailed the party. Their strategy was a common practice, so rehearsed they didn't need to tell each other the plan. As darkness continued to fall, the trio of wolves split from each other and moved to surround their target.

XV.
ENDELYNN

How long would she be made to walk? Endelynn had no way of knowing. Soon it became too dark and they had to stop. At first Endelynn thought that was the end, but one of them just lit a torch and then kept going. It seemed like hours passed to her terrified mind. The image of her handmaiden pierced through by an arrow lingered in her mind, and each time she saw it she would shudder and begin to cry again. The rag around her mouth soon became soaked with her salty tears.

"By the gods, does this little brat ever stop whining?" Rayleigh sneered. "We ain't even cut her up. She got nothin' to be cryin' about."

"Shut up, Rayleigh." The leader said. "These are dangerous woods. It's called the Forest of Wayward Souls for a reason."

"Yeah, yeah. Ghosts and monsters, I'm sure." Rayleigh rolled his eyes. "Fairy tales to put babes to sleep."

"Once there were men. Tribes of savage men used to live out here. Some say they performed human sacrifices to their gods, and ate the flesh of their enemies." The greasy haired falconer said. "Others claim they flayed captives alive and wore their skin like like clothes."

"All nonsense." The leader said. "Those tribes were wiped out hundreds of years ago. Still, there are wolves in this forest. And panthers and bears."

"Yeah, and if this girl keeps crying I'll gut her open and leave her out for the damn beasts." Rayleigh growled.

"She's worth too much." The leader grew more irritated with his lackey. "King Kendrick will pay a big reward for her safe return, so you won't cause so much as a scratch. If this goes right, we'll be set for life. So shut your maggot filled trap and just stick with the plan!"

As Endelynn heard them talk, a thought occurred to her. It was obvious they were holding her for ransom, but why did they send the falcon with demands to Kendrick? Why not her mother? Dadria was closer. Had they somehow heard of her engagement to Sedrick? That was only made official a few days ago, how would a trio of lowly thieves and cutthroats hear about that so fast?

"Hold it." The leader held his torch out and moved it in a circle around him. They had come to a small clearing, a space between the trees where the ground was mostly flat and barren. There were no rocks and nothing grew in this spot. "This is it. We make camp here. Get some twigs and sticks, build a fire." He said to the greasy-haired falcon tamer.

A twig snapped in the woods. Endelynn's heart skipped. Leaves rustled, there was a quick patter of feet in the dark. The three bandits all froze in place. The leader scanned back and forth, holding the torch out before him. He slowly reached across his body and grabbed the sword pommel. "Rayleigh," he said, "put the girl someplace safe. Form a circle around her. Get that damn crossbow of yours ready."

"Why? What's goin' on?" Rayleigh slurred.

"I heard something." The leader drew his sword. "Don't know what, but we should be prepared just in case."

Something moved through the trees, a shadow just on the edge of the torch light. It was there for a second, and then gone the next. The leader swung the flames towards it, but now there was nothing. The woods had fallen silent. And then a growl; a

116

raspy, rumbling snarl emanating from the darkness.

"Wolves." The leader said. The three bandits grouped together, keeping the princess between them. Rayleigh swung the crossbow off his back and strung it, locking a bolt in place.

Endelynn stood between them, all of their backs to her. She realized how similar this was, how all the mounted knights had tried to guard her in her carriage and how they all died. Now her captors were doing the same, and from a deadlier enemy.

A pair of eyes appeared in the dark. Golden amber, almost glowing in the light from the flame. Lips curled back to reveal rows of glistening white teeth, saliva dripped from the fangs. The leader raised his sword, prepared to fight. Then, another growl came from the woods to their left. They turned and saw yet another wolf, this one slinking across the ground and into the clearing. It was big, as large as a man, its shoulders would reach Endelynn's chest. It barked and snapped its jaws, flashing its teeth.

"It's right there." The leader whispered. His voice was harsh. "Rayleigh, shoot it already!"

Rayleigh raised his crossbow. He placed the stock against his shoulder and sighted down at the enormous predator. Just as he was about to fire, Endelynn spotted another moving shadow. It came from the other side of the clearing; a third wolf.

It leapt from the woods, its mouth wide open and fangs bared. The beast pounced on Rayleigh's back, He cried out in shock and pain as the weight of the animal pressed him down. The crossbow flew from his hands, landing too far away to reach. The bowstring snapped forward and shot the bolt harmlessly away into the distance.

The third wolf, a large female with ink black fur, all but roared as it sank its teeth into the bandit's flesh. He cried out in pain, his blood erupted out in a spray, coating the wolf's muzzle red. The other two bandits had almost no time to react before the other wolves lunged towards them. The greasy-haired

117

falconer fell just as quick. A wolf tackled him to the ground, its fangs tore out his throat and he died drowning in his own blood.

The mercenary leader moved to attack. He took his sword and swung at the she-wolf. The beast jumped away, dodging the blade. "Rayleigh, get up!" The leader shouted. Rayleigh stood, but did not go for his weapon. Instead, he raced off into the woods, disappearing in the dark. A wolf gave chase. "Rayleigh, you coward!"

The she-wolf paced around the only remaining mercenary. He held the torch in one hand, his stolen sword in the other. The other wolf, the one who attacked the falconer, moved away from its kill and joined the female in bearing down on their new target.

Endelynn cowered behind the bandit leader. Once her kidnapper, now her only defense. He glanced over at her for just a second, seeing a terrified child shaking in fear. She tugged on the binds holding her hands. She wanted to run, was desperate to run.

Just then, the third wolf, the one that chased Rayleigh into the woods, came racing out from the darkness. It pounced on the man, its jaws agape, and sunk its teeth into his neck. He lost the sword and the torch, falling backwards to the ground, as the vicious beast tore his throat away.

Endelynn caught his dying gaze, horrified eyes staring at her as the wolf stained the ground with his blood. Now alone and surrounded by three hungry predators, Endelynn couldn't handle it anymore. Her head felt light, her vision blurred and sounds became distant. Her eyelids grew heavy and closed. She fainted.

PART II.
WOLVES OF THE WAYWARD FOREST

XVI.
ENDELYNN

Where was she? What happened? Why could she not see? Had the world been swallowed in total blackness? What was the last thing she remembered? She tried to think, her mind raced and images flashed before her. She saw her carriage, her ornate and beautifully painted one, with soldiers and raox surrounding it. Then the swift, streaking birds came, sharp metal tipped bolts shooting through the air and striking them down. The men fell from their raox with crossbow bolts protruding from their mouths and eyes,

Endelynn tried to scream. She twisted and shook her head from side to side. They needed to be warned, had to be warned of the ambush, but it was too late. The three men, more like misshapen ogre creatures then human beings, emerged from the woods and surrounded the carriage.

She watched, unable to step in and stop it from happening again, as they slit the throat of her handmaiden, Winifred, and threw her body to the ground. Endelynn continued to fight, struggling against whatever unseen force compelled her to observe.

The ogre-men tore the carriage door from its hinges and threw it aside. One of them reached inside and grabbed the princess, yanking her outside.

At the moment, three massive shadows began to drift

through the trees. The ogre-men stopped, threw the princess to the ground and formed a circle around her. The shadows, black masses of darkness with glowing yellow eyes and razor-sharp teeth encompassed the ogre-men and consumed them.

Endelynn was horrified, but could not turn away as they were torn limb from limb and devoured. Once the ogre-men were gone, the shadow beasts turned their attention on the princess. They swarmed her and their fangs, still dripping with blood, ripped through her dress and tore at her flesh. Endelynn could not turn away, held in place by some terrible power and forced to watch. Then, they turned on her. They growled and snarled as their gnashing teeth came towards her. There was a loud, echoing howl.

"Wolves!" Endelynn tried to scream, but her voice was caught in her throat and died before it could escape her lips. She lurched straight up, her heart racing and face covered in a cold sweat. A dream. That's all it was, a horrifying, vivid nightmare. She stopped to catch her breath, placing her hands over her chest as she gulped the air.

As her hand touched the fabric of her clothes it gave her pause. This wasn't her nightgown. And why was her bed so hard?

Looking down she found herself still dressed in her lavender formal dress, the one for royal events. Why did she try to sleep in this thing? Her fingertips graced the surface of what should've been her bed, only to find it not soft, but hard and gritty like dirt. Pulling her hand back and staring at her fingers, she found it was dirt.

There was very little light coming from the dying embers of a campfire, but it revealed more than enough. This wasn't Endelynn's room, she was outside. And not just outside, she was beyond the walls of Dadria, somewhere in the Forest of Wayward Souls.

And she was not alone.

Three figures stood at the edge of the campfire's light, all of them stared back at her. Their eyes shimmered an amber-gold hue in the dying light. All were tall, muscularly built with powerful arms and well defined chests, even the solitary woman. Their skin was a reddish-brown, almost a copper hue, and hair as black as raven feathers. Speaking of, they all had a pair of black-tipped white feathers adorned in their hair.

Endelynn felt a scream rise up within her throat, but it could not escape. Who were these people? They didn't resemble anyone from either Kahren or Dadria, so where could they have come from? The answer came to her like a lightning bolt in her mind. They were the people from the paintings in her castle hall, the savage men.

One of them, the smallest of the trio, moved towards her, his gait powerful and undaunted. With a renewed rigor, Endelynn tried to run only for her feet to catch on her dress, causing her to trip and fall back to the ground. Se couldn't catch her fall, as her hands were still bound at the wrists. Instead, she shoved herself away as fast as she could, the backside of her dress dragged against the forest floor, until she found herself pinned against a tree, its rough bark pressed against her back.

The savage reached to the short scabbard on his waist and pulled forth a small dagger made of sharpened black stone that glistened like glass. A flaying knife. It must be, just as the old stories told. She was about to be skinned alive. Nowhere to run and the fierce savage man staring down at her, Endelynn trembled in terror. Tears streamed down her cheeks as she clenched her eyes shut and turned away, unable to face the gruesome death that awaited her at the edge of that blade.

The savage's strong hands grasped her arms and yanked them towards him. This was it, any moment now she would feel the needle-like pain of the black glass-stone slice into her flesh and the agony of her skin being pulled away.

But there was no pain. Only the tearing sound as the fibers of the cloth around her wrists were sawed by the knife. With a final cut, the bindings snapped and fell away. The savage man released his hold on her arm. Once he was finished, he stood and sheathed the knife.

Endelynn rubbed her hands over the swollen red flesh of her wrists. With her hands free, she pulled the gag from her mouth and gasped for breath. "Thank you," she said, then internally chastised herself. There was no way he understood her language. She might as well have told him his feet smelled of tomato paste and it would have meant the same to him. How could she have been so stupid?

"Welcome." The savage man uttered in a powerful voice.

Endelynn froze in place. She could not have just heard that, but she did. He spoke to her in her own language.

"Yes," he said, " I know your tongue and many more. I am a Chaowtee, a speaker of many words." He reached out his hand to her. "Stand."

Unsure of any other action, Endelynn placed her hand, which appeared small and fragile by comparison, within his. He pulled her to her feet faster than she expected and she yelped in shock.

"Come," he said, "we take you to our home. Give you food and clothes and place to sleep." She craned her head back, finding that even while standing, he was nearly a foot taller than her. Eye-level with is chest, Endelynn noticed a patch of raised skin a deeper red that the rest. It reminded her of Prince Sedrick's birthmark, but instead of a deer's antlers, the one on the native man's chest resembled a wolf's head as it howled to the sky. "My name Shunka." The man said.

"Um," she said, speaking for the first time since learning they could understand one another, "my name is Endelynn." Suddenly feeling her ladylike upbringing strike, she straightened herself as much as possible, rubbing her hands along the length of the dress to smooth out any wrinkles, and adjusting her crown before folding her hands neatly together over her waist.

"I am Princess Endelynn of the House Rambourne, daughter of King Cassius the Third and Queen Beatrice, and heir to the throne of Dadria." She took the edges of her dress between her fingertips and curtsied. "It is an honor to make your acquaintance."

XVII.
DARREN

The Black Sword ascended the spiral staircase till he reached the top of the watchtower of Haddrick's Keep. He found Prince Sedrick there, waiting for him, with a copy of the ransom note clutched in his hand. The prince had one foot planted on the stone battlements and was looking out at the mass of dense forest all around them. Even here, at the highest point of the fortress, the trees still towered over them. "My prince," Sir Darren said with a bow, "we are ready to depart."

"Good." Sedrick responded without turning to face him. His fist tightened around the ransom note. "Those murderous thieves stole her from me." He said through clenched teeth. "And now they demand gold or money or status of whatever for her return."

"I know, my prince." Darren said. "I've read the note as well."

"Well, they won't get it." Sedrick took the paper and tore it to shreds before tossing the tattered pieces off the tower. "You assembled the best hunters and trackers in Kahren, didn't you?"

"Of course, your grace." Darren replied. It was as Kendrick ordered.

"Then once we have their trail, we will rescue Princess Endelynn and I will acquaint her abductors with the pointed end of my sword." Sedrick gripped the hilt of his sword for

126

emphasis. Darren had heard this little speech before. Sedrick practiced it several times since hearing of the princess's abduction. The boy was filled with rage at the thought of someone taking his bride-to-be.

"You need not worry, your grace," Darren said. "none of the kidnappers will escape today alive."

"Then let us go." The two came down from the tower to meet with the rest of the hunting party; five members in total including the prince and Sir Darren. Two of the others were knights, and the last was an expert at hunting and tracking. Sedrick mounted his horse and the fortress doors opened. He gave it a sharp kick and the horse moved forward, the trackers and knights falling in line behind him.

This fortress, officially known a Haddrick's keep, had been constructed over two hundred years ago by Sedrick's ancestor, King Haddrick, during the Savage Wars as a resting and resupply position halfway between Kahren and Dadria. It was also to be the place where the prince was to meet Princess Endelynn on her way to Kahren so he could escort her the rest of the way.

The search party, led by Prince Sedrick and Sir Darren, moved briskly along the beaten forest path. The knight kept a watchful eye on the surrounding woods, glancing from side to side careful to note any movement he might see. He didn't want a repeat of their previous venture into these woods. Prince Sedrick, on the other hand, was completely absorbed in the idea of rescuing Endelynn. It was his duty, him being a prince and she a princess, that when she is in danger he must save her.

The caw of a crow caught their attention. The black bird flew overhead and joined a murder of other crows, all circling over something in the distance. "I saw those birds from Haddrick's keep." Sir Darren said. "That could be the sight of the attack."

"Then let us hurry." Sedrick whipped the reins and gave his

horse a kick, driving it faster.

Following the column of birds, it did not take long for them to come upon the scene of the ambush. The princess's carriage stood still in the middle of the road, arrows embedded in it and the doors hung open. Around the empty carriage, the ground was littered with corpses. The princess's bodyguards lay in pools of their own blood, most with bolts sticking out of the eye holes in their visors or the weak spots in their necks. An elderly woman's body, Darren recognized her as Endelynn's handmaiden, was likewise dead, stabbed with so many arrows she bristled like a hedgehog. Crows cawed and pecked at the bodies, they tore away flesh with their sharp beaks.

Prince Sedrick wrinkled his nose in disgust. He placed his arm over his mouth and nose to shield himself from the rotting smell. The bodies had bloated and rotted in the sun, the skin had turned black in places and fallen away where the crows had picked at them. "This is horrible. How could anyone just leave them out here like this?" Sedrick gagged as the stench became unbearable.

Sir Darren pulled a rag from his pocket and tied it around his face. He jumped down from his horse and motioned to the others to follow him. "Come on, men. We have work to do."

The knights steadily gathered the bodies of the dead and piled them together around the carriage, shooing away the birds as they did. Once that was done, they gathered sticks and twigs from the edges of the forest along with whatever dry vegetation they could find, and constructed a makeshift funeral pyre. Sir Darren struck a piece of flint against the tip of his sword and a spark leapt onto the bits of kindling. It ignited into a small flame which steadily grew larger, hotter, and brighter as it engulfed the carriage and the bodies. The fire roared, smoke rose in a black column up to meet the clouds. "There," Sir Darren said as he finally removed the rag from his face, "a funeral fit for a king."

The knight moved in a circle around the pyre, examining the ground. At one point, opposite of the open door, he fell to his knee and placed his fingers against the earth. "There's a set of footprints here." He said. "Not one of ours." He signaled one of the trackers to him and pointed at the depressions in the dirt. "What do you make of this?"

The tracker stared intently at the trail of prints, he followed them a little ways as they left the path and moved into the forest. "I see four pairs of footprints. Three of them are larger and appear to be men, the last is a smaller set and look to be women's shoes. These prints are shallower and seem to have come from shoes that are only worn by royals. No doubt this is the princess and her abductors."

"Good, then let's follow them!" Sedrick said eagerly.

"We'll have to travel by foot. The forest is too thick and ground too uneven for horses to be of much use here." Sir Darren said. The rest of the party secured their horses together at the base of a tree.

Prince Sedrick approached the forest's edge. He gazed off into the darkness between the trees, brows furled with determination, and he drew his sword. "Lead the way, tracker."

The party left the well-beaten path behind and entered the sea of trees. The sun disappeared behind the thick canopy of branches, cloaking them in darkness. The tracker kept his eyes intently on the trail of footprints, making sure not to lose it.

"Everyone keep your eyes open for anything suspicious. And stay close to me, it's easy to get lost in these woods." Sir Darren said. He glanced over his shoulder and counted their numbers in his head. So far, none of them had left the group.

"Sir Darren," one of the younger knights spoke up, "if I may ask, sir, why is it called the 'Wayward Forest'?"

"That is an old legend," the black knight said, "from when the first of our people came to this land. Long ago, this land used to be inhabited by a race of brown and red skinned

129

savages. They were little more than animals, living in the woods and covered in filth. Some say they ate raw meat that they killed with their bare hands and teeth, others state these man-beasts consumed human flesh."

"That's disgusting." The young soldier looked green in the face. "Is any of this true?"

"I cannot say for certainty, as this was over three hundred years ago." Sir Darren continued. "When our ancestors first crossed the Endless Sea to this land, they started to build a new kingdom under the leadership of their captain, Haddrick. But as they ventured farther inland and deeper into the forest, they came into conflict with the native savages. One young woman was killed and skinned by them, and fighting broke out. These would be called the Savage Wars.

"The savages outnumbered our ancestors ten-to-one. But it was us who were better equipped. We built fortresses like Haddrick's Keep where we could rest and resupply, and we used plate armor and swords of steel. We drove the savages back, scoped out their villages and wiped them out. All of them."

Sir Darren stepped over a large root. The prince, younger knight, and the rest of the hunting party followed suite. "But that's when the forest itself turned against us." He looked up at the overhanging branches. A light wind moved through the forest and the trees groaned. "There are stories of strange lights in the woods that lead soldiers away to their deaths. Other tales of people being attacked by enormous beasts. It became such a problem that Haddrick, now the first king of Kahren, ordered the construction of a wall around the kingdom, a wall over a hundred feet high now called Haddrick's Mercy.

"Since then, no one has ventured beyond the walls that wasn't on the trail, and even then only in groups. Whenever someone left the path without a seasoned guide, they are inevitably lost and never found," Sir Darren said. "These woods are haunted. Filled with the lost spirits of all those who never made it out and swarming with beasts and monsters. That's why we need to find the princess and get out of these woods as soon as possible."

"I found their campsite. It's just up ahead." The tracker said. The hunting party emerged into a small clearing and came upon an ugly sight.

The bodies of two of the abductors lay splayed out across the ground. Their throats and gullets were torn open, entrails ripped out and blood stained the ground. One still clutched a knife and stared with white empty eyes towards the sky, mouth open in a silent scream. His left leg had been torn off at the knee, leaving only a bloody stump. Flies buzzed and hovered in a cloud of black, shining wings over the corpses. Sir Darren stared in shock. He didn't speak. The other knights came upon the sight and a collective gasp rose from them. "What is . . . this isn't right."

"What is this?" Prince Sedrick asked in horror and disgust when he witnessed the scene. He sheathed his sword and placed the back of his hand against his mouth. "What happened? Are these the thieves?"

"I don't know, your grace." Sir Darren. "I would assume so. But something clearly got to them before us." The black knight took the rag from his pocket and tied it around his face before inspecting the bodies. The stench was overpowering, even through the rag. "There was a struggle," he said. The knight noticed a series of tracks which littered the ground around the bodies before they disappeared off into the woods. Large prints. He held his hand over one of them, fingers spread out as far as they could, and even then they barely reached the edges. "Wolves."

The prince's eyes widened in fear. He gulped. "Wolves?"

"I think there were three. Maybe more." Sir Darren stood, dusting his hands off. "They came out of the woods in the

131

middle of the night. Attacked these two and killed them where they slept."

"What about the princess?" Sedrick asked.

"I can't tell. There were three kidnappers before, but only two here. It's possible the other one escaped with the princess." Sir Darren turned to the hunter. "Can you find the trail of the missing abductor?"

"Give me a few minutes to scout the area." The tracker said. He stepped into the clearing. He found a depression in the moss and dirt, about the length of a person laying on their back. "This was were the princess was." He said. "It's too shallow to be a full grown man. The only prints around her are wolf tracks, so she didn't walk from this spot. None of the blood is hers, and there are no remains. No sign that they killed or ate her." He tugged his beard in thought.

"What of the third abductor?" The prince asked. "Any sign?" A cry echoed through the trees, a scream like a dying man. A flock of startled birds took flight. Both Prince Sedrick and Sir Darren turned in the direction the sound had come. "What was that?"

"That could be our survivor. We need to investigate."

"That fiend took the princess! He's mine!" The prince charged recklessly off into the woods.

"Wait! Your grace!" Sir Darren called after him, but the boy did not slow. The black knight cursed under his breath, "Insolent child," then gave chase.

Prince Sedrick ran through the forest, he leapt over roots and boulders. He saw a man ahead of him, hunched on the ground with something in his hands as though he was eating. Sedrick came to a stop and drew his sword. "You there," he shouted, "identify yourself!"

The man paid no attention. He continued to chew loudly, his lips smacking together before he swallowed and tore another hunk of meat from the bone in his hands.

"I gave you an order!" The prince grew more agitated. "I am Prince Sedrick of House Stagghart, younger brother and heir of King Kendrick. You will obey when I speak to you."

The man stopped. He stood, his movements slow and deliberate, and then turned to face the young boy. One eye was swollen shut, the other hazed over milky white. His lips were stained red with blood that oozed from his mouth and down his yellow beard. He had a partially eaten leg in his hands, tattered cloth and a shoe hung from the foot.

Sedrick stepped back, his grip on his sword slackened. "Wha . . . you're eating . . ."

"My lord," Sir Darren caught up to the prince and placed his hand on the boy's shoulder. "You should know better than to run off like that. What if you'd-" The knight stopped when he saw the thief, who brought the severed limb back to his mouth and ripped into the flesh greedily.

"Abomination." Darren reached for his sword, but he wasn't fast enough. The man threw the leg at the knight. He raised his arm to defend himself, but the cannibalistic man tackled Sir Darren to the ground, his hands reached for the neck. The knight held him back, but the man's scrawny appearance betrayed his strength. His dirt covered, bony fingers grasped around Sir Darren's throat. The knight gagged and choked, gasping for breath. He kicked at his attacker, but the man didn't seem to notice even when Darren struck him in the groin.

Sedrick gritted his teeth and bit his lower lip. It hurt, but the pain brought him out of his stupor. He lunged forward and thrust his sword into the assailant's back. The man howled, a chilling shriek of surprise and pain. He slammed Sir Darren's head back against the ground before releasing his grip and turning on Sedrick.

The prince yanked his sword back and swung at the crazed man, but the attacker caught him by the wrist and twisted.

Sedrick cried out and dropped his sword. The cannibal threw the young boy to the ground and pounced on him like a vicious cat, then sank his teeth into the soft flesh of Sedrick's neck. The prince screamed, blood seeped from the hole, his skin torn away by jagged teeth. He struggled, but couldn't get free.

Sir Darren regained his strength. Seeing the young prince in danger, he jumped back to his feet and unsheathed his sword. Giving the cannibal no chance to react, he kicked as hard as he could in the man's ribs and forced him off Sedrick. He felt a few of the man's bones crack when his foot hit.

The man didn't stay down for long, he was back on his feet and racing for Sir Darren, growling and gnashing teeth. The knight waited for just the right moment, then dove to the ground and rolled just as the attacker charged past. Then rose to his knees and slashed his sword through the man's neck.

The head fell from the shoulders and rolled across the forest floor before finally coming to a stop at the base of a tree. Its mouth opened and closed as if still hungry, then slowed and finally stopped. The body collapsed against the ground, blood spurted from the stump of a neck and painted the green foliage red. Soon, that stopped too.

Sir Darren took a moment to rest. After a few deep breaths, he retrieved the rag once again from his pocket and cleaned the blood from his sword before sheathing it. "Your grace," he ran over to Sedrick's side and helped the prince stand. "Are you alright?"

Prince Sedrick groaned, his hand pressed against the wound in his neck. Blood seeped between his fingers. "I'll be fine. Don't worry about me. We need to find the princess." He pulled away from the knight, but his legs gave out and he fell back to his knees.

"You're losing blood, your grace." Sir Darren pulled Sedrick's arm over his shoulders and lifted the boy back to his feet. "We can't stay out here anymore today."

"But what about Princess Endelynn?" Sedrick's voice was weak and quiet.

"The hunters and I will continue our search tomorrow. Right now we must get you back to Haddrick's Keep." The knight said.

"That's nonsense. I won't leave her out here." Sedrick pushed away, but lost his balance and fell. He tried to catch himself, but his arms were too week and he collapsed to the ground. His breathing was labored, body felt heavy, arms and legs as weak as water. Cold sweat appeared on his forehead.

"My prince, we have no choice." Sir Darren lifted the boy, one arm around Sedrick's shoulders and the other under his legs. "We are going back to Haddrick's Keep now."

The knight moved quickly. He regrouped with the other soldiers and hunters then backtracked out of the woods as quickly as possible. They came to the trade route, found their horses still hitched to the same post, and remounted the beasts. Prince Sedrick could hardly stay in the saddle, he fell against the horse's neck.

"Give him to me!" Sir Darren ordered. Once on his horse, the others lifted Prince Sedrick onto the saddle in front of the knight. A flow of blood ran down from the boy's neck, his tunic already stained red. Darren gritted his teeth. He whipped the reins and kicked his horse, driving it forward even before the others had a chance to stride their mounts.

With the horse's reins in hand and the prince seated in front of him, Sir Darren galloped back to the fortress as fast the horse would go. Foam accumulated at the edges of the animal's lips as Daren kicked it again, forcing it to run far more than he knew he should.

Sedrick's skin grew warm, his hair was damp with sweat. He'd fallen ill just a few minutes after being bitten, lost consciousness and was now almost completely unresponsive. If the prince didn't receive aid from a healer soon, he would certainly die.

Haddrick's Keep soon appeared before them. "Open the gates! The prince has been injured!" Sir Darren shouted. As they approached, a loud horn was blown and the doors opened, the rusted hinges groaned in protest. The horse raced inside and Darren jumped from its back, bringing Sedrick with him. The exhausted animal staggered before it fell to the ground, it convulsed and shuddered, then fell still.

Sir Darren watched the animal die. He should not have pushed it so hard, but he had no choice. "Quickly, get the healer!" Three aides ran over to the prince, they carried him together up to the prince's chambers and lay him across the bed. Darren watched from the doorway.

The healer rushed in. He sent everyone out from the room, then knelt beside the prince's bed and examined the wound. Deep wrinkles formed in his forehead. "How long ago was Prince Sedrick injured?"

"An hour ago, no more." Sir Darren said.

"The infection appears to be spreading quickly. Already it has begun to fester." The healer gingerly pressed his fingertips along the teeth marks. The blood that oozed out was deep dark red, almost black. "We need to clean this. You!" He pointed to one of the aides still standing in the room. "Prepare a basin of hot water and bring as many towels as we have."

The aide hurried off. Darren watched anxiously. "Can you help him?"

"There is little I can do for him here." The healer said. "I have a few herbs that might help him, but we need real medicine to treat this."

"I'll send a falcon to King Kendrick immediately." Sir Darren headed off to the aviary. He stormed past everyone in his way, shoving those not fast enough out of his way. His worry and frustration built the closer he got. How did he plan to explain this to Kendrick? Not only were the bandits not at the rendezvous, two of them had been killed and the third gravely injured the prince. And what's more, the Princess Endelynn was still missing. This plan was growing worse by the moment.

XVIII.
ENDELYNN

Each step sent a throb of aching pain through her feet. These shoes were not made to be worn in such a place, or even for much walking in the first place. They were fashion pieces, meant to accentuate the princess and show her for the high class royal she was, not to be worn in the woods. And especially not to be walked in for long distances. Endelynn gripped the tattered and torn edges of her dress in clenched fists as she walked, holding it above her ankles to keep herself from tripping and falling to the ground. Two of the forest people, the larger man and the woman, walked ahead of her, leading the way. The third man, younger and slimmer than the others, walked at her side. Shunka was his name, and he moved at a faster pace than her. He had to stop every so often so she could catch up to him.

The fact that these people still existed was an amazing fact to the young princess. She'd been taught all her life that the native barbaric tribes of this land had been wiped out long ago, but here they stood before her. How had they managed to survive out here for so long? And what about the vicious beasts in these woods? Just last night she and her abductors had been ambushed by three black wolves, and Prince Sedrick's caravan had likewise fallen under attack from a similar pack of wolves on his way to Dadria. But these three seemed unconcerned about any dangerous beasts.

138

Endelynn was so caught in her thoughts, she didn't notice the uneven roots weaving through the forest floor. Her foot snagged on one that jutted up from the ground and she pitched forward. She cried out, startled, and flung her arms out to brace her fall, but her tumble was stopped when the native man, Shunka, caught her by the back of her dress. She hung there, dangling by the seams of her old dress, before Shunka tugged her back to a steady stance. "Keep eyes on path," he said, "and you will not fall."

Endelynn held herself steady, a little shaken, but otherwise alright. Aside, of course, from having to sleep in the woods, being covered in dirt and grime, wearing the same clothes as the day before, and being hungry and exhausted. She couldn't remember the last time she had walked this long or this far, and certainly not in these kinds of clothes or shoes. She hiked up her dress again and started off after the other native people. She looked back at Shunka, then turned away quickly.

Last night she found him scary; a hard, angry face cloaked in shadows. Now in the daylight, she found him to be much less intimidating that he had been in the dark. She thought of the paintings and portraits in the castle, along with the history tomes about the Savage Wars, which were obviously about these people, but they didn't match the descriptions given in the old stories. For one thing, those books always said these people had skin dark as pitch, that they moved in a hunched fashion like animals, and they had no grasp of language. But they all stood as tall and proud as any Dadrian noble. And while they didn't speak her language very well, she'd overheard them speaking amongst themselves and they could communicate pretty well. As for their skin, while it was not as fair as her own, they were in no way black as pitch or coal, rather more like a copper hue. The only part of them that was actually black was their hair that shimmered in the sunlight like raven feathers.

139

"How much further?" She asked, pressing her back against a tree to rest. She ran a hand across her forehead and wiped away the droplets of sweat that gathered at her hairline. She felt gross, like she needed a long soak in her warm bath. It sounded nice, letting the warm water envelope her while servant girls ran soft sponges and rags across her skin to remove all the dirt and grime. Right now, she wanted nothing more.

"Not far." Shunka said. "You will know when we are there."

"I hope so. I'm starving." Endelynn turned to the native man, who stood beside her waiting impatiently for her to continue. "I don't suppose you have anything to eat?"

Shunka moved in a deliberate motion, he face as steady as stone betrayed none of his thoughts, as he flipped open the satchel which hung from his shoulder. Reaching in, he pulled out a strip of dried animal meat and handed it to her. "Food." He said. "Eat. Keep strong and walk far distance."

Endelynn looked down with disgust at the food offered her. It didn't even look like food, more like a flaked off chunk of black tree bark. It looked greasy and revolting, even the thought of touching it twisted her stomach. Her revulsion only grew as he pushed it closer. "Said was hungry. This is food. Eat it."

"I don't want that!" Endelynn said, pushing herself harder against the tree. "It looks horrible!"

The tribal man grasped her wrist in his hand and yanked her towards him. She stumbled and cried out in shock. He then forced her hand open and placed the dried meat in her palm before enclosing her fingers around it. "Eat." He said, then turned his back to her and continued after his comrades.

She stared down at her hand, the strip of meat clutched between her fingers. It didn't feel nearly as greasy as she'd thought, and was in fact more appealing as she held it. It had a smoky scent, as though it had just come from a fire. Her

140

stomach grumbled again, and this combined with the flavorful smell of the meat made her decide to take a chance. Tearing off a small chunk with her fingers, she opened her mouth and placed the small piece on her tongue.

The meat didn't taste bad. In fact, it was rather nice. That might have just been because she hadn't eaten in over a day, but right now it was the most delicious thing she had ever tasted. Endelynn bit into the dried meat and tore it to shreds with her teeth, going back for more almost before swallowing the first mouthful. Soon the meat had been completely devoured, leaving only the small bits of flavor left on her fingers which she greedily licked up. It only briefly dawned on her how much Mother would be ashamed of her manners, but right now Endelynn didn't care.

Upon finishing, the princess felt a resurgence of energy. Taking the edges of her dress again in hand, she strutted off through the forest after the trio of natives. Shunka, the one who seemed most concerned about her, was waiting not too far away still within sight. As she approached, he followed beside her, easily keeping pace.

They continued on their way through the forest. Now with some food in her stomach and without the threat of eminent death, Endelynn began to truly notice the beauty of the trees. The way the rust colored bark contrasted with the deep green of the pine bows. She'd never seen the forest from this perspective before, not from within.

The ground evened out into a dirt path that wove through the trees and Endelynn found it easier to walk. She no longer had to bring her feet up to her knees just to step over a root. It almost made walking bearable. Her feet still ached, though.

A murmur of voices rose from the path ahead of them, along with the splashing and babbling of water. The voices spoke in the same odd language Shunka and his companions had the night before. Was that a settlement or village? And the

141

running water, could that be a stream? Maybe even the Blue Serpent river? If so, then she might be allowed a boat or canoe to take her all the way to the Serpent's Mouth and Kahren.

The idea was enough to put an extra spring in her step. Endelynn lifted her dress a little higher and her strides lengthened. She wanted to be on her way down that river so much she almost didn't hear Shunka calling to her.

"Stop! Don't enter alone!" His voice rang out, but it was too late. Endelynn emerged from the woods and found herself in a clearing. The trees appeared to pull back creating a large, circular patch in the forest of flat earth. A stream wove through its rocky bed on the far edge of the clearing, casting small rainbows in its spray as the water struck rocks.

Endelynn froze in place at the sight before her. The village was larger than she could have expected. A dozen different styles of structures from long, dome shaped houses to smaller huts. Intricately carved and painted tree trunks depicted animals and strange faces. There were fire pits, some still burning, with meat and food suspended over the flames to smoke.

Most incredible of all were the people. Dozens if not possibly hundreds of men, women, and children milled about the village. They all had the same characteristics as Shunka, the same copper skin and glossy black hair. And although it was hard to see, every one of them had the same amber-gold eyes. Some stoked fires to cook meat. Others moved from one hut to another with woven baskets upon their backs. A few even stood along the banks of the stream with sharpened pronged spears waiting for fish.

She realized these were Shunka's people. His tribe, or clan, or whatever they were called. And there were so many, a thriving community of hidden people living within the Forest of Wayward Souls. How was this possible? With the beasts and the evil spirits that haunted the woods, how could these people

142

survive out here?

A small child sat on the ground playing with a wood carving of a wolf. An older woman, Endelynn assumed her to be the boy's mother, stood nearby observing him. The child made growling and barking noises as he ran the toy wolf across the ground in front of him. He looked up for only a moment and saw Endelynn standing at the edge of the clearing. He froze, dropping the toy, and his golden amber eyes grew wide in shock.

The boy jumped to his feet and pointed at her. He shouted something, words Endelynn couldn't understand, in a shrilling voice that brought pain to the princess's ears and caused the entire village to fall silent. The gaze of every native villager was upon her. Each stopped what they had been doing and stared at this new pale-faced girl in the tattered dress with the disheveled red hair.

This brought a new level of anxiety Endelynn had never felt before. The old stories came to her again, tales of bloodthirsty savages who would scalp and flay their victims and wear the skin as cloaks, who made human sacrifices to their pagan gods and ate the flesh of the slain. Is this the fate that awaited her now? Had she been brought to this village just to be tortured and killed?

An older man stepped forward. His hand gripped a bow made of hardwood and a quiver fashioned from animal hide hung across his back. He pulled an arrow from the quiver and nocked it, the sharpened stone point aimed for her. He said nothing and his hard face betrayed no emotion as he readied to shoot her.

Before he could fire, Shunka burst from the woods and threw himself between Endelynn and the villagers. He stood with his arms outstretched as he shouted a warning. At least, Endelynn assumed it was a warning, as he was speaking to them in their language which she couldn't understand.

The bowman responded, still speaking the native language, as he lowered his bow and slipped the arrow back into the quiver. Endelynn could only watch and listen in fear and confusion as they exchanged words, their conversation growing fiercer and more heated as it went on. Looking passed them, she found the villagers still fixated on her, some looking on in fear and others in anger. The boy with the wooden toy wolf clung to his mother's side, his face hidden behind her leg.

The argument between Shunka and the bowman came to an abrupt end as Shunka said three words. The old archer's eyebrows jutted up sharply and a collective gasp rose from the villagers. After what seemed like a long while, but must've only been a few minutes, the elder bowman conceded. He gave Endelynn one final angry glare, then turned and stormed away.

As he walked away, Endelynn let out a relieved sigh. She hadn't realized she'd been holding her breath for most of that conversation, even if she couldn't understand it. Her relief was lost, however, when Shunka turned to face her and his eyes were filled with just as much anger as the rest of the tribe. "Told you not rush in. Almost killed you."

Endelynn couldn't think of a response. Standing there, with Shunka's angry judgmental face gazing down at her, she felt like she was being scolded by her parents. "I'm sorry." She said at last.

"Not matter now." Shunka said, quietly readjusting the satchel across his shoulder. "Come. Must speak with elders."

"About what?" She asked as she followed him towards the largest dome-like structure in the village.

Shunka pushed aside the draped, tanned animal hide that served as a door and held it open to allow Endelynn entrance. "Your fate."

XIX.
KENDRICK

He strolled down through the halls of his throne room, flanked on either side by a pair of Black Swords, watching the work being done. Servants with straw brooms swept the dirt while others with buckets of hot water and bristle brushes scrubbed the stone floor behind them. Masons on scaffolds installed iron rungs in the ceiling and columns, intended to string chains through and support chandeliers covered in candles. A red carpet was in the final stages of being sewn. It would run all the way from the great wooden doors to the throne. Preparations were well on their way to being finalized for the wedding.

"How many candles are on each chandelier?" He asked.

"Fifty, your grace." One of the masons on the scaffolds called down in reply.

"I want more." Kendrick said. "At least sixty. This room needs to be bright and well lit. Install ten more candle stands on each one."

"My king," a mason said as he knelt down before Kendrick. "With the wedding so soon, there may not be enough time."

"I'll decide what there is time for." Kendrick said, walking past the man without looking in his direction. "Tell the blacksmiths that every chandelier used in this wedding is to have at least sixty candle stands. Understood?"

"Yes, your grace." He man bowed again, then hurried off to

145

relay the king's commands.

The wedding was scheduled for a few days from now. That would give enough time for Sir Darren to return with both Sedrick and the rescued Dadrian princess, and to allow the girl some recuperation time. She would be a little shaken, but mostly unharmed. Being held captive would do that to a young lady, but to be saved by a prince such as Sedrick was a dream come true for any little girl. The trauma she'd endure would be offset by the daring, fairy tail rescue.

"Your grace," a messenger came into the hall with a small scroll in his hands, "a falcon has arrived from Sir Darren at Haddrick's Keep."

"Ah, good news indeed." Kendrick took the scroll and used his nail to break the seal. He knew what the letter would say. That the mission was a success, the kidnappers were all slain, and the princess was safely in their midst, being guarded and courted at the fortress by Sedrick. Everything was moving forward perfectly.

But that was not the message sent by Sir Darren. As he read the letter, Kendrick's face grew long and dour, brows furled and lips pressed tight. He read the scroll twice, and then a third time to be sure. Every time, it remained the same.

"My King,

I regret to tell you the mission was a failure. The rendezvous spot was attacked some time in the night by a pack of wolves, and two of the mercenaries were found dead. The third we found alive, but under some kind of spell. He attacked and wounded your brother, who has fallen ill and been confined to bed. The princess was nowhere to be found. Our guide suspects the wolves took and consumed her elsewhere.

146

-Sir Darren, Black Sword of the King"

Kendrick stared at the parchment in his hands. Failure? How could it be? None of his plans ended in failure, it was inconceivable. And yet, here was this message from Sir Darren, still his most loyal knight, that stated otherwise.

He crumpled the paper in frustration and threw it to one of the burning braziers. "Sir Carch!" He shouted.

The Black Sword at his left straightened up at the sound of his name. "My king."

"Prepare a squadron of your best knights. You are to go to Haddrick's Keep and reinforce Sir Darren. Bring a physician with you to tend my brother. And find out exactly what happened out there." Kendrick ordered.

"As you command, your grace." Sir Carch said with a bow. He turned on his heels and marched from the throne room.

Kendrick climbed the steps to his throne and collapsed in it. He slouched to one side and pressed his fingers into his forehead, as if he had a headache. In a sense, he did, just not a physical pain.

"Wine." He muttered. The room had fallen silent. None of the servants or workers dared to move. Kendrick lifted his face from his hand and looked around. "Is everyone deaf!? I said Wine! Bring me some wine!" His voice roared off the walls.

A young aide hurried off quickly and returned with a goblet and a pitcher. He filled the cup and held it out for the king. Kendrick took it, snatched it from the shaky hands of his worthless servant and drank.

What was he to do now? The wedding was set for only a few days from now. The princess's mother, the widow Beatrice would be expecting an update on her daughter, and would soon be departing for Kahren. She could not know that the princess was missing. And if his brother had fallen ill, what then? For

147

now, he would have to remain silent. No falcons would be sent to Dadria until the girl was found.

Kendrick held out his already vacant goblet. "Wine." He said. "Fill it. I don't want to see the bottom of this cup."

XX.
SHUNKA

"In complete honesty, this is most irregular." His father, Ahote Chaa, said from the head of the council. Shunka stood at attention in the center of the Longhouse. All the village elders were here; the Den Mother, Head Builder, Lead Warrior, Shaman, and the Chaa all gathered to discuss his actions.

"Irregular?" The Warrior Elder, Kitchi said. "It is down right wrong!" He turned his focus on Shunka. "You, foolish child, have endangered all our lives and the lives of every single person in our nation. Every man, woman, and child is now at risk because you brought that back with you!" The elder pointed forcefully at the girl.

She called herself Endelynn. This was only one of the many names she seemed to have, all focused on her heritage, but even the first was difficult to say. This girl, Endelynn, stood at his side, her small, soft hands clung tightly around his arm. He wanted to push her away, but to do so would convey regret in his decision, and that was not the case. Although given how things were going and the direction they were taking, he might have to change that conclusion.

"You should have killed her when you had the chance." The elder warrior said.

"I chose not to." Shunka stood his ground. Now, when not only her life but his own might be in danger, he needed to show strength and conviction.

"And that's what we need to learn," Onatah, the Elder Den Mothers spoke. "You know our ways. You know what is to be done when the pale man ventures within our borders. Do you not?'

"I do." Shunka answered.

"And what is that?" She continued her questions.

"Kill on sight."

"And yet you did not." The old woman narrowed her gaze. "You say you chose to spare her life, and then chose to bring her back to our village."

"I did." Shunka said.

"And again we ask why?" The Den Mother asked.

Silence filled the Longhouse. The eyes of all the village elders fell upon him. Shunka did not speak, even as he felt the heat rising on his neck and sweat collect on his brow. He could not say, for even he did not fully believe or understand the reason. The shaman had told him things, and those things caused him to act, but Shunka found those things to be so unlikely. That this girl; an outsider, pale-faced, invader, childish weakling could be the Aleutsi; the Great Mother, was still unbelievable.

The silence was finally broken when the shaman rattled the bones and small colored stones that decorated the end of his staff. He closed his eyes and hummed a quiet chant. The council's attention shifted from Shunka to the shaman. The old medicine man hummed and chanted, whispering ancient words that only he understood as he waved his staff back and forth through the air over Shunka and Endelynn. At last, the old man opened his eyes. "It matters not why. The matter is only that the girl is with us."

Ahote Chaa nodded in agreement. "Very well. Then what are we to do with her?"

"She must still be killed." The Head Warrior said.

"Whether in the woods or the village center matters not. She has crossed our boundaries and entered our lands. She has seen too much. Her life is now forfeit."

Shunka moved without thinking. He pushed the foreign girl behind his back and placed himself between her and the old warrior. "You try, and I'll kill you myself."

A clamor arose from the council. The Head Warrior jumped to his feet and stared down at the younger man. "You dare challenge me? You are out of line, boy."

"I am protecting my charge." Shunka said. "I will have no harm come to her while I live and breathe."

"Then I will have to stop you from breathing." Kitchi growled.

This was ridiculous and Shunka cursed himself for his stupidity. He was no match for the elder warrior, even in the old man's advanced age. If they were to fight now, no matter if they took human or wolf form, it would be Shunka who would die.

"You'll not harm my son." Ahote Chaa stood and raised a hand to the other council member. The Head Warrior glanced at the Chaa, then back to Shunka, and finally seated himself. "If the boy needs to be disciplined, it will come from my hand and no others."

"My Chaa," the shaman spoke again, "your son has already given us the answer to our dilemma."

"And what is that?" Ahote asked.

"He called the girl his charge. Let it be so." The shaman said. "Let him care for her, feed her, bathe and provide for her."

Even as he heard these words, they settled heavily on Shunka's mind. His father crossed his arms and gave a slow nod. "You speak well, Alo. So shall it be." The Chaa stood. "Shunka," he said, "you brought the girl here, now you will tend to her. She is your responsibility from now until her last day. Is that understood?"

"Yes." Shunka said. "Understood, sir."

"Then this council is adjourned. You are free to go." Ahote waved them away. The council stood, each leaving the Longhouse in their own time. The Head Warrior stopped just a moment to shoot Shunka an angry glare before departing.

Only now that it was all said and done did Shunka feel the tightened grip of the young red-haired girl on his arm. "What happened?" she asked in her own language. The entire conversation before had been spoken in the tongue of his people, leaving her in the dark about what was decided. "What did they say?"

"You are to be given to me." Shunka replied in her tongue. "You are to be my charge."

"Charge?" He could hear the fright in her voice. "What does that mean? When can I go home?

"I'm afraid you cannot. It is too dangerous to let you return after everything you've seen." Shunka explained.

"But I don't want to be here. And no one else does either. Just let me go home."

Shunka did not respond to her pleas. He turned away as the old shaman walked over, his gait was slow and hobbled, relying on the staff for support. "You did well. You found the Aleutsi and protected her while in need." The shaman, Alo, spoke.

"Is my task finished? Must I wait upon this child the rest of her life?" Shunka asked, again speaking in the tongue of his people.

"It is your destiny, as well as hers. You can fight it, but not escape it." The old medicine man said. "You will be compelled at the strangest times to follow, just as you did when you set eyes upon her face."

The shaman then turned to Endelynn, her fingers tightened against Shunka's arm, leaving grooves in his skin as she pulled herself closer to him. The shaman just gave a kind, grandfatherly smile, and bowed to her. He then spoke in the tribal language, ending with the phrase "Chaneewah Ishde," and left the Longhouse.

"What did he say?" Endelynn asked.

"He said he was honored to meet you," Shunka hesitated for a moment, then relayed the last phrase the old man had said. "Woman-with-fire-for-hair."

Her fingertips graced the length of her hair. It was as the old shaman said, as bright and red as flames. Was that the only reason? Had Alo chosen her as the Aleutsi, the Great Mother, merely for her red hair? It seemed ridiculous. And yet, here she was.

XXI.
TALA

Three days came between the foreign girl's arrival and her first escape attempt. While Tala had almost no direct interaction with her during that time, the pale child had an effect on everyone in the village in one form or another. The most contact she had with the foreigner actually came on the very day of her arrival. Shunka had taken the girl to see the Council of Elders, and afterwards brought her to the central communal Longhouse. Tala watched them from a distance, her long-time close friend, Naomako, beside her.

"So it is true," Naomako said, her unblinking eyes followed Shunka and the redheaded girl as they traversed the village on their way to the communal house, "I heard rumors, but I did not believe them. The Chaa's son has taken a pale-faced girl as a bride."

"She's not a bride," Tala corrected, "she's his charge."

"What is the difference?" Naomako asked.

"He doesn't bed this one."

Naomako shifted the basket of corn and squash in her arms. A cradle board hung across her back with her sleeping five month old child nestled inside. She'd just returned from the fields when Tala and Mingan came back from their patrol. Unlike Tala, Naomako was a home keeper who spent most of her days tending the crops, mending clothes, and raising the children, a few were even her own. Not everyone was cut out

154

to be a warrior, after all.

"You were with him when he found her, right?"

"I was." Tala nodded.

"Did he give any reason as to why he brought her back?"

"None." Tala explained. "While on patrol, we found a few other pale men and they had taken this girl hostage. Mingan's plan was to ambush and kill them all, but Shunka insisted we leave the girl alive. He wouldn't give a reason why."

Shunka emerged from the communal Longhouse at that moment and walked over to them. "Tala," he called out to her, "I need your help."

"With what?" She asked with her arms crossed.

"Chaneewah Ishde needs help changing her clothes."

Tala tilted her head and raised an eyebrow. "Chaneewah Ishde? Is that what she's called now?"

"It is the name your father gave her." Shunka explained.

"My father?" Tala asked. "Why would he give her a name in our language?"

"You can ask him yourself later. As for now, the girl needs help out of her dress."

"Why do you need me? You should be more than capable of helping her on your own."

A reddish tint came over Shunka's face as he averted his eyes. "She requested a woman's help. She said it would be improper for an unwed girl to be seen unclothed by any man other than her father."

Tala gave a roll of her eyes, and then an amused look over at Naomako. Her friend raised a hand to her mouth and laughed. "Does she know how many girls you've seen unclothed and how many have seen you? Is she shy? Is she perhaps, misshapen in some way?"

"Tala!" Shunka's voice grew angry.

"Alright, I'll help you." She walked with him back to the communal lodge and found the girl in one of the small alcoves

155

within the Longhouse. A bearskin hung draped over a rope to offer the child some privacy.

Shunka waited outside as Tala helped the foreign girl undress. Using her sharpened flint knife, she tore the back of the girl's dress and helped pull it off her body. As she removed layer after layer of soft silk fabrics it was obvious why this girl needed help. The fasteners and strings were pulled so tight in places she probably couldn't even get into this dress without the aid of others. So impractical.

Once the pale child had been stripped down to her skin, as bare as the day of her birth, Tala took a brief moment to examine her. The girl tried to cover herself with her hands, one arm across her chest and the other at the point where her legs met her hips. There was nothing misshapen or unusual about this girl, aside from her skin being almost blindingly white, like the first snows of winter, and with less muscle definition that Tala was used to seeing. A sheltered child.

Tala took the old dress and bundled it together in a small pile she tossed on the ground. She then helped the foreign girl dress in a new set of clothes consisting of leggings, a slip dress with a belt around the waist, and pair of moccasins all made from tanned and toughened deer hide.

As the girl finished dressing, Tala took a step back to look her up and down. The clothes were designed for someone a bit taller, but otherwise fit her well. Tala reached for the glittering gold crown on the girl's head, only for her to pull away. "No!" It was one of the few words of the foreigner's tongue Tala understood.

Shunka pulled the bearskin drape aside. "What is it?" He looked from the red-haired girl to Tala, and back again. "What happened?"

Before Tala could say anything, the foreign girl rattled off a string of words. She took her crown and ran her fingers delicately over it, before clutching it close to her chest. Tala thought she could see a twinge of tears start to form at the corners of the girl's eyes.

Shunka nodded, then turned back to Tala. "She wants to keep that. She says it was the last gift from her father before his death. It has sentimental value."

Tala understood. Not in a direct fashion, as both of her parents still live, but a special gift from a loved one carried great importance to her. "Very well," she said, "if nothing else, she is dressed."

"Gwomu." Shunka replied, and Tala left the Longhouse.

That night around the fire, her father told the story of Wahyuk, the warrior hero of the Wolf Tribe. Stories about how he fought monsters of the forest, and protected his people from the invading armies of pale-faced men. Of how he was first granted the gift of Skin-changing by the Great Spirit, their Father in the Sky, and then taught it to not just his own clan but all the others in their nation. The shaman ended the story by telling of how Wahyuk was always reborn in the times of greatest need, and that he would next return as a wolf with fur as bright and red as flames.

This was an old story, one Tala had heard many times before. The children of the village always listened with great interest when her father recited the many old tales and legends of the the past, but for Tala it had grown stale. A person could only hear the same thing so many times and not be bored of it.

The next day brought nothing out of the ordinary, at least not for her. She practiced with her bow, went searching for new flint to make arrowheads, and even managed a little hunting. She shot a pair of rabbits and brought them back to the village to skin and cook. All the while, from the corner of her eye, she watched as Shunka tried to control his strange new companion.

Any task he gave the girl, she tried to refuse. He enlisted her help in skinning the rabbits Tala caught, and the girl almost heaved when he cut the belly of one open. He tried to show her how to start a fire, and her hands were so tender she could not rub the sticks for more than a few seconds at a time. He would shout at her in the foreign tongue, and she shouted back. Eventually it just became funny to watch Shunka struggle.

On the third day, the foreign girl was sent to gather blackberries with the young children and their den mothers. Shunka and Tala were assigned as their guards. Each child was given a woven basket to gather the berries. The baskets each had a pair of straps to secure it over the gatherer's back when it was full.

Tala and Shunka stood side by side as they surveyed the children. Both he and she carried a spear with them for defense. Tala watched with bemusement as the foreign girl struggled with her basket. Some berries she picked were too green, and others she crushed with to much force, smearing her hands dark purple.

"She is completely helpless," Tala said, "like a child. No, not even that. Like a baby." Shunka said nothing, just grunted. Tala turned to him. "Why did you bring her back anyways?"

"I have my reasons. Although, at the moment, I am starting to have regrets." Shunka replied.

"Reasons, huh?" Tala shifted her weight from one foot to the other. "Care to share them?"

"I'd rather not." He clutched at his spear, his fingers tightened around the shaft. "All you need to know is it was my choice."

Tala pursed her lips and narrowed her eyes. She loved Shunka as her brother, although they did not share parents, but at times he annoyed her like a brother, too. "I think I deserve an explanation." She moved to stand right in front of him. "Of all the warriors in our village, you have more reasons than most to hate the pale invaders. After what they did to your mother– "

"Don't bring my mother into this!" Shunka snapped. Tala took a step back in shock. Shunka did not often lash out at her like that. After a moment, he calmed. "Sorry," he said, "I didn't mean to attack you like that."

"You are forgiven, but you still haven't answered anything." Tala said. "Did you bring her back as some treasure of war?" She continued. Then another idea came to her. "Or is this some kind of rebuttal against your father for agreeing to wed you to the Hawk Clan? Is this your way of telling them you'd rather have a foreign girl as a wife than Orumaku Chaa's daughter? And what do you think the Hawk Clan will do when they hear of this?"

"It has nothing to do with that." Shunka struck back. He sighed and turned away. "In truth, I hadn't even thought of the Hawk Clan's proposal when I brought her back."

"Really? Because it's been the only thing on my mind since we found that girl."

"I guess I'll have to explain it to them." Shunka said.

"How? You haven't even explained it to me yet." Tala rebuked.

"I'm not sure yet." Shunka admitted. "I'll figure something out before they get here."

"Maybe you could start with me." Tala said. "From the moment you saw that girl, you've been trying to keep her from danger. Even when Mingan wanted to attack the other pale-faces with the girl, you argued to not attack her. All I want to know is why. I think I deserve that much."

His shoulders slumped as he exhaled. Tala watched him, trying to read his face and eyes. "I want to tell you, but I can't." Shunka said at last. "You would think it ridiculous."

As she studied him, she saw the truth in his words. He wasn't lying, even if he was withholding the truth. "Any more that what is already happened?" Tala asked.

Shunka turned to face her, and his eyes suddenly snapped wide. "Where is the girl?"

Tala turned around and found the foreigner was gone. A

half-filled basket of blackberries on its side on the forest floor, the berries spilled out on the ground. "I guess she chose to leave." Tala said. "I suppose that problem has been solved then."

"What?" Shunka asked, his eyes were full of panic.

"She's gone. Not a problem anymore. From here, we're five days walk back to the walls of her city, and that's if she knew which direction to go." Tala said. "There is no way she'll survive in the woods by herself."

Shunka raced past Tala, nearly knocking her to the ground, to the spot where the fire-haired girl once stood and knelt in the ground, examining her footsteps. "I was distracted," he said. "You distracted me and now she's run away."

"What does it matter?" Tala asked. "With the girl gone, you won't have to worry about explaining anything to the Hawk Clan. We can pretend like this never happened."

"No." Shunka stood and gazed in the direction the footprints led. "I can't. I'm going after her." He didn't wait for any response, and charged off into the forest.

Tala sighed. That was so like him, to just leave her to finish the job by herself. She waited, alone, surveying the other children and the den mothers as they gathered berries.

Just as they were about to head back, a wolf's howl climbed through the trees. Tala's brows raised as the sound reached her ears. It was a distress call. Shunka was in danger.

XXII.
ENDELYNN

She ran as hard and as fast as her legs could go. Her chest heaved, legs burned, heart raced, still she ran. Endelynn's face was covered in sweat and coated with the salty tears that streamed from her eyes. All she could think of was home.

How was she planning to get there? She had no idea where she was, or how to get out of this accursed forest. She didn't care. She just had to get away, away from the village, away from the forest's people, away from everything.

Her foot caught on a root and she lurched forward. She had a brief flash of memory to when Shunka caught her on their first day together. There was no one to catch her this time, and she fell to the forest floor. She braced her fall with her hands, her left palm slammed into a jutting rock which pierced her skin. She winced and pulled back, holding her hand close to her chest.

A fresh set of tears flowed from the pain. Lifting her hand before her eyes, a smear of blood had formed in her palm. She was disgusted, angered, and exhausted all at once. Clenching her fist, she punched the trunk of a nearby tree. This only caused her knuckles to bruise.

She started crying now. Not the quiet, lonely tears from before, but now a full wailing sob. She brought her arms around herself, curling up in a ball and laying on the ground,

161

weeping. This was the first real cry of this kind she'd had since she was a child, but she didn't care.

She hated it out here. This accursed forest where you slept on the ground or a bench or maybe a mat of reeds if you were lucky with no pillows and the only blankets were made of animal furs, and you woke up far too early. The food was tough and tasteless, and you had to eat with your hands. Even the shoes, which at first she appreciated because they were softer and less constricting than her heels, offered little protection against the stones and hard roots underfoot and she almost had to take ginger steps.

But worst of all were the people. Ever since she was brought to this place all she'd gotten were angry glares and sharp words. Not that she knew what any of those words meant, the only one who spoke her language was Shunka, but even though she didn't know the meaning she understood the intent. They hated her, all of them, and she had no idea why.

All she wanted in the world was to go home, just to see her mother again, sleep in her own bed, take a warm bath, eat honey-glazed sweet cakes. The thought of home only made her weeping more intense.

The rustling of foliage alerted her. She jumped up, startled and in fear. Hearing the sound grow closer, she scrambled across the ground, crawling until her back was pressed against the tree trunk. She braced against it, her breath coming in shallow, rapid bursts of fear, and slid around to the other side of the trunk away from the sound.

Peering around the edge, she saw the source of the rustling. It was the tribal man, Shunka. He was alone, a spear held in his left hand which he used as a hiking stick. His eyes were fixed toward the ground following her tracks.

Endelynn hid behind the tree again, her heart raced. What was he doing here? Why did he have to follow her? She didn't want to go back. Two days in that accursed village and she'd never been more eager to leave anywhere. She hated these vile, horrid, dirty, bug infested woods, and just wanted to be home. Taking a step away from the tree, she tried to move in a stealthy and quiet manner. She didn't do it very well, as each step squished into the wet forest floor and her legs brushed against the ferns.

She hadn't taken more than five steps from the tree when a strong hand grasped her by the shoulder. She tensed and became rigid. He'd gotten her. How he managed to sneak so quietly when earlier she could hear the rustling was a mystery, but that didn't matter now that she was captured once again. His hand tightened around her shoulder and he yanked her back. Endelynn twisted and slipped, falling and hitting her head against the ground.

As she looked up, wincing and rubbing her sore spot, she saw this man wasn't Shunka at all. He was taller, if only by a little, and more muscular. His head was shaved bald aside from a stretch of short black hair that ran from the top of his forehead to the base of his skull, with a pair of feathers sticking out from the back. His eyes stared with an intense anger and lips turned down in a hateful scowling frown. He was bare chested, and on his pectoral muscles he had a pair of red birthmarks that resembled scarred slash marks, like a big cat had made them. The man had an axe in one hand, one made of sharpened stone and a wooden grip.

Once she saw the weapon, a new wave of fear swept over Endelynn. She flipped over on her knees and elbows and tried to run, but the forest man grabbed her and forced her back to the ground before she could get more than three feet. Endelynn yelped as he grasped her hair and forced her face into the dirt. Her mouth open, she tasted the dank, wet soil. Her heart hammered in her chest, she struggled but he was too strong. From the very corner of her eye, she watched as he raised the stone axe and held it over her neck.

"Leave her alone, Katsalgi!" A voice broke the calm of the forest air. The man who held her stopped. He lowered the axe slowly and turned to face the source of that voice, but did not release his hold on the princess.

Endelynn shifted her eyes the best she could and saw Shunka. He stood a few feet away, his legs crouched and the spear now grasped in both hands aimed for the man holding her down. "Let go of the girl." Shunka said, not as loud as before, but more forceful.

"Fine." The tribal man with the slash-marked chest said at last. He stood, lifting Endelynn by the hair. She cried out in pain as if her scalp were being torn off. He then released his hold, throwing her back down where she landed face first again in the dirt. "You may kill her if you wish."

Endelynn crawled across the space between the two men, clawing at the ground as she scurried to get away from the one with the axe. She came to Shunka and hid behind him, clinging to his back out of fear. Only a few minutes ago she was doing everything to escape, now she held to him like a frightened child, trembling and quivering from of fear.

"Now leave." Shunka said, jabbing with his spear. "This is Wolf territory. Go back to your own tribe."

"You're mistaken, young pup." The axe man, Katsalgi as he'd been called, replied. "If you'd been paying attention, you'd have seen or smelt the markings of the Panther Clan. You're the one out of place." He lifted his axe again and spun it around in his fingers. "The girl," he motioned to Endelynn, who slunk further behind Shunka, "she is an invader to our lands. Why does she cling to you like a child?"

"Not your concern." Shunka said. He turned and draped an arm around Endelynn, pulling her close and pressing her to his chest. Her eyes grew wide with shock. "We'll go now."

"Is she yours?" Katsalgi pointed with his axe to Endelynn. "A captive of a raid? Maybe spoils of war? I was unaware the

Wolf Tribe did such things."

"Only you Panthers commit such horrid acts." Shunka said. Endelynn could feel a growl rising within his chest.

"And yet you've not killed her." Katsalgi continued. "What is she to you? Have you taken a pale-faced girl as your wife? Have you Wolves fallen that far from the oaths of our fathers?"

Shunka did not answer.

"Very well." Katsalgi swung his axe at a tree, the stone blade embedded in the bark, and he left it there. He fell to all fours, crouching on the ground like a wild animal stalking prey. His lips pulled back and Endelynn thought she saw his teeth lengthen into fangs.

She watched, entranced by the sight before her. The forest man changed right before her eyes. His shoulders hunched as sandy-brown fur sprouted along his back and grew to encompass his entire body. A long tail grew from his back and curled up around him like a cat's. His feet and a hands became paws with talons, and his face shifted to that of a predatory feline. The man was gone, and in his place was a large panther.

Endelynn jumped as Shunka held his spear out for her. She took it with shaking hands. The young warrior stepped between her and the panther that now stood before them, and likewise crouched to his hands and feet. Endelynn stared with a mixture of shock and bemusement A similar change swept over his body. His body bristled with black fur, his ears stood tall and pointed as they shifted up the sides of his face to rest on the top of his head. A bushy tail grew from the base of his spine, claws sprouted from his fingers and toes, and his face lengthened into a muzzle full of sharp teeth.

Endelynn couldn't believe her eyes. Shunka had shifted into an enormous black wolf. The same wolf that attacked her abductors. Her heart pounded harder than when she'd tried to run, but her blood felt cold. She wanted to run away, but her legs were paralyzed with terror.

165

The snarling roar of the panther startled Endelynn from her trance. She jumped and fell backwards, the spear landing across her lap. The wolf barked, its jaws snapping open and closed, flashing the long white fangs.

It charged forward, rushing for the big cat. As it neared, the wolf leapt and pounced on the panther. The two predators rolled end over end, clawing and snapping at one another. They came to a stop with the wolf on top, pinning the panther to the ground with its jaws clamped around the cat's neck. The panther growled, it kicked up with its powerful hind legs under that wolf's stomach.

A yelp arose from the wolf as claws tore at its exposed gut. It released the cat's throat and leapt away to a safe distance, blood stained its muzzle.

The panther twisted back to its feet and snarled. The two predators circled one another, each waiting for the other to make the first move. This time, the panther was the first to strike. It rushed forward and leapt onto the wolf's back, its claws slipping easily though the black fur and sinking into flesh. There was a yelp of pain as the cat enclosed its mouth around the back of the wolf's neck. They collapsed to the ground, this time with the panther holding the wolf down. It kicked and snapped, growling and yipping, but the wolf could not escape the panther's grasp.

Endelynn could only watch as the two beasts that had once been men fought. The wolf and panther bit and clawed at one another, but the longer they struggled the more obvious it became that the wolf could not win. Shunka was smaller and lacked the flexibility or claws of the big cat. He was going to lose. He was going to die.

She caught his gaze, the terrified look of desperation in his eyes. He yelped again as the teeth sank deeper into his neck and claws tore at his skin, whining like a trapped dog. Endelynn's hands tightened around the shaft of the spear. A

166

new surge of energy filled her, not one of fear, but of a desire to fight back.

Before she knew, she was on her feet again and running towards the fighting predators. Endelynn raised the spear over her head and screamed an angry, wrath-filled battle cry she didn't know she had. The panther's eyes widened with surprise as it saw her charge. It released its hold of the wolf and jumped away just as Endelynn stabbed down. The spear point stuck in the earth right where the big cat had been moments before.

The panther looked back at her, its eyes still filled with shock. There was blood around its lips and on the tips of its claws. Endelynn yanked the spear from the ground and held it out before her. She shouted at the cat, jabbing with the spear. It swiped back at her, hissing and snarling.

The wolf limped back to its feet and joined Endelynn at her side. It lifted its head to the air and howled. The sound rose up through the trees and drifted away into the deep woods. At first, Endelynn was confused why the wolf would do such, but she soon realized it was a signal for help. Soon, there would be more wolves and the panther would be outnumbered. As strong as it was, the big cat could not fight them all by itself.

The panther let out one last vicious growl, and then turned and raced away into the woods. Endelynn watched as it ran, its sand-colored fur stood out against the green foliage and red bark.

Her energy surge started to fall. Endelynn's arms fell at her sides, the spear slipped from her grasp. The wolf at her side, fur black as the underside of the night and matted in places with blood, looked up at her with golden-amber eyes. There was a quality to them, something she couldn't explain, that made her sympathize with him.

The wolf limped away, his fur sloughing away in bits and pieces as his human self gradually started to reappear. His tail shrunk, muzzle fell away, and ears receded. By the time he slumped against the base of a tree to rest, the wolf features were all gone, save for the color of his eyes.

Endelynn took back up the spear and approached with caution. He didn't seem dangerous, at least not at the moment, but he had just changed into a wolf and back right before her eyes. It was true what the old stories said, these people of the forest were something between man and beast.

There was a rustling behind them. Endelynn turned just as two more wolves came rushing through the trees. They stopped as they came within sight of their wounded compatriot, looked at the painful state he was in, and then turned on her. Their fur bristled and lips pulled back to reveal the bone white fangs underneath.

Endelynn looked at the spear still grasped in her hands and realized they thought she had been the one who injured him. "No!" She tossed it to the ground and held out her hands. "No, I didn't do it!" They did not seem to hear, nor did they seem to care, as they continued to approach with menace. At least, not until Shunka spoke up.

He said something, Endelynn could not understand it, but it caught the attention of the two wolves. The only word she recognized was Katsalgi, the name of the panther shifter. The two wolves glanced back and forth between the princess and her wounded protector.

At last, they moved away from her and towards their comrade. Gingerly, the wolves prodded his cuts and injuries one by one, licking up the blood and cleaning the wounds.

Once they had cleaned him off, the two wolves began to shift. Even having just saw it, Endelynn was still shocked to witness the transformation. In the place of the wolves now knelt two members of the tribe. The same man and woman who had found her along with Shunka. She did not know their names yet, but she recognized them nonetheless.

The woman stood and came to approach Endelynn. The

princess took a defensive step back, her heart rate spiked with fear. The native woman stood a fair distance away. Her chin was held high, and hands placed at her side. At last she said one word, "Gwomu," and then left to tend to Shunka some more.

Seeing the obvious confusion on Endelynn's face, Shunka spoke up. "She said 'Thank you'." He explained.

"Oh," Endelynn said. "Um, you're welcome."

Shunka translated for her, but the woman did not seem to care. Together, she and the other native man lifted Shunka and draped his arms over their shoulders. They helped support him as they headed back in the direction they'd come, returning to the village.

Endelynn picked up the spear again. Her fingers gently tightened around the smooth shaft of wood. She watched them go, then turned to look in the other direction, away into the forest. She thought of running again, trying to leave while they were distracted, and then decided not to. Her earlier feelings of anguish that made her run in the first place were gone. And besides, she still had no real idea where she was or where she'd be going to. Plus there was the panther shifter, Katsalgi, and all the other creatures and monsters of the forest she had no names for. She could not defend herself, even if she stole Shunka's spear. It would be better to stay with the tribe of forest people. She may not like it, and they might not like her, but at least she was safe. Resolved to her new state, she followed after the three warriors.

XXIII.
DARREN

The torch light flickered across stone walls outside Prince Sedrick's chambers. It was late, already full dark outside. Sir Darren stood by the door, his arms folded over his chest. His watch, two hours standing guard for the injured prince, was almost over. Only two hours but it felt like an eternity he'd been standing in this hallway.

A clank echoed through the hall as the door unlatched and the healer stepped out. "I've done all I can." He said with a bow to the knight. "The best thing we can give him now is rest." He hurried down the hall, leaving Sir Darren to finished his guard duty alone.

The healer had arrived three days ago along with an entourage of fellow soldiers and knights led by Sir Carch of the Black Swords. Kendrick sent them as reinforcements. The rode into the fortress on their black stallions with a carriage trailing behind them. "Where is he?" Darren shouted as he approached, not caring about greetings or protocols. "Where is the healer?"

"I am right here, Sir knight." The healer, a man of advanced age but still spry and strong, stepped down from the back of the carriage with a bag clutched in his hands. "I was told the prince's condition is dire. I must see him right away."

"This way," Sir Darren turned and lead the old man through the fortress, along the hallways and corridors until they came to the chambers of the ailing prince.

170

"Tell me what you know of his condition?" The healer asked before entering the room.

"He's gotten worse since I sent the message." Darren replied. "He neither eats nor sleeps. What food he does eat doesn't stay down for long. And he's been soiling the bed every few hours."

"I see." The old man grasped the iron handle of the door and pushed it open.

The room stank like a chamber pot, even with the shutters open to allow fresh air. Flies buzzed around the prince's bed in a humming swarm of black and silver wings. Sedrick lay with his mouth open, his breath coming in barely audible wheezes. His skin was yellow and clammy, covered in a film of slick sweat that made his hair cling to his scalp, and drawn so thin his bones were beginning to show. He looked less like a prince and more like a corpse.

Darren was forced to hold a hand over his mouth and nose to keep from heaving. The healer pulled a cloth mask from his back and tied it around his face, followed by a pair of gloves. "I need to examine him in private. You and the rest of your men need to wait outside."

The knight did as he was bid. He left Sedrick in the healer's care and took himself back down to the courtyard where he met with the other Black Swords as they unpacked the carriage. "You brought supplies?"

"Yes," Sir Carch answered. "Some to help restock the fortress."

"What about wine?" Darren asked.

"We have a barrel." Carch replied.

"Good." Darren said. "I've been in need of a drink." He helped unload the wine barrel and brought it to the galley. They opened it, filled their cups, and sat down to drink.

The healer came down to the great hall a few hours later, his robes, gloves, and mask covered in bile and feces. "I have finished my initial examination."

"What have you learned?" Darren asked.

"I believe it to be a disease of the stomach. I have some herbs that may remedy this. I found the bite mark where he was assaulted, and I fear the wound may have begun to fester. Some of the flesh surrounding it may need to be surgically removed." The healer explained. He peeled the gloved from his hands. "Did the prince receive some head injury?"

The question confused Darren. "No."

"Strange." The healer said. "I found a pair of raised bumps on his head beneath the hair. They were on either side, roughly between the eyes and ears on the crown of his skull."

"But can you treat him?" Darren asked.

"I will do all I can. I have some medicines and potions for the pain, but I don't know what all can be done."

And so, for the past three days, the healer tended to Sedrick's care from the breaking of dawn to the fall of evening. He would call upon the aid of the Black Swords to bring fresh bedding and take away the soiled ones. They would also bring hot water when called upon. During these days, at least one guard was to remain outside the prince's chambers at all times.

Darren braced his back against the stone wall of the corridor, his arms folded across his chest and eyes stared at the floor but not seeing anything. The prince's groaning continued to come from behind the door. It was a near miracle the boy could make any noise at all with how weak he'd gotten these past days. He had not lain eyes upon Prince Sedrick in person since the healer's arrival, so he did not know how bad he the boy had gotten. But from the smell and the continued descriptions given, it was not improving.

Suddenly, a crash came from behind the door. The sound of splintering wood. Darren reacted instantly, he threw the door open and stormed into the room, his sword drawn.

Instantly, he was struck by the rank smell, like a rotten

corpse covered in excrement. He had to clasp his hand over his mouth and nose. The next thing he noticed was how Prince Sedrick's bed was crushed, the legs smashed and frame in shambles. The sheets and linens torn to shreds. The shutters on the window were likewise shattered, a few stray pieces of wood hung limply from the hinges.

And in all the destruction, Prince Sedrick was gone.

Sir Darren moved around the room, looking for any sign of the prince. Somehow, in the few moments between the healer leaving and him entering, someone had come in through the window, abducted Sedrick, destroyed the room, and then made their escape out the same window. How could anyone be that fast?

He noticed something odd about the window. Not what was there, but rather what wasn't. He approached it wearily, placed one hand on the stone of the windowsill, and looked down. The remains of the shutters were scattered across the ground outside, not the floor inside. They were broken outward from within.

A scream echoed throughout the fortress, followed by a crash and a blood-curdling shriek. Sir Darren charged out of the room and raced down the hall. Something was attacking the fortress, something had taken the prince, and he would not let it get away.

As the knight came out into the courtyard, one of the soldiers stumbled out of the galley. Tears streamed down his face. He left a trail of blood behind him from the gash in his arm. "My lord!" The young soldier called out when he saw the knight. "Help! There's something in there!"

The frightful wail screamed out from the galley door. The soldier backed away, he stuttered and hyperventilated on the verge of pure panic. A shadowy figure appeared on the edge of the doorway, tall and lanky with long arms ending in clawed fingers and a small pair of horns sprouting like a crown upon its head. Shining red eyes stared back at them from the darkness. It snarled and hissed, lips on its short muzzle pulled back to reveal rows of white, sharp teeth dripping with saliva.

Sir Darren drew his sword. The air grew cold, his breath was visible before his eyes, but he paid it no mind. His attention was focused solely on the monstrous aberration before him. "This beast," Sir Darren sneered, "it murdered the prince." He raised his sword and charged at the creature, screaming a vicious battle cry. He swung and caught the monster in the arm. Black sludge gushed from the wound, it shrieked in pain.

Pulling back, he brought his sword to bare again and slashed at the beast. Again and again he attacked, his blade cutting into the monster's flesh. Like a cornered animal, it lashed out. The creature swung at Sir Darren. Its claws struck the knight across the chest and tore easily through his armor. Before he could react, the creature struck again. It grabbed him with both hands and lifted the knight easily over its head, then tossed him into a wall.

Sir Darren slammed against the stone. He cried out in pain and slumped to the earth. The creature leapt away, it ran on all fours hunched like an animal.

A bell rang throughout the fortress, the alarm for intruders. The other soldiers emerged from their barracks. They surrounded the creature in the courtyard and attacked, firing arrow after arrow into the monster. It hollered in pain, sharp points of metal pierced its skin and embedded in its back. The monster scurried across the courtyard as the barrage of arrows rained down. It ran for the sealed gate, throwing the full force of its weight behind the impact as it crashed. The large wooden doors shook and buckled, but held.

An arrow struck the creature at the base of the neck. A spurt of black ooze gushed out. It shrieked and turned to face the archer. With a mighty leap, the beast jumped straight up and latched itself to the stone wall, its claws digging into the rock. It crawled vertically along the fortress wall, arrows bouncing off the stone all around it. The creature screamed a horrible shriek, something that reminded Darren of a beast's death rattles. It leapt down and landed atop one of the bowmen, crushing him beneath its feet. Bones crunched and blood splattered across the walkway.

Another arrow swooshed past the monster's face. It hissed and snarled in frustration. It grabbed a severed arm from the man beneath it, and tore flesh away with its ragged teeth and swallowed.

Darren struggled to his feet. His legs trembled under him, weak and feeble, but he held himself. As he watched the onslaught, he came to realize their weapons were useless against this monster. They did little more than annoy it. He could think of only one weapon in the fortress that could kill it.

He tried to run and a bolt of pain shot through him again. Clutching his side, he limped as quickly as he could down to the storage cellar. He took a torch and carried it in his free hand until he came to a great latched door. A wooden beam ran through three pivots along the wall and the door itself. Nestling the torch on a slot on the wall, be braced his shoulder against the beam and lifted it away. His teeth clenched and his feet scraped against the stone floor as he struggled to lift, as the weight was greater than he expected.

The beam clattered to the ground and Darren shoved the door open. Inside were wooden barrels stacked three or sometimes four high, all filled with whale oil. The fishing villages and whale hunters had gathered it long ago and planned to use to light lamps, but Kendrick had seen its potential as a weapon and had all oil collected from whales declared the property of the crown.

Darren reached for the nearest barrel and had just gotten it over his shoulder when he heard a man's horrified shriek, followed shortly by a cracking of bones as the soldier fell end over end down the stones steps leading to the cellar. The body landed at the bottom of the stairs, the head split open and blood gushed out.

Darren stared at the body, then heard the snarling growl of the creature as it descended the steps. He saw its shadow, long and inhuman, with rows of horns like deer antlers protruding from its head, cutting off most of the light from above. As the beast itself came into view, all Darren could see were the shining red eyes as they stared back at him.

He snatched the torch from the wall and swung it out before him like a sword. The flames swished through the air, causing the monster to flinch. As he slashed at the creature with the fire, he stepped steadily to his left, forcing his opponent to mirror his moves and shift to the right. He did this until his back was to the stairway and the monster was backed against the room full of oil. He took three steps up the stairs, then took the barrel on his shoulder and threw it to the ground.

The wooden planks splintered and shattered, fish-smelling whale oil splashed out all over the floor. The monster hissed and recoiled. Taking this chance, Darren tossed the burning torch into the puddle, which erupted into a sea of flames.

Darren turned and hobbled as fast as he could up the stairway. Below, the monster hollered in anger and fright. He did not turn to look back. Sir Darren emerged from the cellar, his heart racing and forehead beaded with sweat. Men were standing at the ready, arrows nocked and aimed at the cellar door. "Stand down, men!" Darren panted as he emerged from the shadows. "It is merely I."

The men lowered their bows. "Sir," one of them approached, and in the dark Darren could not tell which it was. "The creature, what's happened to it?"

"I have detained it." Sir Darren responded. "Trapped below with burning oil. But we should evacuate the fortress before the oil either burns out or ignites everything else."

There was a roar from the cellar. Darren turned just in time to see a flaming barrel come flying up the stairway towards him. He threw himself to the ground just as the barrel flew past his head. It burst open upon contact with the ground, spewing more oil which instantly caught ablaze. It was soon followed by yet another barrel. And another after that. Soon, the entire central courtyard was engulfed in a sea of flames. The fire was spreading quickly, climbing up the support beams and moving along the wooden walkways.

"To the stables!" Sir Darren ordered. "Free as many horses as you can and get out of here!"

The men did as commanded. They reached the holding pens to find the horses kicking and roaring in terror as fire consumed the straw and hay.

Sir Darren forced a bridle onto the mouth of one of the frightened animal and managed to lead it out of its stall just as he saw the creature emerge from the cellar door. He found himself caught in the gaze of those hungry red eyes, too frozen in fear to move. Smoke rose from the lightly charred patches of fur on the creature's body, but it was otherwise unharmed.

The pull of the horse against its reins brought Darren out of his trance. The beast had no saddle, but he would have to do without. He pulled himself onto the horse's back and dug his heels into the animal's side. "Yah!" He shouted, and the horse took off at a run. He charged through the open gate just as the walking platform above it came down in a jumbled heap of burning, smoldering wood.

The horse galloped into the darkness, its hooves thundered against the well worn dirt path. Sir Darren glanced back only once to see the fortress of Haddrick's Keep engulfed in flames, yellow tongues of fire reaching for the sky as smoke billowed up to block out the stars. He could hear the shouting and screaming of men and horses as the flames swallowed them, along with the shrieking cry of the monster. He turned away, leaning forward on the horse and deafening his ears to the death behind him.

XXIV.
ENDELYNN

She was in the woods again, running as fast as her legs could carry her, ducking under low branches and jumping over fallen logs, trying to escape the pursuing creature. Each glance over her shoulder seemed to bring it closer. A cold, white mist seeped through the trees as it approached. The grass and ferns of the forest floor withered beneath its cloven hooves.

Endelynn caught sight of the thing, an emaciated deer-like creature with arms too long for its body and red eyes sunken into its skull. Half the creature's fur was molted off, the skin beneath a sickening ash gray. Bones protruded from the taut flesh and organs pulsated under the skin. She had no name for this creature, except that it was a monstrosity, an abomination of nature.

And it was reaching for her. Her legs couldn't move, as though they had been frozen in place, paralyzed by fear. Its clawed hands grasped her by the shoulder and lifted her off the ground. The monster opened its lipless mouth filled with dozens of twisted, razor-sharp teeth and sank them into her neck. She tried to scream, wanted to cry out in agony and desperation, but as the flesh of her throat was torn away no sound could escape.

Her eyes snapped open. Endelynn shot up in bed, clutching the blanket to her chest. She was short of breath and covered in

179

sweat. A dream. That's all it was. A horrible, vivid, chilling nightmare. She took a deep breath, trying to calm her racing heartbeat.

What was that thing? Some kind of monster, but she'd never seen or heard of anything like that before. There was no name for it. Why would she dream of something for which she had no name?

It didn't matter. Already the terrifying image was slipping from her mind like dreams always did, like fog in the early morning sun.

Endelynn shifted, only to notice how hard her bed was. This wasn't her bed, not her real bed anyway. She was in Shunka's hut, in the Wolf Tribe village, laying on a reed mat rather than the mattress she was used to. And instead of her soft silk sheets, she had a woven blanket and bear skins as covers. Her back still ached from sleeping on the ground, no matter how many nights it had been.

They must be searching for her by now. The kidnappers had sent a falcon to Kendrick of Kahren with their ransom demands, Endelynn could image whole squadrons of soldiers, hunters, and trackers teeming through the forest, scouring for her. She wanted to be home, wanted to see her mother again, and she wanted to see Sedrick.

He was probably leading one of the search parties himself, the young dashing prince that he was. It shouldn't be long now, soon Sedrick would find her and rescue her from her captors. Then they would return to Kahren and be wed at last.

Looking across the small hut, she caught sight of Shunka's sleeping form. He was curled up with his back against the wall, his legs crossed and arms folded over his chest. His chin rested on his chest and she could hear the low rumble of his snore. He'd let her sleep on his bed, which was kind of him, and he'd also rescued her from the panther shifter Katsalgi yesterday, which was even nicer.

180

But he still wouldn't let her go home, and that was cruel. If he would just take her back to the forest trail, or even to Haddrick's Keep, she could convince her mother to give his tribe any reward they wished for. So why was he so stubborn about it?

A sliver of light fell in through the smoke hatch in the roof, signaling the sun rise. Endelynn still found herself unused to waking at such an early time. The days of being awakened by her handmaiden long after the rest of the castle was up and about were behind her now.

She shifted again on the less than comfortable floor, only to have a sharp jab of pain spike in her abdomen. She recognized it, a familiar but unwelcome pain. Endelynn knew her time was close, even before she left Dadria for Kahren, but she'd hoped to make it in time before her cycle began. Obviously, it was too late now.

Lifting the blankets, she came upon a grisly sight. The clothing around her hips and inner thighs were soaked through and dark red, almost black with blood. Even the blanket above and mat beneath her were discolored. Her bleeding cycle had begun.

Shunka groaned in his sleep. His face twitched. Endelynn's stomach lurched at the sound and she pulled the blankets back up to her chin, covering the blood. The native man awoke, his eyes blinked as he turned to her.

They gazed at each other in silence. Endelynn didn't want to address her condition, but the longer they stared at one another the more anxious she became. He would see the mess as soon as she stood, and then she knew she would face the rage of an uncultured, wild, wolf savage.

"Your cycle of blood has started." Shunka said. Endelynn's eyes snapped open and her jaw fell slacked. Before she could say anything, he continued, "I could smell it."

Of course he could. A man who could change into a wolf

would have some kind of incredible nose and could find any scent, even in human form. At least, that's how she saw it. She pulled the blankets tighter.

Shunka stood, the top of his head almost reached the roof of his hut. As he approached, his imposing figure gazing down at her from above like a sentinel. He grabbed the blankets and pulled them away. Endelynn's fingers betrayed her and released there hold.

He looked down at her blood-soaked legs. She tried to cover herself, bringing her knees together and turning away, only to wince as another jolt of pain stabbed through her abdomen. "More blood." Shunka said. "Greater than expected. Not problem." He rolled the blankets into a bundle and set them aside before holding his hand out to her. "Come."

"Where to?" Endelynn asked, more confused now than afraid.

"Bleeding house." He said.

That name brought her concern. It sounded like some sort of torture chamber or slaughter house. Even so, she took his hand a allowed him to pull her up. Standing hurt, like a hot spike being driven through her stomach, and she almost lost her footing, but Shunka caught her and helped her stay upright.

He lead her by the hand like a child. They stepped out into the early morning light, the sun's rays creeping over the distant Dragon's Teeth mountains, catching the mist and fog that hung in the air. Many of the other villagers were already awake and teaming about the village. A trio of men were heading out into the woods with their spears, bows and arrows. A small number of women and children likewise set off into the forest, but with baskets for gathering seeds, nuts, and berries. Days started early here.

Everyone they passed stopped to watch. Endelynn could feel their eyes on her as they all looked down at the bloodstains that ran the length of her legs. Her face and the back of her neck grew warm with embarrassment.

Shunka stopped when they came to a large lodge. It was taller and longer than many of the others, with smoke rising from the vent in the roof. As they came to the wood panel door, Shunka placed his hand against it and spoke a few words in the tribal language. The slotted panel door lifted away and an old woman with gray-white hair and deep wrinkles stepped out. Endelynn was shocked when she saw her, as this woman wasn't of the tribe. She was Dadrian.

The old woman turned to Endelynn. She looked the princess up and down, taking particular notice of the blood on her legs. She nodded to Shunka, stepped to the side and held the plated door open. "Come inside, child." She said in the language of Dadria.

After a moment's hesitation, and a reassuring nod from Shunka, Endelynn stepped inside. The old woman dropped the door behind her, cutting them off from the outside world. The first thing Endelynn noticed was the warmth. A fire burned in the central fire pit, with baskets of steaming water placed throughout the room.

Rows of benches and hammocks lined the walls, and resting on them were other women. They all stared at Endelynn as she came inside, and much to her surprise, they were all nude.

"Come along," the elder woman placed her hand on Endelynn's shoulder, "let's get you cleaned up."

"What is this place?" Endelynn asked.

"This is the House of the Moon."

"The what?"

"The House of the Moon." The older woman said. "It has a few other names, such as the Bloody Lodge or the Red House. It is the place where woman go when their cycle begins, and they stay here until it is finished." She pulled a curtain along the ceiling to block them from the rest of the lodge. "Now, disrobe."

Endelynn did as she was told and peeled the soiled clothes from her body. The trousers were the most difficult, and gross. The old woman took the clothes and left, returning a moment later with a clay bowl of warm water and a rag.

The princess crossed her legs at the knee and held her arms over her chest. "There's no need to be shy, child." The woman said. "You have nothing these ladies haven't seen before, and no man is allowed in the House of the Moon." She took the soaked towel and rung out the excess water. "This is a sacred place, a spiritual place for when the moon calls to us."

"I never thought of it like that." Endelynn said. "All I know is it's gross and ugly and painful."

"Is that what they say in Dadria now?" The woman placed the rag against Endelynn's back and started to rub in circles.

The tightness in her muscles began to relax. Endelynn hadn't realized just how tense she'd been until now. "You're from my country, then? From Dadria?"

"I was." The woman said. "I used to live in a small village just within the walls. My father was a merchant, trading in spices. He was delivering goods to Kahren, and I insisted on going with him. We were halfway there when we were attacked by bandits. My father was killed. I would've been too, if my raox hadn't panicked and raced off into the woods. These people took me in, and I've been living here ever since."

"What is your name?" Endelynn asked.

"I used to be called Hallie. The tribe gave me a new name, Uyoonta." After a bit of scrubbing, the woman placed the towel back into the clay bowl and rang it out again. "Tell me, who is king of Dadria now? When I was last there, it was Leothuldus, but that was years ago. Has his son, Cassius, risen to the throne?"

"He has," Endelynn answered, and then paused. "Well, he was the king. He died recently."

"That's sad to hear." The woman, Uyoonta, said. "How did he die?"

She didn't want to talk about this. The thoughts of her father's final moments only brought more grief. "He just got sick one day." She answered.

"So then who is king now?" Uyoonta kept pushing the subject.

"No one, I guess." Endelynn said. "It would have been whomever I married."

"Oh, my goodness," the elder woman dropped the towel to the floor. "That makes you the princess. I'm sorry, I didn't know. I shouldn't have been asking such questions about your father."

"I'm just glad I have someone to talk to." Endelynn said. "I can't understand a word these people say. It all just sounds like nonsense words to me."

"And you sound the same to them." The old Dadrian woman said. "The words of the pale-faced men are just as confusing and disjointed to the people of the forest. Shunka can only speak it because he is a Chaowtee."

"And what is that?" The princess asked.

"It means he's a speaker-of-many-tongues." Uyoonta said. "He has the gift of language and can learn them quickly. There are a few like him in each village."

"I think we met one." She said. "There was a man in the woods yesterday. He was similar but different, he changed into a panther and tried to attack me, but Shunka fought him off."

"The way I heard it, you helped him a little." The older woman ran the towel along the length of Endelynn's legs, wiping away the blood. Until now, the princess had almost forgotten about it. The pain in her abdomen had lessened since entering the lodge. "I heard that you took Shunka's spear and attacked Katsalgi yourself. That was a brave thing to do."

Endelynn didn't think herself brave. Her actions had not

been really to save Shunka's life, at least she didn't think they were, but rather for self preservation. The panther shifter would have turned on her as soon as it finished off her wolf protector. "If I hadn't, then Shunka would've been killed."

"But you saved him." The woman finished washing the last of the blood from Endelynn's legs. The rag, now stained red, drifted in the bowl of warm, pink tinged water. "You saw a chance and choose to help. Not everyone could have made that choice."

They sat in silence for a while. The woman, Hallie or Uyoonta or whatever name she wanted to call herself, Endelynn thought about her words, but they didn't offer much comfort to the trouble princess. "All I want is to go home. I want to go back to Dadria. I miss my old room, I miss the old stables and my raox, Sleppa. I miss my mother, but mostly I miss my father." She wrapped her arms around her chest, as if embracing herself, but it was less an embrace of joy then sadness. "I'll never see them again, will I?" She asked. "I mean, I know I can never see my father again, but everything else is still out there. It all still exists, but I can never be there again."

"I'm afraid not." The old woman said. "The forest tribes greatest defense is secrecy. If word somehow got back to the Walled Cities that these people still lived out here in the woods, it could spell death for them all."

"Why?" Endelynn asked.

"You saw, didn't you? Yesterday you witnessed Shunka and the man from the other village change shape into the giant beasts." Uyoonta continued. "You should try remembering your history. A royal born girl such as yourself should know how the Savage Wars ended."

"The savage forest dwellers were all cleansed." Endelynn recited from her lessons.

"Is that the word they use now? 'Cleansed'?" The woman said in a dismissive tone. "You may find the histories kept in the castle library differ greatly from what the Forest Tribes remember." She shook her head as if Endelynn were a small child who didn't know better.

The princess's face burned hot and her cheeks flushed. She felt embarrassed, like she'd given the wrong answer during one of her mother's tests. She hated being wrong on those tests, it always made her feel stupid.

"But then what happened? After the savages were 'cleansed', why did the people of Dadria and Kahren build their great walls?"

"It was the beasts." Endelynn said. "The enormous wolves and bears and panthers and . . ." Wolves. The wolves like what she'd seen Shunka change into. Like the panther shifter from yesterday. "The forest savages became the beasts."

"To protect their villages and their people. And it has worked rather well. Over three hundred years later, and no one within the walls know these people still exist." Uyoonta explained. "So, you see, to preserve their villages and their way of life, the warriors will kill or capture anyone that sees them or ventures too close to their settlements. If word reached the wrong ears, everyone in this tribe could die."

"I could swear." Endelynn said. "I could make an oath on my honor as a Rambourne, as a princess, and as the next queen of Dadria to never reveal their secrets."

The older woman shook her head. "No oath would be enough." She said. "In the past, our ancestors made many promises and treaties with the Sequoia people and none of them were ever honored. Hundreds of thousands died by trusting the words of a foreigner. They will never do it again."

Endelynn's heart sank. She slouched lower on the bench. "So I'm trapped here forever."

"It won't be as bad as that." Uyoonta said. "You may even find you like it better here."

"I'm not sure of that." Endelynn said. "The day I consider

this my home will be the day the wolf and lamb lay together in peace." It was an old saying in Dadria, one Endelynn had heard from her parents many times. It referenced an old story in the book of the All-Father, that the coming of the Hero of Ages would be foretold by a wolf and lamb lying together with no contest. Nowadays it was mostly used as a euphemism for something that was never going to occur.

The elder Dadrian woman produced a small bundle of leaves from the pouch at her waist. She held them out for Endelynn. "Here, chew on these. They will help ease the pain." She said. "And, if you would like, I can help make your stay easier."

Endelynn took the leaves and placed one in her mouth. It was bitter, but she chewed it anyway. "How so?" She asked.

"I can teach you the language."

XXV.
KENDRICK

"**A** creature," the king said, repeating the phrase spoken by Sir Darren. Kendrick was seated in the throne room, a goblet of wine clutched in one hand, the braziers ablaze around him. He propped his head on the closed fist of his other hand while he listened to the knight's report. "What kind of creature?"

"I cannot say." Sir Darren knelt at the base of the steps leading to the throne. He had one knee planted on the floor and his left arm draped over his other leg, his head was bowed.

The knight's face was ragged, black rings circled his eyes and he looked as though he hadn't slept in days. The guards found him in the earliest hours of the morning just outside the walls. Darren was pounding on the gates, demanding to be let in, with his exhausted horse lying on the ground behind him, foam dribbling from its mouth. Off in the distance, a column of smoke rose into the sky.

Kendrick had been awoken not long after when Darren demanded to speak with him. The news had not been good. The destruction of Haddrick's Keep, the deaths of many loyal Black Swords of the King, as well as the disappearance of his brother. And the bad news kept coming, as Sir Darren told of this bizarre creature that he claimed to be responsible.

"Can you at least describe it?" Kendrick asked, then took another sip from his goblet.

189

"It was emaciated." Darren explained. "Brown, matted fur over thin skin with protruding bones. It walked on cloven hooves, had claws on each hand, and antlers atop its head. It killed all others in the fortress."

"What of Sedrick?" The king asked. "My brother, was he among the slain?"

"I know not." Darren answered. "I believe the monster attacked him first, as I first encountered it after the prince's bed chambers had been ransacked, but the prince himself was nowhere to be found."

Kendrick drank the last of the wine in his cup, then tossed it aside. It clattered to the floor, a sound that echoed off the great, stone walls of his throne room. A heavy silence fell over the hall. "Leave me," Kendrick said at last, "I need time to think."

Darren stood and walked back the way he came, his footsteps were the only sound. Once he was gone, Kendrick allowed himself to slouch low in the stone chair. He pressed his fingers into his left temple as his head began to throb with a pounding headache. Nothing was working as planned, nothing ever worked as planned. The last time anything had gone Kendrick's way was when he ascended the throne, when he removed the old king from power with just a few drops in his wine and ordered his dear brother; Roddrick's hunting accident. Those orchestrations were the last time anything happened the way Kendrick intended. And even those weren't without their issues.

When Sir Darren returned to inform him of Roddrick's demise, the knight was compelled to admit he did not witness the elder prince's death. A bear had attacked them during the hunt and killed Roddrick's horse. Sir Darren and the other surviving bodyguards had fled before the beast came after them, but that left Prince Roddrick's fate uncertain.

Kendrick had ordered his men to scour the kingdom in

190

search for the lost prince. He even offered a reward, one hundred gold coins for his brother's safe return. At long last, a man came forward claiming to be Roddrick. But beyond a superficial resemblance, this man was clearly not the missing prince.

Kendrick was so enraged by this conman's scheme, he had the impostor's tongue cut out and the man thrown in the dungeon. A public execution was held, where Kendrick revoked the reward and declared the missing Prince Roddrick dead. On that day, he had gone from acting king to the absolute monarch of Kahren, and his rule remained uncontested ever since.

Another man entered the throne room. It was an old man, one of the bird keepers from the aviary. He shuffled along, his hands tucked within his sleeves and back bent from age. A beard hung down to his belt. "My king," the old man spoke with a rough, withered voice, "a falcon has come for you."

Yet another headache. What ever happened to the days when a king was allowed a moment of silence? Why even be a king if everyone kept coming to him with their little, petty problems? "From whom?" he asked with as much interest as he could muster, which wasn't much.

"It appears," the bird keeper said as he pulled the scroll from his sleeve, "it was sent by her majesty, Queen Regent Beatrice of Dadria." The old man extended his wizened hand, weak fingers held the scroll.

Kendrick shifted in his seat. He lifted his head from his fist and eyed the messenger. "Beatrice?" He asked as he took the parchment. "What does she want? A message for the princess?" Of course, he knew what she wanted. This letter must be intended for Princess Endelynn, a concerned mother reaching out to her child to find to make sure she'd arrived safely. He would have to find some forgers to impersonate the Dadrian princess, craft a response and delay the queen's arrival.

191

"It seems not, my king," the aviary keeper said. "This falcon was meant for you."

Kendrick broke the wax seal and read. Once he was finished, the paper crumpled in his fist. He could feel the heat rising on his neck. To add to everything, now the girl's mother was on her way. Not just that, somehow she claimed to know about the princess's abduction and was demanding answers of him. Even without knowing the tone of the words, he could tell the queen was incensed.

He tossed the ball of paper into the brazier and watched it burn. It was too late to send a reply falcon, the queen would be halfway to Kahren by now.

"Be gone." He waved a tired hand at the bird keeper. The old man bowed, slowly, as if he could do it any other way, and then shuffled out of the throne room. The king resettled in the throne, a cold chair carved from stone ages ago. After a long while, how long he couldn't tell, he stood and climbed down the steps. He needed to prepare for her majesty's arrival.

XXVI.
SHUNKA

Shunka found himself seated on a smoothed log that served as a bench at the edge of the great central fire pit. The coals inside were white and cold, coated in ash. No fire would burn there until tonight. He looked across the pit to the massive totem pole, the tallest in the village, that told of the war between his people and the pale invaders.

Three days. That's how long the pale girl had been in the House of the Moon. In that time, life had returned to a state of normalcy. Shunka helped to fashion reed nets, hollow out logs to make canoes, and sharpen pieces of flint to make spear points and arrowheads. Simple tasks. Plain tasks.

Boring tasks.

The monotony of day to day living was starting to wear on him. Never before had he really thought or cared about how things changed, or rather how they stayed the same. He used to just take each day as it came, do the work that required doing, and go on patrol to protect the village. He hadn't really given much thought to the future.

All that had started to change now that the girl was here. The future was upon him, and he was unsure how to feel about that. What was this girl to him? What was he to her? He didn't know. When Alo said he would find the Aleutsi while on patrol, Shunka did not believe it. The appearance of the Great Mother was supposed to signal the change of times, the coming of the

Red Wolf, and the salvation of their people. The idea that this person would be a foreigner, one of the pale-faced invaders, would be enough to make most men's stomach turn. It wasn't until Shunka saw the girl with his own eyes, saw how she matched the description given by the old shaman, that he started to have second thoughts.

He had to admit, there was some strength in her. There was a fire inside her spirit, and Shunka saw it briefly when she protected him from the Panther warrior. The name Alo gave her, Chaneewah Ishde, seemed suitable. The Flame-haired maiden.

Shunka was so lost in his thoughts, he didn't notice how he was being stalked until Mingan's arms snaked under his shoulders. Mingan's fingers laced together behind Shunka's head, catching him in a hold. Shunka lurched upwards, tried to pull free, but the elder warrior's grip was too strong.

"Caught you daydreaming again, little brother!" Mingan laughed, but did not release his hold. "You ought to watch your surroundings better. This is why you only have two feathers in your hair."

"Let me go." Shunka struggled. Mingan did as he was bid and pulled his arms away. Shunka fell forward managing not to land on his face, then shot his brother an angry glare.

"I was just playing, don't get mad." Mingan said. "Ever since news of your upcoming union, you've been so dour."

"The union." Shunka repeated as he sat back on the bench. Even now he'd given it little thought. What was he going to do about Endelynn when he had to leave for the Hawk Tribe? Orumaku Chaa was far less lenient about bringing captives back to his village than most of the other Chaas. "That's soon, isn't it?"

"Envoys from the Hawk Tribe could arrive any day." Mingan replied. "Maybe even your feathery bride herself." The older brother stepped around the log and seated himself beside

Shunka. "Are you excited?"

"Not the word I would choose," Shunka admitted. He glanced up at his brother. Sitting beside him, Shunka couldn't help but feel small. Mingan had always been taller and stronger than him, even when they were boys. Even sitting, his elder sibling had at least a six inch height advantage and more than fifty pounds of muscle. He was everything a Wolf warrior should be; strong, confident, capable, a natural leader, someone you would follow in an instant but also able to take orders if needed. Basically, everything Shunka wasn't.

A pit formed in his stomach. A part of him hated his brother for it, for just being so perfect. But there were many times when Mingan came to Shunka's defense when no one else would. When they were children and Mother and Father were trying to teach them to adopt the wolf's skin as their own for the first time. Mingan got it right away, but Shunka struggled with it for days. For all of their parents' berating, Mingan offered nothing but kind words and encouragement. He would even talk back to Mother and Father in Shunka's defense, despite how it might anger them. That was when Mother was still alive, of course.

"Not excited, huh?" Mingan said, bringing Shunka back to the present. "Why not? You think she might be ugly?"

"No," Shunka said, incredulous.

"Afraid she'll be stronger than you?" Mingan nudged his brother with his elbow. "They say Hawk women are better fighters than the men."

"It has nothing to do with the union." Shunka stated.

"Ah, I see." Mingan straightened his back and folded his arms, a smug smirk came over his face. "Well, then, how about we go for a run?"

"A run?"

"Just the two of us. Nothing much, not even a patrol. You and me, to the forest path and back." Mingan slapped his palms on his knees and stood. "What do you say?" He reached back with one outstretched hand.

Shunka smiled. "Yeah," he said and took the hand. Mingan pulled him to his feet. "That sounds nice."

"Then let's go." Mingan released his grip, then shoved Shunka back to the ground and started running. "Last one to the path is the loser!" He shouted back as he left the village.

Shunka hopped back to his feet and took off after his brother. He charged out of the village and into the woods, the sunlight choked off by the enormous trees. Once they were in the forest, Shunka allowed the wolf to take over. He leapt forward with his arms outstretched, and his hands became paws before they touched the ground.

As a wolf, sleek and black against the trees' shadows, he easily overtook Mingan. He ran full bore, racing across the ferns and grasses that covered the forest floor. It wasn't much later, however, when a second wolf came to his side. Shunka could smell him and knew it was his brother, keeping pace just as easily as before.

They ran together for miles into the forest. Sometimes side by side, and other times far enough that Shunka could not see Mingan. But all the time, he felt his brother at his side.

Eventually, they came to the well-worn packed earth road. Shunka stopped at the forest's edge, finally out of breath. His heart hammered fiercely in his chest, and his tongue rolled out to hang from his mouth as he panted. Mingan trotted up to his side, also panting for air.

Shunka shifted back to his human form and braced his back against a tree. A tingling sensation ran up and down his arms and legs, his body was coated in sweat. He rolled his head back and gazed up at the canopy, the sunlight that was both too bright and not bright enough. "I guess that means you win," Mingan said as he changed back.

Shunka shifted his eyes over to his brother, he was too

exhausted to move much else. Mingan looked winded, but not as tired as Shunka felt. "Yeah," Shunka muttered under his breath.

The clop of hooves and creak of wheels alerted them to an approaching caravan. With a new burst of energy, Shunka and Mingan backed into the shadows between the trees. The first to come was a man covered from head to toe in shining, bright, metal armor. He rode on the back of an armored ram, its spiral curved horns nearly as wide as the creature's shoulders. The man carried a red banner that depicted a white ram against a purple shield.

Mingan and Shunka crouched close to the ground, observing the single mounted knight from the shadows. "It's just one," Mingan leaned close and whispered, "you think we can take him?"

They might. It would be two against one, and even with his armor and weapons, a pair of wolves would be more than a match for a single foreign soldier. The problem, as far as Shunka could see, was the beast. A full-grown male raox, especially one trained for combat, would be more than enough to turn the tide of battle. And besides that, armored men like this never traveled alone. "We shouldn't," Shunka said, "there might be more of them coming up the path."

"We can bring this one down before they get here," Mingan goaded. "Come on, if we shift right now we can knock him off the beast and drag him back into the woods before the rest arrive."

"No." Shunka's tone was stern, more than he expected. "We'll not. Not this time."

Mingan shot him a shocked look. Shunka couldn't blame him, he surprised even himself with his words. It didn't matter anyways as two marching rows of mounted knights followed the first along the path, each carried either a banner like the first, or a steel-tipped spear. An ornate coach, pulled by four raox, rested in the middle between the rows of knights. The pair of brothers watched in silence as the carriage and its entourage of guards marched through the woods until they disappeared from sight and the sounds faded into the ambiance of the forest.

Once they were gone, Shunka released the breath he didn't know he'd been holding. The muscles along his back relaxed as the tension lifted. He was only briefly aware of the foliage rustling as Mingan stood.

"What happened to you?" The older warrior glared down at him with his arms crossed. "The brother I knew would never hesitate to defend his homeland."

"I told you why." Shunka stood, brushing the dead needles from his hands and trousers. "We were too outnumbered and they were too heavily armed. We might've taken one or two, but then they would overwhelm and kill us. Attacking them would've been suicide."

"As if that ever stopped you before." Mingan retorted. "As I recall, it was you who attacked that black-garbed man and the boy first. You nearly clawed his eye out."

"And I got a knife in the gut for it," Shunka said, and ran his fingers along the scar across his stomach for emphasis.

"Is it the foreign girl, then?" Shunka did not respond. Mingan continued. "You didn't talk with Tala about it, maybe you'll talk to me. Why didn't you kill her when we first found her?"

Shunka snorted. "Did Tala put you up to this?"

"Our sister is just curious. As am I." Mingan shifted his weight and turned to face Shunka. "I was there," he said, "I watched as they took our mother. I saw as they cut her head off and ripped the skin from her body. I can never forget and will never forgive what those pale-skinned demons have done to our people. So then, why did you choose to bring one of those monsters back to our village?"

Shunka's jaw tightened. His chest rose and fell with a heavy breath. "I can't tell you." He confessed. "No more than I could tell Tala."

"Why not?" Mingan's voice rose with anger. "It doesn't make any sense to me. If you took her as spoils of war, that I could understand. But you haven't. What is she to you?"

"She is my charge." Shunka answered. "And I will not discuss it anymore with you." He turned and started to walk away, but was wrenched back when Mingan grasped him by the shoulder and yanked.

"I am your brother!" Mingan shouted. "We were born from the same mother and sired by the same father! We've grown and fought at each other's side for years. I've put my life in danger for your sake. I am owed an explanation."

Suddenly filled with rage, Shunka shoved back. Mingan lost his balance and fell to the ground. "I owe you nothing!" Shunka stood over and glared down at his brother. "I will talk no more with you about the foreign girl. She is under my protection and that is all you have to know." He turned away and started the long walk back to the village. Once he was a fair distance away, he shifted into his wolf form and darted into the deep forest. He could still hear Mingan calling to him.

"This is what she's done to us! Turned brother against brother! She's poisoned you! Made you forget your true purpose!"

He tried to ignore the angry words of his brother. He wanted to tell Mingan the truth. Really, he wanted to tell anybody just so he didn't have to carry the secret alone. But Shunka knew that if the truth were known, that the foreign princess was foretold to be the Aleutsi, most would think him delusional, some would try to kill the girl for casting some horrible spell over him, and others would take her to use to their own ends. It was best for all that the truth remain a secret.

XXVII.
BEATRICE

From the moment she stepped down from her carriage, the queen was in a rage. As a matter of fact, her anger had been building ever since she prepared her journey to Kahren, from the moment news arrived of her daughter's disappearance.

When the bird-keeper came down from the aviary that morning with the letter in hand, she was more than a little surprised. It had been only a few days since Endelynn's departure, not long enough for the wedding to take place, or even for the young girl to reach Kahren. "Your grace," the old bird-keeper said, he shuffled through the hall of the throne room to find Beatrice in the Queen's Chair. Her bodyguard, Sir Aridain stood at her side. "A message has just arrived by falcon. From Kahren, it seems."

"A message from the king?" Beatrice asked as she took the roll of parchment from his hand.

"I do not believe so." the bird-keeper said. "The seal is wrong."

Upon a quick inspection, Beatrice found what he meant. Kendrick's royal seal had the antlered head of an elk buck facing to the left with a crown over its head, but this seal was the opposite, the elk facing right. As well, a capital letter "R" was displayed in the wax just below the elk's head. The queen broke the seal and unrolled the message.

"Your Highness,
I regret to inform you that your daughter has
gone missing. She never made it to Kahren, and
it appears she's been taken hostage by bandits.
Kendrick has not told you, and he does not
intend to, for he was the one who orchestrated
the princess's disappearance.
-The Exiled King."

The letter fell from her hands. It drifted slowly, almost as if time was moving at a crawl, before finally handing at Beatrice's feet. Missing? Kidnapped? Hostage? Her daughter, her only child being held prisoner? Could it be true?

"Your grace?" Sir Aridain asked, snapping her from her daze. "Is everything alright?"

"Read for yourself." She said, scooping the paper off the floor and handing it to the knight.

Sir Aridain quickly scanned over the letter, his eyes grew wide with shock, and then twisted in anger. "This is an outrage! My lady, this must certainly be a jest." He said, crumpling the parchment in his hands.

"What if it is not?" The queen said. "My daughter's in danger, I can feel it. Last night I had a terrible dream, monsters killing her bodyguards and taking her captive. And then, three vicious shadow beasts appeared from the trees and devoured the monsters before swarming on her." Beatrice stood, meeting the gaze of her knight. "She's in danger, and we need to help her."

Sir Aridain wet his lips, hesitant to speak, "Your grace," he said, "if I may be so bold, your dreams may very well just be a case of nervous thoughts brought on by Endelynn's upcoming wedding. Can we really trust the word of an anonymous letter? How do we know this wasn't sent as a cruel prank? Who even is this 'Exiled King'?" Aridain said, flashing the name on the crumpled paper.

"I don't know, but I intend to find out." She turned to the bird-keeper, who was still in the throne room, "I need a letter sent to King Kendrick immediately. Tell him I am on my way to Kahren, that I know what's happened to my daughter, and I will expect answers when I arrive."

"Yes, my queen." The bird-keeper bowed and departed, shuffling his feet as he went.

"My lady, you cannot be serious." Aridain said. "You are under pressure, the death of our beloved king has been hard on us all, as well as Endelynn's wedding, you cannot let this simple message get the better of you. We need you here. Dadria needs you here, you are the only one in power now. You cannot abandon the kingdom so simply."

"Do not lecture me!" She snapped, silencing the knight. "You are not a mother. You have no children, you do not understand the lengths I will go to to ensure her safety." She stepped passed Sir Aridain, then turned to say, "You should prepare your raox for departure. You're coming with me."

They had spoken very little since then. Sir Aridain rode the entire journey from Dadria to Kahren aside the queen's carriage, his eyes ever watchful and ears ever listening, but still he did not believe this was a serious deal. He did not, however, voice this opinion to her majesty during the trip.

And now, as they reached the walls of King Kendrick's castle, he still stood at her side. It was his loyalty, not his opinions, she needed right now, especially as they came into the king's throne room.

"Your grace," a young man dressed in the garb and the gold sigil of the Black Swords of the King said as he approached, "it is an honor to greet you. My name is Sir Mordrane." He gave a courtly bow. "We received your falcon, although we were quite shocked by the urgency of your message."

"I don't have time for pleasantries." Beatrice silenced the man with a wave of her hand. "Or for exchanging words with one of Kendrick's mouthpieces. I will see the king now."

"I am sorry, but I cannot allow you before the king so heavily armed." He motioned to Sir Aridain, still astride his raox. "If you would please disarm, I would gladly take you before his majesty."

Aridain looked over to her, and Beatrice gave a quick nod. With her command, he dismounted his raox and began the process of removing his weapons. The sword came first, pulled from its scabbard and set inside the queen's carriage. Then the scabbard itself and the belt that held it. Followed soon by the pair of daggers at his waist. Once his weapons had been set aside, their greeter nodded and directed the two of them inside.

They soon came to the throne room, finding all the windows shuddered. The only light came from a row of torches along the pillars and a brazier besides the throne itself. Behind the throne hung a tapestry which depicted the sigil of House Stagghart, a red elk against a gold shield on a blue background. Kendrick himself was seated below the tapestry.

It had been a long time since Beatrice had last seen Kendrick in person, not since his coronation. He had grown considerably since then, as he came to the crown quite young. It appeared, however, that the years he spent on the throne had not been kind to him. While he was at least ten years her junior, the Kahren king looked as though he were closer to forty than she.

"Your highness," Kendrick said as he stood, his robes flowing down around him, and crown settled on his long ash-blond hair, "I am pleased to see you, although I must admit I was surprised to get your message."

"Kendrick, as I just told your servant before, I don't have time for pleasantries." Beatrice cut him off. "My daughter. Where is she?"

The king let out a low sigh. He rubbed his hand against his forehead as though he had a headache, although Beatrice doubted if that was the case. "Right to the point, I see. In truth, I do not know where the princess is. A search party has already been assembled and gone looking for her. My brother is among them. They are using the fortress of Haddrick's Keep as their headquarters while they conduct the search."

"That's not good enough!" The queen spat, her voice rang throughout the halls. "Your brother comes to my kingdom and my husband dies! Then a marriage is arranged between that same brother and my daughter, only for her to be taken hostage on the way to her own wedding! How are you to account for all of this?"

"Your husband's death is regrettable. I am sorry for your loss. But we cannot allow our emotions to drive our actions." Kendrick's response was cold. He stepped down from his throne to meet Beatrice on her level. "I can see that you are tired from your long journey. I will have a room prepared and some food and wine sent up to you. We can discuss more once you are rested." Kendrick turned away from Beatrice and towards the Black Sword. "Sir Mordrane."

"Yes, my king?"

"Would you be so kind as to escort our guest to the bed chambers we've prepared for her?"

"Of course, your majesty." The young Black Sword, younger than the knight who accompanied Sedrick, bowed to Beatrice. "If you would follow me, your grace." His cloak swirled behind him as he moved for the exit, his footsteps echoing through the hall.

Was this all? She traveled all the way here, barely stopping to rest during the three day journey, just to get pawned off on another one of Kendrick's lackeys? "I've not finished with you, Kendrick."

"I am aware." The king replied. "We will talk more on your

daughter and our plans to retrieve her after you've had some rest." He turned his back to her and walked up the steps to his throne. "Until then, I wish you a pleasant evening." Beatrice sneered. She turned to follow the Black Sword knight, Sir Aridain close behind her.

They left the throne room and followed their guide through the various halls of the castle before he stopped at one of the doors. "This will be your sleeping quarters while you are staying with us. I hope they are to your liking." He procured an iron key from his pocket, used it to unlatch the door, and held it open as the queen and her bodyguard entered. "I will have a pair of guards outside your doors at all times. If you are in need of anything, do let me know." He closed the door behind them, but did not leave.

Trapped. Imprisoned like criminals.

The sleeping quarters were smaller than she expected; there was a single large sitting room with a lounging couch, a circular table with two chairs, and a stone and brick hearth with the cold ash and coal remains of a long dead fire.

Adjacent to the sitting room was a smaller bedroom with a single, massive bed stuffed with goose down covered in scarlet silk linens and pillows. A thin beige curtain separated the two chambers of the room.

With the tension and emotions of the meeting with Kendrick now behind her, Beatrice allowed herself to relax. Although she had never felt less relaxed in her life. She did not feel at ease, but instead was more drained. She collapsed on the lounging sofa. Kendrick was right about one thing, at least, she was exhausted. Not just physically from their journey, but mentally and emotionally from everything that had happened in the last few days. Prince Sedrick's visit and the disturbances that came from it, her husband's sudden sickness and death, and now Endelynn's abduction. It was all weighing on her mind and steadily pushing her towards despair.

"Go away, boy." Sir Mordrane's voice came from the far side of the door. "The visiting queen is trying to rest and does not need your disturbances."

"But I brought food and drink." A child's voice replied.

"I do not care. Take it back." The black knight's voice grew angrier.

"Wait," Beatrice called out to them, "some food sounds good right now. Open the door. Let him in."

The door swung inward as a young child, no older than seven, stood in the open doorway holding a silver platter of pastries and a flask of wine. "I hope I'm not intruding."

"Not at all." The queen said.

The boy moved briskly across the room and set the pastries and wine on the table. "I hope you enjoy them." He bowed to the queen, then departed as quickly as he'd appeared. The door closed behind him.

Beatrice's eyes lingered over the pastries, soft warm dough covered in honey and a fine layer of powdered sugar. Some of them even with custard or jelly filling. They looked delicious, and right then she wanted nothing more than to gorge herself on them, until she noticed the small folded paper placed right beside them.

It was the same kind of parchment as the letter that had brought her to Kahren. This letter was also closed with a wax seal which bore the same reversed royal sigil as the previous one.

Another message from her mysterious friend. Although she didn't know if this person sending messages was a friend at all, or even a distant ally. For all she knew of him now it might be some castle servant with too much time on their hands and a penchant for tormenting a grieving woman. After all, the last letter she received from them brought her here, and for what purpose? Should she open it? What strange directions would they try to give her this time?

She shifted her eyes from the platter over to Sir Aridain. He was fixated on the letter as well. "My lady," he said as he picked up the letter, "should I dispose of this?"

"No." She held out her hand. "Whoever has been sending these messages wanted us to come here. Let's find out why." Aridain placed the letter in her open palm. Beatrice broke the seal and unfolded it, only to find the paper blank.

Somehow, she felt disappointment and relief at the same time. There was nothing here, so it was all just a means of tormenting her and there was no reason to come to Kahren. On the other hand, that also meant that Endelynn's captivity was not some plot orchestrated by Kendrick and he was, in fact, using all his kingdom's resources to find her, just as he said he was.

As she moved to set the paper down, her thumb brushed against the folded portion and she felt a sticky residue. Running her fingers over it again, she found this same sticky substance all over one side of the page. "Maybe it's not so blank after all."

"My lady?" Aridain asked, confused.

Beatrice quickly moved off the couch and walked over to the cold fireplace. She took a handful of soot from the floor of the hearth and sprinkled it over the letter. The ash stuck to the residue. Letters and words began to form. She blew away the excess soot and could now see the message.

"Your Highness,
Do you know how your husband truly died?"

The first line struck her and she didn't know whether to be shocked or infuriated. The image of her husband on his deathbed, writhing in pain with his skin burning to the touch, listening to him long for death, it all flashed before her mind again.

She wanted to destroy the letter, tear it to shreds and burn the pieces in the fireplace, but something stopped her. The small twinge of curiosity in her wind was piqued. Beatrice wanted to know if anything this mysterious writer said was true. She continued reading.

> *"If you really want to know the truth, come to the tavern of The Starving Bear after sundown. There is a secret passageway out of the castle hidden behind the fireplace of your bed-chambers that will lead you into the marketplace. The tavern is not far from there.*
>
> *Once you get there, order the mackerel with a pint of mead. After it arrives, I will come to your table and ask how it tastes, and you should answer "The salt is heavy." Then I will know it is you and we can discuss what's really happened with your husband and daughter. I look forward to speaking with you in person.*
> *-The Exiled King"*

The message ended there. Beatrice folded the paper twice before ripping it in two. She tore it five more times in multiple ways before tossing the small fragments into the cold ash of the fireplace. She stood, staring into those long burnt out coals for a long time, contemplating.

Who was this Exiled King? Two separate messages, both sent to her, although they did not mention her by name, and no name given for himself. In fact, the only person mentioned by name in either letter was that of Kendrick. She didn't even know if the one sending them was a man, they might be using the title of King to throw off suspicion.

But she wanted to know. The same way the first letter had compelled her to come to Kahren, so to did this one compel her to find answers. And from what she'd read, Beatrice could find answers at The Starving Bear.

"Aridain," she said at last.

"Yes, my queen?" He stood at attention.

"I want you to check the back of this hearth for any loose stones or latches, anything that might contain a secret passage." Beatrice commanded. "And once it is found, I will need you to accompany me."

"Your grace?" Aridain asked in confusion.

"Tonight," Beatrice said, "we're going to meet this exiled king."

XXVIII.
ARIDAIN

The queen had moved behind the curtains of the bed chambers to change her clothes while Aridain remained in the siting room. She'd ordered him to check the back wall of the fireplace for any loose bricks, latches, or other signs of a hidden passageway. This was how he found himself standing in soot, running his gloved fingers across the stone.

Something on that letter had enticed her, and now drove her to these actions, although she never shared its contents with him so Aridain didn't know what that could be.

His fingers brushed against a brick and it wobbled in place. He heard the distinctive sound of it clinking against the others as it did. He pressed on it, and the brick slid deeper into the wall. There was a click and the back wall of the hearth rumbled as it descended into the ground, revealing a long, dark, passage leading away from the room.

"My queen," he said in surprise, his voice echoed down the dark corridor. "I found it."

"Very good." Beatrice said from the other room. "We need to travel in disguise, so you should remove your armor. A Dadrian royal guard would stand out too much. We need to pass as commoners."

"I understand, your grace." He stepped out of the fire pit, kicking as much soot from his boots as he could, and began the process of unlatching his armor. He was grateful he wore light armor today rather than his fine armor. This way he didn't need a squire or other servant to help him remove it.

Aridain undid the straps under his wrists to remove the gauntlets first, followed by the plating on his arms and shoulders before untying the restraints for the breast plate. Then off came the armored boots and shin guards.

The air in the room suddenly felt cold. How the queen had managed to stand it was beyond him. Once the plate was off, he removed the chain mail as well and the protective padding. Soon, the knight had stripped down to only his trousers. As he reached for a plain brown tunic, Beatrice stepped out from the bed chamber. "Aridain, are you ready?" She saw him and became unusually still, her eyes wide.

"My queen?" Aridain asked. "Is something the matter?" She did not respond. The room fell silent. Sir Aridain then realized the his state of undress. Hastily, turned his back to the queen and pulled the tunic over his head. His face felt warm.

"I'm sorry. I didn't mean to walk in on you." Beatrice said in a hurried tone, her face turning red.

"No apology is required, my lady." Aridain said. He strapped a short dagger to his waist. Even in disguise, he still preferred to have some form of protection. "I am ready."

The queen fully emerged from the other room. Her usual fine silks and extravagant clothes were gone, replaced with a dress made for a servant girl. It was drab gray and plain, even smudged with stains. A headdress the color of dirt covered her hair. "Then let us depart."

They stepped into the passageway, shadows engulfing them. Along the walls were rows of unlit torches, their flames long since extinguished. Aridain took a piece of flint, one that had been left in the bed chambers to light fires, and struck it against the point of his dagger to ignite a spark. A small flame burst onto the tip of a torch which soon engulfed the oils covering the end.

He slipped the dagger back in its sheath and took the torch, leading the way down the hall with the flames casting their dancing light across the stone walls. They walked in silence, the only sounds coming from their footsteps, the fire on the torch, and the occasional drip of water somewhere further down these catacombs. The ceiling was low, barely above their heads. Other passageways branched off from the main hallway, likely leading to other rooms in the castle.

Aridain glanced over his shoulder every few minutes to check on the queen, always finding her just a few steps behind him. The awkward moment in the sitting room still lingered in his mind. He hadn't expected it, or even known it was there before, but something passed between them just then. A thought, maybe even a feeling or an attraction.

He tried to brush it away. She was the queen, far above his station, and he was a knight. He was her bodyguard, and she was his charge. And now, with so much having already taken place and still going on, they needed to focus on the task at hand.

Finally, after what seemed like an eternity of walking in darkness, a point of light appeared in the distance. They approached and came to a door. Upon opening, they found themselves in an abandoned, broken down old shop. Dust and dirt clung to everything inside. Aridain extinguished the torch and set it by the door. They would need that to get back, but it would seem strange to walk around with it in the city streets.

They stepped out into the streets. the common people moved at a hurried pace back and forth along the road; some pushing carts, others with packs on their backs, but most carrying nothing. The roads were paved in stone, but uneven and with rocks jutting up from the ground to meet their feet. Walking was difficult and trying to push or pull one of the carts appeared to be near impossible. This was a dangerous part of the capital city, and not someplace a queen such as Beatrice should frequent.

"That's the place." Beatrice motioned past Aridain's head, pointing to a small tavern with a creaky old sign which read The Staring Bear.

They moved across the street, having to maneuver between the waves of people and dodging carts, before finally entering the tavern. The air was thick with the pungent smell of stale beer, ale, sweat, and dirt. Aridain brought his arm over his face and Beatrice had to bring her hand over her mouth and nose. As rancid as the tavern was for Aridain, he could only guess as to how the queen would handle this strange environment.

There was one empty table with two chairs. It was small, square shaped, made of wood which appeared to be splintering, and the nails holding it together had started to rust. Beatrice walked over to this table and Aridain pulled her chair out for her to sit. He then took the seat opposite her.

The room was loud with the roar of patrons, their drunken chatter and laughter, shouting and screaming. All the while, Beatrice sat quietly in her chair with her back held straight and hands laced together in her lap. This was no place for her.

A tavern girl came by the table. "Evening, y'all." She said, her tone attempting to be happy, but only coming off as strained and forced. He could tell just from the woman's voice that she didn't want to be here any more than they did. "What'll ya be havin' tonight?"

Beatrice answered before Aridain could interject. "The mackerel." She said. "With a pint of mead."

"Comin' right up." The server girl took the order and went to the kitchen.

The queen trembled in her seat, as though a cold drop of water had fallen down her back. Her hands clenched tighter around the front of her dress. "Remind me to burn these clothes when we get back," she said.

213

The plate of food was soon brought before her, although Aridain questioned greatly as to whether or not it was safe to eat. Two grilled mackerel with their blank eyes staring up at her and a crust of stale bread adorned the plate. As for the pint of mead, specks of dust and dirt floated in the bubbles. Beatrice quickly thanked the service girl, then once she was gone the queen had to hold her mouth closed with her hands to keep from vomiting.

"My lady," Aridain said, his voice barely audible even to his own ears over the deafening noise of the tavern crowd. "What are we doing here?"

The queen took several deep breaths, keeping her hands placed over her mouth so as not to taste the foul air any more than she had to. After composing herself, she turned to answer. "We are hoping to meet our mysterious messenger. This 'exiled king', as he calls himself."

"And what makes you think he would be here?"

"In that letter." She said at last. "There were instructions to meet with him. To come to this tavern and order this . . ." she paused, as if choking on the thought, "meal." She strained on the last word.

"How do we even know he will show?" Aridain said. "That letter could have been sent by anyone. It could be a trap to draw you out and have you killed."

"Could've been. But it wasn't." Aridain jumped to his feet at the sound of this new voice, his hand instantly reached for the dagger at his waist. A man approached their table, he wore a long green cloak that reached to his ankles and bore a hood which covered his face except for his mouth and dark blond beard. He had a pair of leather vambraces on each forearm which depicted a set of elk antlers, and brandished a battle axe in his hands. He set the top of the axe on the ground and supported his thick, muscular arms on the handle.

"Who are you?" Aridain asked, his hand never leaving the

dagger's grip.

"Before I answer that, might I ask a question of my own?" Without waiting for a response, the man turned to the queen and asked, "How does the fish taste this evening?"

Beatrice straightened her back as she turned to address him. "The salt is heavy."

The man smiled, revealing a mouth full of stained yellow teeth to match his beard. "Good." He let out a small chuckle. "Very good. That's exactly what I wanted to hear." He took the chair from Aridain, leaving the knight standing. "I'm glad you could meet me on such short notice. Getting that message to you inside the castle was no easy feat." He leaned the axe handle against the table and eyes the plate of fish. "I don't suppose you're going to eat that?"

"Absolutely not," Beatrice said scathingly and pushed the plate away.

"Then I'll help myself." The man grasped one of the fish with his dirty hands and brought it to his mouth, biting half of it of at once. Small bones crunched under his teeth as he chewed. "You were right," he said between chewing and swallowing, "the salt is rather heavy tonight."

Aridain had just about enough. He pulled his dagger from the sheath and held it over the table. "Before we go any further, you should explain yourself." He growled at the cloaked man. "Who are you, and what do you want from her majesty?"

The cloaked man froze in place for a brief moment at the sight of the dagger, then set the other half of the fish back on the plate and dabbed the sides of his mouth with his cloak. "First, sir knight, I suggest you not go about pulling knives on people like that. It could start a fight you can't win.

"Second," he continued, "I wouldn't give away the identity of your charge so obviously. There are plenty of folks who would love to take a foreign royal hostage, either for ransom or just for the joy of it." He turned away from Aridain to face the queen again. "And as for you, your highness, I commend your effort, and you were right to disguise yourself, but no one here would assume you were a commoner. You don't move or hold yourself like one."

Beatrice stared at him with her steely gaze. "My bodyguard asked you a question," she said as though she hadn't registered his previous statement. "Who are you?"

"I am the Exiled King," the man said, "the first son of King Osrick the second, the elder brother of Kendrick and true king of Kahren. I am Roddrick."

Beatrice's eyes snapped open. She turned to Aridain, who was just as shocked as she, and then back to the cloaked man across from her. "Prince Roddrick?"

"Former prince," Roddrick corrected. He took a swig from the jug of mead, set the mug back down with a thud on the table. "Future king."

Aridain would not believe his eyes, nor his ears. That this man, this grungy, filthy, uncultured, disgusting, vile man could be the first born son of his late majesty Osrick and the true heir of Kahren seemed impossible. He brandished the dagger again. "My lady," he said, "you can't seriously believe these lies. Roddrick is long dead. He died even before his father. This figure cannot be the prince."

The cloaked figure pushed himself away from the table and stood. He was tall and strongly built, his arms displaying thick, powerful muscles. He stared at Aridain, his eyes glimmered in the shadows cast by his hood. "Let me show you." He untied the straps on the underside of his left vambrace. Once it was loose enough, he pulled it off to reveal a red birthmark on his arm that took the shape of an elk's head and antlers.

Aridain and Beatrice both recognized this mark. Every member of the royal house of Stagghart shared this same birthmark on their left arm. It was definitive proof that this man was, at the very least, a direct descendant of Haddrick, the first

216

king of Kahren.

"As I said," the cloaked man said, "I am Roddrick, the exiled King and eldest son of Osrick. And I have come back to claim my throne."

XXIX.
RODDRICK

He had recognized them from the moment they walked into the tavern, both the queen and her bodyguard knight. While he had only seen Queen Beatrice once before, and that was from a distance, there was no mistaking the way she moved. All the ratty, dirty clothes and rags in the world could not hide the precision and confidence she emitted just from her presence. She moved and behaved like a queen.

Not like him. He had to learn long ago how to move and act like a commoner. Ever since the attempt on his life, he'd been forced to stay in the shadows, ever watchful that the Black Swords not find him and finish the job they'd started. Even showing off the birthmark on his arm was dangerous.

"I have to keep it hidden." Roddrick pulled the vambrace back over his arm and tied it closed again. "If any of the Black Swords saw this, I would not live to see tomorrow."

"I apologize." The queen's bodyguard quickly sheathed his blade. He moved to stand beside his queen, his hands now placed behind his back.

"Your grace," Beatrice said as she turned to Roddrick. Aridain took notice that this was probably the first time in almost twenty years that the queen had used that phrase while addressing someone else. "What are you doing out here? If you're still alive, why have you not taken the throne?"

218

Roddrick took his seat at the table and continued eating as noisily as before. "Because," he said between bites of fish and stale bread, "Kendrick's had me declared dead."

"Why would he do that?" Beatrice asked.

"It's in his best interest." He said as he drank from the mead. "After all, he was the one who tried to kill me. Even meeting with you is dangerous, his spies are everywhere. But that's not what we're here to talk about." He pushed the plate away, having eaten the last of the fish and bread. He belched and dabbed his mouth again with the corner of his cloak. Roddrick placed his hands together on the table and leaned forward. "Now then, my lady, you remember what I wrote in that letter."

"Of course I do." Beatrice said. Roddrick noticed the twitches in her face, the lowering of her brows and thinning of her lips as she pressed them together. "You wrote of my husband's death."

"Yes," Roddrick said. "I didn't know Cassius well. My father and mother used to tell me he was a good man, but I'm sure you've been told that many times since his passing."

"I have."

Roddrick nodded. "Now I have a theory pertaining to his death. But I need more information from you. Tell me, were you with your husband when he passed?"

"I was." Beatrice's voice grew darker, more sorrowful. He could feel her unease. She hadn't had time to properly mourn the king's death, not with the following announcement of Princess Endelynn's wedding and then her subsequent disappearance. To speak of it was still painful. "He became suddenly very sick. He was fine at first, but then a few days later he was dead."

Roddrick let out a long sigh. He did not speak for what felt like at least a full minute. "Now," he said at last, "I know this will not be easy for you, but can you describe what his state

219

was like before he died? What were his symptoms?"

The pain twisted on Beatrice's face. Her eyes clamped shut and lips quivered. She was trying to hold back the pain, trying to keep her composure, but it was falling apart. She braced her elbows on the table, held her face in her hands, and sobbed. Her cries and weeps muffled by her hands. In that moment, Roddrick caught the hate-filled glare of the queen's bodyguard.

"My lady, maybe we should go. This might not be the best time to-" He tried to place his hand on her shoulder, only to have her pull away.

"No." She wiped her tears away and straightened herself. "This is important." Beatrice turned to Roddrick. "It started on the second day of Prince Sedrick's visit. My husband started to develop a fever. Nothing bad at first, but it didn't go away. At night he would begin to sweat, and no matter how many wet towels we brought to him, it wouldn't cool him down. By the next morning he couldn't get out of bed.

"His fever grew so hot he was burning to the touch. We brought healers and Faith Lords to try finding the source of his ailment, but none of them could find anything. By that next sunset, he was gone." She looked down at her hands, now smeared with her tears. "I held him as he died. He was so hot to the touch, I could hardly stand it, but I couldn't let go."

Roddrick's lips twisted in a thoughtful expression. He tapped his thumbs together. "I have a thought, but first I need to know who came to Dadria with Sedrick. Was one of the Black Swords of the King with him?"

"Yes," The queen's knight answered. "He called himself Sir Darren. He was Sedrick's bodyguard."

"I figured." Roddrick said. "I believe guarding Sedrick was only his secondary purpose. Most likely, Kendrick sent him to Dadria to murder your husband."

"Murder?" Beatrice said in shock.

Roddrick nodded. "Assassination by poison. And I think I

know what kind." He leaned back in the chair, placing his hands down on the table. He knew these symptoms, and he also knew what caused them. "All the symptoms you described match the effects of Blood of the Fire Rose."

"What's that?" Beatrice asked.

"A deadly concoction. Odorless and tasteless if mixed in wine, which is how it's usually given."

"But my husband didn't drink wine." Beatrice stated. "He hated the taste. He always had ale instead."

"And both of those were tested by the tasters for poison." The queen's bodyguard interjected.

"It needn't be in wine to kill. It could've been in the food itself. One way or another, the poison found its way into your husband. The primary ingredient is the juice extracted from the Fire Rose flower, hence the name." Roddrick explained. "By gathering enough of the flowers and compressing them in a vice, the tiny amounts of fluid contained in the petals can be extracted. There are other ingredients, of course, but that's the main one that causes death."

"In the food?" Beatrice's bodyguard said, and a horrified look of realization came over his face.

"What is it?" The queen turned to her knight. "What do you know?"

"I am sorry, your grace. I have a confession to make." Aridain spoke. "The night of the great fest, after Endelynn shouted and threw her crown to the floor, and while you went to speak with her, I caught the Black Sword giving a vial of pink fluid along with a handful of silver coins to one of the servant girls."

The queen's eyes grew wide. Her fingers tightened into a fist and a sneer curled on her lips. "You caught this in action and did nothing to stop it?" She spoke with restrained anger.

"He claimed it to be for the prince's food allergy. And I tasted it to be sure, and it had no effect on me." Aridain defended himself. "I didn't want to trouble you or your husband with anymore problems."

"I think I understand." Roddrick interjected, drawing their attention back to him. "The potion you tested must've been the antidote." He met Beatrice's eyes. "You said your late husband didn't drink wine, is that correct?"

"Yes," she replied.

"With what your knight has said, I believe I know how the king was killed." Roddrick explained. "Trying to poison one person can be difficult, so I think the Blood of the Fire Rose was put in all the food at once. But to make sure no one else died, the antidote was placed in the wine. And the only one who had no wine to drink that night was Cassius." Roddrick folded his hands on the table again. "It's entirely possible the poison was already in the food, and if your knight had told you of what he saw, everyone would've died."

"But why would he do it?" The queen asked. "Why would Sedrick's bodyguard assassinate my husband?"

"Probably on orders from Kendrick himself." Roddrick explained. "How much do you know about the Black Swords?"

Beatrice shrugged. Her face was still streaked with the grooves of where her tears had flown. "Not much. Only that they were established during Kendrick's reign and are considered elite knights."

"Less like knights and more akin to secret enforcers." Roddrick said. "The Order of the Black Swords of the King was established while Kendrick was still a prince. He wanted his own organization of followers, people he could call on to carry out his dirty work. The 'hunting accident' that supposedly killed me was in actuality an arrow from a Black Sword's crossbow that killed my horse and nearly killed me. I only wasn't killed that day because a bear stumbled upon the scene and frightened off my assassins." Roddrick scoffed at the irony. Despite their name, the Black Swords hardly ever used bladed weapons, choosing instead to kill from a distance with crossbows or poison.

"My brother didn't just inherit the throne, he took it." Roddrick continued. "He had my mother assassinated in the delivery room by the very midwives who were helping birth Sedrick. The Black Swords had found these women's families and held them hostage to force their compliance. Then, when I was older, he tried to kill me as well. And lastly, our own father was given the same Blood of the Fire Rose and died just like your husband. He schemed and killed and blackmailed his way to the crown, and all with the Black Swords to do his bidding. That's also why I didn't take it back once I returned."

"And what does all this have to do with my husband's death?" The queen grew more angry and frustrated. "You brought me out here, and all you've done is bring up painful memories and spout about your obsession with taking back Kahren. But what about my husband?"

Roddrick was taken back by her words. "I'm sorry." He said. "I'll get to the point." He laced his fingers together again as he leaned across the table. "The truth is, Kahren is in serious debt. Once Kendrick took the throne, the crown began to hemorrhage money. He threw lavish parties and wasted the kingdom's funds on ridiculous things. You've been to his throne room, yes?"

Beatrice nodded.

"And you saw that tapestry on the wall, the one just behind his throne? Well, all the gold threads used in that tapestry are, in fact, real gold. He's constructed numerous statues of himself. All sorts of things to his glory. But to pay for it all, he's increased the taxes so high on the common people that most of them can't afford food every day."

He pointed out the broken window of the tavern. "And all the while, the kingdom is falling apart. Even the capital is in ruins. This used to be a prosperous and lively center of trade with a thriving market. Now, the roads are falling apart and the shops are in shambles. Because that tax money isn't going to repair the streets or buildings, but instead to his vanity projects.

"He's pushed Kahren so far to the edge, he feels the only way out is to take the wealth of the only other large kingdom around. But he can't just conquer Dadria, your location in the mountains makes that next to impossible. So he chose a more subtle approach."

The queen's eyes snapped open. He saw the realization in her eyes. "Endelynn." She said. "Once my husband was dead, he would wed my daughter to his brother."

"And through that union, he would take control of Dadria by proxy," Roddrick said. "A little at first, but then over time his influence would grow greater and greater until he ruled the kingdom in all but name. And if you, or Endelynn, or even Sedrick started causing problems he would simply have one of the Black Sword's remove them."

"But then why would he have Endelynn abducted?" Beatrice asked. "In your letter, your stated that Kendrick had orchestrated her kidnapping. If he needed my daughter to marry Sedrick, why have her abducted on the way to the wedding?"

"That part I do not know yet." Roddrick said. He leaned forward and laced his fingers together. "This is my proposal. I can help you find your daughter and return her, as well as bring justice to those that murdered your husband. And in return, you help me remove Kendrick from power and restore me to the throne."

The queen did not hesitate for even a second. "With all my power, I will see it done." She stood and stretched out her arm to him. Roddrick lifted himself from the chair and grasped her outstretched arm as she did his. The pact was forged.

"Many thanks, your majesty." He said. "And please, don't worry about the food. I can pay for that." He took three gold coins from his purse and set them on the table under the empty plate. "You should be heading back now, someone might have noticed your room is vacant. Don't worry about how to contact me, there are those loyal to me all over the city, even a few of them in the castle. After all, I managed to get the letter to you. If you ever need, send a letter through that boy."

"We will." Beatrice said. She and her bodyguard set out to moved towards the door, stopping only once as they exited tavern when she gave him a thankful smile, before they disappeared into the street and back into the secret passageway to the castle.

XXX.
ENDELYNN

"Hello," Uyoonta said. The old woman stood behind Endelynn, running an antler comb through her wet, tangled, red hair. Every morning they started like this, the princess would be bathed and scrubbed by the older women in the lodge and the morning blood of her cycle washed away. Then, as she dried off, the Dadrian woman would quiz Endelynn on the words of the Sequoian language.

"Aneewa." The princess replied.

"Good bye."

"Hootu."

"Thank you."

Endelynn paused, going through her sleep deprived brain searching for the right word. She chewed on her lower lip and wrinkled her nose as if she smelled something foul. What was that word. A flash went off in her head and she blurted out the word. "Gwomu!"

"Good." The elder woman said. "You are learning."

"Gwomu." Endelynn couldn't help but smile. Not just smile, she beamed with pride. She'd always been good with languages, her parents had told her so.

Every day as a young child, Endelynn would go to the library in the castle with her father. They'd sit together for hours at a time poring over old books and scrolls. She loved

226

listening to her father's voice as he read the old stories to her. Occasionally he would stop, point out a word for her, and ask her to tell him what it was. If she had trouble, he would help. By the time she was four, Endelynn could read most of the simpler books in the library. By age seven, she had stopped learning to read and began reading to learn.

Of course, that had been years ago. She was much older now, and not learning to read anymore. Plus, she'd only spent the last five days trying to speak the language of the natives, not five years. Her progress was decent, but nothing incredible.

The language itself was a major issue. It had almost no similarities with her mother tongue, aside from the few words that her ancestors appropriated from the natives. Endelynn had been shocked to learn that the name of the black and white whales that swam up and down the coast, Orca, had come from the indigenous population's word Orukwa which literally meant Black Fish. But aside from things like that, the language was tough to grasp. Nouns and verbs came in different places in the sentence, almost like she was speaking backwards. If she needed to say I ran through the forest, it would be phrased more like I forest ran through.

On top of that, some words had multiple meanings. The word Quoi meant both person and tree. If she added an A sound on the end, it became plural. So, Quoia could mean many trees or many people. Even further, the sound Se meant something that had come earlier or first. If she used it at the beginning of Quoia it applied only to the old; so an old person or an old tree. All together, the word Sequoia had even more meanings. It could be a grove of many old growth trees or a group of old people, but it also could refer to the forest itself or to the concept of a person's ancestors. Most often, however, the word referred to the entire race of people who lived in these woods. All the tribes and clans collectively were called the Sequoia people.

"Why is that?" Endelynn asked.

"Why is what?" The older Dadrian woman said.

"The word Sequoia. Why does it have so many different meanings?" Endelynn explained.

"That is a long story." Uyoonta said. Incidentally, Endelynn now knew that the name given to this woman by the native tribe translated as White-skinned.

"I think I have plenty of time." Endelynn said. "Besides, I like stories."

"Very well." The elder woman continued to comb out the tangles. "Long ago, in the time before time, the land was dark and still. There was no sun, nor moon neither stars in the sky. The Great Spirit, our Father in the Sky, saw the darkness and resolved to change it. He took a piece of flint and struck it against an iron stone. The sparks flew into the air and became stars.

"He was still not yet pleased, for the world was still very dark. So he took a chunk of the iron stone and carved it into a circle, then threw it into the sky. It stuck in place and became the moon. And for a while he was happy because it brought light. But the circle would spin in the sky. It would be bright only part of the time, and then go dark.

"The Sky Father then tried again. He struck the flint against the iron stone again and made a fire. It roared and blazed, growing larger than the world could endure. He wrestled with the fire and threw it into the sky, where it stayed and became the sun." Uyoonta explained.

Endelynn turned back to face the older Dadrian woman. "That has nothing to do with what I asked."

"I'm not finished." Uyoonta said with a bit of annoyance in her voice. "You should mind your elders and let me continue."

"Sorry."

"Now that the world was covered in light, Sky Father could finally see it. But now, he was even more saddened. The land was dry and barren, without even a single tree or drop of water. Filled with grief, the Great Spirit began to cry.

"He cried for a long time. So long, his tears became ponds and lakes. They flowed across the land as rivers and streams, crossing this way and that. Eventually, his salty tears filled even the great salt waters of the sea.

"His tears also seeded the earth the same way a man might seed his wife. For the earth itself is alive, and she is also a Great Spirit, our Mother Earth. Plants began to grow across the land, spreading down from the mountains all the way to the shore where land meets water. Our Sky Father was pleased with the trees, but Mother Earth felt alone. So she opened a great chasm and out from that spilled all the animals of the world. All except for humans."

"Why not humans?" Endelynn asked. Her original question had been forgotten, she just wanted to learn more.

"Because I have named only two of the Great Spirits. There is a third, the Wicked Spirit, Chaa Ruk. He lives beneath the earth, deep underground, and is the cause of pain and suffering. He grew jealous of the joys of Father Sky and Mother Earth. Wanting to destroy it, He tore off the top of a mountain and unleashed a wall of fire and ash. The forests burned, animals tried to run but could not escape. It seemed like all was lost.

"But Father Sky and Mother Earth fought back. They used another mountain as their weapon, hurling balls of fire and bolts of lightning back at Chaa Ruk. The battle lasted for days with no rest. At long last, the Wicked Spirit was forced back underground and his mountain collapsed on top of him. Father Sky then filled the land with rain water, creating a lake now called Wikeke Sakwa, the blue water. The mountain Sky Father and Earth Mother used for the battle is the place they meet, now called Uyoontooku, the white mountain.

"During the battle of Great Spirits, one of Sky Father's lightning bolts struck a tree which exploded in a splintery burst of wood, with only a smoldering stump left behind. But from this stump emerged the first men. The slivers and splinters were taken by Mother Earth and likewise became humans. The people of this land were made from the trees, and so the language reflects it."

Endelynn listened, enamored with the story. "Wow." She said at last. "Is any of this written down? I'd love to read it."

"Sadly, it is not." Uyoonta said. "The Sequoia people do not have a writing system. Every story is simply told and retold across the generations. Sometimes a legend is depicted on a mural painting or carved into a totem pole, but that is all."

"What about the places in the story?" Endelynn asked. "The White Mountain and the Blue water, do these places exist for real?"

"Of course." The elder woman set the antler comb aside and separated Endelynn's hair into three segments. "Far to the north of here, following the Blue Snake River all the way back to its origins, you will find Uyoontooku, the place where the earth meets the sky." She pulled the hair taught, eliciting a brief whine from Endelynn. "And even further north, far beyond the borders of the Sequoia nation, is the Wikeke Sakwa. The lake that traps Chaa Ruk. You will never see water so blue in all your life, not even the sea compares." She began braiding the hair together.

"Have you seen these places?" Endelynn asked.

"Only when I was younger. And then, only in my Moon Dreams." The elder woman replied.

"Moon Dreams?"

"Yes." She said. "Your moon cycle is a special time when girls and women are more receptive to the spirits of the land. We can see and hear things in our dreams that no one else can. Sometimes visions of far away lands, other times it can be a memory of things that once were or of things yet to come."

Endelynn's shoulders tensed and her hands clenched into

fists. Her dreams had been frightful of late. The image of that creature, that horrifying skeletal deer corpse, still lingered in her mind long after she woke each morning. That thing with no name, but a desire to kill and consume her.

The princess's stiffness did not go unnoticed. As Uyoonta tied a string around the end of Endelynn's braid, she said, "You've been having strange dreams, haven't you?" Endelynn nodded, and Uyoonta continued. "What have your dreams been like?"

Endelynn did not turn to face her. "They've felt wrong, somehow. Like I'm seeing something I'm not supposed to."

"What is it?" Uyoonta asked. "What do you see?"

"I don't know." Endelynn explained. "In my dream I'm being chased through the woods by something. A monster of some kind. It's cold and getting dark the more I run, and I can hear it behind me. The sound it makes," Endelynn shuddered at the memory of it, "like some kind of dying scream, and the scent it gives smells like a rotting corpse." Her stomach felt weak and gross. She lurched as though she might puke, but managed to keep herself under control.

Uyoonta moved around Endelynn to face her, placed her hands on the younger girl's shoulders, and met her gaze. "Do you see this thing?" Endelynn looked up and noticed the fear in her eyes.

"I do." Endelynn said. "At the end of the dream it finally come out of the trees and catches me. That's when I see it. A rotten, walking carcass of a long dead deer. It grabs me and is about to swallow me whole, and then I wake up."

"And when did these dreams start?" The elder woman asked.

"The night I started bleeding." Endelynn replied. "Do you know what this is? Or what it means?"

Uyoonta remained silent, but Endelynn could see the fear linger on her face. The older woman moved a short distance away, her back to the princess. Endelynn felt a new terror rising inside her, which only grew as the silence lengthened. "The creature you describe," Uyoonta said at last, "has been dead for many years."

"It has?" Endelynn asked.

"Yes." The Dadrian woman continued. "It is a wicked spirit and a servant of Chaa Ruk. And it has many names. Some call it the Consumer of Men. Others say the Devourer of Worlds, or the Starving One. All its names speak of the monster's hunger. But its name in the tongue of the Sequoia is Wendigo."

"Wendigo?" Endelynn repeated the word and it left a foul taste in her mouth, like the word itself was cursed. "Have you ever seen one?"

"Once," Uyoonta admitted, "a long time ago when I was a younger woman. The last one appeared almost as if from nowhere. Many people were killed, maybe even a hundred. I saw when it was captured and slain. A piece of Rainbow Obsidian pierced through its heart and the writhing body thrown onto a burning pyre."

"You said they were all dead."

"They are." Uyoonta said.

"Then why would I dream of one in my Moon Dreams?"

The older woman returned to Endelynn's side and placed a comforting hand on the girl's shoulder. "As I told you, the dreams can see things both in the past as well as the future. They are not always a perfect vision of things. I am no shaman or medicine man, but I would believe that this dream showed you someone's past encounter with the monster."

Endelynn sighed and a weight lifted from her chest. Dead, They were all dead. "But what about the dreams?" She asked again. "How long to they persist?"

"Your Moon Dreams will end when your cycle does, which may be as soon as tonight. Once that is over, you will have nothing to worry about."

232

Endelynn didn't push the subject further, and Uyoonta did not elaborate on the creature, or the nature of Moon Dreams anymore. By sundown, the last traces of bleeding had stop and her cycle had ended.

She was given a new dress. It was fashioned from two sheets of tanned animal hide that had been sewn together and came down to a point in both the front and the back. The sleeves were short, only reaching halfway to her elbow. A belt wrapped around her waist. Along with the dress, she had a new set of leggings and a pair of toughened moccasins for her feet. Once she was fully dressed, the princess was allowed to leave the House of the Moon.

As she walked thought he village, she once again felt the eyes of the people crawling across her skin. There was little malicious intent, however, more of an innate curiosity, and once she past them they returned to their previous task. She found Shunka crouched beside the large central fire pit, two pieces of stone in his hands. He was striking one against the other, sharpening the edges of the shiny black stone.

She approached him from behind, her hands clasped together behind her back. "Aneewa." She said as she stepped to his side.

He glanced up at her, a look of mild surprise in his eyes. "Hello," he replied in the Dadrian language, then turned back to his work. "I thought you were close to finished."

"Yes," she replied in the Sequoia tongue, "my bleeding is finished." She crouched at his side, resting on the balls of her feet with her hands on her knees. "And I learn little words in your talk."

Shunka smirked and let out a small chuckle. "Yes, little words." He replied in the language of his people, and continued to strike the two stones together.

XXXI.
RODDRICK

Sparks flew from the red-hot iron horseshoe as he brought the hammer down upon it. A metallic clang rung though the air with each strike. Taking the metal pincers, he grasped the horseshoe and dunked it in a basin of water. Steam bubbled and hissed from the rapidly cooling iron.

His skills as a blacksmith had grown greatly in the last few years. He no longer caused the steel to shatter upon its first contact with water. It was something he took pride in, this work he did. Everyday he made things, crafted and created with his own two hands. It didn't make him a rich man, but it made him happy.

With that last shoe, he was finished for the day. He put his hammers away and wiped the sweat from his brow with the back of his soot covered forearm. Taking his heavy leather apron off, he splashed his face with water to wash away the worst of the soot and ash.

He said goodbye to the owner of the blacksmith shop, the man kind enough to take on an apprentice of Roddrick's age and give him work, and set out on his way home. The hairs of his beard were singed from the years he'd spent working here, hammering iron. It all worked in his favor, disguising his true identity. The one thing he couldn't change, the birthmark on his left arm, was kept hidden under a vambrace.

Living these past eight years in secret, hidden from the ever watchful eyes of his brother's Black Swords, had not always been so easy, not when everyone still recognized him as Prince Roddrick, eldest son of King Osrick and heir to the throne of Kahren.

If he had been more vigilant this never would have happened. He wouldn't be hiding in the lower slums, hammering out horseshoes to survive. If he had been watchful, and recognized the actions of his brother, than it would be him sitting on the throne instead of Kendrick. It still wrecked his mind at times, the day he was banished in all but name.

He'd been on a hunt, him and three members of the Black Swords of the King. They served as the new royal guards ever since his brother, Kendrick, and the newly appointed knight, Sir Darren, uncovered the conspirators who murdered the queen. Once that happened, Prince Kendrick had convinced their father to phase out the Stag Knights and replace them with the Black Swords. It was counter to Roddrick's advice, but the king would not hear him. King Osrick was too distraught over the loss of his wife, and Roddrick could sympathize, she was his mother after all, but despite their name, the Black Swords of the King had little actual loyalty to Osrick.

But they served their purpose. It had been five years since Queen Diane's death and there were no harmful incidents involving the Black Swords. So, on that fateful day, Roddrick had gone hunting on the verges of the Forest of Wayward Souls with three Black Swords.

It was supposed to be a simple day out and back. Roddrick and his hunting party had set out on horseback that morning. He'd found the tracks of a deer and followed it deeper into the woods until they saw it in the distance. It was a buck, five-point antlers. The animal chewed on the low-lying ferns at the base of a tree. Its ears flicked back and forth, listening for any sound of approaching danger. At that moment, it had not heard them.

Roddrick held up a closed fist to signal his party to stop. Once they had, the young prince dismounted his horse, took his bow and quiver of arrows, and attempted to approach the deer on foot.

He'd not taken three steps before a bolt struck his horse. The animal roared in pain. Roddrick spun around to find his horse on the ground, convulsing and spasming as two of the Black Swords shot it full of arrows.

"What is the meaning of this?!" Roddrick shouted.

"Nothing much, your highness," one of the Black Swords, Sir Darren, directed his horse forward. He carried no crossbow, but a sword still hung in its scabbard at his waist. "This is just a hunting accident."

The other Black Swords formed a half circle around Roddrick, their crossbows all loaded and aimed at him. "An assassination, is more like it." Roddrick said. He clutched his bow, his gloved hand twisted around the grip.

"Call it what you will, your highness." Sir Darren said. "It's the command of the king."

"The king?" Roddrick stammered in shock. "My father would never– "

"Osrick's reign is as good as over." Darren cut him off. "The king is dead. Long live the king."

"Yes," Roddrick said, "long live the king." He swung his bow around and loosed the arrow. It struck one of the Black Sword through the eye. A short scream escaped the man's lips and blood spurted from the eye socket as he fell from his saddle.

As Roddrick reached for another arrow, a bolt struck his shoulder. He winced, dropping his bow and quiver. Roddrick grasped at his shoulder, blood seeped out around the bolt and stained his tunic red.

"How did you miss? He's right in front of you!" Darren scolded the other Black Sword.

"He moved, sir."

This was his only chance. While they were distracted, the young prince ran to the dismounted horse and pulled himself into the saddle. He dug his heels into the beasts sides and grasped the reins with his good hand. "Yaah!" He shouted, and the horse jumped forward.

"After him!" Sir Darren's voice rang behind him. Roddrick heard the gallop of hooves as they pursued, and the ring of metal as Sir Darren drew his sword.

He jostled back and forth as the horse ran. Each movement of the horse sent another jolt of pain through his shoulder. He gritted his teeth to endure the pain and leaned into the gallop.

A sudden roar and a flash of brown fur brought a new level of terror to Roddrick's mind. An enormous brown bear, nearly six feet tall at the shoulder, came charging out of the woods. Its claws tore chunks of earth from the ground and it bellowed an earsplitting roar. Roddrick's horse came to a frantic halt, stomping the ground and flipping its head from side to side. The bear stood on its hind legs and roared. It towered over Roddrick and the horse at a height of ten feet.

Roddrick pulled on the reins, trying to get the horse under control, but the beast was too frightened. It kicked and bucked, and Roddrick lost his grip. He was thrown from the saddle and slammed against the ground. The bolt shaft in his shoulder snapped as he rolled end over end and finally came to a jolting stop against a tree.

His head struck the trunk. Roddrick groaned, a loud ringing filled his ears and the world swam in blurred images around him. He could barely see as the bear swung one huge paw and slashed his horse's throat open in a fountain of blood. The two Black Swords came into view, and immediately pulled their horses away. He couldn't keep his eyes open anymore. Roddrick slumped against the tree and passed out.

When next he woke, Roddrick found himself lying on a

mattress of straw. His head throbbed, his shoulder ached, his entire body felt like a sore muscle. One eye was covered with linen bandages along with a good portion of his head.

The room was plain, simple wooden walls and a dirt floor. The beams of the roof were visible along with the straw. This was a poor peasant's house. He tried to move, but raising his arm took all his energy. With a gasp, he let the exhausted limb fall back to the bed.

The front door to the house opened with a pillar of sunlight too bright to look at, causing Roddrick to wince and turn away. A pair of women entered, one older and one younger, both with black hair and wearing plain-looking wool tunics and skirts. Each carried a pail of water. "Declared himself king already?" The younger woman proclaimed. "But, what about the missing brother?"

"They say people took advantage of his generosity and tried to steal from him." The older, possibly the mother, responded. "He's declared Roddrick dead."

Roddrick tried to shout at the mention of his name, but it only came as a muffled grown. He wasn't loud, but the noise was enough to catch the attention of the two women.

"Oh, dear, you're awake." The older woman said. They set the pails of water beside the hearth and both came to his side. "How are you feeling? We tried to patch you up as best we could."

"How long?" Roddrick forced himself to speak. His throat felt raw, like it was full of sand.

"You've been here for about five days." The elder said. She turned to her daughter. "Get some water for our guest."

The young maiden brought him a cup and he drank deeply from it. The water felt like sweet wine to his parched throat. Some of it dribbled down his chin, but he did not care. After his second cup, he felt well enough to speak again. "Where am I? How did I get here?"

238

"This is the farmstead of Amerstien." The old woman said. "I am the widow Amerstien, and this is my daughter, Charon."

"Amerstien," Roddrick repeated, "I'm afraid I don't know where that is. Which province is it in?"

"None." The daughter, Charon, said. "Our farmstead is located outside the walls of Kahren, on the borders of the Wayward Forest."

"Outside the walls?" Roddrick shouted, and a sudden spike of pain drove into his chest. He was still not well enough to raise his voice.

"A strange man brought you to us from out of the forest." The young maiden spoke. "He very tall, almost seven feet. He was also old but still strong. He was dark skinned and wore animal leather clothes. He just came out of the forest with you draped in his arms and asked us to keep you well."

A strange man? Dressed in animal leathers? None of that sounded right. The last he remembered was the massive bear killing his horse and driving the Black Swords away. "I'm sorry." He said. "I've forgotten my manners. You've introduced yourselves, but I have not. My name is Roddrick of the House Stagghart."

"Roddrick?" Lady Amerstien's eyes grew wide and she stepped away. "The missing Prince Roddrick? The dead prince?"

"I am not dead," Roddrick said, "although I might wish to be." He winced as he adjusted himself on the bed. "Who declared me dead?"

"The new king. Your brother, Kendrick." Charon stated.

"What happened to my father?"

"It's horrible." Lady Amerstien shook her head in sorrow. "Your father, King Osrick, past away in his sleep just recently."

"When you went missing, your brother offered a massive reward for your safe return, but all that did was bring out con artists. One man even dressed up like you to get the reward, but

Kendrick brought the sword upon him. He retracted the offer of gold and had you declared dead. Anyone coming forward and claiming to be the missing prince is to be treated as an impostor and executed."

"I am no impostor." Roddrick stated. He lifted his hand and showed them the birthmark on his forearm. "This is the mark of the royal line. The red elk of House Stagghart."

Charon placed her hands on the birthmark, examining it closely. "Is that what this means?" She asked. "I noticed it before, but didn't know it had any true meaning." She turned to Lady Amerstien. "You know what this means, mother? We've found the missing prince. We can return him to the castle and claim the reward for our own! We won't have to live out here anymore!" Her voice was full of hope and optimism.

"I'm afraid you can't." Roddrick said. He'd already put the pieced together in his mind. "I didn't go missing. My brother tried to have me killed. And when they didn't bring my body back, he had me declared dead and executed some poor sap in my place."

"I'm afraid he's right." The widow said. "There is no reward to be had. If we brought him to the capital, he would be killed and we would be imprisoned. And that is the best we can hope for."

"But," Charon started, but her sentence trailed off.

"Curse him." Roddrick's good hand clenched in a fist. It shook with gathered rage. "May all the gods damn him to hell!" He shouted, and slammed his fist against the frame of the bed. "He planned all this! He murdered our father and stole the crown from me!" Roddrick could taste the blood in his throat. The world around him started to fade again, images turned blurry and voices grew distant. He collapsed on the bed again, lost to sleep.

Over the next several days, and as they stretched into weeks, Roddrick recovered and offered his services in tending the farm of this kindly woman and her daughter. He let his hair and beard grow long to better disguise his true identity, and later found work with a blacksmith in the capital city. Under Kendrick's rule, the kingdom began a steady decline. By the end of the first year, the treasury was empty and taxes spiked.

Roddrick made connections with the oppressed and impoverished people of Kahren and started an underground peasant rebellion. By the time of the missing Dadrian princess, he had a network of spies all across the kingdom and even in Kendrick's castle.

A loud whistle caught his attention and brought him back to the present. He looked up and saw Charon, her black wavy hair bouncing as she ran towards him. He smiled and opened his arms to catch her. They embraced and he planted a soft kiss on her forehead.

"I was hoping I'd catch you before too late," she said.

"I was just finishing up. Did you learn anything?"

"I have." They walked side by side through the streets, his hand in hers. "Those who were hired to abduct the princess."

241

XXXII.
SHUNKA

The shrill of a hawk's scream caught Shunka's attention. He was a fair distance from the village, kneeling beside the creek with a stone in each hand. He was using one to sharpen the other into an arrowhead. Looking up, he saw the dark feathers of the large hawk against the clear blue sky. It circled over the village, slowly descending. The day had come at last. He'd been dreading its arrival, knowing what it meant, but there was no delaying now.

"Oh, wow." Endelynn said as she approached. She carried a bundle of small branches and kindling in her arms. Still being unskilled in many of the tasks needed to sustain the village, she'd been sent to gather firewood. "You see?" She motioned with her head up at the enormous hawk in the sky. "A bird."

"Yes, I see." Shunka slipped the unfinished arrowhead into the pouch at his waist as he stood. "But is not a bird, not really. No more than I am a real wolf."

The pale princess tilted her head at his quizzically, then her brows raised as she understood. "A Skin-changer." She said. "Person changed into bird from other tribe."

Shunka nodded. "Come, we should return." They set off towards the village, Shunka in the lead with Endelynn following close behind. They walked in silence, Shunka only giving the briefest of glances over his shoulder to make sure she was still there. A pit formed in his stomach. How was he going to explain to her what was about to happen? Until now, he'd never brought up the agreement made between his father and Orumaku Chaa. Before they reached the village borders, the princess called to him.

"Are you well?" She asked.

"Hm?" Shunka turned back, his thoughts distracted him and he missed her words.

"You seem sad." Endelynn said. "You are not well. What is wrong?" Her words were stilted and broken, her grasp of the tribal language weak. But she knew enough to see there was something off about him.

A breathed a heavy sigh. "The hawk brings with it an unsettling truth I've been avoiding." He said. "Today is my last day as a true member of the Wolf Clan."

Endelynn's brows raised and lips parted in a look of surprise and confusion. "I do not understand." She said. "Not of your clan?"

"I will join in union with Shikoba, daughter of Orumaku Chaa of the Hawk Clan, and leave to join their tribe." Shunka explained. "The bird we see in the sky is most likely my escort back to their village."

"Union?" Endelynn repeated the word, fumbling over it like one might trip over a large rock or root on a path. Her eyes snapped wide open. The sticks and branches tumbled from her arms and clattered to the ground at her feet. "Marriage?" She said in her own tongue.

"Yes." Shunka replied. "A marriage. I am to leave, and live with my bride and new family among the Hawks."

The girl moved to gather the fallen branches. She lifted them almost with not real conscious thought. "Leaving? To join the Hawk Clan." She repeated, further ingraining the idea in her mind. "Why are you going to them? Why is she not coming to live with you?"

243

"That's not how it works." Shunka said as he helped her pick up the firewood. "When a man and woman enter a union together, the husband always joins the wife's family. To secure the lineage."

"Huh," Endelynn uttered to herself. "It's the opposite in Dadria. Back home, the woman would take her husband's name and sigil as her new house." Just as she gathered the last of the fallen wood, she looked to him and said, "so, we will be leaving for the Hawk village? I just gotten used to this one."

"No." Shunka said. "You're not coming with me."

She paused again, one knee still planted in the dirt, looking up at him. "No?"

"No. The Hawk Clan is much less tolerant about outsiders than my tribe. If I tried to take you, a young woman from the Walled Cities, to their village as I'm about to wed the Chaa's daughter, they would kill you for certain. No, you will have to remain here."

"But," she stuttered, unable to find the words she wanted. She shook, clutching the branches to her chest. "You can't do this to me!" She shouted, no longer trying to speak in the tribal language, but screaming in the words of her people. "You're the reason I'm here! You brought me to your village and took charge of me, and now you want to toss me aside to go live with your new bird bride?" She threw the firewood to the ground in a huff. "You can't just abandon me like this!"

"I did not choose this." Shunka responded, his own voice growing sharper. "This union was decided before I found you. And I'm not too happy with the arrangement myself. I didn't ask to be joined with the Hawk Clan."

"But you agreed to go along with it nonetheless." Endelynn said.

"Because that is the way of things! Orumaku Chaa offered his daughter's hand to one of my father's sons and they agreed on me. To defy their will would've been a grievous insult."

"More than you've insulted me?" She shouted again.

Shunka straightened up, looming over her with his brows scrunched together and lips twisted in a frown. "There is no insulting you." He said. "Nothing could bring you down. You are a foreign girl, a pale-faced demon whose ancestors invaded the land of my people and slaughtered them." He turned his back to her. "There is nothing I can say or do that would be insulting to filth such as that. And it was a mistake to bring you to my village." He walked away, leaving her alone in the forest beside the jumbled pile of broken sticks and twigs.

He marched back to the village alone. When he returned, Shunka found most of the villagers had gathered around the entrance of the Great Longhouse. They murmured and whispered amongst themselves.

Tala emerged from the crowd. "There you are." She said as she came over to him. "We've been wondering where you were. The envoy from the Hawk Clan is inside, speaking with your father. They're expecting you."

"I am sure." Shunka said. He stepped past her and made his way through the crowd. Just before he entered the Longhouse, Tala's voice reached him again.

"Where is Chaneewah Ishde?" She asked, using the Sequoia name her father had given the pale girl. Shunka did not answer. He lifted the door flap and stepped inside.

He found his father seated at the far end of the lodge. A flame blazed in the fire pit, casting dancing shadows across the wall and a column of smoke up into the air and out through the smoke hole in the ceiling. The elder Chaa sat with his legs crossed and arms folded over his chest.

Across from his father, there was a young maiden Shunka did not recognize. A pair of black-tipped white feathers were woven in her hair, black and shiny as obsidian, which flowed in a braid down her exposed back. She wore a dress fashioned from tanned buckskin that looped around the back of her neck, and was adorned in turquoise of red and blue. Her tribal birthmarks, patches of raised, red flesh in the shape of folded eagle wings, began on her shoulder blades and fell down until they disappeared beneath her dress.

Both the maiden and Ahote Chaa turned to him as Shunka entered the lodge. In the dancing glow of the fire, Shunka saw her eyes the same amber-gold as his, with a fierce quality that reminded him of the intense stare of a predatory bird. Her exposed arms, shoulders, and back all bulged with muscle. She was just as much a warrior as he.

"My son," Ahote Chaa said. "I'm glad you've come. Allow me to introduce your betrothed. Shikoba, daughter of Orumaku Chaa of the Hawk Clan."

The woman stood. There was a beauty to her, Shunka had to admit, a statuesque quality of strength and power mixed with grace and elegance common to women of the Hawk Tribe. She closed the distance between him and herself, then placed a closed fist against her open palm and bowed to him. "It is my pleasure to meet you at last, Shunka of the Wolves."

He returned the gesture, bowing at the waist with his fist cupped in the palm of his other hand. "As am I, Shikoba of the Hawks. I hope our union will be filled with mutual happiness and respect."

"My children," the Chaa said, and he rose to his feet. "Come, we must announce your union to the rest of the tribe." Ahote led them both to the entrance of the Longhouse. They stepped out into the sunlight and the Chaa raised his hand to silence the people. "Brothers and sisters, sons and daughters," he spoke with a powerful, reverberating voice that brought silence to the village. "It is my honor to announce the union of my son, Shunka, to Shikoba, maiden of the Hawk Clan! With this, the bonds of fellowship with our Hawk brothers is strengthened, and we grow closer in brotherhood!"

A cheer and whooping of voices rose from the gathered

villagers. Shikoba glanced over at him, the hint of a smile on her lips as she reached over and took his hand in hers. Her eyes betrayed her, and Shunka could see she was happy, truly happy, as this was what she wanted. He returned the smile. Perhaps this arrangement wouldn't be so bad after all. He might find joy in it.

In the distance, at the far edge of the village, he spotted Endelynn returning with the armful of twigs and branches for firewood. She caught his gaze for the briefest of moments before turning away in anger. She tossed the firewood on a pile of branches and then retreated off to the small hut they shared.

"Tonight, a feast will be held in their honor!" Ahote Chaa continued, bringing Shunka back to the moment. Another cheer rose from the gathered villagers. Any excuse for a feast was welcomed.

Shikoba leaned in close, her lips beside Shunka's ear. "That girl over there," she whispered, "that pale-face, what is she doing here?"

"She's just a captive." Shunka said. "Found on patrol and brought back by some foolish young warrior."

"You wolves were always too lenient when it came to the foreigners. In my village, such a thing would never be tolerated. She'd have been killed on sight." Shikoba said in a hushed tone. "I think this young warrior needs to be reminded of who we are. Can you point him out to me?"

"He is not here." Shunka said. "And he will not return before we leave tomorrow."

"A pity." Shikoba said. "I would've liked to question his motives."

XXXIII.
ENDELYNN

That night left Endelynn in a sour mood. A great fire had been built in the central fire pit of the village, the flames reached up high into the air. As the Chaa had promised, a feast was prepared. Rows of corn and squash, fresh caught fish from the river along with deer and wild boar. There was even some baked bread from the clay oven.

During the feast, the old shaman told stories to entertain the villagers. He would throw some powder into the fire and cause explosions of smoke to rise up. In the clouds of soot, the shaman would cast shadows with his hands to act out the stories.

Tonight's story was the tale of how Killer Whale, hungry and greedy as he was, ate all the fish in the sea. He even ate the other whales, and the people on land were forced to go hungry. Mighty Thunderbird, father of all the great birds of prey, saw the strife of his people and fought against Killer Whale to save the people from starvation. The battle raged, storms and floods and earthquakes shook the land, and eventually Thunderbird was victorious and threw Killer Whale back into the ocean. From that day on, Killer Whale did not trouble the people anymore, and there were always plenty of fish to eat.

This story was carved into one of their totem poles. Shunka had pointed it out to Endelynn and told her of the legend. It was likely the Shaman was retelling it now because of their guest, the woman from the Hawk Clan.

Shikoba, Endelynn heard the name from some of the other villagers, sat beside Shunka, his father, Ahote, and brother Mingan. She and Shunka had new necklaces made of animal bones, claws, and turquoise. They feasted together.

Endelynn, however, was down in the crowd. No one spoke to her, and whatever food she got was just the remains that were left over by the time it got back to her. Scraps compared to the succulent meats and fruits enjoyed by the rest of the tribe. She was alone again, truly alone.

"Are you alone?" A voice asked. Endelynn almost jumped from her skin in startlement. Looking around, she found Tala standing next to her, the wolf warrior's hands tucked behind her back. "Do you have no one to share this feast with?" She asked.

"No one." Endelynn answered in the native tongue.

"Then you won't mind of I join you." Tala seated herself beside the princess. From behind her back, she produced a pair of smoked fish skewered on sticks. "Hungry?"

Endelynn took it with ravenous intent. "Gwomu." She said and began tearing into the fish with her teeth. She'd gotten used to eating with her hands and not having to wait on manners in her time with the tribe.

"You're language skills are improving." Tala commented. She took a more restrained bite than Endelynn. "I'm a little surprised you picked it up so quickly."

Endelynn swallowed and wiped the scales that still clung to her face away. "Uyoonta taught me." She explained. "And I've always been good with languages. My parents told me so."

"Even so." Tala turned away to gaze at Shunka and his soon to be wife, Shikoba. "What are you going to tell him when he leaves?"

Endelynn pulled her legs up close to her chest and wrapped her arms around her knees. She clutched the fish skewer in one hand, the fish left half eaten with her appetite gone. "I don't know." She said at last. "I guess I'll just wish him happiness."

Tala nodded. "That would be best. It's not like he could love you anyways."

Endelynn's eyes snapped wide in shock. "What?" She sat up straight and turned to face Tala. "What did you mean?"

"This is probably for the best, is all." Tala continued. "When he leaves for the Hawk Tribe, there will be no chance he could fall for an outsider."

An outsider. That's all she was to these people, the stranger who didn't belong. The pale-faced girl from the Walled Cities who was brought back by a warrior who forgot his people's ways. "And what about you?" Endelynn asked. "Did you ever love him?"

"As my brother." Tala explained. "While we did not come from the same mother, nor do we share the same father, Shunka and I are siblings nonetheless. And I wish only what is best for him."

"Which is not me." Endelynn said.

"Exactly. He will be happy with the Hawk Clan, and you should do nothing to upset that."

"Why did you think I would?" Endelynn pointed one end of the fish skewer at Tala's face. "I also have a betrothed back home, a handsome and daring prince who is probably searching these woods day and night looking for me."

"Good." Tala stood. "That means you don't love Shunka, and won't do anything to upset this union. I am glad to hear that." The wolf maiden walked off to join the rest of her village in the festivities, leaving Endelynn alone again.

As the evening wore on and the villagers began to disperse, Endelynn soon found herself alone by the fire pit. She stared into the dying coals, watched them glow and occasionally spark. Craning her head back, she gazed up at the black sky filled with more stars than there were numbers for. All the many trees in this vast forest could not number the stars seen in her small patch of sky between the forest canopy.

Why was she restless tonight? The day had been long, even before the woman from the Hawk Tribe arrived, and usually she would be exhausted, but tonight she did not feel like sleeping. She took another piece of wood and tossed it on the glowing embers. Not much, but just enough to keep it burning for herself. After all, it wasn't like she could go back to Shunka's lodge tonight, not with his new bride there. No, tonight she was staying under those thousands of stars.

"Restless night?" An unfamiliar voice called to her. Endelynn shifted on the log that served as a bench and looked behind her. The statuesque, muscular form of the Hawk woman emerged from the darkness, her face illuminated in the orange glow of the embers. "Don't you have some place to sleep?" She asked.

"I not tired." Endelynn answered, and returned to facing the light flames that sprouted across the new wood.

"You can speak like a real person." The Hawk maiden, Shikoba, approached and seated herself on the far end of the log. "Almost like a real person. Was it the Wolves' other pet pale-face who taught you? That old crone?"

"Uyoonta teach me, yes." Endelynn confirmed. "She say I learn good."

Shikoba laughed. "Yes. Learn good, for a foreign invader."

They sat in silence together, the only sound that of the crackling flames. Neither one turned to face the other. Endelynn's heart began to beat faster the longer the other woman sat beside her, the same way it would when her parents quizzed her on something and she didn't have the answer. She felt like she was being tested, but she didn't know on what. "Why you still awake?" Endelynn asked at last.

"I don't need to explain myself to some pale-faced foreign girl." The Hawk maiden's voice was quick and harsh, nothing

251

like it had been before. "And you have no place to ask things of me."

Endelynn hunched her shoulders in and pulled her legs up. She felt small, like a mouse cowering in the death glare of a hungry raptor just before it struck. "Sorry," she uttered in a low voice.

"Good." The Hawk woman said. "You know your place in the tribe. The lowest of the low, someone's delicate pet and nothing more. Glad to see these Wolves have some sense, even if they were foolish enough to bring you back to their village." Shikoba stood and walked towards Endelynn, and even in the dancing light of the small fire, the princess could still see the angry glare in her eyes. "I have some questions for you."

Endelynn gulped in fear. She began to tremble and couldn't stop herself. The Hawk warrior moved behind her and placed her hands almost delicately on Endelynn's shoulders.

"Now, you better not lie to me. I'll know if you lie." Shikoba leaned down beside her ear, and Endelynn could feel her hot breath against her cold skin.

"I not lie." Endelynn said.

"Good." Shikoba's fingers tightened. Endelynn felt the nails dig into her skin, almost like raptor talons. The Hawk warrior placed her face right beside Endelynn's and asked, "which was it that brought you here?"

Endelynn's heart leapt into her throat. What should she say? She couldn't implicate Shunka, she knew that much, but Endelynn was too blinded by fear to know what to say. "I don't remember." She said at last, forgetting herself and speaking in the tongue of Dadria. "I can't remember his name."

Shikoba rolled her eyes, then tightened her grip on Endelynn's shoulders and shook her. "Speak like a human being, you filthy foreigner!"

She winced and bit her lip, her eyes clamped shut. Tears threatened to flow, but she blinked them back savagely. She mustn't cry now. "I don't remember name." She reiterated in the Sequoia language.

"You're lying!" The Hawk woman shoved Endelynn off the log.

She tumbled forward and landed with her face in the dirt. As Endelynn struggled to get up, Shikoba grasped a handful of hair and yanked her head back. She cried out in shock and pain.

"A member of the Panther Clan found you, didn't he?" The Hawk maiden asked, but it wasn't a question so much as an accusation. "He came to my village and told my father all about you. About how a lone Wolf warrior came to your defense when he tried to fulfill his sacred duty and rid this forest of your kind." She tightened her grip on Endelynn's hair and twisted, eliciting another shriek of pain. "And how you took one of our spears and tried to attack him with it."

The Panther shifter? Endelynn could not bring up his name right now, but she couldn't forget the encounter and how Shunka almost died protecting her. How much did Shikoba already know?

"I'll not ask again." Shikoba pushed her face closer to the fire pit. Endelynn's face tinged and the hairs closest to the flames twisted and melted in the heat. "I will burn your hair off and melt the skin from your bones. Tell me who brought you here."

She winced, her eyes closed. She didn't want to give his name, but the thought of those coals on her face was too much to bare. "Shunka!" Endelynn shouted at last. "He brought me!" And the tears began to flow.

"I knew it." Shikoba hissed. She pushed Endelynn closer to the fire, and the princess's felt a new rush of fear.

"No, no, no!" She pleaded. Endelynn struggled, but she was no match for the raw strength of the Hawk warrior. "I told you the truth!"

"I know. And I will still burn your hair and melt your face.

We'll see how much Shunka likes you after that." Shikoba said.

The fire crackled and danced before her. As much as Endelynn tried, all she could do was slow the steady progression towards the flames. She shut her eyes and turned away, trying not to see it before it happened. Any second now, she would feel the raging flames across her scalp and burning into her eyes.

A loud bark, almost like a roar, split the air. Shikoba released her hold and jumped away just as an enormous black wolf emerged from the darkness. It leapt out of the night, teeth bared and glistening in the dancing light of the fire. Its eyes seemed to glow, and a deep snarl rumbled in its throat. It stood over Endelynn, putting itself between her and Shikoba.

Endelynn trembled. She hugged the ground, the wolf's legs forming almost a cage around her. Protecting her. She could feel the rumble of its growl deep in her chest.

"What is this?" Shikoba snapped once the shock had worn off. "Why do you protect this invader?"

The black wolf began to change, it shrank and its fur sloughed away. The muzzle fell away to a simple human nose, ears slid down the sides of its face, tail retracted back into the spine. Once it was small enough, it rose from a four to a two-footed stance, but continued to stand over Endelynn. "I protect her," Shunka said as his mouth reformed, "because I choose to."

Shikoba's eyes grew wide, but otherwise betrayed little emotion, as Shunka grew out of the wolf. He crouched beside Endelynn, one knee planted in the dirt, and rested his hands on her. "Chaneewah Ishde," he said, calling her by the name the shaman had given her, the Flame-haired girl.

Endelynn took his hand, still frightened, but no longer trembling in terror. Shunka helped her to her feet, then pulled her against his chest, his strong arms wrapped around her.

Shikoba's jaw clenched tight. "I see." She said, and

Endelynn could hear the hurt in her voice. "The rumors were true then. The envoy of the Panther Clan was right." The Hawk maiden turned away, maybe to stop herself from another outburst or to hide her tears, Endelynn could not tell. All the princess could see were the warrior's tense shoulders and clenched fists as she stormed off into the dark.

"Where she going?" Endelynn finally allowed herself to ask once Shikoba was gone.

"I'm not sure." Shunka said. His arms still held tight around her. "Probably back to the Great Lodge for the night. She might be gone by morning."

"I sorry," Endelynn buried her face in his chest, "I ruin everything."

Shunka breathed a heavy sigh. Not one of relief, but rather of resignation. "I'm not sure how things will turn out now." He admitted. "I just threatened my betrothed for the sake of a foreign invader girl, and in so doing insulted a very powerful clan."

Endelynn pulled herself closer to his chest. More dangers, more enemies who wanted her dead, and only a single protector. But right now, in his arms, she felt safe. And utterly exhausted. Now that the excitement was over the sleep that she'd been holding off was starting to wash over her, even more so while Shunka held her.

"Come," Shunka said, "we can think more on things in the morning. Sleep is needed." He lead her by the hand back to his small lodge, where fortunately Shikoba had not returned, and he gave her the bed to sleep on. Less than a minute after pulling the blankets over herself, Endelynn was asleep.

Her dreams, those that she remembered, were short and meaningless. She dreamt of home, of her mother and father in the banquet hall greeting her as she came down to break her fast. But as she moved to sit, she saw a third person at the table with them. She saw Shunka, but he was dressed like Prince

Sedrick. Aside from this strange image, Endelynn did not remember anything else from her sleep.

It was mid-morning by the time Endelynn awoke, and she was not alone. As she blinked the sleep away from her eyes and started to shift, she noticed the extra weight across her chest. Shunka lay beside her on the bed mat, still asleep, with his arm draped over her. He wasn't under the blankets with her, but still close enough to bring her pause.

As she tried to push his arm away, his eyes fluttered open. They looked at each other, her green eyes locked with his amber ones, before Shunka turned away and sat up.

"I'm sorry," he said, "I did not mean to disturb you."

Endelynn sat up, letting the blankets settle in her lap. "You did no wrong," she said. Her mouth felt dry and her voice crackled, the way it usually did when she woke up.

Shunka stood and stretched his back. Endelynn caught herself staring at him, watching as his muscles tensed and flexed in the early sunlight. He turned to her and held out a hand. "Come," he said, "we should see if any food is waiting for us."

Her cheeks felt warm and she was sure they burned pink. Endelynn took his hands and allowed him to pull her to her feet. He lifted the flap to his lodge and a flood of bright, morning sunshine flooded though. Her eyes burned and she winced, holding her free hand before her face. As they stepped outside, and as her eyes adjusted to the light, she found them confronted by the angry face of another Wolf warrior.

"I told you not to interfere." Tala's words were harsh. She stood with her arms crossed over her chest and hips jutted to one side. She frowned and glared at them both. "I told you not to do anything to upset the union, but you did so anyway. And because of that, you may have started a blood feud with the Hawk Tribe."

Endelynn blinked. She was still confused and caught off

guard. "But I . . ." she started, lost her words. What was she supposed to say in her defense?

"She did nothing wrong," Shunka interjected. "Shikoba came up to her in the night and attacked her. I merely stepped in to stop it."

"It doesn't matter," Tala said. "She's gone. Left early this morning after a heated argument with your father. Threats were made, and there's a good chance they'll be carried out." Tala leaned in close and glared at Endelynn. "You've been warned."

The Wolf maiden strutted off, leaving Shunka and Endelynn alone. The princess's heart was racing for the second time this morning, and for a very different reason.

XXXIV.
ARIDAIN

The knight held a scroll in his loose fist. He'd read it thrice already, and it took great pains for him not to read it a fourth. It had been beside his bed when he awoke, sealed with wax that bore the reverse elk sigil of Roddrick. Upon discovering its contents, he dressed himself and hurried to the queen's chambers without even stopping to break his fast.

He arrived to find two of Beatrice's personal guards, his fellow Dadrian knights, standing watch outside her room. They were talking amongst themselves, one bragging of a tavern girl he'd met the night before, when Aridain approached. They stood at attention and saluted him. "Sir Aridain," the one who'd been bragging said. "Good morning to you, Captain."

Aridain saluted them in return. "At ease," he said. "Stand aside, I need to speak with the queen."

"We're afraid her grace has not yet awoken, Captain." The second stated.

"I don't care, I need to speak with her. It is a matter of some importance." He held up the small scroll, but was sure not to display the broken seal.

"News from Dadria?" The first asked.

"Does it concern the missing princess?" The second's voice was filled with concern.

"All you need to know is it is of great importance to her

grace, and I have to speak with her directly." Aridain stated. "Now, stand aside." The guards did as they were bid. Aridain brought it fist to the door and gave three harsh knocks. "Your grace," she called, "I must speak with you!"

There was a creaking of the bed from within the room. Queen Beatrice's voice was groggy and scratchy. "Sir Aridain? What is the matter?"

"A message," he said, looking at the scroll, "from your secret ally."

The lock unlatched from the inside and the door pulled open. "Enter." Beatrice said.

Aridain stepped inside the queen's sleeping chambers. The curtains over the windows had been drawn open to allow sunlight in. Beatrice pulled open the bedside drawer and pulled out a match. She attempted to strike it against the wooden table top, but the match wouldn't light. Aridain closed the door behind him and turned the key to lock it. "Please, your grace, allow me."

He set the scroll on the seating table, moved to his queen's side, and took the match from her. "Is you insist." Beatrice stated, pulling her gown closer around her body as she moved away. He fixated on the task at hand, trying his hardest not to notice his queen's womanly shape within that sheer sheet of fabric with sleeves. There were more important matters to attend to. "You have a message?" She asked.

He struck the match not against wood, but the rougher surface of the stone hearth. It flared in an instant. He used it to light a small candle on the table before whisking the match out and tossing the burnt stick into the ashes in the fireplace. "Yes, your grace," he retrieved the scroll from the table, "it bares the reverse sigil on the seal," he said as he held it out to her.

Beatrice took the scroll and unrolled it to read. He watched with practiced patience as her eyes scanned back and forth across the paper. Aridain noted how her eyes grew wider and her brows scrunched lower, indicating her growing unease. "He found a lead."

"Yes," Aridain confirmed. "He claims to have found the mercenary organization hired to kidnap Princess Endelynn."

"And he's arranged a meeting with their leader." Beatrice read. She looked up from the paper and her eyes met his. "He wants you to accompany him."

Aridain nodded. "As extra muscle, should it come to that. And he knows he can trust me, as I am not under the employ of his brother."

Beatrice rolled the scroll back up, then held one end over the candle. "I won't allow it!" She spat and tossed the flaming paper into the hearth. "I will not send my most skilled guard out on a dangerous mission without knowing what we'll get in return."

"What we'll get is information on the last known location of your daughter." Aridain argued. "And perhaps some definitive proof that Kendrick organized her abduction, as well as the murder of your late husband." He kept his voice low, speaking barely over a whisper. There were the two guards outside, but he had no idea who else might be listening in on the private conversations of the visiting queen.

"I can send any of my other guards. All are perfectly able to handle themselves if things get rough." Beatrice paced back and forth through the room, her gown sweeping behind her and exposing her elegant legs.

Aridain raised his eyes to her face. "And they should stay behind to protect you, my queen." He saw the worry in her eyes. Something deep inside him said that her concern was greater than she let on, that there was more than she said. "If things get bad, I am more than capable of taking any single man in a fight. And besides," he continued, "he requested me specifically."

Beatrice turned her back to him and placed a hand over her

eyes. "Very well." She said at last. "Go. Meet with him and tell me what you learn." Aridain bowed and turned to leave when her grace called to him again. "And Aridain," she said, "come back to me alive. I can't bare to lose someone else dear to me."

"Of course, my queen." He unlocked the door and stepped out into the corridor. The pair of Dadrian guards stood diligently at their post. "You heard nothing of this, is that understood?"

"Yes, Captain." They both answered in unison.

"Good." Aridain said, and returned to the barracks of the visiting Dadrian knights. He joined other members of his garrison in the galley hall to break his fast.

The better part of the day was spent with the queen, standing by her side in his full plate armor to serve as her bodyguard as she traversed the castle, spoke with Kendrick and otherwise performed simple royal duties. They didn't speak of the letter, or of what Roddrick meant by it. Hopefully, that would all be explained when he spoke with the exiled king.

The day wore on. Finally, late in the afternoon, Aridain's shift ended and he returned to the barracks. He quickly changed his clothes, putting on the plainest trousers and tunic he could find, along with the dullest boots. He secured a single dagger to his waist, a double-edged blade about the length of his forearm, the only weapon he would take with him. Once he had himself dressed, Aridain when back to Beatrice's chambers and used the hidden passage behind her fireplace.

As the stone wall behind her hearth slid away to reveal the long, dark passageway, the queen called to him. "Sir Aridain," she said.

"Yes, your majesty?" Aridain replied.

"I command you to return to me safely." She said. "You are not to take any unnecessary risks or get into unwarranted danger. Am I understood?"

"Of course, my queen." Aridain bowed.

"This is an order." Beatrice stated with all the regal authority of her status. "If I find you have disregarded me, you will be discharged from my service. Am I understood?"

"Absolutely, your grace." The knight said, and then stepped over the threshold into the secret passageway.

He followed the long, dark corridor all the way out to the abandoned shop. From there, the disguised knight walked to the tavern of The Starving Bear. He found an empty table, seated himself, and settled down to wait for Roddrick. He asked for a jug of ale from the serving girl as she passed. She nodded and continued on her way.

His drink came soon enough. He sipped from it, making sure not to get himself inebriated. He needed his head clear for whatever the job was tonight. Besides, he had no idea how this ale was brewed.

A girl screamed from the end of the tavern and a plate crashed to the floor. Aridain snapped to attention. It was the serving girl, her tray lay on the ground surrounded by a mess of broken dishes and food. One of the other patrons, a rather disheveled looking man, laughed along with his friends. "Oh, come on, girly," he said, "it was just a little pinch. You should be flattered." From the man's slurred words and red face, Aridain could tell he was drunk.

"You grabbed my ass!" The serving girl shouted, her face full of outrage.

"And it was nice." The man and his group of buddies laughed. "May I have another one?"

"No!" The girl scoffed. "This isn't that kind of tavern. If you're going to do that, you can take your business elsewhere."

"Now, really," the man stood and advanced towards her, "don't be such a prude. Maybe I can help you loosen up." He reached out for her. "By the time I'm done with ya, you'll be loose in more ways than one."

The girl brought her open palm against her aggressor's face

in a hearty slap. The strike was loud enough to bring the otherwise rowdy tavern to silence, and the man recoiled. He stared at her in shock, his cheek already turning red.

The man's surprise soon turned to anger. He moved towards her and when she tried to slap him again, he grabbed her forearm and twisted, forcing her arm behind her back. The girl cried out in pain. "I was going to be gentle, but now I don't think so."

Aridain could take no more. The longer he watched, the more his blood boiled. He pushed his ale away and stood. "Halt." His voice carried like a boom through the tavern, instantly bringing everyone's attention to him. He, however, focused completely on the ruffian with his hands on the serving girl. "Release her."

"Who are you supposed to be?" The man asked, his hands still clinging to the girl.

Aridain ignored the question. "The girl has expressed her displeasure with you. You will take your hands off her, or I will take your hands."

Uproarious laughter filled the air from the man and his four friends. "Look at this, boys," the man said, "this guy thinks he's some big hotshot."

"Yeah, boss," one of his friends said, "what does he think, he's some Black Sword?"

"I am no Black Sword," Aridain said as he approached, his shoulders stiff and both hands clenched into fists, "but I don't have to be. A knight isn't needed to deal with the likes of you."

The man's face turned sour, his lip twisted to a sneer. "Not as funny the second time." He said, then turned to address his compatriots. "Deal with him, will ya? I want some alone time with the lady."

"Sure thing, boss." One of the goons, a big man with a bald head and missing teeth, slammed down his mug and stood. He was taller than everyone else in the bar, with a thick body that ripped with muscle and fat. He stepped towards Aridain, and each of his foot falls could be felt through the floor.

The tall brute gave no warning as he swung a fist as large as an ale glass for Aridain's head. The knight ducked with ease as the closed fist and bulging knuckles whisked past his head harmlessly, then delivered a well-placed kick to the back of the brute's knee. The big man stumbled and lost his balance, he landed with a thunderous crash to the ground which shook the tavern.

The hall fell silent, the crowd looking between the fallen man and the unassuming nobody in the plain clothes that just took him down. Aridain paid them no mind, his attention was still focused on the remaining fighters. "I'd take my wounded and go, while you are still able."

The vile man spat on the floor. He tossed the serving girl aside. "You think I'd be intimidated by some no name-"

The heavy thunk of an axe head hitting the floor brought a new level of dread to the room. A new figure approached, dressed in a hooded green cloak, with a pair of leather vambrace on each arm, and a short, singed blond beard. He braced his hands on the handle of his axe, the heavy steel blades of which rested on the ground. "Evening, fellas," the cloaked figure said, his yellow teeth showing behind his yellow beard, "we're not getting into trouble are we?"

"N-no," the ruffian stammered, his voice suddenly trembling and legs wobbly, "no trouble at all."

"That's good." The man in the dark-green cloak said. "I'd hate to have to break up a fight." His fingers gripped around the leather binds of the axe handle. "I think you boys have had enough to drink for one night, how about you head home and sleep it off?"

"Y-yeah," the ruffian complied, "yeah, okay. Let's go boys." The helped their injured friend back to his feet and quickly hurried out of the tavern. Once they were gone, a low murmur of voices and talking rose from the other patrons.

The green cloaked man rummaged a silver coin from the pouch at his waist and handed it to the serving girl. "For your troubles. I'm sorry you had to deal with that." She took the coin, bowed quickly, and hurried off to the kitchen. "Well," the green cloak moved towards Aridain, keeping his axe low, "I am obligated to ask," he pushed his hood back just enough to reveal his eyes, "how is the fish?"

"I don't know," Aridain replied, irritably. "I haven't had the chance to order it yet."

XXXV.
SHUNKA

"**Y**ou hold it like this." He cupped the stone in his hand lengthwise, with the long end pointed away from his body. "Then you take the other one and hit it like this." He struck one stone against the other at an angle, chipping away pieces to make a sharpened edge.

The foreign girl watched with intense focus. She held a piece of flint similar to Shunka's and by his example, was trying to shape it. They crouched beside one another on the banks of the river, the gentle waves lapped over the smooth stones at their feet.

She brought one stone down against the other and a flake fell away, leaving a flat, glossy, sharp edge. "Like this?" She held it out for him to inspect.

He eyed the stone, then smiled and nodded. "Very good," he said, "for a first attempt. Try to keep the strokes shorter and the flakes smaller." Shunka returned to working on his arrow point, steadily chipping away the unnecessary stone.

Endelynn watched him and tried to follow. Shunka watched her progress, and could tell her workmanship was weak at best. But she had an interest in learning, and the more she watched and practiced, the better her stone shaping became. This was the third day they'd been working together to make spear points.

With each day that passed, Shunka could feel the growing

apprehension in the back of his mind. When Shikoba of the Hawk Tribe left, she swore that her father would answer the insult in turn. However, no word had come from the Hawk Clan since then. But Shunka knew better than to be complacent. The Hawks were not known for their charity or mercy, nor their forgiveness. This exercise with the Flame-Haired Girl was as much to help distract his mind as it was to craft new weapons.

"When will I get to work with Obsidian?" Endelynn asked.

"When you get better at it." Shunka chipped a few small flakes away from his stone. The basic shape of an arrowhead was beginning to appear. "Obsidian is rare. Only the most skilled are allowed to fashion weapons from it."

"Does that make you especially skilled?" She asked. "I know you have knife made of it. And I seen your spear, the one I used to force the panther away. Remember?"

Shunka smirked. "Yes," he said. Of course he remembered. He'd had aches and pains for days after that fight, and a few new scars to show for it. "That spear is special. It was my initiation spear."

"Tell me." Endelynn said. "I want to know more."

He looked away from his work and saw her eyes full of wonder. It was true. She had a drive for knowledge he'd not seen outside of a young, curious child. "Very well." He set his half-finished spear tip on the smooth stones of the riverbank and adjusted himself so he was sitting instead of crouching. "Every young warrior goes through a series of trials before they are deemed a true warrior. Tests of bravery, endurance, patience, strength. Tests for how well you follow orders and how well you think for yourself, as there are times for both."

"Can you tell me the tests?" Endelynn asked.

"Well," Shunka leaned forward and rested his arms over his knees. He stared out across the river, listening to the rushing water. "An endurance test might mean standing naked in the

267

river for a day and a night without food or drink."

"Couldn't you just drink from the river?"

"No." Shunka said. "It tests your will power as well. To see if you are strong enough to be surrounded by all that water and not drink a drop. You enter the river at first light, and don't leave until the sunrise of the next day."

Endelynn listened with great interest. Shunka continued.

"A skilled warrior must also be able to hunt on their own. So one of the tests is to track, kill, and dress a deer all by yourself." He said. "That is especially important for the next test. At a certain age, all young warriors-in-training set out to live alone in the forest. They are not to visit any village of any tribe for assistance, they have to survive only on their own skills."

"Wow," the red-haired girl exclaimed, "what age?"

"Usually thirteen winters." Shunka said. "And the young warrior must live on their own for a moon. Usually they set out from their village when the moon is at its brightest, and return home when it is bright again."

"A moon?" Endelynn asked. Her eyes lit up almost instantly as she came to understand. "A month."

"The final test is to craft your own weapon. The weapon of choice is yours, or course, but you have to make it yourself. I chose a spear. I had to carve the shaft myself, sand the wood so it became smooth, find the obsidian and then craft the spear point myself. I even had to gather the tree resin and tan the deer hide to make binds to secure the point to the shaft."

Shunka's eyes slid closed and a light smile grew across his lips. A wave of nostalgia washed over him as he thought back to those days, all the time he'd spent crafting his own weapon. For days at a time it was the only thing he did, not stopping for food and only sleeping when he passed out from exhaustion. "Of course, that wasn't the hard part."

"Then what was?" Endelynn asked.

He brought one hand to his hair and brushed his fingers lightly over the white and brown feathers. "Getting these."

"Feathers?"

"Eagle feathers." He elaborated. "The final test of a young warrior is to climb to an eagle's nest and take a pair of feathers. One is for completing the warrior training and crafting your weapon. The second feather is earned for making the climb." He rested his arm across his knee again. "The more feathers someone has, the more great feats they've achieved."

"Like the Chaa?" Endelynn asked.

"Yes." Shunka said. "To become a Chaa, or any member of the Council of Elders, the person must achieve many great feats. Enough feathers that a special headdress is needed to hold them all."

"Why can't they all be woven in the person's hair?"

Shunka gave a sly smirk. "Because by then, they may have no hair left."

He laughed. She laughed. They laughed together and Shunka came to realize he was happy right now. Just sitting and talking with this girl, this foreign child with all her curiosity and willingness to learn, brought him happiness he hadn't known before.

The moment was broken when a hawk's shrill cry split the air. Its shadow passed over them, bringing their laughter to a premature end. Shunka shaded his eyes as he looked skyward to see the great bird circling overhead. It came in to land on the banks of the river and Shunka noticed it had a quiver of arrows and an unstrung bow slung over its back.

He stood, placing himself between Endelynn and the giant hawk. On the ground, standing at full height, the crown of the predatory bird reached to the center of his chest. It stared back at him with intense, angry eyes. As they watched each other, the bird's feathers gradually began to shrink and disappear. It changed shape, as he knew it would, from a bird into a woman.

"I'd hoped I'd find you out here." Shikoba stood on the riverbank where the hawk had been. "I thought we might talk."

"About what?" Shunka said. He felt Endelynn press herself against his back, her fingers clutching his arm.

"My father's proposal. My proposal." Shikoba pulled the bow shaft from the quiver on her back and a bow string from the pouch at her waist. With practiced ease, she strung the bow in one quick motion.

"Orumaku Chaa is still seeking a union between us?" Shunka asked with shock. Given the Hawk Clan's leader's reputation, he would never have expected to hear that.

"No. My father wanted to dissolve all relations between our tribes after your rejection." Shikoba explained. She drew an arrow and nocked it. "I spoke with him and asked him to reconsider." Her eyes met his, and Shunka saw not just the anger and frustration, but what appeared to be sadness. "He is willing to overlook this whole affair. We can still join and it will be as if nothing happened. There is only one condition."

"And what is that?" Shunka asked.

Shikoba motioned with her eyes to the girl standing behind him. "The foreign child must die."

Endelynn's fingers tightened around his arm. Shunka reaffirmed his stance and his jaw hardened. "I cannot allow that." He said. "She's my charge and my duty is to protect her."

"If you don't agree to these conditions, my father will take it as an insult and bring the entire strength of the Hawk Tribe down on your people." Shikoba stated. "Is this invader's life truly worth more to you than those of your clan?"

"It doesn't have to be that way." Shunka rebuffed. "There's no need for violence."

"You are right." Shikoba raised the bow and aimed. "It can all be corrected with a single arrow. I can make it quick and painless so no one has to suffer."

"You'll have to put that arrow through both of us." Shunka

said. While he tried to speak with confidence and strength, his heart was racing. He knew Shikoba's reputation with a bow and arrow, how she could pin a pheasant to a tree at a hundred paces without killing it, if she wanted to she could easily hit the both of them with a single arrow.

She lowered the bow and for a moment, Shunka felt relief. "No. I won't." Shikoba said.

Hidden beneath the sound of the rushing river and the wind through the trees, Shunka heard the straining of a bowstring as it was pulled taught. His eyes shifted to the line of trees to his left and he understood. Twisting around, he shoved the princess to the ground and covered her with his body just as an arrow burst from the forest. He felt the rush of wind as the arrow flew just over his head and splashed into the river.

Of course Shikoba hadn't come alone. She would never do something so foolish. There could be as many as six or seven other Hawk archers in the woods, all ready to shoot them full of arrows.

"Endelynn, when I return, you'll need to get on my back." Shunka said in a low voice.

"What?" She asked.

"Just do it."

He jumped off the princess and began to shift. Black fur rippled across his body as the wolf took shape. He raced for Shikoba. As he did, she lifted her bow and pulled the arrow back. As she took aim for the foreign princess, Shunka tackled her to the ground. The bowstring snapped forward, sending the arrow flying wildly off course.

He pinned her to the ground beneath his powerful wolf body. His jaws clamped around the bow shaft, splinters of wood scrapped between his teeth as he wrestled it away from Shikoba's grip. The bow slipped from the her fingers and Shunka flung it into the river, where it splashed and sank.

He raced back to Endelynn, making sure to keep himself

between her and the line of trees. The princess jumped to her feet as he approached and threw herself onto his back, one leg on either side and grasping two thick handfuls of fur.

Another arrow loosed from the tree line and bounced off a rock by Shunka's paw. He snarled as he pulled his foot back, and started to run, following the flow of the river. The extra weight on his back slowed him down. Out in the open like this, running along the stone covered banks of the river, they were exposed. Normally he would retreat into the safety of the woods, but he had no way of knowing where the Hawk archers were hiding. If he approached the trees, it would leave them more vulnerable. They would probably never make it to the forest before being filled with arrows.

His sharp wolf ears caught the sound of another bowstring and he veered to one side. The arrow struck the ground where he had been. Endelynn cried out in fright and shock each time he made a sharp turn like that, and her grip always tightened.

A hawk's shrill screech echoed through the air. Its dark shadow appeared on the ground and kept pace beside him. He dared not look back, but he knew it was Shikoba.

Ahead of them down river, the once smooth water grew swift and choppy. Spray shot into the air wherever a rock jutted up from the stream bed and broke through the surface. The current was growing stronger. Although it was still a fair distance away, Shunka's powerful ears could make out the roar of the waterfall. The falls were short and the pool beneath it was deep. If they could get there, they could hide until dark when the Hawks were at a disadvantage and they could escape.

Between the roaring of the upcoming waterfall and the continuous screech of the hawk overhead, Shunka didn't notice the next attack until he felt it stick into his side. Not an arrow, something much smaller and sharper. He yelped as it dug into his skin under his ribs. A poisoned dart. Although he couldn't see it, he knew what it was. Already, his vision was starting to swim and blur.

The hawk shrieked again and the shadow beside them grew larger. It would be on them soon. With no other choice he could see, Shunka veered towards the river and dove beneath the surface.

The water swept them along. Endelynn tried to keep her grip, but the force of the current tore her away. Shunka fought against the river's pull sucking him to the bottom, paddling with all four legs until his snout broke the surface and he gulped the air.

A little further downstream, he caught sight of the princess as she breached the water's surface and gasped for breath. Shikoba in her hawk form circled overhead. She cawed again, a signal to the other Hawk warriors that she'd found them.

Shunka struggled forward, trying to reach the princess before the current pulled them over the waterfall, but he could hardly see her anymore his vision was so blurry. He could only make out the mess of tangled red hair against the white foam of the river. Trying to swim grew harder too, his legs felt heavy and weak like he could hardly move them at all. Whatever poison was in that dart was starting to more greatly affect him.

He managed to paddle beside her, nuzzling the tip of his snout against her arm. Endelynn first pulled her arm away in fright, then once she saw him, wrapped both arms around his body and clung to him.

The current grew swifter and the roar of the falls was deafening now. He hadn't realized how close they'd come, and he didn't have the strength to pull them away. The world around him grew dark. His wolf body slipped away and he reverted to his human form, not that he was conscious of it. Soon, he wouldn't be conscious at all. As the waterfall grew louder and closer, Endelynn wrapped her arms around his waist and buried her face in his chest. He was barely awake to feel the river's pull as they fell together over the waterfall.

XXXVI.
ENDELYNN

Her eyes snapped open, confused and disorientated. She was upside down, water swirling all around her. Her lungs burned for air, her vision blurred. She kicked and struggled, but the current forced her beneath the surface.

The water pulled her along, dragging her down stream. She could see the sunlight dancing through the water. There was air, there was life, but she couldn't reach it.

A rock jutted up from the riverbed ahead of her and burst through the surface. She kicked towards it, managing to brace herself against the bolder and push herself skyward. She broke the surface and with a strong gasp, filled her aching lungs with air. She coughed and sputtered, spitting out up water.

The roar of the river deafened her. Water sprayed as it splashed against the rocks, casting rainbows and turning to white foam. Endelynn clung to the rock, pressing her face against the rough surface. Her whole body ached. If only she could stay like this, just to rest for a moment. Just to let her mind at ease and fall asleep.

Shunka!

Her eyes grew wide with realization. He'd fallen down the waterfall into the river as well, but where was he now? Had he resurfaced? Was he even alive?

Endelynn pushed and dragged herself up the rock's face.

She came to the top and peered out over the river. White foam mixed with the water as it crashed against the boulders and stones that burst out from river and strewn along the banks. She couldn't see him, but in the turbulent waters he might have been dragged down to the bottom as she had almost been.

Her breathing grew quicker and shallower as the thoughts flowed into her head. Was Shunka drowning on the riverbed, forced under by the terrible strength of the river's current? Or worse, had his bones been shattered against the rocks? Did he hit a rock with his head and bash his skull open?

"Shunka!" She shouted. Her voice barely reached her own ears, smothered by the roar of the river. Taking a deeper breath, she screamed, "SHUNKA!"

It hurt her throat, but still the sound was lost. She couldn't call for him, and it wouldn't matter if he was trapped underwater.

A dark shape emerged on the surface further down river. It was Shunka, he lay face down in the water. "Shunka!" Endelynn cried out again. Without thinking, she climbed to the top of her rock and leapt back into the river. Using the current, she kicked and clawed at the water as she fought her way to him.

She grasped him, hooking her arms around his chest, and started to kick towards shore. The river began to spread out and the current slowed. Ahead was a bend in the river, and a patch of sand between where the water ended and the forest began. Endelynn struggled. Even in the water, Shunka was heavy and hard to move. As she approached shore, her feet scraped against the riverbed, now covered with a fine sand. Using the more secure footing, she began to hop for land.

Endelynn drug Shunka's limp, listless body onto the dry, coarse sand. Laying him on his back, she placed her ear close to his mouth and listened. He wasn't breathing.

She felt a new surge of fear. Sitting up, she pushed against his shoulders. "Shunka?" She said. There was no response. Endelynn shook him harder, smacking her hand on his cheek, trying to wake him. "Shunka? Please, wake up!" There was an urgency in her voice she didn't know she had. Not since her father died had she been this afraid of losing someone. Winifred's death was sudden and terrible, and she never had time to react to it alone. But now, staring down at the lifeless body of Shunka, she didn't know what to do.

A roar erupted from the trees, followed by a frightened flock of birds taking to the sky. Endelynn jumped in startlement, falling back on her haunches. Branches snapped and groaned, a small tree splintered and came to a thunderous crash as it was torn from the ground.

Her heart raced. Whatever was in those trees was coming closer, she could hear the breaking of twigs and sticks grow louder as it approached. She wanted to run, but if she did, Shunka would be left alone and at the mercy of whatever was coming for them. Endelynn spotted the knife on Shunka's waist. She took the black blade and grasped it in both hands, holding it out in as much fear as desperation.

It emerged from the woods. An enormous bear, plodding along on four massive legs which each ended in a set of curved claws. Its lower lip drooped and a trail of saliva dripped to the ground. Endelynn could see the rows of huge, sharp teeth behind those lips. Its fur was a chestnut brown with a twinge of gray and silver along the hunch in its back, signaling the animal's advanced age. It sauntered over to her, claws digging into the earth, snarling as it approached.

The bear was massive. Even walking on four legs, it still stood taller than her. There was no point in trying to run, it could chase her down in seconds. As for the short dagger in her hand, it might as well have been a blunt stick. Endelynn threw herself over Shunka's unresponsive body, dropping the stone knife in the sand and leaving it forgotten.

She tensed up, clenching her eyes shut and lacing her fingers together behind her head. Short whimpers escaped her tightly closed lips. "Please," she said in the wolf's tribal language, "please don't hurt us."

She spoke mostly to herself, her words were a desperate plea to an uncaring world, but as she huddled in terror over Shunka's body and no pain came, the seconds seemed to drag on. What was the bear waiting for? She gave no resistance, only cowered in fear, so why did it hesitate to kill her?

Endelynn lifted her head ever so slightly and saw the bear sitting on its hindquarters, looking back at her and tilting its head like an over sized dog. Its ear twitched and it blinked, but otherwise the big animal did not move. They stared at each other, both waiting for the other to say or do something first.

At long last, the bear stood up again, balancing on its hind legs so it came to a total height of over ten feet. As it approached, the animal began to shrink. The fur sloughed away like old clothes, and the animalistic features softened to nothing. The bear was gone. In its place stood an old, Sequoian man.

Endelynn stared slack jawed and wide eyed at the man. He was another like Shunka, or like the Panther and Hawk Clans. A Skin-changer. And from what she saw in those painted murals and totems in the village, this man was of the Bear Tribe.

He was tall, standing at least six and a half feet tall and possibly more, even in human form. His hair was a faded black, with signs of gray and silver along his temples. He had many wrinkles, and while his face appeared as hard as stone, his golden eyes betrayed an inner sadness. His body was muscular, well toned especially for a man at least fifty years old. On his chest were a pair of red markings, elevated areas of skin on his pectoral muscles that took the shape of bear paw prints.

277

The man knelt in the sand beside Shunka. He brushed Endelynn aside, placing his hand on her shoulder and giving a light shove. He then placed his ear beside Shunka's mouth, and upon hearing nothing moved lower so his head was at the young man's chest. Sitting up again, he raised a fist over his head and brought it down on Shunka's chest.

Endelynn gasped in shock. "What are you doing?" She screamed, forgetting for a moment to use the tribal tongue. "Stop it! Don't hurt him!"

The bear man gave her no regards. He brought his fist down on the younger man's chest again, causing him to lurch with each impact. Water gurgled up from within Shunka's throat. He coughed and sputtered, spitting up river water.

After a few deep coughs and gasps for breath, Shunka collapsed back to the ground. His breathing returned, loud enough for Endelynn to hear without having to get close. Still, he remained unconscious, his eyes closed and otherwise unmoving.

She turned to the elder man, whose attention remained focused on Shunka. He'd just saved the young wolf warrior's life. While she'd been horribly inept to do anything, this man saves him in just a few moments. A wave of relief swept over her. "Gwomu," she said, a gesture of gratitude.

She was more shocked, however, by his response. "You're welcome." The man replied in her language. Endelynn was taken back by his words. "Yes," he continued, "I can speak your language. I am a Chaowtee, same as Shunka."

"A speaker of many words," Endelynn said.

"Yes. I see you have learned that word," he said. "Your dialect if of the Wolf Clan, as to be expected, but all the tribes speak the same basic tongue."

"You speak my language very well." Endelynn said, relieved to be able to talk fluently again. All that time spent only being able to say halting, stilted words had been driving her crazy. "Better than Shunka."

"I've had a long time to learn. I was the one who taught the words to him." The man moved to inspect Shunka's unconscious body. He found the small dart stuck in his skin and pulled it out. "I know this poison." The bear-changer held the dart up. "Could be deadly, but I can treat it." Sliding his arms under Shunka's listless body, the Bear Tribe man lifted him from the ground. "Come," he said, "I'll take you to my home."

Endelynn followed behind him as they headed into the forest again, having to take a step and a half for every one of his strides just to keep pace with him. "So, do you have a name?" She asked.

"Of course." He said. He continued walking, seeming to ignore her question.

"Can you tell me?" Endelynn asked.

"I could. But I would rather not. Names are personal, and given specifically to those of the tribe. Some are more willing to share with others, but I am not."

"Then what should I call you?" She asked.

"Anything you want." He said, all interest lost in his voice.

She thought for a moment. Coming upon an idea, she blurted out, "Beary!"

The tribal man came to a stop. His eyes shifted over to her with a look of annoyance. Endelynn turned away and tried to avert her eyes, hiding her sheepish face.

"You may call me Kuruk." He said, and continued walking in silence.

"Yes, Kuruk." Endelynn repeated. "That sounds better." She followed Kuruk through the forest, this way and that, until they came to a village much like the Wolf Tribe's. This village, however, was smaller. Most of the Longhouses were in horrid states of disrepair, the wood was rotten and falling apart. The totem poles, unlike the vibrantly colored and painted ones in the Wolf village, were faded and dull. Cracks split down the length of the totems.

Only a single Longhouse was still in good condition. Kuruk went to this one, and Endelynn followed. Inside it was modestly furnished, much like those from the Wolf Tribe. There was an empty fire pit with only some long cold ash in the center, a simple bed composed of blankets and animal furs, a stack of wood and kindling for fires, racks for drying meat and cooking fish, assorted weapons for hunting and defense, and bowls and baskets. It appeared that everything of use had been gathered in this one lodge.

Endelynn sat down beside the cold fire pit. Kuruk laid Shunka down on the floor, then set about gathering wood for a fire. He set a bundle of sticks in a cone shape with some dried leaves and twigs in the middle. Using a fire board with a notch, he placed a dry stick into the notch and rubbed his hands back and forth across it. Endelynn watched as smoke began to rise from the wood. Kuruk pulled the thin stick from the notch and blew into the hole. A small, glowing ember, rested in the bottom. He lifted the fire board and dropped the ember into the nest of twigs and leaves. A small flames appeared, which spread and grew. The kindling caught ablaze, and Kuruk added more wood.

The fire burned bright in the pit. Endelynn stretched her hands to it, warming herself. Her clothes were still wet from the river, and they chilled her straight through. The fire was welcome.

"Your friend has been poisoned." Kuruk said as he rummaged through the plant supplies. "Your people call it the Blood of the Fire Rose." He took a bowl and filled it with red berries, a few leaves, and some crushed root powder. Taking a stone pommel, he ground them all together until they turned into a mushy paste.

"Can you save him?" Endelynn asked.

"Yes. Blood of the Fire Rose is deadly if untreated, but the antidote is easy enough to make." Kuruk brought the bowl with the mixture back to Shunka and smeared a little on the raised skin where the dart had stuck him. Then, pushing the younger man's mouth open, he dabbed more of it on his tongue. "Why would they try to kill him?"

"They didn't," Endelynn said, her voice filled with guilt. "The dart was meant for me."

"Oh," Kuruk muttered under his breath.

"He's protected me," Endelynn continued. "He's suffering to protect me."

"You needn't worry. Shunka is strong," Kuruk said. "Much stronger than even he, or his father, suspects."

"But why?" She asked. "The Hawk Tribe offered to forgive him if he let them kill me, but he turned them down. He defied their Chaa and even took the poisoned dart for me." Her heart ached. It pained her to watch him suffer on her behalf. She turned to face Kuruk, tears formed in the corners of her eyes. "Why would he do so much for me?"

The bear shifter shook his head. "I cannot say." Kuruk said. "That of all the members of the Wolf Tribe, he would be the one to take a foreign captive is a mystery."

"Why do you say that?" Endelynn dried her eyes.

Kuruk set the bowl and pommel aside. He crossed his arms and stared into the fire. The light danced off his old, worn face casting shadows along his deep creases. "How long have you been with the Wolves?"

"Um," Endelynn muttered. She honestly couldn't remember now, it felt like months. But she'd only had one Moon cycle, so it couldn't be that long. "A few weeks, I think."

"And this boy has been at your side that whole time?" Kuruk asked.

"He has." Endelynn nodded, and then, "well, except when I spent a week in the House of the Moon. And when he left to marry that Hawk lady. Her name was Shikoba."

"Shikoba?" Kuruk said with astonishment. "The daughter of Orumaku, Chaa of the Hawk Tribe?"

"I suppose. I don't know everyone's names yet." Endelynn admitted. "Why? What does that mean?"

"It means Shunka has greatly insulted the grand elder of a powerful clan, all for the sake of what most would consider some foreign girl." Kuruk said with a empty shaking of his head. "I don't know why he would do this. Shunka has more reason than most to hate the pale men."

More reason than most. It wasn't as though the others in the tribe treated her with any great kindness. Endelynn sat across the fire from the old man. "Tell me."

Kuruk shook his head again. "I should not say. It concerns the boy's mother."

"His mother?" Now that she thought of it, Endelynn didn't remember seeing, or even hearing of Shunka's mother. "What happened to her?"

"I just told you," the old man stood, he looked down at her with hard eyes that betrayed no emotions, "it is not my place to say. If he ever wants you to learn, it will come from his mouth and not mine." He turned and walked towards the door, stopping only to grab a two-pronged fishing spear and a net of reeds. "You may stay here until he has recovered," the bear man stood in the door frame, his massive body blocking the light, "but the two of you will leave my village after that." Then he stepped outside, leaving Endelynn alone with Shunka.

XXXVII.
RODDRICK

They made an unlikely pair; one disguised knight from another kingdom and one disguised prince living in exile. They walked together in silence. The back alleys and crowded ghetto streets of Kahren's capital, the Fang, made for a dangerous, difficult journey. The houses down here were little more than shacks, sometimes stacked four high on one another, with rickety ladders leading up to the higher floors.

This was another symptom of Kendrick's mismanagement of the throne. All this rampant poverty. More than one person they passed huddled in a doorway dressed in rags and holding a half empty jug.

Roddrick couldn't bring himself to look upon such a depressing sight for more than a few moments before having to turn away. He could do nothing about it now. He would work to fix all this once he was king. Until then, all he could do was observe.

"How much further is this place?" The Dadrian knight, Aridain asked.

"Not much." Roddrick said. He tugged on the leather strap across his shoulder and resettled the axe across his back. He kept his weapon hidden under his green cloak.

"Who are these people we're going to meet anyways?"

Aridain continued his questions.

"They call themselves the Red Brothers. A mercenary organization." Roddrick replied. "A small band of cutthroats and murderers. Folks who will do almost anything if there's a suitable price."

"You think they're the ones who took the princess?"

Roddrick turned around and held up a single finger. "Don't talk about that." He said. " I don't know how it is in Dadria, but there are eyes and ears all over Kahren and most of them belong to the king. And he would love nothing more than to see my head removed from my neck and placed on a spike above the castle walls. And he would probably not be upset if yours was beside it."

They came to an alley. The heavy smell of rotting trash and human refuse wafted out between those buildings and hung in the air. Roddrick lifted the collar of his tunic to cover his nose, then stepped inside. He walked a fair distance down this passageway when he realized his companion wasn't with him. Turning around, he saw Aridain standing at the mouth of the alley, his hand over his mouth.

"You can't be serious." The Dadrian knight took his hand away to speak, then retched and gagged, quickly covering his face again.

"I am." Roddrick called back, his face still under the collar of his tunic. "Now, come on." He continued down the filthy alley. He'd learned long ago not to worry about dirt and grunge, if anything it only further hid him from Kendrick's spies.

A man sat on the ground, his back against a wall with with a clay bowl at his side. Roddrick stopped beside him, and the man looked up. His beard was ash colored with specks of black, but his head was mostly bald. The old man's clothes were little more than rags. "You have any coin to spare?" the beggar asked.

Roddrick reached into the purse at his waist and pulled out

a silver coin. He dropped it in the bowl where it landed with a loud clang. "Take me to your boss. He's expecting me."

The beggar took the coin from the bowl and inspected it. After a few twirls between his dirty fingers, he slipped the coin into his shirt and stood. "You're late." He said, and tapped his knuckles against the wall behind him.

Just then, the wall opened to reveal a hidden door. Roddrick blinked, then regained his composure. "Come along, then." The beggar said as he stepped through the doorway. Roddrick followed him inside just as Aridain reached his side. Once they were all inside, the door closed, encompassing them in darkness. The pair walked down this new dark hallway, lead by their mysterious guide.

They came to a large, circular room. There was a stone hearth with a blazing fire within, and a large, soft cushioned chair with a man seated in it. He held and was reading from an open book when he heard their approaching footsteps.

"Boss," their beggar guide said, "the exile is here."

The book closed in the man's pudgy hands. He rose from the chair, which creaked and groaned as his weight lifted from the frame, and tucked the book under his arm as he turned to face them. "Roddrick," he said in a raspy voice, "fancy meeting you." He gave a dismissive wave to the beggar man, who turned and disappeared into the shadows.

"Evening, Jorne." Roddrick tilted his head forward in a slight bow. "I've been looking forward to seeing you in person for quite some time."

"Yes, I know." The large man, Jorne, crossed the room in three great steps and placed the book on a small shelf. He seemed to flow rather than walk, strange for a man of his size. "I've heard rumors about you, they circle all throughout Kahren. People everywhere talking about the Exiled King. Some think you're only a myth designed to inspire the poor. Others think you exist but are merely a liar claiming to be the

285

lost prince to gain power. So when word reached my ears that you wanted a meeting with me, I was a little shocked." He came back into view, holding his hands behind his back. "So, how may I be of use to the leader of the underground resistance?"

"I need some information." Roddrick said. "Concerning a job some of your men took recently."

"We've taken many jobs." Jorne smirked. "I can't remember every single one. You may have to refresh my memory a little."

"It concerned the Dadrian princess." Roddrick continued. "She was abducted on her way to marry Prince Sedrick. I want to know by whom, and for what reason."

"Hm." Jorne closed his eyes, then moved back to his chair and seated himself. The chair groaned under his weight. "Before we get to anything, I'm gonna need some proof that you are who you say you are."

Roddrick snorted, then loosened the ties around the vambrace on his wrist. It slipped away and he raised his arm into the fire light, exposing the deer antler birthmark. "Is this good enough?"

"Ha! Hardly." The mercenary leader scoffed. "House Stagghart always claims that mark signifies their royal lineage, but half the fools in this band have the deer antlers on their arms. There was an idiot that worked for me named Rayleigh who had a mark just like that, does that make him the lost prince?"

"I can't make a claim for Rayleigh, nor of the illegitimate born children of my House." Roddrick pulled the vambrace on his wrist and laced it up. "All I can say is I was not killed in the hunting accident as my brother proclaimed."

"If you say so." He shifted in the chair and placed one foot across his knee. "It doesn't matter too much. I happen to remember the job you speak off. It's not often we get hired for something so high profile."

"It was your people then!" Aridain stepped forward, pushing past Roddrick and reaching for the dagger at his belt. "You who took her!"

Roddrick grasped the Dadrian knight and yanked him back. "Stop." He hissed. "You can't blame the hands for what the head told them to do." His grip on Aridain's shoulder tightened. "Leave the talking to me." Roddrick turned back the the mercenary boss. "Sorry, he's a little over zealous."

"That's fine. Aren't we all just a little excited at times." Jorne said with a sly smirk.

"But you were hired to kidnap the princess?" Roddrick asked. "That is what you said, isn't it?"

"Aye, we were." Jorne confirmed.

"When? And by whom?"

"About a month ago, if I'm not mistaken." The mercenary said. "It was before the young prince and his entourage set out for Dadria. A man dressed in black with dark hair and a beard approached us with a bag of gold and a job."

"A Black Sword." Roddrick observed. "What did this job entail?"

"We were to wait at Haddrick's Keep while he and the prince journeyed to Dadria, and when they came back and we learned of good ol' King Cassius's death, we were told to wait about a single day's ride from Dadria to intercept the princess."

"And what were you to do with her?" Aridain asked, and Roddrick could hear the anger boiling just under his voice. The knight grasped at the handle of his dagger.

"The instructions were to kill her guards, take the girl to a rendezvous point, and wait for the prince. The boy and his knights would attack, my mercenaries would retreat before the young prince's might, and the girl would be smitten by her dashing rescuer." Jorne answered. "And once we were finished, we would be paid three more bags of gold coins."

"That sounds rather lucrative." Roddrick commented.

"It would've been, if my men ever came back from this mission." Jorne replied. "But that was weeks ago, and nothing came of it."

"Do you have a record of this?"

"Of course. We take all our contracts in writing, as a preemptive just in case they try to weasel us out of our money." Jorne said.

"I'd like a copy of that contract." Roddrick placed his hand on the pouch of silver coins at his waist. "I'll buy it off you if you'd like."

"I'm sure you would, but I already have a buyer." The mercenary said.

The door behind them, the same one they came in through, creaked open again. Roddrick and Aridain both turned and saw a man emerge from the shadows, dressed all in black with a gold crown and sword emblazoned on his tunic.

"Ah, what perfect timing!" Jorne rose from his seat and raised his arms in the air. "Sir Mordrane of the Black Swords of the King, I have the contract right here, just as you requested." He pulled a scroll from his robes.

"Good." The Black Swordsman said. He eyed both Roddrick and Aridain. "And a pair of traitorous rebels, it looks like."

"Nay, not just rebels." The mercenary boss said, almost unable to contain his excitement. "This one here claims to be the long lost eldest son of the late King Osrick." He pointed towards Roddrick.

"The lost prince?" Mordrane said with astonishment. He turned to more directly address Roddrick. "An unexpected situation. I would tip my hat to you, your grace, but as you can see my head is currently bare."

Roddrick did not reply, simply ground his teeth. He reached one hand behind his back and grasped the handle of his battle axe.

288

The Black Swordsman shoved his way past Roddrick and Aridain. He took a pouch of coins from his waist and upended its contents into his hand. A pile of gold coins spilled out into his gloved palm and slipped between his fingers to land with tings and clangs against the floor. He then cupped the coins and poured them back into the purse before pulling the string taunt. "Is this sufficient?"

"Absolutely." Jorne replied. Sir Mordrane offered the bag of gold and extended his open hand. The two men swapped items in an instant. "Glad to do business with you."

Mordrane turned back to Roddrick and unrolled the scroll. He examined it silently to himself, smiled, and rolled it back up. "It's authentic, if that's what you're wondering. It even bares his majesty's seal." His fingers tightened around the parchment, and then he tossed it into the fireplace, where the paper blackened to ash.

The next incident happened almost too fast for Roddrick to follow. The Black Sword drew a dagger from his belt, spun around on his heels, and slashed the throat of the mercenary leader. Jorne's eyes grew wide with shock. He dropped the bag of gold and reached for his neck, waves of red already pouring from the gash and down his front. A gurgling noise came from his throat as he tried to gasp or scream, and then slacked in the chair.

Mordrane turned back to them, the bloody dagger still in hand. "No witnesses." He reached across his body with his other hand and drew a long sword.

Roddrick slid the strap of his battle axe off his back and took the grip in both hands. Aridain drew his dagger. "Yeah, no witnesses." Roddrick's grip tightened. "Just like the last time you tried to kill me."

"A mistake." Mordrane said. "I shouldn't have left you to the bear. I won't make it again." He tossed the dagger in the air, snatched it by the blade, and threw it at Roddrick's head.

The exiled prince jumped back. The twirling blade flew past his head and stuck in the wall behind him. In that instant, the Black Sword charged forward with his sword at the ready. He raised it over his head and brought it down with all the strength he could muster. Roddrick lifted his axe and the two weapons met in a ringing of steel and a flash of sparks.

Aridain slashed at Mordrane. The Black Sword grabbed his black cloak and threw it out in front of him. Aridain's dagger tore through the fabric, but soon became entangled. Mordrane smirked and brought his fist against the Dadrian knight's face. Aridain recoiled from the hit and tumbled to the ground.

Mordrane snatched the knight's dagger from his cloak and twirled it between his fingers. Before Aridain could regain his footing, Mordrane took the dagger and threw it like he did before. This time, the Black Sword hit his target. The steel blade ripped straight through Aridain's clothes and embedded itself in his left side. Blood spurted up from the wound.

Roddrick took up his axe again and swung in an upward arc. The Black Sword dodged easily, taking step after step backwards as Roddrick pushed forward. Mordrane dove to the side just as Roddrick brought his axe down. The steel blade of his axe buried in the skull of Jorne's corpse.

He tugged and yanked on the axe handle, but the blade remained lodged. It's what Mordrane wanted, of course. Roddrick had let his frustration take over and swung with enough force it didn't matter what he hit, his axe would've gotten stuck anyways.

Mordrane let out a soft chuckle and spun the sword in his hand. "Kendrick will be quite pleased when I bring him back your head." He raised his sword again and prepared to attack. The Black Sword came to a sudden halt and his eyes bulged from their sockets. He lurched, the sword dropped from his hand and clattered to the floor.

Aridain stood behind the Black Sword. One hand clutched

the gash in his side, blood still oozed between his fingers and dripped to a growing puddle on the floor. His other hand clutched the hilt of his dagger, the blade of which was buried to the pommel in Sir Mordrane's back. The Black Swordsman fell to his knees, gritting his teeth in pain.

Roddrick took the fallen sword. He said nothing, merely raised it over his shoulder, then swung with all his strength and took Sir Mordrane's head from his shoulders. The decapitated body fell to the floor.

Roddrick threw the sword to the ground. He grabbed the handle of his axe and placed his foot on Jorne's chair for better leverage, and wrenched the axe head free with a wet plop.

"Are you alright?" Roddrick asked the injured knight. "Can you walk?"

"I think so." Aridain said through clenched teeth. He took two steps, then his legs gave out from under him and he collapsed to his knees. "No," he muttered, "I can't."

"Come on." Roddrick slung the axe across his back and pulled Aridain's free arm over his shoulders. "We've got to get you to a healer."

"I don't think I can make it." Aridain's voice grew weaker. He tried to walk with Roddrick, but soon his legs couldn't even do that. "I want you to give a message to her highness from me."

"Whatever you have to say you can tell her yourself." Roddrick dragged the dying man back through the long, dark corridor. They came out the hidden door into the alley and Roddrick had to step over the dead body of the old beggar man from before. So, it appeared the Black Sword killed him first.

"Tell her I'm sorry." Aridain's speech weakened. "I couldn't keep my promise." His hand slipped from Roddrick's grasp and the knight collapsed.

XXXVIII.
ENDELYNN

She slit a flint knife along the underside of a large trout. Her nose wrinkled and face twisted with disgust as yellow-orange eggs spilled out onto the wooden cutting surface. Close by, Kuruk did the same. He showed no sign of discomfort as he scraped away the fish's scales, gutted it, and cut off the head. When he'd returned with his reed net full of fish, he'd enlisted Endelynn's help in preparing them.

"Are they dead?" Endelynn asked with trepidation, eyeing the net of motionless fish.

"Mostly." Kuruk said as he set them on the ground. As he opened the net, one of the trout wriggled, thrashing up and down. The old Sequoia man grasped the fish by the tail and bashed it against the ground. "Now it is."

Endelynn placed her hands across her mouth, both in shock and in disgust. She could see the blood leaking out of the fish's burst eye. "I don't think I can do this."

"If you want to eat tonight you will help me." Kuruk took a chiseled piece of flint and held it out for her to take. "I will show you."

They had two wooden bowls full of water for cleaning and another to place the severed heads and entrails in. Endelynn found herself almost puking at the sight of Kuruk preparing them. The smell was overwhelming.

292

Of the seven fish the old bear caught, four had been gutted and cleaned by Kuruk. He just finished with the fifth and set it aside when he looked back up at Endelynn. With his direction, she had managed to finish one and was in the middle of preparing her second. As she worked, the tribal man spoke. "You remind me of my daughter."

"What?" She said, caught by surprise. The fish almost slipped from her grasp, but she caught it and placed it back on the prepping surface.

"My daughter." Kuruk reiterated. "She also hated cleaning and gutting fish." At first he laughed, then a look of sadness came over the old man's face. It was mournful, almost like happy memories had been tainted by harsh reality. "Whenever the men and I came back with salmon from the river, she would groan and stomp her feet like an anxious child."

"What was her name?" Endelynn asked before she could stop, and winced at her own stupidity. She hadn't meant to ask, it was just one of those things you say. If the old bear had been so adamant about keeping his name secret, he would never share the name of someone so precious to him. "I'm sorry," she said, "forget I asked."

"It is fine." Kuruk answered. "Her name was Miska. She was about your age when she died, along with the rest of my tribe." Kuruk stood up and started setting up a spit rod to cook the fish.

"Oh," Endelynn uttered the word quietly, with regret. "I'm sorry." She finished cleaning the trout and gave it back to the older man, making sure not to meet his eyes.

"You want to ask, but are afraid to." It was a statement, not a question. "You want to know what happened to my people, but are worried about sounding rude." Kuruk impaled the fish along a pair of wooden rods and placed them over the fire.

Endelynn dipped her hands in the bowls of water to wash away the stray scales. She continued to keep her gaze averted.

"That's not it at all." There was an aching in her chest as she cleaned her hands. "I just know..." she tried to talk, but could not find the words to say when she wanted. "What happened to your tribe, it was the fault of my ancestors, wasn't it?"

"Is that what they've told you?" Kuruk said. He stood and walked to where Shunka lay in his comatose state. The old bear pulled a blanket up so it rested across the younger man's chest. "The other clans have a much harsher view of the pale men than I do. The Wolves are the most lenient, but that is not saying much compared to the harshness of the Panthers and Hawks. No, it was not your people. At least, not as directly as you might think."

"Then what was it?" Endelynn asked.

"It was the Creature." Kuruk's voice dropped as he said it. He returned to the fire pit and sat across from Endelynn, the flames cast dark shadows across the lines in his face. "It was the consumer of man. The monster that devours the world."

Endelynn's eyes grew wide. Her heart began to beat faster and her fingers tightened into fists on her knees. She'd heard some of these names before when the older Dadrian woman, Uyoonta, last spoke to her. "The Wendigo."

"You know of it." Kuruk said without looking at her.

She nodded. "The old woman, the one who helped teach me your language, she spoke of it briefly while I was in the House of the Moon. She said they killed the last one."

"And that was almost twenty summers ago." Kuruk took a stick and prodded at the fire. "A Wendigo appears every so often, when the hearts of our people are filled with greed and corruption. When the tribes are in conflict with one another and fighting amongst themselves."

"Where do they come from?" Endelynn asked before she could stop herself.

Kuruk pulled his stick from the fire and rested it over his knees. He locked his gaze on her, his eyes betrayed nothing.

"Why do you wish to know?"

"It's just," Endelynn's thumbs fidgeted on her lap. "In my Moon Dreams I saw it. A monster that looked like a rotting deer carcass chasing me through the forest. No matter how I tried I couldn't escape this thing, and in the end it would always catch me and start to eat me. That's when I would wake up." She explained. "I guess, since then, I've had it on my mind."

"A dream of blood." Kuruk said.

"A what?" Endelynn asked.

"A certain kind of Moon Dream, one foretelling of death." Kuruk said, his eyes now wide with fear. "Very well. I will tell you." He stood and walked to one of the clay jars that lined the walls of the lodge. He scooped a handful of blueish-gray powder and brought it back to the fire, then threw it on the coals.

A burst of white smoke filled the air. Endelynn fell backwards, bracing herself with one arm as she threw the other across her face to shield her eyes.

"Hundreds of years ago," Kuruk's voice rang out, "the first Wendigo came down from the north." Endelynn pulled her arm away from her eyes. Smoke filled the lodge, shadows cast by the fire light danced along the underside. Images of the forest and of a mountain appeared in the shadows. A village grew out from the shadows, with shapes of people walking around. Suddenly, the trees began to sway in a fierce wind as snow fell and a blizzard settled over the village. "One day, the weather began to turn cold, harsher than the worst winter any elder could remember." Kuruk's hypnotic voice spoke. Then the trees parted as an enormous creature appeared. It towered over the trees themselves, and had a thin, skeletal body with a deer skull for a head.

The people in the village tried to run, but the creature reached with its clawed fingers and snatched them by the handful. Its mouth full of gnarled, fang-like teeth gaped open

295

and devoured the villagers. "The Wendigo suffers from insatiable hunger. It can never consume enough to fill its belly, as the more it eats the larger it grows." Endelynn saw it was true. As the monster in the shadow ate more and more of the villagers, it grew in proportion. Soon, the entire village was gone.

Kuruk swished his hands through the smoke. The shadows reformed and the Wendigo reappeared, this time surrounded on all sides by different animals. Some wolves, panthers, hawks, and bears. The animals all attacked it, but while they appeared to overwhelm it, the monster just stood up again and knocked them back. "Our warriors fought bravely, and many died. For there is only one way to kill a Wendigo."

Another wave of his hands and the shadows changed again. An archer appeared. He pulled an arrow from his quiver, and even in the shadows Endelynn could see something different about the arrowhead. It seemed to shimmer and glisten more than flint or regular obsidian. "An arrow or spear made from Rainbow Obsidian is the only thing that can restrain the creature, but it can not be killed except by fire. For the Wendigo is a beast of the cold, frozen north." The archer fired his arrow and it struck the Wendigo in the chest. The monster's jaws flew open as if roaring in pain and it fell back. As it lay on the ground, clawing at the arrow in its chest, a trio of hawks flew over the fallen beast and dropped burning torches on it. Soon the Wendigo was engulfed in flames. The fire in the shadows dissipated and in its wake remained only a human skeleton, that then dissolved into dust.

The smoke began to clear as it drifted up through the smoke hole. The fire settled back down, burning low but steady in the fire pit. "This was the creature that killed my people." Kuruk said at last.

Endelynn stared at the place where the smoke shadows had danced long after they were gone. The images lingered in her mind. A horrible monster that couldn't be killed, but consumed all in its path.

"You have nothing to say?" Kuruk asked, and his words brought Endelynn back to the present.

"I don't know what to say." Endelynn said. "You've confided a lot in me, and I know that takes a lot of trust. Especially to trust an outsider."

"You are not the first foreigner I've come to trust." Kuruk gave a smile.

"No?" Endelynn asked in shock. "The Wolf Clan always said I could never leave once I learned of them. That it could spell doom for their people. Who did you befriend?"

Kuruk ignored the question. "The other tribes hold onto the past too rigidly. I've lived a long life, seen many things and lost many friends. Something I've learned in all those years is that I cannot hold on to old grudges forever."

"But, what my people did–" Endelynn began but was stopped by Kuruk's raised hand.

"Is all in the past. None are alive today that fought in those wars. To look to the future, the past must be understood, but ultimately forgiven. Hate is like a poison, but instead of giving it to your enemy you drink it yourself. Is that wise?"

"Why would anyone drink poison?"

"Why indeed." Kuruk said.

The scent of cooked fish filled the lodge. The skewers had been roasted quite effectively and were ready to eat. Kuruk took the cooked fish and gave one to Endelynn. She peeled the skin away and ate it delicately, picking the bones from the meat and setting them aside.

"That last figure," Endelynn said between mouthfuls, "the one who shot the arrow that killed the Wendigo, was that anyone in particular? Or was it just a representation of the warriors as a whole?"

"It was a single person." Kuruk explained. "You are still

eager for knowledge, aren't you?"

"If you are willing to share, I'd like to know more." Endelynn said.

"The Wolves have a legend," Kuruk said as he poked at the glowing coals with a stick, "it is very old, going back even before the war with your people, and it tells of a heroic figure."

Endelynn listened to his words with great intensity. She leaned forward, as if getting closer could make the story better.

"He has had many names throughout the ages, as he has been born and reborn many times. A brave warrior of the Wolf Tribe. To most, he is simply called Wahyuk." Kuruk explained.

Endelynn blinked in confusion. "But Wahyuk just means wolf," she said.

"Just as Kuruk means bear." The older man replied. "What you haven't come to understand yet is how names are important. Most of the time a person doesn't give out their own name, a close friend or family introduces them instead. I have no living family or real close friends, so I tell you to call me Bear, as I am the last of my people. In that same vein, the hero of wolf legend has had so many names, he is best just called Wolf." He set the stick aside and looked across the flames to Endelynn. "Do you wish to hear the story or not?"

"Yes, please." Endelynn said, and settled back to listen.

"The last time Wahyuk came to his people was during the days of the War of Invaders." Kuruk explained. "The fighting was going bad for his people. For my people as well. All the clans were suffering and dying at the steel weapons and overwhelming power of the invading men. They rode through villages on their horses and raox, cutting down men and women with no remorse.

"Along the coast, the tribes of Orca and of Raven were completely destroyed. Every settlement burned and every child slaughtered. The Elk tribe had been cut down to only a few still alive. Sometimes a battle could be won, but this was no longer

298

a war. It had become a massacre. Soon, all would be dead.

"But that's when the Sky Father sent a vision to a young Wolf warrior. He told the boy to craft a blade from rainbow obsidian, the rarest kind of obsidian in the world, and then take it to the greatest redwood in the forest, the Tree of Life. Once he got there, he was beset by a large black wolf. They fought, and in the end he managed to kill the beast by stabbing it through the heart with his rainbow obsidian knife.

"He placed the wolf's body at the base of the tree and offered a prayer to the Sky Father. As soon as his prayer was complete, the young warrior knew what he had to do. He took the knife, still covered in wolf's blood, and plunged it into his own heart."

Endelynn gasped and placed her hands over her mouth. She hadn't realized just how engrossed in the story she was until that moment.

"And then it happened," Kuruk continued. "He pulled the knife from his chest and the Mark of the Wolf appeared over his heart. And he changed, his skin fell away and became that of the wolf. He was the first Skin-changer.

"The young warrior returned to his village and told his elders what had transpired. Some thought it a sin and wanted him condemned, but others recognized it as the gift from the Sky Father. The gift was soon transferred to all members of the Wolf Clan, and all who followed in the bloodline would inherit this power.

"As the Wolf Clan began to turn the tide against the invader army, the other tribes heard of the power they possessed. The remaining clans of Bear, Panther, and Hawk all repeated the ritual at the Tree of Life and were granted the power of the animals as well. It became known as the Ritual of Beasts. Because of this, the war turned in our favor and the foreigners built their walls to hide behind.

"The young Wolf warrior, however, was horribly injured in

the battle and succumb to his injuries After his death, the shaman of his village foretold of his return as a wolf with fur red as flame, born to a woman called the Aleutsi, the Great Mother. To this day, those of the Wolf Clan wait for the appearance of the Aleutsi and the birth of the Red Wolf, for it's said the Red Wolf would arise when his people were in their greatest need."

"He was the one who shot the arrow and killed the Wendigo." Endelynn exclaimed.

"He was." Kuruk said.

A low groan came from the far end of the Longhouse. Endelynn turned and saw Shunka squirming. "Is he alright?"

"He is fine. Sometimes when a person is poisoned with the Fire Rose, they may have fierce dreams and visions." Kuruk said. "He'll awaken in time."

XXXIX.
TALA

"This was an attack on our village!" Kitchi, the Warrior Elder's, powerful voice rang through the council Longhouse. He, the Chaa, and all the other elders had gathered. "The boy was attacked by a squadron of Hawks while still within our borders. That is an act of war. Reprimands must be made!"

"Shunka was not our target. Only the foreigner girl." The Hawk warrior maiden, Shikoba, retorted. "We were only fulfilling our duty, which you Wolves seem to have forgotten."

"We have forgotten nothing." Kitchi shouted back. "How this tribe deals with the invaders is only the business of this tribe, and none other."

Tala stood at the back of the Longhouse. Mingan, and a few other Wolf warriors at her side. They shared a mutual glance, but remained silent. They'd been the ones to bring Shikoba and her entourage of Hawk Tribe archers to the village. They'd heard the commotion down at the river and came to investigate, only to find a massive hawk circling the waterfall and five archers crouched in trees. One of those archers had a dart shooter and a pouch full of darts, all coated with Blood of the Fire Rose.

"It becomes the business of the other clans when it affects them." Shikoba snapped. "And your insults to the Hawks will

301

not go unanswered."

"Then we will answer them." Ahote Chaa stood and raised a hand to silence the hall. "But as long as I am Chaa of the Wolves, then I will deal with the actions of my people. I do not need the interference of another tribe on my lands."

"And what of the boy?" Kitchi said. "Your own son, attacked and possibly killed. Will you not answer this insult?"

"It will be dealt with." Ahote Chaa directed his words as the Warrior Elder, then turned back to the Hawks. "One of you will go back to your village and speak with Orumaku. Tell him he and the rest of his Council of Elders are summoned to the village of Ahote to finally deal with this issue of the foreign girl."

"How are you to deal with her if you do not have her?" Shikoba asked.

"On the morrow, the rest of you will lead my warriors to the last place you saw the girl and my son. They will finish tracking them down and bring them back to this village." Ahote said.

"Very well." Shikoba answered.

"And if my son is brought back dead, I will have your life as recompense." The Chaa stated, his eyes as cold as ice as he stared down at The Hawk warrior maiden. "Is that understood?"

"It is." Shikoba said, then turned to leave. She and her Hawk archers strutted past the wolf warriors, each giving the other a look of defiance.

The sky was ablaze with reds and purples as the sun slowly sank below the tree line. It was too late to start searching tonight, the Hawk's vision would be useless. They dispersed into the village, the Hawks all going to the communal Longhouse to wait until morning, except for the one who shifted to his animal form and took off flying back to his village.

302

"What do you think happened to them?" Mingan came to Tala's side.

"Washed down the river." Tala said flatly. "How far, who knows. Maybe all the way to the sea. The Hawk woman said she did not see them surface."

"Shunka wouldn't fall like that." Mingan said. "He's too strong. Maybe he's hiding behind the waterfall itself, just waiting for sundown."

"Maybe." Tala replied. "And if he is, then we will learn later tonight."

"I'm looking forward to it." Mingan hissed. His fists clenched and shoulders tensed. "I can't believe our brother was supposed to be joined with that wicked little bitch." He cursed. "If I get the chance, I will take it to kill her myself." He then stormed off, leaving Tala alone.

She stood alone by the central fire pit for a while afterward. There was to be no gathering and feasting tonight, nor any stories. In light of recent events, no one was in the mood. Tala came to wait beside the entrance of the Council Longhouse for her father. Raised voices drifted out, and she couldn't help but listen in.

"Every decision you've made since choosing to form a union between Shunka and Shikoba has ended poorly!" The angry voice she recognized as Kitchi, the Warrior Elder. "Who is really to blame for this situation?"

"What do you insinuate?" Ahote Chaa retorted.

"I think the time has come to choose a new Chaa." Kitchi said. "Someone who won't cave so easily to the whims of other Chaa or undisciplined children."

"We haven't held a Chaa Rantuuk in fifteen years." The voice was familiar, that of her father. "There is no reason to hold one now."

"On that matter, I must disagree." That was a woman's voice, that of Onatah the Elder Den Mother. "A new, stronger leader is needed now."

Tala listened with apprehension. For as long as she could remember, Ahote had been Chaa of their village. The idea that that could change brought a new level of stress she did not want. She held her breath, eager to hear more even though she did not want to know more.

"To hold a Chaa Rantuuk requires either the sitting Chaa to die, step down, or a majority of council members to call for it." Her father, Alo, stated. "Kiyiya, you are the only member who has not voiced their opinion. What do you say?"

Kiyiya was the Elder Builder. He had been a long time friend of Ahote, as far as Tala knew. There was no way he would fall on the side of displacing the current Chaa.

"I withhold my opinions." Kiyiya said. "I will not oppose Ahote Chaa at the moment. But depending on the next few days, I may change my mind."

A new tremor shook through Tala. They were so close, on the precipice of taking Shunka and Mingan's father from leadership, stopped only by the indecision of one council member.

"We can discuss this later," Ahote's voice rang out again, "after the matter of the foreign child and the Hawk Tribe is settled. Right now, I believe rest is required."

Tala jumped away from the door of the Council Longhouse and returned to the cold fire pit. Her father was the first to exit, moving along using his staff as a walking stick. The bones and colored stones on his staff rattled with each step.

"Father," Tala said when she saw him.

"I trust you heard what we were discussing," he said with no hesitation or pretense.

She'd been caught. "What? No. I mean . . ." Tala stumbled over her words.

"You shouldn't worry yourself over it," her father said with a kind smile. "All you need concern yourself with is finding

Shunka tomorrow. Come, you need your rest."

That night, Tala did not sleep well. Usually, sleep came easily for her. As soon as she crawled into bed and pulled the blankets over her, she would be asleep. But her mind was too full of thoughts and worry for rest to come. She tossed and turned, tugging the blankets this way and that as she searched for a comfortable spot.

She must've slept at some point, as she was awoken by her father the next morning. "Daughter," his hand pressed against her shoulder and pushed her lightly, "daughter, Mingan and the others are waiting outside for you."

She groaned and sat up, the blankets collapsing in her lap. Her eyes ached, her body ached. She'd never felt lest rested in her life. "Alright." Her voice scratched. She stood and raised her arms high above her head, stretching her back and chest muscles.

As soon as she finished dressing and straightening her braid, Tala stepped outside and was greeted by the faces of her fellow Wolf warriors, including Mingan, as well as those of the Hawk Clan.

"You overslept." Mingan said. "They wanted to leave at first light, but I made them wait for you."

"Thank you." Tala said.

"Come on, then. Let's move out." Mingan ordered.

They headed out into the woods, following the flow of the river. Everyone shifted into their animal forms, the Hawks soaring overhead while the Wolves moved along the riverbanks.

By midday, they came upon the waterfall. Tala let out a snort and scraped her paw at the rocks beside the thundering falls. She glanced up at the circling hawks overhead and felt a low rumble form in her throat. This was were they attacked her brother, those hypocritical feathered fiends. They kept talking about how wrong it was to bring the foreign girl to the village

305

and how Shunka had forsaken his oaths, but the pale girl had done nothing to harm him. The same could not be said of the Hawks.

Mingan barked at her and they started to move again. They eased down the stones and jutting rocks beside the waterfall until they came to the pool below. Tala climbed the slick, wet rocks behind the falls and scented the air and ground. It was musky and dank, the smell of wet earth, but the cave held no scent of either Shunka or the girl.

They continued down river. Not much further, Tala noticed something dark against the tan sand. As they approached, her heart raced when she recognized it. That was an obsidian knife, one of Shunka's. She raced ahead, leaving a confused Mingan behind.

Coming upon the knife, she found it in lying beside a depression in the sand about the length of a body. She pressed her nose to the ground and sniffed. It was Shunka's scent. All around it were a series of further prints. They smelled of the foreign girl. And someone else. Looking away from the knife, she spotted the enormous footprints in the sand that lead out of the forest. Pressing her nose to them, she caught and recognized the scent.

Tala shifted from her wolf back to human form as Mingan approached. The Hawks landed nearby and likewise returned to their human selves. "This is where they came out of the river," she said, taking up the obsidian knife, "and that's the way they went."

"Then you got their scent, like a good dog," Shikoba smirked and Tala narrowed her eyes. "Well, get along. Follow the trail."

"I don't have to." Tala flipped the knife in her hand and fixed a glare on the Hawk warrior. "I already know where they are." She gave a knowing smile. "With Kuruk of the Bear Tribe."

XL.
SHUNKA

His eyes snapped open and he found himself in the Sequoia. The mighty red-barked trees jutted straight up in the sky, reaching for the clouds like the arms of so many children.

Shunka turned around in a circle to gauge his surroundings. He stood in a clearing, the trees at least fifty feet away in every direction, and the ground covered in a blanket of grass that reached his ankles. He had no memory of how he came here. This part of the Sequoia was unknown to him. He didn't even know what direction he should go.

Looking up again, he found there was no sun. The sky was as bright and blue as midday in summer, but the sun could not be found. That struck him as odd, but not as odd as it should. It seemed normal, like that had always been the way of the world. Still, none of this helped him find his way.

A low bark caught his attention and drew him back to the trees. At the edge of the forest, resting on their haunches, were a pair of wolf pups. They were young, a couple of months old at best, and staring at him.

Shunka found himself staring back. The had the same amber eyes of his tribesmen, making him assume they might be Skin-changers, but he could not help but notice their most striking feature; their red coats. The fur of these pups almost seemed ablaze in vibrant, flaming red against the green of the forest.

One of the pups, the older brother although Shunka did not know how he knew that, stood up and let out a quiet whine. It yipped at him, then turned and walked into the shadows between the trees. The other, the younger sister, watched as her brother left. Then, with a final look back to Shunka, she lifted from her seated position and followed the other pup.

Shunka found himself watching as they walked into the darkening woods, their fur still bright against the shadows. Though he couldn't understand why, and was barely conscious of the thought, he felt compelled to follow.

For the first time since he awoke, he left the clearing and entered the woods. The trail was easy to follow, a wide path of bare dirt snaked through the ferns with two sets of paw prints running down the center. Ahead, the pair of wolf pups stopped every so often just long enough for him to get close, and then continued on their way.

He wandered like this for quite some time, the path never grew wider or narrower and the tracks never deviated. With the ever present and unchanging sky, it was impossible to tell how long he followed, but it was long enough to make his feet sore and legs ache. He stopped to rest, his hands braced against his knees as he gasped for breath. Why did he feel so tired? He was a trained warrior of the Wolf Tribe, a man of the forest. Walking along a steady path at an even pace should be easy, but here he was having to rest and catch his breath.

As he looked up, he saw the pups staring back at him. They had stopped and appeared to be waiting. Then, the elder brother lifted his head to the sky and howled. Both he and the sister took off in a sprint down the path and out of sight.

Before he could think, Shunka gave chase. He dropped to all fours and shifted to his wolf form, taking off like a black streak between the trees. His sense of smell was stronger now, and he easily caught the scent of the pups. There was something oddly familiar about them, like he had smelt it before. But from where, he did not know. He spotted them in the distance and increased his pace. They weaved and wove along the dirt trail. Shunka did not give up the chase. He wanted to catch these pups now, although he did not know why.

All around him a landscape began to change. The thick forest started to thin as the trees spread farther from one another. The ground leveled, no longer the gradual hills and gentle slopes, but now a flat field, and the dirt replaced with polished white stone. Shunka stopped, his claws tapping on the stone floor, and looked around. He was no longer in the Sequoia, but instead he found himself in a garden of pampered trees and trimmed hedges and flowers.

He was standing at the base of a wide, stone staircase which lead up to an ornate palace. Shunka looked up these steps and came face to face with two children. Twins, a boy and a girl almost identical to one another and no more than six years of age, stared back at him. They both had the same amber-gold eyes of his people, but fairer skin and vibrant red hair.

A woman appeared at the top of the steps. She wore a long, flowing dress of deep lavender trimmed with gold and white, and a dazzling blue sapphire at her throat. Her skin was more fair even than that of the children, as pale as freshly fallen snow by comparison, with hair as intense as red flame and eyes a startling green. A crown rested upon her head, large and ornate, forged from gold and precious jewels.

This woman descended the stairs and embraced the children, who laughed at her touch and clung to her. She smiled and kissed them lightly on the cheek while running her fingers through their similarly vibrant hair. She then turned to Shunka, seemingly unfazed by the sight of an enormous black wolf in her courtyard.

"My love," she said with a voice as sweet as honey, "you've found us."

Shunka knew that voice, and he knew this woman's face. It was the girl, the foreign child, the princess from the Walled City, the Flame-haired maiden, Endelynn.

She appeared older now, a woman grown rather than the child on the cusp of adulthood that he knew, but what did this mean? What was she doing here? And who were these children with both tribal and foreign traits?

"Wake up, Shunka." Her lips mouthed the words, but the voice came from all around. "Wake up!" It grew louder, more frantic. Suddenly, some great unseen force grabbed and shook him. His eyes clamped shut, and then snapped open again.

He found himself no longer in the courtyard or garden, but now looking up at the ceiling of a Longhouse. He was on his back, lying on a bed of blankets and furs. And he was in his human form rather than his wolf skin.

But the same face stared back at him; the face of the princess. Her cheeks were flushed pink and eyes filled with fear. Tears welled at the corners of her eyes as relief replaced her fright. She wrapped her arms around him and pulled his face tight against her chest. "Bless the gods," she said, "you're awake."

Awake? Yes, it had been a dream. The two wolf pups of red fur, the twin children of mixed traits, the elder princess, all had been a fever dream brought on by his illness. Or, perhaps, a vision? And if so, he still could not understand its meaning.

All those would be questions for later. Right now, he was alive, conscious, recovering, and in the arms of the Flame-haired maiden. He raised his arms, they ached and throbbed with stiffness and felt heavy, but he lifted them anyway, and embraced the foreign girl. "I, too, and glad to be awake. Thank the Sky Father."

A shadow fell over the both of them. Shunka looked up to see an old man he recognized as Kuruk of the Bear Tribe. "I see you've recovered some." He said "Good. There are a few visitors waiting for you."

"Visitors?" Shunka asked. "Who? For that matter, where am I?"

"You've been a guest in my home for the past few days." Kuruk explained. "I found you and the girl on the banks of the river, you had almost drowned. She was the one who pulled you to shore, and probably saved your life. I just brought you back to my village so you could recover enough to return to your own."

As the old bear spoke, it started coming back to Shunka. He remembered the encounter with the Hawk warriors, their ambush and the dart when it dug into his skin. He could recall grabbing hold of Endelynn and pulling her into the water with him to escape, but after that there wasn't much else. "How long have I been asleep?"

"Three sunrises and sunsets. Today is the fourth sunrise. And, as I said," Kuruk stepped aside and held out an arm, "you have people eager to see you."

A collection of warriors stood at the far end of the lodge. Some were from the Wolf Tribe, and Shunka recognized both Mingan and Tala amongst them. Most, however, were of the Hawk Clan. First and foremost of the Hawk warriors was Shikoba.

"If you are fit to travel, you've been summoned by Orumaku Chaa to answer for your insults against his tribe." The Hawk maiden spoke with a neutral, formal tone. Even so, Shunka could see the stiffness in her jaw and neck along with the slight twitch of her lips and the furl of her brows that betrayed the rage burning within her.

Shunka's legs trembled as he struggled to lift himself from the blankets and furs. Endelynn grasped him by the arm and helped pull him to his feet. "The Hawk village of Orumaku is far from here." Shunka placed his hand on Endelynn's shoulder to steady himself, as his legs were still weak. "I don't believe I'm ready to make that kind of journey right now."

"Orumaku Chaa is in our village." Tala stepped forward. "He's been speaking with Ahote Chaa. Your judgment will be held there."

XLI.
BEATRICE

The hour was late when the queen brought Sir Aridain into her sleeping chambers. The bandages around the knight's torso were soaked red with blood. He found it hard to breath and he couldn't wear his armor until the injury healed. It could be weeks until then. Looking at them, Beatrice knew the bindings needed to be changed. Usually that would mean calling a healer to tend to the injured knight, but the Dadrian queen didn't trust any of the healers in Kendrick's service.

"Sit down." She told him. "That needs to be cleaned."

"My lady, with all due respect," the knight protested, "you should not concern yourself with my well being. I can have a physician do it."

"No." The queen stated. "I'll not have my captain of the guard tended to by the very people who tried to kill him. And besides," Beatrice removed the pot of heated water from its hook over the fire and poured the water into a bowl, "your well being is my well being. I am safest when you are at your strongest. So, I will keep you well." She placed the steaming bowl of water on the small circular table in the center of the room and pulled out the chairs. "Now, your queen commands you to sit."

Overruled, Aridain did as he was bid. He was shirtless, as

he was to remain while the wound healed. Beatrice sometimes caught herself staring at him, enthralled by his physique. His chest, arms, and back were all well toned and coursing with muscles.

Over a hundred scars covered those muscles. Some were small and barely noticeable amidst all the rest. Others were huge and ragged. One in particular stretched all the way from his left shoulder to his right hip. A diagonal cut along his back that nearly split him in two.

Beatrice remembered when and how that scar came to be. It was during the tourney of Endelynn's birth celebration. Back then, Aridain was a young squire serving her husband during the jousts. One match had just ended and Cassius had won, dismounting his opponent. The king paraded around on his raox, back and forth to the cheers of the crowd. Beatrice had smiled and applauded. She was so taken with her husband at the time she didn't notice the other knight.

The man King Cassius had dismounted, Sir Malgorne of Southhaim, had a reputation as a braggart, a sore loser, and a quick temper. While everyone was distracted, he drew his sword and advanced on the king. No one seemed to notice him, and no one moved to stop him.

No one, that is, aside from the young squire Aridain. He was only a child of ten, but the boy had a heart of courage and devotion to his king. Young Aridain took up a short sword, one too small for a grown man, and threw himself between the defeated knight and his king. "Not another step, sir!" The child shouted with trembling fear in his voice.

Sir Malgorne paid no attention to the boy's words. He raised a hand, still encased in its steel gauntlet, and struck the child across the face hard enough for the sound to resonate across the tournament field. The crowd fell silent in shock. Aridain cried out in pain and fell to the ground, while Malgorne stepped over him without another though and continued his advance toward the king.

Cassius wheeled his raox around to confront the disgruntled man. "Stand down, Sir," the king said, "you were beaten fairly on the field of battle. Accept your defeat with dignity."

"I accept no defeat," Malgorne said, "not even from the king."

As the knight raised his sword to strike, young Aridain made his move. He thrust his sword into the calf of Malgorne's leg, crippling the man and bringing him to his knee in pain. The knight lashed out, slashing his sword at the boy. Aridain turned to run, but the sword caught the child across his back. By some miracle, Aridain wasn't cleaved in two, but a huge red gash extended the length of his body and blood sprayed from the wound. The boy screamed in agony. Beatrice clasped her hand across her mouth in horror and the crowd gasped.

That was enough for the king. Cassius took his own sword and stabbed through Malgorne's unprotected neck, killing him in seconds. The young squire was taken straight away to a healer and the gash was sewn closed. Lord Marigold of Southhaim demanded reprimand for his dead knight, but Cassius would not hear of it. After all, his life had been threatened by that knight. Aridain, on the other hand, was to be commended. The king swore an oath to continue the boy's training, rather than just as a one-time squire, and someday make him a full knight in his own right.

That day seemed like a thousand years ago. In that time, the princess had grown from a squalling babe to a woman of marrying age, and Sir Aridain had risen from a squire and knight-in-training to the Captain of the Royal Guard. He was no longer a little boy, but a man. And that inner strength remained.

Beatrice took the knight's side dagger and gently cut the very tip of the bandages. She started to unravel them, releasing the pressure they placed on the wound. It had been cauterized and stitched closed, even so an ooze of pus flowed out as the bindings came off. It had begun to scab, the edges were black with crusty, dried blood. She took a towel and soaked it in the bowl of hot water, then twisted it in her hands to drain the excess water and began dabbing it against the raw flesh. Aridain winced, but otherwise made no sound.

As she cleaned the wound, Beatrice found herself thinking painful thoughts. She should never have let Aridain go with Roddrick. Any of her other personal guards would've sufficed, but the Exiled King had been insistent on Aridain. This was as much his fault as it was the man who wielded the knife. And her fault as well. If she had been more steadfast, she would've made Aridain stay behind and sent another in his place.

She applied just enough pressure to push the pus out and wipe it away. She did this several times until the swelling had lessened and the oozing stopped. She soaked the towel again. "I haven't thanked you."

"There is no need, your grace." Aridain replied. He gasped a little as the towel was pressed against his back. "It's my duty to serve you."

"It still deserved gratitude." Beatrice placed the towel into the bowl to rinse it, and placed it against the injury to clean the bleeding. "You've been strong for me. With so much happening at once, I don't think I'd be able to cope with it if I didn't have you with me."

"I am only strong because you need it." Aridain replied.

Beatrice placed the towel in the basin again and noticed how the water had taken on a reddish tint to it. She stared at her hands, where the skin had turned red as well both from the blood and from wringing the cloth. "I don't know how much longer I can go on like this." She fell forward, bracing her hands against the tabletop. Her legs felt as weak as water and arms were as heavy as lead. "I'm a widow and a childless mother. The two things that gave my life meaning have been taken from me. I don't know what I can do anymore. Is it all pointless?" The words were flowing now, even if she wanted to stop, she couldn't. "Everyone looks to me for strength. If the queen is confident, then everything will be alright." She took a fresh bundle of linen and started wrapping it around Aridain's torso. She pulled them tight to keep the wound closed. "But I'm not. I can't be strong all the time. I'm not like you."

She finished the binding and then fell back to her chair, her hands folded in her lap. Was this what had become of her? The great queen of Dadria reduced to a quivering child?

A sudden shock flushed through her body as Aridain turned around and cupped her hands in his. A quiet gasp escaped her lips. She looked up and her eyes met his. They were filled with sadness and compassion. Aridain knelt before her on one knee. "Your grace," he began, then paused, and started again, "my queen, I'll always have faith in you. If you asked it of me, I would go to the ends of the earth. And if you need, I will be your strength."

The next moment shocked them both. Before she could stop or second guess herself, Beatrice leaned forward and kissed him. Their lips met. Her eyes closed, heart raced, and face flushed. It was wonderful, exhilarating, a pure moment of bliss she's been missing.

At long last, she pulled back. Her eyes opened again and saw the surprise upon the knight's face. They stayed that way for what seemed like an eternity before Sir Aridain stood. "I should be heading back." He reached for his tunic. "The other guards will be wondering where I am."

Beatrice's fingers brushed against his arm and lightly clung to his wrist. "Stay with me," she said, pleading with her eyes as much as her words. "I would have you guard me tonight. I don't want to sleep alone anymore."

"My queen, please," as he spoke, she could sense his

resolve weakening, "it would be improper. I am not worthy of you."

"You are the most worthy man alive I know." She stood and allowed the corner of her night gown to slip from her shoulder, revealing bare skin. "I would have you warm my bed."

"But," Aridain fought between his urges and his duty. "Your husband– "

"Is dead." Beatrice finished. If she had been steadfast before, he wouldn't have been injured as he was. She wasn't going to waver on her decisions anymore, starting with this one. Her gown slipped from the other shoulder and fell to the floor. Aridain's eyes were drawn to her body and his jaw slacked. She took a step towards him and took his hands in hers. "Comfort me tonight. Your queen commands it."

XLII.
SHUNKA

The whole council had gathered. Not just of his tribe, but of the Hawk Clan as well. Shunka's own father, Ahote Chaa, sat in the middle of the gathering of elders with Orumaku Chaa to his left. Their emotionless faces, as if carved from stone, gave no indication of their thoughts. But as the Chaa's stared down at him with those fierce amber eyes, he knew their hidden anger.

The soft, delicate grasp of Endelynn's hands clasped around his arm as she clung to him for safety and comfort. She was here, too, also a target of the council's judgment. It was because of her that he was in this situation. It did not escape his notice that this was the second time they were here, twice before the council awaiting their judgment and twice because of the foreign girl. Shunka stood firm, his back held straight and chin raised, unwilling to let his fear be seen.

At long last, Orumaku Chaa stood. He glared down at Shunka and Endelynn, eyeing her for a moment with contention, then turning his fury towards the young warrior. "Shunka," he spoke in his deep voice which resonated throughout the Longhouse, "you have insulted me. You have insulted my people, and you continue to do so by bringing that pale demon in here with you." The Chaa motioned to

319

Endelynn, who's fingers dug into Shunka's arm as she ducked out of sight behind him. Whether she could understand everything they were saying was unclear, her hold on the language was still weak, but she could tell when things were directed at her.

"Worse yet, you have insulted your own tribe, and the memory of all those who gave their lives to keep our villages and our people safe from those heathenish murderers." Orumaku continued. "Have you anything to say in your defense?"

Shunka glanced over at Endelynn, her big green eyes pleading for his protection like a frightened child. He needed to protect her, it was his charge and his destiny, her life was in his hands.

But was it worth it? After everything that happened, all the anguish and hardship he'd brought his tribe, was she really worth the suffering? He could give her up, stop trying to defend this foreign girl and abandon her to her fate. What was she, anyways? Just some pampered child from behind the Stone Walls, descendant of those that slaughtered his tribesmen and uprooted their lives. If he gave her up now, he might be able to regain some dignity and salvage the situation.

Shunka scanned over the Council of Elders, all of them stared intently with aggression waiting for his response. One face, however, was filled with concern rather than anger, and that was of the shaman, Alo. It was his words and guidance that sent Shunka down this path, and the words of a shaman were never to be taken lightly.

"Answer me, boy," The Hawk Chaa growled. "What do you have to say for the insult of your people and mine? Or the insult of my daughter? Have you anything to say in your defense?"

Shunka steeled himself. He closed his eyes and took a deep breath, then fixed his gaze upon Orumaku Chaa. "I only did what I felt was right. If given the chance, I would do it again."

Orumaku sneered. "And now you continue to defile our ways." The Hawk Chaa turned to address the council. "The laws of our people require action! We cannot let such a disgrace go unpunished!" He then focused specifically on Ahote, Shunka's father. "You know what must be done."

It was cheap and cruel, dragging his father into the judgment like that. As strained as the relationship between Shunka and Ahote was, forcing a father to pass judgment on his own son was too painful a burden to bare.

The Chaa's eyes clamped shut as lines of stress formed across his forehead. He pressed his fingertips together against the bridge of his nose. Shunka saw how his father was grappling with the decision, not wanting to go through, but unable to turn away. It had to be done, by the laws of their people.

At long last, Ahote moved his hand from his face and opened his eyes. "My son," he said, and Shunka could hear the strain in his voice as he struggled to keep his personal feelings suppressed, "your actions have shamed me and have shamed your people. You have insulted our brother clan, who need retribution. In the interest of preventing conflict, there is only one choice for me."

Shunka knew what was coming. He knew from the moment he returned to the village. He thought he'd readied himself to hear it, but now at the moment of truth, it still made him anxious.

"Shunka, son of Ahote, it is the decision of the council that you are to be banished from the Wolf Tribe," his father said, "exiled to live out the rest of your life as a lone wanderer in the Sequoia, never to return to this or any other village under pain of death."

Endelynn gasped beside him. As weak as her grasp of their language was, she understood what his father had said. He'd expected this, tried to prepare for it, but hearing the words coming from his own father's mouth was much more difficult than making them up in his head. They weighed him down, pressed heavily on his chest and he for a moment felt himself smothered under those words.

"As for the girl," Orumaku Chaa said, perking up Shunka's attention again. Endelynn's hands clutched tighter around his arm when she heard them address her. "She will be dealt with as she should have from the start. Execution."

Shunka's eyes snapped open with shock.

"At the dawn's first light tomorrow, she will die." Orumaku's voice rang throughout the Longhouse, and continued to echo in Shunka's mind long after his actual words had fallen silent.

He turned to Endelynn, and upon meeting her eyes he knew she understood. And she was afraid. Terrified. She had the look of a frightened lamb backed into a corner just before being sprung upon by a predator. Wasn't that what she was? What she had always been? A sweet, kind, demure lamb trapped amongst a pack of wolves? He couldn't let it happen. Wouldn't let it happen.

"No." Shunka declared. "You can't kill her! I won't let you! She's mine and you can't have her!"

"Silence, boy! Your words mean nothing!" Orumaku glared down at the former wolf warrior. "You are an oath breaker. A blood traitor. To choose the life of a pale-faced invader over those of your own people is worse than murder. Your father has been merciful to only banish you. If you were my son, you would share her fate."

The Chaa of the Hawk Clan raised a hand and motioned to the pair of hawk warriors at the back of the lodge. They descended upon Shunka and Endelynn, grabbing the young princess and pulling her away.

Endelynn let out a frightened yelp as their hands grasped

around her arms. "Aah! Shunka!" She cried out for him, eyes filled with fear. The second Hawk warrior shoved Shunka to the ground, he pressed his foot down on Shunka's chest to keep him in place.

"Take the girl, tie her hands and feet, and keep her guarded. She dies at first light." Orumaku ordered. He then turned to Shunka, who lay on the ground with the Hawk warrior standing over him. "And as for you," the Hawk Chaa said, "you are to leave tonight. Take all your belongings and depart this village before the sun sets. And if you attempt to rescue the foreigner you will both be killed tonight."

Endelynn kicked and screamed, thrashed and flailed, as she struggled against the hold of her captor. "No! Unhand me!" She spat in both her own tongue and the tribal language. "Shunka, don't leave me!" She pleaded as they dragged her from the lodge. Outside, Shunka could still hear her defiant shouting as she was taken away. At long last, as her voice grew further away, the Hawk warrior stepped away and allowed Shunka to stand.

As he stood, the entire council of both the Wolf and Hawk Clans rose to their feet in unison. And then, one by one, they crossed their arms over their chests in an X motion, and turned their backs to Shunka. Even Alo the shaman, the same man who put him on this path. At the end, after all the other council member had disavowed him, Ahote Chaa, his own father, met Shunka's eyes with shame, and then turned his back to his son with arms crossed.

It was official. All ties were severed. He was banished.

Shunka left the central Longhouse. As he walked through the village back to his own hut, the judgmental stares of every tribesman burned into his skin. He felt their glares, their anger, more than that he felt their hate.

Once in his hut he began to gather everything he owned. Every set of buckskin trousers and vests, his quiver and arrows, his bow, his obsidian knife, his waterskin, his satchel with the small supply of food and antler comb. Everything he owned that wasn't a part of the tribe could be carried on his back.

Shunka froze as he reached for the last item. His spear, leaning up against the wall just as he had left it. The day he finished crafting it had been the proudest day of his life. The hours spent shaving the wood from a massive hardwood branch to make a suitable shaft, days searching along the riverbeds for the perfect obsidian shard, and even longer hammering away at the stone to make it the right shape and sharpness. And then the most difficult part, climbing to an eagle's nest to retrieve the pair of feathers that adorned the spearhead. It was the final test of every warrior-in-training. Shunka had never felt as elated, and his father had never been prouder.

But that was over, the effort all for naught. His time as a warrior of the Wolf Tribe had been short and disastrous. He grasped the spear, and with nothing left, stepped out of his home for the last time.

"Shunka," Tala stood before him just outside his door, causing him to jump in shock. "Why did you do it?"

"You shouldn't talk to me." Shunka said, ignoring her question. "You could be banished too just for speaking with a traitor." He tried to move away, only to have Tala block his path again.

"Answer me." She demanded. "I asked you once, and you never told me. You turned your back on centuries of tradition, spat in the faces of our ancestors, and even defied the elders for the sake of some outsider girl. And now it's gotten you exiled. Why did you do it?"

"It was the right thing to do." He brushed past her and this time didn't stop. Just as he reached the edge of the village, he heard her call to him once again.

"According to whom?" Tala shouted.

Shunka stopped. With his back to her, he replied, "Why

don't you ask your father?" And without another word, Shunka left his village, the only home he'd ever known, never to return.

There was one part of his banishment that he had to complete on his own. Once he had walked a fair distance from the village, far enough that he could no longer hear any voices, he stopped and set all his belongings on the ground. He pulled his vest off and threw it atop everything else. Looking down at his chest, he ran his fingers over his wolf birthmark, an elevated patch of red skin which bore a striking resemblance to a wolf's face.

All members of the Wolf Tribe had this same marking over their heart, placed there by the spirits of the forest when the Skin-changer ritual was performed as a physical reminder of the oath their ancestors made to protect the forests and tribes from invaders. Shunka had forsaken that oath. Tradition insisted he make a physical sign of it.

He took his obsidian knife. The shimmering black stone blade glistened in the dying sunlight. He placed the sharpened edge against his chest directly over the mark and slashed downward, leaving a bloody tear in his flesh over his heart. Switching hands, he made another slash in the other direction, forming a red crisscrossed gash in his chest.

Blood poured down his chest. The blade was so sharp the slicing itself was almost painless, but now the open wound stung in the chilling air. The injury would eventually heal, but it would forever leave a grotesque scar, a permanent reminder of his disgrace.

XLIII.
TALA

She stood at the edge of the village and watched him leave. Staring at his back and all the things he carried on it, not just the physical but also the burdens on his soul. How much was he carrying, and what kind of weight did they hold? The burning thoughts seethed within her mind.

Ever since that patrol, the night they came upon the girl in the woods, Shunka had not been himself. All his waking moments had been spent tending to the foreign child and waiting on her every need. The only time Shunka had not devoted to the redheaded girl was when she was in the blooding lodge, and that was only because men were not permitted to enter.

There must be a reason for his devotion. Tala knew him well; they had grown up together, hunted and fought together, done patrols and killed the foreign invaders together. Shunka's murdered mother gave him more reason than most to hate the pale-faced men. He would not dedicate so much of his efforts towards protecting this outsider if there was not a good explanation.

The day of that fateful patrol, as she and Mingan had been waiting patiently by the village outskirts, her father had taken Shunka aside and spoken with him. She never heard what they discussed, but now with his final parting words resonating in her mind, it must have something to do with the girl.

Tala headed back into the village. She stepped into her father's meditation room, threw the draped animal-hide tarp aside and stormed over to where the shaman sat by the fire. Alo's eyes were closed and his hands rested on his knees. His staff lain across his lap. "Tell me the truth." She demanded.

"Of what do you speak?" he asked without moving.

"The girl. The fire-haired pale-faced foreign girl from the walled city." Tala said. "Shunka said you had something to do with her. He chose not to kill her when we found her on patrol, and then brought her to the village and gave up everything for her. You know why. Tell me."

Alo remained silent, his breathing a consistent rhythm. Tala waited, the crackling of the fire hung heavily in the air along with the smoke as it drifted up to the circular hole in the ceiling. She knew her father well enough. He would answer in due time.

At long last, the shaman spoke. "Shunka has been chosen by the Sky Father for a wondrous task. Destiny surrounds him and binds him to the girl. They are forever linked."

"It's rather hard to be forever linked with someone who's dead." Tala said.

"She will not die tonight. Nor at first light. Or any day soon to come. The Flame-haired child will live and follow Shunka north to the White Mountain. I have foreseen this."

Tala snorted. "You're avoiding my question. I know you spoke with Shunka the day of our patrol when we found her. What did you tell him?"

"The truth." Alo said.

"And what is the truth?"

"That this girl is our salvation. She is our future, and she will be the one to protect us." The shaman took his staff and used it to stand.

"What is she protecting us from?"

His gaze shifted down to the fire, his eyes filled with sorrow. Tala thought in that moment, for the first time, he appeared old and tired. Despite his ash colored hair and the creases on his face, she had never thought of her father as an old man until now.

"The old ways are dying. Ahote, Orumaku, the other Chaas and elders, they cannot see it, or at least choose not to. But I can, and it can't be ignored. I see a storm coming. A rain of arrows will fall on our people from the Walled Cities and the invaders will finish what was started. Our villages and tribes will be removed from the face of this world, and the forest will burn. None will survive." Alo hovered his hand over the wispy columns of smoke that rose from the flames. "It will be as though we never were, the same as the Raven and Orca Tribes. Smoke in the wind."

Tala listened intently to her father's words. The shaman had never been wrong when divining the future, even if it turned out to not be exactly what was thought at the time.

"But this does not have to be." Alo said. "We have the power to change the future and save our people."

"How?"

"The girl."

Tala rolled her eyes and scoffed. "You keep saying she's important somehow, but you won't say why. If the invaders from the Walled Cities do decide to attack us again, we will just push them back as we did before."

"There are more of them now. And fewer of us. We have only survived all these years in secret within our hidden villages. What do you think will happen when they learn that we still exist? When they discover our Skin-changing?"

"They won't." Tala stated without hesitation.

"Are you so sure?" Her father asked, pushing the topic. "They grow bolder all the time. More and more they venture into the Sequoia, and we no longer have the numbers to properly patrol the forest. Eventually they will find us. And once they do . . . ”

He let the sentence trail off, leaving Tala to reach her own conclusions. And those that she came to were not comforting. “Then what are we to do?”

“You must do what you think is right.” Alo said. “I told Shunka the same thing, and he made his choices. Now I tell it to you, and you must likewise make your choice. That is all I can say.”

And with that, her father fell silent again. It was useless to argue with him, he had told her all he would. She left him, heading back outside into the dying light of the setting sun, left to stew with her thoughts.

Make her own choices. She needed to make her own choice is what her father said. But how could she do that when she didn't even know what that choice was?

The old ways are dying and the Chaas and elders refuse to see. If that was true, then keeping to the old traditions would bring their ruination. Things would have to change if they were to survive. And somehow, the foreign girl was at the center of it all.

Tala then knew what had to be done. It would not be easy, and she wasn't looking forward to it, but there was only one course of action. And it would require help.

She found her help down at the banks of the stream, kneeling by the water and striking one stone against another to fashion a sharpened point. “Mingan,” she said as she approached.

He glanced over his shoulder upon hearing his name, then rose to his feet when he saw her. “Tala, what is it?”

“I need your help.” Her jaw tightened and heart raced as Tala tried to keep her composure. “Something must be done tonight.”

"Tell me," He reached out his hand to hold hers offering comfort. "Anything you need, I will do it."

She wanted to take it. For what she had in mind she would need all the courage she could get, and all the support. But she needed to show conviction as well. She decided not to take his hand. "You have to swear to help me. Before I tell you what it is, you have to promise. And you cannot back out or change you mind after I've told you."

Mingan closed his hand and pulled his arm back, a concerned look came over his face. "What is this about?"

She paused, mulling over him her mind what to say, and then spoke. "We can't let them execute the pale girl."

"Why not?" Mingan asked in a harsh tone. "She should never have been brought here. Shunka was wrong to keep her. She's done nothing –"

"Exactly." Tala cut him off. "She has done nothing. There is no reason to kill her."

Mingan froze in shock. Tala surprised even herself with what she was saying, and she realized there was a difference between thinking a thing and speaking it. Mingan's expression hardened. "There needs to be justice. The laws of our people were broken."

"The law is wrong." She said before she could stop herself. Now the words began to flow, spilling from her lips like a river she was unable to stop. "She has done no harm to us. We've always considered ourselves wiser and more enlightened than the pale-face foreigners, so when did the murder of an innocent child become the enlightened thing to do?"

"When her ancestors murdered entire villages and burned them to the ground. When the Raven and the Orca were wiped from existence. When they tortured men, women, and children!" Mingan's voice rose. "When they felt that our lives were worth less than theirs!"

A moment of silence passed between them. They locked

eyes with one another, a challenge for who would back down first. "I'm sorry, but I can't go through with this." Tala said at last, breaking contact. She left in a huff.

Her mind was made up. Marching across the village, she soon came to the storage lodge, which was being used as a makeshift prison. A pair of Hawk Tribe warriors stood by the entrance, each with a spear and a wooden shield. As she approached, they crossed their spears over the door, blocking her path.

"Stand aside," she said. "I wish to see the prisoner."

"No one is allowed to enter. Orders from Orumaku Chaa." The elder of the warrior's said.

"Last I checked, I'm not under Orumaku's command."

"But we are." The guard said. "And he has ordered not to allow anyone entrance."

Tala stepped closer, crossing her arms over her chest. "I am of the Wolf Tribe and this is a Wolf village. Now, stand aside. I wish to look into the eyes of the girl once more before she dies."

"You will have plenty of time to do that in the morning once they remove her head." The Hawk warrior stood rigid.

"I also wish to look upon the foreign girl."

This new voice caught the attention of both the warriors and Tala. She turned around in surprise to find the source, a young woman from the Hawk Tribe whom she'd met before. Orumaku Chaa's daughter.

"Shikoba." Tala uttered in a whispered voice under her breath. What could the Hawk Chaa's daughter be doing here? While Tala knew Shikoba was in the village with her father, she hadn't expected to see her here of all places.

The Hawk woman stepped forward to address the two warriors. "I want to see this girl who stole Shunka from me." There was a brief glance from Shikoba to Tala, before she turned her attention back to the pair of warriors.

The warriors looked at one another, briefly confused, and then nodded. "Very well." The elder said. "Be quick." He pulled the drop cloth aside.

Shikoba waited and let Tala enter first. The Wolf woman dipped her head down as she hesitantly walked under the doorway, still unsure and concerned about the Hawk woman's intentions.

She found the girl within, the foreign princess's hands were bound behind her back to a post in the center, and her head hung low with the girl's fiery hair strewn around her face. A circle of moonlight fell in from the smoke hole in the roof of the lodge. She looked up as the they entered, at first her eyes filled with confusion, and then they snapped wide in surprise. "Tala?"

The wolf warrior woman nodded. "Don't look so shocked. You should've expected visitors."

The pale girl slumped lower against the post to her back. "You come to gloat?" She spoke in the tribal language. Her words were broken and stuttered, but understandable.

Tala shook her head. "Just to look upon you one last time."

Shikoba came over and stood at Tala's side. Her hands were placed together across her waist, lips pressed and jaw tight. Her eyes narrowed down at the foreign girl, like those of a hawk targeting prey.

The pale girl looked up at Shikoba and her eyes grew wide in surprise. "I know you." She said. "You are Hawk woman. You supposed to marry Shunka."

"I was." Shikoba sneered as she looked down her nose at the girl. "Until you came along."

"I sorry. I know what you feel."

"How?" The Hawk maiden hissed.

"I supposed to marry prince from Walled City." The foreign girl said. "On my way, taken captive by evil men. Shunka, Mingan, and Tala rescue me from them. He then keep me safe

332

and save me when in danger. He would make good husband."

Shikoba made no response, none that Tala could discern anyway. She began to move slowly, taking very deliberate steps as she walked around the foreign princess. "Do you remember my name?" She asked as she walked.

"I do not." The outsider girl confessed.

"I am Shikoba." She said. "My father is Orumaku Chaa of the Hawk Clan. When I want something, I get it. And you have taken something that I want from me." In a flash, Shikoba grasped the girl by her flame-colored hair and yanked her head back. The princess cried out in shock and pain, then gasped as the sharpened edge of an obsidian blade knife pressed against her neck.

Tala's eyes grew wide. This was what Shikoba wanted all along. She didn't come to look upon, or even speak with the foreign child, she came to murder her.

The princess gulped in fear as the knife brushed against her throat. "I want something else now." Shikoba's voice barely rose above a whisper as she leaned down to the girl's ear. "I want my face to be the last thing you ever see."

Without thinking, Tala grasped Shikoba's hand holding the knife and forced it away. She held her grip around the Hawk maiden's wrist. "Stop," she commanded. "We do not spill blood in here."

At first, Shikoba was shocked. Then her eyes filled with rage and her jaw tightened. "Release me, you filthy dog!" She said with a sneer. "The white-skinned witch has cast some foul spell on my betrothed. She deserves to die."

"That is not your decision to make, nor is it yours to carry out." Tala held firm.

"I can call the guards." Shikoba threatened with a wicked grin. "They are loyal Hawk warriors, not your traitorous Wolf bastards. They will do as I say, and not forget the vows they've made."

"And what will they think when they see you holding the knife?" Tala retorted. She tightened her grip on Shikoba's wrist. She was stronger than the Hawk woman. Tala could feel the bones in Shikoba's hand start to pop and dislocate as her fingers enclosed around it. Eventually, the Hawk maiden was forced to drop the knife.

They pushed away, releasing their holds on each other as well as the foreign girl. Shikoba cradled her dislocated wrist as she would a child, glaring daggers at Tala. "I will not forget this day, she-wolf." She spat at Tala's feet. Just as she was about to leave, Shikoba turned her attention once again to the flame-haired girl. "Be grateful. Your life has been extended for one more night. But tomorrow at first light, you will still die." She stormed out, leaving Tala alone with the frightened girl.

After Shikoba had left, Tala could hear her speaking with the pair of guards. No doubt telling a warped version of what just happened. Not something she wanted to deal with.

"Thank you." The foreign girl said once she'd calmed.

"I haven't saved you yet." Tala looked down at the obsidian knife, still laying in the dirt where Shikoba dropped it. "You have to escape tonight."

"How? The guards see me if I try leave." The flame-haired girl said.

"I don't know." Tala nudged the knife with her foot until it rested next to the girl's bound hands. "You don't want to die tonight, do you?"

"No."

"Then you'll have to find a way." Tala's voice fell to a whisper as she crouched low and placed her lips beside the pale girl's ear. "Once you're out of the village, find Shunka. He'll help you escape. Tell him he needs to go to the White Mountain."

"Where's that?" She asked.

"He'll know." Tala stood. "Now go before someone else

334

tries to take your life prematurely." She left, stepping out through the same door she came, catching the angry looks of the Hawk guards. She paid them no mind. Her only hope was that this wasn't in vain.

XLIV.
ENDELYNN

Her fingertips brushed the antler handle of the knife. She fumbled for it, smacking her hand against the ground as she groped around. Endelynn winced as the sharpened blade left tiny slices on her fingers the more she tried to grab it. A warm liquid, which she knew to be her blood, spilt out onto her hand.

Readjusting her grip, she took hold of the handle. Tilting her hand at an awkward angle, she began to saw through the ropes binding her wrists.

The binds were thick, but the knife was sharp. It wasn't long before the ropes snapped and slacked. She gave a small cry of elation and relief. Though just as she did, Endelynn had to bite her tongue. Quiet was the goal now. Couldn't give herself away while freedom was within reach.

With her hands free, she quickly severed the ropes at her ankles. The skin around her hands and feet were red and sore, but relieved. As she stood, the question remained in her mind of how to get out of here. This structure had only one doorway, and the pair of Hawk warriors were still guarding it. She needed some way to get past them.

And she would have to do it soon. It was only a matter of time before someone else came in, wanting to gawk and laugh at the pale-faced invader.

As she stood there, contemplating her escape, she came upon a realization. It had to do with the circle of moonlight in the center of the floor. It encompassed the post to which she had been tied. Looking up, she saw a hole in the roof of the Longhouse, probably a way to let the smoke out from the fire pit below. And the post reached almost all the way up. That was her way out. She couldn't get past the guards, but she could get around them.

After wiping her bloody hand on her leggings, Endelynn placed her fingertips against the post. It was smooth, no trace of splinters or grain at all. How she was going to keep a grip on this was a mystery. She grasped the post with both hands and tried to lift her legs up, only to find herself planted on the ground.

She gasped for breath. She hadn't even started yet, and already she was winded. Pressing her forehead against the post, her eyes fell on the knife by her side. How could it help her now? She didn't need to cut anything else. What good was it?

Unless it could help her. But how? It couldn't lift her to the hole in the roof. But, she thought as she stared at it, it might make for a good handhold.

She grasped it again and, using all her strength, stabbed it into the post. The blade sank about halfway into the post before it stopped. She tugged and jostled it, but the knife was stuck fast. A grip. Something for her to hold onto.

With renewed vigor, Endelynn grabbed the knife handle and used it to pull herself up. Her arms strained, beads of sweat grew on her brow and around her temples. She clamped her legs around the post and used them to steady herself, as well as push herself further up.

She got herself high enough to drape her arm over the knife handle. Her heart was pounding, she felt light-headed as she panted for breath, small after images swam before her eyes.

After a brief rest, Endelynn repositioned herself just high enough to use the knife as a foot stand. If she stood all the way up, she could reach the top of the post. She hooked her fingers around it. Just as she did, the knife began to lean. Her complete weight was too much for it to hold, and the blade started to slip from the post.

With no time to think, she jumped and grasped the lip at the top of the post just as the knife slipped out and tumbled to the ground. She hung there by her fingertips, staring down at the black blade that lay so far below her.

No turning back now. No starting over. If she fell, she wouldn't get another chance. Fastening her legs around the post again, she strained her arms and pulled herself up little by little.

At last she found herself laying across the top. She lay on her stomach, gasping for air. It hurt, the post's blunt end dug into her midsection, but she needed to rest. Her hair was a matted mess, stuck to her face and neck with sweat, loose strands hung in front of her eyes. The only thing even remotely keeping her hair in place anymore was her crown, the gold circlet her father gave her.

What would he think of her now? What would anyone from Dadria or Kahren think of her? Was this the life of a princess?

Questions for later. Now she just needed to get out. Looking up from where she lay, she could see the edges of the smoke hole. Although, now that she was here, she found it to be a bit further away than she thought. Pushing herself up, she crouched on the top of the post with her knees bent to keep her balance. Endelynn reached for the lip of the hole, but it was just out of reach.

She would have to jump. There was no other way out now. If she didn't make it out that smoke hole, then all this was for naught. If she missed and fell back to the ground, the guards would hear and she'd still be killed. Only a single chance to make it out.

She took several deep breaths to steady her racing heart and wiped the sweat from her forehead. Then, before she could change her mind, she shoved off, jumping away from the post with her arms outstretched and hands reaching.

She seemed to float in mid air. Her mind was racing, all the bad scenarios played out through her head. She was going to fall and crash to the ground, the guards would rush in and find her untied, then run her through on their spears. Or maybe fate would be kind and the fall itself would kill her. Or the guards might take her before the Chaas who will then decide to flay her alive.

Her hands caught the edge of the smoke hole. She let out the breath she'd been holding in a humph. Endelynn found herself more amazed than she could imagine. She'd done it. She hung in the air, her fingers starting to slip. After everything else, there was little strength let in them. Mustering what she could, she pulled herself up and hooked her elbows over the edge. Then swung her leg out, and before she knew it, she was outside.

The air was cold against her warm skin. The full moon shone brightly in the sky and cast the world in a silvery blue light. It was night. The world looked beautiful out here, although she had never quite appreciated it before.

The prison lodge was located near the center of the village. From her position, she could survey every possible escape route. But she would still have to be quick and silent. If anyone raised an alarm, then it was back to the post again. Luckily the lodge was a dome shape, much like all the others in the village. She sat down on the roof and pushed herself, sliding down the outside of the wall until her feet planted in the dirt.

She maneuvered through he village, slinking past every lodge and Longhouse between her and the forest's edge. Ahead of her was the line of trees that marked the border between the native's village and the Wayward forest. She was almost there.

Just beyond that was her freedom.

"You!" A voice shouted at her. She froze in place and her heart jolted in her chest. Her eyes shifted back as she turned to see, and found the source. It was one of the Hawk guards. "What are you doing out here?" He shouted.

She didn't answer. Overtaken with fear, Endelynn bolted. She charged into the woods, disappearing into the darkness between the trees. Her heart was racing, her mind lost in white terror. As she ran, some part of her registered the trumpeting of a horn and the shouting of the Hawk warrior. "Prisoner escape! Call to arms!"

ACKNOWLEDGMENTS:

This book has been my most ambitious project yet. It grew so massive I had to split it in two just to reach my deadline. I have so many people who helped me I need to thank. First, Hope Hill who spent three weeks meticulously editing the manuscript and finding my mistakes. Second, Steve Ferchaud who made the gorgeous cover artwork. Third, Kathryn Azevedo of the Butte County library for hosting Open Mic night and listening to me read chapters from this book and offering feedback for over a year. And lastly, to the North State Writers for all their support in my fledgling writing career.

And of course to my Mom, Dad, sisters, and everyone else who has supported me. Thank you, everyone.

THE ADVENTURE CONTINUES . . .

THE
KINGDOM
OF

DADRIA

THE BLOOD OF WOLVES
AND WAR

COMING SOON.